Portrait of Change

ENDORSEMENTS

With a poignant pen, Maggie creates a vivid story of yesterday reminiscent of Laura Ingalls and Anne of Green Gables. Settle in for a sweet story that will capture your heart.

—**Kari Turbo**, *USA Today* bestselling author.

Portrait of Change is a sweet story of a young woman's journey from bitterness and pride to understanding that life is not always as it appears and that love is worth the wait. I enjoyed the peek into Minnesota history and look forward to more from this author!

—**Shannon McNear**, 2014 RITA® finalist, 2021 SELAH winner, and author of *Daughters of the Lost Colony: Elinor*

Portrait of Change

Maggie R. McKenzie

ELK LAKE PUBLISHING INC

PUBLISHING THE POSITIVE
Plymouth, Massachusetts

COPYRIGHT NOTICE

Cover and Interior Design:
Editor(s): Sue Fairchild, Deb Haggerty
Author Represented By: Dunamis Words Literary Agency

PUBLISHED BY: Elk Lake Publishing, Inc., 35 Dogwood Drive, Plymouth, MA 02360, 2022

Library Cataloging Data

Names: McKenzie, Maggie (Maggie McKenzie)

Portrait of Change / Maggie McKenzie

376 p. 23cm × 15cm (9in × 6 in.)

ISBN-13: 978-1-64949-575-4 (paperback) | 978-1-64949-576-1 (trade paperback) | 978-1-64949-577-8 (e-book)

Key Words: Minnesota; Late 1800s; small town; homesteading; family saga; unique characters; Christian values

Library of Congress Control Number: 2022937813 Fiction

DEDICATION

To my Lord and Savior Jesus Christ. He gives us dreams and then he brings those dreams to reality.

To my mother and father and Grandpa Ray who were the storytellers of their generation. Their stories expanded my life experiences to include another place and time.

ACKNOWLEDGMENTS

Thank you to Bridget Powers from Light's Scribe whose suggestions and edits helped bring this book to fruition and the friends at Write Now writers group who listened to many of these chapters. Thank you also to ACFW Mn. N.I.C.E. writers.

Thank you to Doris, my sister-in-law who patiently reads my manuscripts and cheers me on. For friends, who read and listen and offer prayer, and my agent Cheryl Ricker at Dunamis Words for believing in me.

CHAPTER ONE

SOUTHEASTERN MINNESOTA LATE 1870S

Beth's mother ran a hand down the front of her bodice, smoothing the fabric against her corset and straightening her back. "We've voiced our wishes. You know we don't believe you and John Bader are a good match, and I won't discuss that further." She lowered herself in a nearby rocker and set the chair in motion. "You'll be leaving on the morning train to stay with your Aunt Nora."

"Why must I leave? I don't want to go live with a stranger."

"Your father and I told you this would be the result if you persisted in your willfulness." Pursing her lips, her mother clamped her jaw tight.

Beth untangled her feet from her skirts and whirled away, wishing to hide the tears that swelled at this rejection from her mother. During their weeks of discussion about John, her mother had remained insensitive and rigid. If it didn't mean being sent off to a stranger, Beth would almost welcome leaving. She clutched at the broach pinned to her bodice. John had given it to her only last week. She wished she had a more fanciful dress to wear it upon but had to make do with what she had.

Finally, her mother stopped rocking. "I'm sorry, but you'll like Nora." She turned in her chair to glance at Beth. "Your father and I believe you should be away for a time."

"You just don't like John." Beth pressed her fingers to her lips, stopping a scream of frustration.

"We don't know him but are concerned with what we see. We asked you to stop seeing him, until he proves he could support a family." Her mother dropped her hands on the arms of her chair. "You'll stay with Aunt Nora for six months, working and helping her for your room and board. If you want to take up with John again when you come back"—her mother closed her eyes—"Well, then it's your choice."

"But, Mother, listen to me!"

"I'm done listening." Her mother rested her elbow on the chair, her head in her hand. "You need to pack today— no more delays."

The words dropped like a bolt, allowing no more argument.

Beth shook her head. If her mother were patient, John would win her over. It's not like he'd asked Beth to marry him—yet. She wrenched her brown cape off the peg by the door. "I promised Papa I would be there this morning."

Her mother pushed herself from the chair. "You know perfectly well he didn't ask you to help at the mercantile today."

Beth turned her back, dropped the cape over her shoulders, and hurried out the door. She wouldn't give up her beau without a fight. Maybe her father would listen.

"Beth, come back here."

She heard the demand, but sprinted toward the store, hiking her dress to keep it out of puddles. She cringed when she stepped in a pool of cold water, soaking her high-button shoes. They would have to hold her until warmer weather. Yanking the hood on her cape over her head, she jumped over water-filled ruts and dashed through the door. Her father, his arms piled with goods for a customer, stopped when he saw her.

2

"What are you doing here? I thought Mother had something to talk to you about."

Beth shook out her cape and hung it up, taking her time to formulate an answer her father would accept. When she turned back to him, he was face to face with a customer. She blew out a breath and rushed to straighten a counter where Mrs. Ward rummaged through a rack of trim.

"Hello, Mrs. Ward. What did you need today?"

"Well, missy, I'm looking for thread and trim for the dress goods I bought a few days ago." Her eyes squinted at the display while her head shook in a perpetual rhythm. "I don't remember what shade it is exactly."

"Yes, ma'am." Beth walked around the counter. "Here is the thread you need." She showed the old woman the spool she'd chosen. "I'll take this to the counter for you, and the trims are arranged here." She pointed to shelves containing trims of varying styles. "You should be able to find something here, Mrs. Ward."

The widow furrowed her almost bare brows, making the two tuffs remaining stick out above her nose. "Can I return the thread if it's not right?"

"If you haven't used it, ma'am." Beth knew Mrs. Ward's idiosyncrasies. It's unlikely anyone else would cater to her as Beth did. And Mrs. Ward was one of several difficult customers who demanded extra attention. Her father's disapproval of John had taken over his good sense.

"Thank you, my dear, and greet your mother for me." She waved her hand as if shooing away a fly. "Go ahead and help others while I ponder these trims."

Beth returned to the counter where her father finished helping a customer. When the shopper walked away, he faced her. "You're leaving in the morning. Now go to the house and pack."

"But, Papa, why do I have to leave?" Maybe if she appealed to his business sense. "What will you do for help here at the store when I'm gone?"

"I'll hire someone." He glanced around the crowded room and whispered, "We've been through this, daughter. I'm disappointed at your willful disobedience, and that is precisely why you're going away for a visit. Maybe Aunt Nora can talk some sense into you."

Beth turned from his sharp reprimand, her nose burning while tears filled her lashes. She wouldn't cry in the store, but what had happened to her dear father to make him hard-hearted toward her?

Beth helped with customers and cleaning throughout the day, avoiding her father. If she kept busy, maybe he would see how important she was to their business and let her stay. Her relationship with her parents had always been good, but that changed a few months ago when Beth began to spend more time with John.

Their relationship—if you could call it that—had begun with a stupid move on her part. John had rescued her from a runaway horse that escaped from the smithy. She'd stood in the street while one person after another yelled at her. She had been frozen in indecision, not understanding the danger until she turned and saw the horse coming right for her. John's quick move had controlled the horse.

After the horse was secured, John had helped her to a bench and sat with her, holding her hands. Others in town showered him with attention for his quick thinking. She'd felt special, sitting there while he was congratulated. She normally meant nothing much to the town's people—only if she could serve their needs at the mercantile. The men in town became his best friend immediately, and his attention made her feel special—not the simple shop girl she really was.

But as time went on, her parents objected to John's lack of ambition. He didn't come to church, he didn't work with his father at the bank, and yet he had money to gamble and bring her gifts. She wasn't worried, though. John was handsome, popular with everyone in town, and seemed to care for her in a special way.

Beth rubbed her hand against her throbbing forehead. It had been a long day, and she hadn't had lunch. As the end of the day neared, she longed for a bit of supper. Just then, the bell above the door tinkled.

Her father glanced toward the door, and his look changed to one of anger. She turned to see John advancing across the room toward her. A thrill flashed through her. She grinned at his swagger, and he smiled back. The few other patrons in the building readied to leave, so her father totaled their purchases, leaving Beth alone with her beau.

"Hello," she spoke softly, noticing a few customers glancing their way. She liked for them to see him with her. It made her feel significant in town.

He flashed his dimple at her. "So what's this I hear, Beth Townsend?"

Beth's brows puckered as she shook her head. "What?"

He balled his fist and gave her a playful punch on the arm. "You leaving?"

Her teeth clenched, glad her mother hadn't seen the gesture. It was something else her mother didn't approve of. "How did you hear?" She'd planned to tell him herself this evening.

"Emileah."

"Emileah? And how did *she* know?"

"According to her, the two of you are traveling together." He waved to a customer leaving the store. When he turned back, his eyes narrowed. "She says that's why you're leaving so soon."

"Oh, really, she said all that, did she? And what else did Emileah have to say?" Beth stepped back from him, annoyed to have someone else tell him her business.

John's hand rose to the tie at his neck, and he turned his head one way and then the other as if it strangled him. His tone had cooled when he continued, "So you're going then?"

"How would I change that?" She had used every method she could think of to keep from leaving.

"Refuse to go." He beamed like he'd solved all her problems. "They can't force you onto the train."

"I can't do that. What kind of girl do you think I am?" She flung her arms in the air. "It's not that simple."

"I thought you liked to spend time with me." John gave her that special smile—maybe because he knew how devastating she found his grin.

"I do like you, but I have to go." Beth wished she had the strength to defy her parents, but she didn't want to hurt them either. They were her only family, and though she was eighteen and disagreed with what they required of her right now, she couldn't refuse to get on the train.

"John, we're closing up now." Her father walked up to them and handed Beth her cape. "Time for you to leave."

She took the wrap from her father, but when she glanced at John, the knot in her belly clenched. John's eyes had turned cold. He spun on his heel. "See you sometime."

Her father said, "Go to the house."

"Don't we have to straighten up?" She shook at John's dismissal. Stunned at his cold rejection. Not even a goodbye?

"Not today." Her father dismissed her. "Tell your mother I'll be along soon." He turned his back and busied himself with the store ledger.

Beth wasn't in any hurry to get back to her mother's recriminations and packing. She slipped the cape over her shoulders and trudged toward their brick house, her head down, her heart breaking. John really wouldn't wait for her? All this worry and trying to change her parents' decision and he wasn't even going to put up a fight? He used his charisma to get what he wanted, but if it didn't happen, he shrugged and moved on. Maybe it would be best to go away for a while. Absence makes the heart grow fonder, after all.

The rain had stopped, and the air held the fresh scent of spring, but it didn't please her as it usually did. Instead, she moped and picked her way around puddles, taking her time. The weight of John's dismissal pressed hard on her chest. She wanted her life back the way it had been.

Her mother flung the door open when she stepped up on the porch and greeted her in a falsely cheery tone. "I packed your trunk and have food for you to eat on the train tomorrow." She pulled her into the house. "Your father on his way soon?"

"Papa said he would be a few minutes." Beth removed her cape and hung it on the hall tree. "Mother, why are you pushing me away? I don't want to visit this Aunt Nora woman."

"Your father and I have discussed this." Her mother straightened the rag rug with the toe of her shoe and crisscrossed the shawl over her chest. "Emileah will be with you, so you won't be alone. We feel certain it's in your best interest to go, and it's also important for you to meet our few relatives."

Beth sat on a stool to unbutton her shoes and remove her damp footwear. "If I haven't met her in all this time, she could hardly be a close relative."

"No matter. Now hand me those shoes before you get mud all over." Her mother left the room and disappeared into the kitchen.

So typical of her mother to walk away instead of listening. Beth debated going to her room, but she always helped set the table, and she'd been disobedient enough today.

Her father arrived home, and they sat down to dinner as usual. The air hung tense, like a hawk ready to swoop on prey. No one spoke after the blessing. Beth pushed her food around. When the subdued meal was finished, her parents removed to the parlor, instead of doing dishes together like usual.

Beth cleaned the kitchen alone and hurried to her room. She opened the door, stepped in, and halted.

The room was bare—like she had moved out completely with her trunk sitting in the middle of the room. She closed the door. Why had her mother packed a whole trunk for a visit of a few months? Beth plopped on her bed, lay back, and closed her eyes. The pain in her heart hurt like a gaping wound. Her parents were ruining her one chance for happiness.

Men's voices from the next room intruded on her thoughts. Had John come one last time to see her? She got up from bed and listened at her door. A tenor, not her father's, spoke from the porch. Beth eased her door open. "Let me know and thank you," her father said.

"I'll keep an eye out, Grant. Be in touch," the visitor replied. Footsteps let her know her father came back to the parlor.

"Merin, you promised to tell her the truth. Why didn't you talk to her today?"

Beth held her breath as her mother responded. "I just couldn't get it out."

"You've nothing to be ashamed of," her father answered.

Beth covered her mouth to stop an outburst.

"All these years of not telling makes me ashamed." Her mother sniffed and Beth pictured her pulling a hankie from her sleeve, mopping her eyes.

"Yes, it's gotten worse for the lack of telling. It would have been better if we'd told her years ago." Her father sounded defeated and resigned. "It appears he's leaving town."

Beth leaned forward. Who left town? Why would such a thing be important to her father?

"That's good, right?" her mother said.

"Maybe." The rest of his words sent shivers down Beth's spine. "Unless he plans to follow her."

Beth bit down on her knuckle to keep from crying out. Were they talking about John? Maybe he had plans to follow her. Her parents didn't tell her she couldn't see him, just that she needed to go away for a while. She bit her lip. Her father sounded worried, sad, and beaten. If only she could throw herself into his arms and feel safe against his chest. Instead, she threw herself onto the bed, buried her head in her blankets, and cried.

CHAPTER TWO

The hissing engine stood ready to go as Beth stepped up into the train. She leaned back for one last look and to wave at her mother and father. They huddled together, wrapped and covered against the damp mist, their shapes melting into one.

She'd pleaded one last time with her mother this morning, but she'd heard none of it.

A porter, waiting to assist her into the railroad car, cleared his throat. "Miss, it's time."

Beth gave one last wave and glanced around for John. He hadn't come to see her off. She grasped the skirt of her traveling garment in a gloved hand and ascended the remaining steps onto the train. Her breath pulled in hard through her constricted chest. The facts were too obvious to ignore—her parents didn't love her, and John no longer cared.

Hissing sounds and the scraping of metal-on-metal accompanied the struggle of the engine to thrust the train into motion. The car jerked back, and Beth grabbed at a nearby seat to keep from falling. When the train lurched forward again, Beth steadied herself before making her way toward her traveling companion, who had agreed to find them a seat.

Emileah had saved a set of seats facing each other. Beth plopped down across from her companion and turned to wave at her parents as they passed from sight. Why hadn't they stopped this madness? They were supposed to change their minds. How could she be living her perfect life one day and on a train to some stranger the next?

"Took you long enough," Em said.

"What?" Beth shook out her damp shawl.

"You kept us all waiting."

Em had been challenging in their years together at school, and her personality hadn't changed.

"Believe me. I don't have that much power." Beth pulled off her leather gloves, one finger at a time, and stowed them in her bag. She had more important things on her mind than whatever Em might be going through—like the mystery at home. What did her mother have to reveal? What couldn't she tell her own daughter?

Beth brought the sleeve of her dress to her face. It smelled of the store—coffee beans, leather, wooden barrels, and spices. Even shiny new pails had a smell. She should be there right now, where she'd spent almost every day for the last five years. They needed her, didn't they?

She was no longer a child, but their abandonment crushed her. Couldn't their differences be resolved without these drastic steps. And why out west—with Em of all people? Just one more thing decided for her.

A man staggered between the narrow seats, jolting Beth, and bringing her headache to a new intensity. She glanced down, her father's long list of safety instructions running through her mind. *Put your reticule on your wrist, away from the aisle.*

The handbag contained her money to return home and the only security she had should the woman she was to visit be unbearable. Tucking the reticule out of the way, she massaged her temples to ease the hammering behind her eyes as she remembered her mother's pushy behavior this morning.

"Hurry. You need to have breakfast before you board the train." Her mother had bustled around her room, picking up the dress Beth had discarded the night before. Then she'd pressed the traveling clothes into Beth's hands and left the room. She'd barely spoken to her at breakfast, only asking what she wanted to eat. When would her mother allow her to fix her own breakfast?

Why had her parents rushed to get her away as if they were tired of her or didn't want her around?

She brushed her hand over her dove gray traveling dress and smoothed the skirt, checking to make sure the bottom ruffle didn't drag on the dirty floor. She'd begged her mother for a new dress, which would take weeks to make, preventing her departure and giving her time to change her parents' minds. But her mother had foiled her plans, insisting this dress was perfectly serviceable.

To be sure, the dress fit her figure flawlessly. The skirt draped and swooped toward the back bustle, giving her room to sit while remaining narrow and sleek when she stood. The square neckline had braid trim, as did the pleated polonaise, which flared over the fullness of the fashionable bustle. It was a beautiful ensemble, almost new, but Beth wished her ploy to delay this trip had worked.

After a time, the train slowed, signaling their arrival at a growing southeastern Minnesota town. The wait here would be longer than the usual whistle stops. Cars were added and subtracted from an incoming spur, giving passengers plenty of time to disembark. Several crowded the aisle to leave the train, and Em disappeared with the others when the train stopped.

Beth laid her head back and closed her eyes. When the warning whistle sounded, her companion hadn't returned. Many new passengers were boarding, filling the car to near capacity. A porter walked down the depot deck, hurrying a last group of patrons. A young man broke from the grasp of his friends' final goodbyes and hustled onto the train as it began to move. Beth prepared to cry out they couldn't leave when her seatmate dashed from the depot. Holding a package in one hand, she grasped the assist handle with the other and bounded up the steps onto the moving train.

"Now who kept us waiting?" Beth snapped when Em dropped into the seat across from her.

Her companion grinned and held up a pasteboard box—a most satisfied look on her face.

"What on earth?" Beth clutched at her bag when it wobbled close to the edge of the seat as they sped up. "I declare, is that something to eat? I thought you had lunch packed for you."

"Not like this, for sure." The girl tucked the box into her bag and looked around at the new arrivals. She smiled at the boy who had boarded at the last minute.

Beth rested her forehead in her hand and massaged it with her fingertips. "You can eat my lunch too if you like. I couldn't eat a thing."

"Sure." Pulling at the neck of her dress, Em turned to Beth. "Now tell me why you got shipped off."

"I don't want to talk about it." Beth retreated to the barrel of water at the back of the car. She filled the dipper and drank, wiped water off her chin, and peered out the window at the drab landscape. The train moved out of town, and in no time, they were on an open plain dotted with farms and homesteads. They passed a young boy beating rugs with a stick. Several homemade braided and woven cornhusk mats hung nearby. The rugs reminded Beth of

Mrs. Simonson who was particularly clever with cornhusks. She made dolls and toys for her children from them and often traded her mats and baskets to the mercantile for supplies. Everyone needed a gathering basket, but some women didn't have the ability or time to make one.

Beth's shoulders drooped—if only she were home, arranging Mrs. Simonson's wares at the store. The mercantile was the one place where she didn't feel gawky or odd. She wasn't good at small talk but helping customers was easy, and they didn't expect more.

The moment Beth returned to her seat, Em resumed her topic. "I noticed your parents seeing you off."

Beth turned away. Why couldn't her old schoolmate leave her alone to think?

"I wondered—how are your parents going to manage with you gone?"

"Why?" Beth snapped her head around. "What makes you ask?" Did this girl know more about the situation than she did?

Her companion bounced in her seat, as if trying to adjust her bustle into a more comfortable position. "Nothing in particular. They seemed old today. I never noticed it before."

Beth chewed on her thumbnail. "They are older, I guess, but they said they're fine."

"They've always been kind to me."

"Thank you." Her parents were caring to their customers. Beth had always appreciated their kindness, but lately her mother, and even her father, had been rigid and uncaring. She couldn't think of their treatment as kind.

Em threw her arms wide to encompass the train. "I want adventure."

"This could be an adventure." Beth stifled a yawn. She'd once cherished a vague sense of something exciting on the horizon and hadn't been able to wait for it to come. Now, she wished she'd never longed for such a thing.

"Not this trip," Em said. "I hate my life."

"Yes." Though Beth didn't agree with Emileah often, this time she gave her complete approval. She hated being here on this train, she hated leaving John, and she hated being sent away to a stranger.

"You have it nice," her companion said, tugging at the neck of her dress. "You can go back home anytime."

Beth shrugged. It was none of Em's business, but she could not. Her mother demanded a long separation. Six months with a stranger? Impossible to contemplate.

"I could never leave anyone as dreamy as John, that's for sure." She coyly flipped her curls and smiled at a boy behind Beth.

As if Beth had a choice. She'd spent every moment trying to stop her eviction. If only her seatmate would quit talking and let her think.

Em gripped the neck of her gown and pulled at it again. "I can't see why you would leave John. He's so handsome."

Beth furrowed her brow. Her nose scrunched when she turned to study her traveling companion and the clothing she appeared ready to rip from her body. "What on earth is wrong with your dress?"

"I hate this thing." She yanked at a sleeve.

"Obviously, but I think it's lovely. Did you order it from St. Paul?"

The girl snorted and shifted in her seat. "It may have come from there, all right, but it wasn't ordered for me."

Beth studied the well-made, paisley-print dress. It appeared a costly ensemble not available in their small town. "Whom would it have been ordered for?"

"My step ..." The girl scrunched up her face as if something tasted nasty. "You know, the woman Father married."

Beth pictured her schoolmate's new stepmother, a small woman who wore extremely high-heeled, high-top boots. The result was the strangest, most knock-kneed, bustle-out walk Beth had ever seen.

"It does look a bit small."

"A bit?" Her companion snorted and pulled at the bodice. "I'm a normal sized, grown woman, but not to her. This is two sizes too small, at least. Do you see it's supposed to belt at the waist, but it's too short? I have to keep pulling it …" She tugged it down to her waist, then slumped over to keep it there.

"Did your stepmother order it from Owen's?" Beth's family had a policy for perpetually disgruntled people like Em's stepmother—pay in advance for special orders. "I don't remember it coming through our mercantile."

She shrugged. "I don't know where she got the dress, but I refused to wear it. This morning, I put on a different gown, and she went into a rage. She dared to say, 'I won't have my *daughter* walking around in a housedress. This gown is beautiful, and you will wear it.'"

Beth smiled behind her hand. Her classmate's mimic of her stepmother was shockingly accurate.

"Can you believe it? She treats me like I'm something stuck on her shoe and then, 'Oh, my *daughter* will dress appropriately.'" She wrinkled her nose, and her lips puckered as if she'd bitten into a sour apple. "It disgusts me that she called me her *daughter*." She shuddered. "Father sided with her, and now, he doesn't want me around."

"Maybe he wants time with his new wife." Beth thought her old schoolmate would be happier away from the woman. There were whispers around town regarding the difficult stepmother, and though Beth wasn't close to Emileah, she understood how awful it was to live in a household where you were not wanted—at least lately.

"They're sending me to work for a relative of hers." Her seatmate fingered the ribbon on her bonnet. "If this person is anything like she is, I'm not going to stay."

Beth had contemplated such a solution herself. "What would you do for money?"

"I may have an idea. I'll think of something." She gave Beth a sly look from the corner of her eyes.

"I'm sorry." As much as Beth hated to admit it, they were in similar situations. But Beth's parents loved her and needed her, didn't they?

She closed her eyes, resting her head against the seat. Her dear father doted on her for as far back as she could remember. Since she was an only child, her parents discussed all family matters with her. She sighed, a wave of panic engulfing her at the memory of her father's sadness. The hurt in his eyes could not be on account of her, could it?

Her brows drew together, reliving the recent goodbye. Her mother had given Beth a fierce hug before she boarded the train. Her father too had clung, pulling her against his chest so she could hardly breathe. They seemed desperate to hang onto her, yet they put her on this train and sent her away.

The cries of an unhappy baby across the aisle woke Beth. A young mother struggled to comfort a fretful infant while a little girl stood next to her, swaying with the rolling train. The girl stared at Beth and Em while sucking her thumb and clutching an old piece of woven blanket.

"John seemed annoyed you were being shipped off," Em said, as if their conversation hadn't paused at all.

Beth smiled at the child and turned to glare at her seatmate. The whole situation made her weary, and discussing it further didn't solve anything. Her companion's obsession with John didn't make sense either. She wished her old classmate would find something else on which to focus. "I'll be home again in no time."

"Do tell." The girl rolled her eyes. "He sounded angry when I talked to him."

Beth's stomach tightened, and she pushed down the jealousy that surfaced. John had discussed this with another girl but not with her? "We don't have a pledge. We're friends."

"Good, because Alice has her eye on him and seems determined to get what she wants."

"I'm not worried about Alice." Em sounded jealous. Is that why she kept pressing? They weren't close girlfriends, and now it seemed their differences were more significant than ever.

Beth glanced out the window, her attention drawn by a young couple waving at the train. The two sat close together on a wagon seat, waving and grinning as the patrons on the train waved back.

The train moved on, and the couple passed out of sight, but their joy lingered with Beth. Would she ever share such a moment—with John or someone else?

"I don't get it." Em threw her hands in the air. "Why did you agree to leave?"

"I have to obey my parents." Beth grabbed her lap robe to ward off the chilly wind blowing through the window. The acrid smell of smoke stung her nose and made her eyes water. The train took a turn around a vast slough, and she noticed, on a rise of ground, a man resting on his horse, watching the train. Prickles went down her spine. Was that John? She lost sight of him as the train turned, and when she glanced over her shoulder—he was gone.

Her seatmate continued talking, and finally, Beth forced her mind back to the conversation.

"You're old enough to make up your mind."

"Defy my parents? How would I live, for heaven's sake?" Beth snapped.

"Well, I wouldn't leave, that's all. If I had a beau as rich as John, I'd marry him quick and move a long way from here."

"I'm not ready to get married," Beth said. "Besides, he hasn't asked me."

"It doesn't make any sense to me why your folks wouldn't approve of someone as rich as John. Look at the house he'll live in, and the money his parents have. Think of the way you'll be able to shop and dress when you marry him. As his wife, you would have the means to do whatever you want."

Beth drew in a deep, cleansing breath when the train, at last, finished its turn and straightened out, bringing a fresh breeze through the window. "That's not the point." She searched for the sentry on the horizon, but no horse waited on the skyline. "I'm not with John because he has money."

"Sure, he's lovely to look at," the girl said. "And everyone likes him, but I'll be after a guy for his money—believe me. If he's good looking to boot, so much the better."

Beth turned to her. "Emileah! Don't you want love?"

"Oh, sure." Her companion pulled again at the confining sleeves of her ensemble.

"Don't you *believe* in love?" Beth asked.

Em slipped her fingers under the tight neckline of her dress and tugged. "Are you saying you love John?"

"I don't suppose I know all that much about love, but John is sweet, and I think I could love him, given time." It had to be true. She'd pinned her hopes and dreams on him, even to the point of disobeying her parents.

Em snorted. "I guess love is blind, like they say." She slapped her bag onto the seat beside her. "For goodness' sake. Haven't you noticed how John uses people? He's sweet if he can get what he wants, but then, watch out. I can't believe you don't know."

"Know what?" Beth whispered, searching her companion's face for clues.

The sudden blowing of the whistle cut off their conversation. The conductor pulled hard on the brakes, thrusting the passengers forward in their seats. Beth grabbed for her valise, but some of her belongings rolled onto the floor. She let them go, more concerned for the danger she and the others might suffer. Had the rider come back, or was he a watchman for a gang of thieves? Craning her neck to see around those who were standing, she searched for the source of trouble.

"Outlaws?" Em screeched. "It's a hold-up."

CHAPTER THREE

The whistle blew again, and Beth stretched her neck to look for the man on horseback. She clamped a hand on her chest, tamping down the panic. There wasn't a place to hide her reticule and money. What would happen now?

"Of all the ridiculous ... stupid ..." her companion grumbled when a milk cow shuffled away from the train. More cows followed, accompanied by young calves. After several minutes, the train picked up speed.

Beth laughed, almost hysterical with relief. She shook her head when the last of the brown-and-white spotted calves ran to catch their mothers, their tails in the air. How silly she'd been to draw an outrageous conclusion, yet her eyes searched the skyline for a rider. The train gained momentum and soon neared its top speed—twenty miles per hour according to her father.

"Just like buffler," a gruff-sounding old-timer spoke behind her.

Another man answered with youthful authority. "None of those around anymore."

"They still hide out in river bottoms, sloughs, and wallows," the old-timer said.

"I ain't seen any in years, mister," the porter commented as he walked through the car, checking on the passengers.

"Maybe not, maybe so," the old-timer mumbled as he talked around a chew. "Those buffler be hiding in some backwater meadow. A few could be lost for years, the way these rivers wander about. I hear tell, from time to time ..." The old-timer coughed. When he got his breath back, he said, "Buffler still around."

Beth waited for a reply, but only silence followed. Maybe the other men decided to let the old-timer have his way. Beth had to agree with them, though—buffalo were gone from Minnesota.

"For heaven's sake, will you help me look?" Her companion knelt on the floor, her head under the seat. "My bag tipped over, and I can't reach everything."

Beth bent down to help but stopped to spread her lap robe over the floor. The remains of chewing tobacco, manure from boots, and who-knew-what-else littered the space under their feet. She got down on her knees atop the robe.

"Can I be of assistance to you, ladies?" asked a male voice behind her.

Beth froze at the thought of someone catching both girls on their knees between the seats. She turned to find none other than the boy Em had smiled at earlier.

"Oh, thank you." She moved out of his way with difficulty, considering the abundant fabric of her skirt and her tight shoes.

He didn't seem to mind the floor, retrieving their belongings, handing Beth her book, then settling on the seat beside Em.

The girl fluffed the fringe of her hair and flashed him a coy smile. "My name is Emileah. Well, Leah. That's Beth." She gestured in Beth's general direction. "I saw you board at the last town."

"I'm Lucas. Heading to the goldfields, I am."

Beth shook out her lap robe and folded it away. "That sounds like a dangerous place. Why would you want to go there?"

"Why?" Em batted her eyelashes. "How can you ask such a question? Gold—that's why."

"But we hear those camps are overgrown with thugs. They're short on food and have little shelter. It's spring now, but how will you live when it gets cold?" Beth had argued with John about this very subject. She believed steady work and supporting a family would bring happiness rather than running off for gold.

"Beth, don't kill his dream." She took Lucas's arm.

"I don't mean ... it just seems ... there are safer ways to make a living."

Em slid closer to the boy. "So, tell me all about the place."

"I don't know a lot about it," Lucas said. "I haven't never been there myself, but we had a man in our town who went. I'm going to be his partner."

The girl snuggled close, clutched his arm, and touched her hair. "I think it's a real adventure. If I were a man, I'd go."

Beth watched Lucas's face as he stared at his arm, captured by this girl he'd just met. He looked around. "Time I got going. I might see you both at supper tonight." He disengaged himself, tipped his hat, and left.

"He's nice." Em fluffed her hair. "I think he likes me."

Beth bit her lip to stop herself from blurting out a rude comment. Her companion's mood changed faster than the temper of Grandpa Isaac, one of their customers at the general store. First, she had a crush on John, and then she didn't, now she thought this boy she just met liked her. "I'm sure he does."

"Honestly, you get to see people all the time, but I'm barely allowed to leave the house. So many interesting shoppers come into your store." She waved at the aisle. "I want adventure like these folks."

Beth nodded. "Papa and I enjoy the people. I'll miss it while I'm gone."

"What I don't understand," Em said, "is why you can't recognize the good-for-nothings."

"I try not to judge." Beth hated to fall into her seatmate's trap. Her companion acted as if she had a juicy bit of gossip she wanted to share. "Who do you mean good-for-nothing? You have something you want to tell me?"

"How about John?"

"You just said you'd snatch him up right quick. Now you're calling him a good-for-nothing. I know he doesn't seem to work at anything, but he says he has plans."

"He has plans for sure." She snorted. "I may be siding with the wrong person, but at least I have my eyes open. All your talk of love and not judging makes you blind."

Beth didn't believe herself innocent and immature. She saw plenty of the seamy side of life at the mercantile. All kinds of characters came to their store. Some down on their luck, others creating problems for themselves by their poor choices, yet many were the victims of circumstances—sickness, crop failure, injuries, and debt.

"I mean it, Beth, you're so naïve. You're going to end up like her." Her companion gestured at the woman across the aisle. "Instead of a nice house, you'll be living in a shanty, having a baby every year."

Beth shrugged. Would that woman's life be so bad if she had someone who loved her—a mate to build a dream together? Beth dreamed of a different life, yet she liked the work at her parents' mercantile. It hadn't occurred to her they would follow through with their threat and send her away.

When Beth woke again, afternoon sun slanted across the land. Trees in the distance signaled a swale or river. Now, the scenery within Beth's view revealed a varied landscape as the sun touched high hills, leaving depressions shadowed. She treasured the prairie in all its moods. In the early morning, the grasslands held foggy moisture, while nests and webs sparkled like jewels in the sunshine. Later, in the full sun, it looked almost flat. She loved this time of day best though. It had contour and depth. Often, an evening wind kept the grass stirring and dancing, bending here to speak some secret and bending there to catch each sound.

The train's whistle blew, interrupting her thoughts. They had arrived at their night stop, at last.

"Doesn't look like much." Em rubbed her eyes and peered out the window.

As they came to a stop in front of the depot, Beth stood to disembark, stretching out the kinks and stiffness.

"Oh, miss, I'll lock up your trunk overnight since you're leaving in the morning." The station agent tipped his hat.

"Thank you, sir."

They wandered from the depot, in search of a promising overnight establishment. Up ahead, a large two-story, corner structure with a wide wraparound porch faced them as they approached. Beth liked the way the black trim on shutters and support posts contrasted with the stark white exterior. But when she gazed up at the upper-level windows that peered out from under the low roofline of the second story, she shivered. Those hooded windows spoiled the welcoming effect of the first floor.

A high, false front hid the peak and proudly carried the name of the business: Main Street Hotel. She would have preferred to find another place to stay. Her skin crawled as if someone watched them, and she thought back to the man on horseback.

The hotel entrance sat on the highest point of land, at street elevation. Then, the hill sloped away to a lower level in back. That basement section must hold the kitchen and laundry. Even as Beth watched, a drayman pulled a wagon loaded with supplies right up to the basement door.

"Looks all right," Em said, as they stepped up onto the generous porch.

Beth pressed her lips tight together. She was here to make her way, and it was time to put away imaginary ideas of being watched. Her travel companion marched through the double doors, and Beth followed.

An intense smell of new lumber and fresh paint permeated the structure. The lobby, nestled in the front corner of the building, contained a few stuffed chairs, several colorful rugs, and a fern on its stand in front of a side window. Chairs and tables filled the larger room beyond, defining it as the place to eat.

They moved forward when the manager at the counter finished his conversation with a previous customer.

The dapper little man turned to them and smiled, his mouth almost hidden beneath his drooping, white mustache. "What can I do for you two fine lasses today?" He slipped an arm into the sleeve of a black coat and shrugged it into place over a shirt as white as his full head of hair. A red and green plaid tie provided the only color in his attire.

"Looking for a room, sir." Em rested a gloved hand on the counter.

"The two of you going to share?"

"Yes, sir." Beth untangled her reticule from her wrist.

He grasped the edges of a ledger with gnarled hands. "Got just the thing, I do." He ran a crooked finger down the list. "Top of the stair, take a right—your room will be the second door on the left."

"Thank you." Beth stepped closer to the counter.

"You be wantin' supper and breakfast?"

"Yes, please," her companion answered in a hurry before Beth could say a word.

"Well, now, that's right fine. Pay in advance now, lassies. We not be knowin' you two, and though I'm sure you be honest folk, it's how we operate here."

The price he named was more than they'd been told to expect, but Beth paid the fee.

"Thank you, miss. Now, go ahead and put up your things. Supper is ready any time you are."

They ascended a steep flight of stairs to their accommodations. Beth opened the door and stepped into the room. She bent her head and walked under the slanted roof and glanced out the window that faced the backyard of the hotel. The drayman she'd seen earlier still unloaded supplies at an entrance directly below.

"Small enough." Em dropped her bulging valise on the floor and banged her elbow on the wall. "Ouch!"

Beth detached the ruffles at her wrists and put them away before hanging her nightclothes on the hooks provided. She turned to the bed, pulled back the pieced blanket, and examined the sheets.

Em picked up the pitcher, poured water into the bowl, and washed her hands. "What do you expect to find?"

"I've heard stories you wouldn't believe." Beth lifted the top mattress. It crunched like straw. A layer of flowers lay between it and the bottom, cornhusk mattress. Nothing crawled or moved, so she rearranged the bedding and straightened the blankets.

"Well?" Her companion waited with hands on her hips.

"Looks clean. The sheets are clean, anyway."

"Let's eat."

"Can't we walk some? We've been sitting all day, and it's early yet."

"All right, let's go." Em snatched up her shawl and sped out the door, leaving Beth to follow or not.

They reached the lobby, and the girl turned in the opposite direction from the train depot. She charged down a well-trod path between houses and barns and forged on as if determined to get this over with as soon as possible.

Her companion brought them around to the tracks they'd come in on. Without a word, she hastened to the hotel. Beth panted from the forced walk, and dampness pooled under her arms. So much for the stroll she had imagined.

Beth dug a hanky from her pocket and blotted her damp forehead, but her companion went straight into the diner. Beth hurried after her. They choose an empty table by the window and seated themselves. Beth glanced around, searching for anyone she might recognize. Several women and two young girls scurried here and there with coffee, orders, and refills. Single men, or at least men eating by themselves, took places at a long table and passed bowls back and forth family-style.

"Now, gal, you tell your ma she done herself proud on this here stew," a rotund man with a bushy red beard yelled from the back table.

The girl grinned and dipped a curtsey. "Yes, sir."

"Heh, J.D.!" another man called as he walked through the lobby.

The old gentleman behind the front desk, thrust his head out to peer around the corner. "What you be wantin', Jonas?"

"What'd you hear about that gang?"

J.D. glanced around the room. Beth wasn't the only one curious as several heads rose at the question. His gaze rested on her, and he cleared his throat. "Nothing, Jonas, there's na to worry about."

Beth tensed. Her mouth went dry when Jonas and several other men met up with J.D. and bent forward, leaning in to hear the whispered conversation. She held her breath, hoping to overhear their talk. Was it about the man on horseback?

CHAPTER FOUR

A young girl came to their table and distracted Beth from her worries. She poured a cup of coffee and set it on the table.

"What would ya like?" The girl flipped an auburn braid over her shoulder.

"There is stew?" Beth didn't eat away from home and wasn't sure how to order.

"Mum's hearty stew with bread and pie," the girl said. "We have venison steak and beans, if dat's more to your likin'."

"Stew sounds delicious." Beth picked up her cup.

Em asked, "What kind of pie?"

The waitress smiled, revealing a dimple. "Dried apple is all we have till the berries are ready."

"I'll have that too."

"Pie is part of the meal when you stay here, miss, and our dried apple pie is famous in these parts."

"I'll try it." Beth smiled up at the girl. "Thank you."

They didn't have long to wait before the server returned with heavy white bowls filled to the top with fragrant stew. She also set a blue, chipped plate piled with thick-sliced bread in the middle of the table, along with a bowl of butter. Last, she gave them each a piece of pie, nicely browned with a drizzle of sugary cinnamon on top.

Em dug in like a starved person, but Beth continued to study people. Maybe she would learn more about the man who followed them or the gang someone mentioned. The cook, her blue, flowered dress protected beneath an enveloping white apron, emerged from the kitchen to confer with J.D. at the front desk.

Em tasted her pie. "Mm, this is good. I want to cook like this. Mother couldn't teach me, and father's"—she rolled her eyes—"new wife won't cook, so I never learned."

"You'll learn from the woman you're working for I bet." Beth had never thought about cooking. When she returned home from work, dinner was there. Each morning after a breakfast she didn't make, she picked up the lunch her mother had prepared and went to work.

"Do you think so?" Her friend licked her lips.

"You could learn to make the best-tasting things. Everyone needs to know how to cook." Guilt at her own lack of knowledge surged through her. Maybe she'd better learn too.

"Maybe I will," Em said. "If the woman I'm going to work for is a good cook. Not like her cousin, who's afraid to eat." She spooned another bite into her mouth and closed her eyes. "Father said the family needed me to take care of children."

"Sure, but cooking is part of being a mother's helper. These days, everyone has to make do."

"My mother could cook." Her companion took another bite. "She made wonderful meals before she got sick. I wish I had paid attention to her recipes."

Beth scraped the bowl for the last of her stew and finished eating a slice of well-buttered bread. "Did she have any relatives you could ask?"

"I don't know. There were never any around, and I didn't think about it then. The only people at her funeral were from town."

"Yes, I remember. Everyone liked your mother." Beth tasted her pie. "I didn't think I had any relatives in Minnesota either, but I never asked. It looks like I'm going to be meeting one of them."

Em finished her pie, reached over and scooped a bite off Beth's plate. "I want this place to be different from home, you know?"

Beth sat back and let her companion finish her pie. The girl's eyes were shining and her countenance hopeful. Beth was happy for her and pleased to see the perpetual, sour expression gone—even for a little while.

One of the serving girls stopped at their table.

"I like your pie." Em wiped her mouth with a cloth. "Please tell the cook for me."

The girl smiled at them. "I made the pie."

"You did?" Em's jaw dropped and her eyes flared open wide. "Do you think I could make pie like this?"

"Of course." The girl laughed. "The topping I used is just rose hips with a little sugar and cinnamon."

"Rose hips?" Em asked.

The girl waved her hand like scattering feed for chickens. "No need to add them. You'll do fine," she said. "Just make a dried apple pie, and when you serve it, melt butter with a tiny amount of sugar and cinnamon and drizzle that over the pie."

Em nodded, but when the girl walked away, she said, "Make a dried apple pie?"

Beth shrugged. "I'm sure someone where we're going must know how to make one."

Her companion scraped the plate for the last bit of syrupy cinnamon, savoring the last morsel. Then she pushed away from the table. "Let's walk." Without looking back to see if Beth followed, she headed out the door.

Beth jumped to her feet and hurried after her. "Goodness. You change your mind quicker than the weather."

"Ready?" Her companion waited at the edge of the porch.

"I guess." Beth pulled her jacket into place and straightened her shoulders.

Em stepped off the porch and turned in a different direction this time. They strolled at a more leisurely pace than before their meal. Beth's head turned here and there to observe the businesses. Another hotel, advertised as "Hotel and Boarding House," stood at the far end of Main Street. It appeared older and smaller than the one where they were staying. Beth would have liked to stop at one of the general stores to compare them with the merchandise her parents carried, but they were closed this time of night.

"Do you wonder how it happened we're traveling together?"

Beth stopped walking and stared at her. The hair on the back of her neck prickled. "As far as I know, my parents just decided I needed to visit my aunt."

"I wondered how we're going to the same town."

"I didn't think of that." Beth began walking again. Was the woman she was to stay with even a relative? How was it that Em's stepmother had a relative in the same town Beth did? Why had Beth's mother decided now was the perfect time to send her away? Trepidation knotted her stomach. "How long ago was your trip planned?"

"I'm not sure."

They stepped up onto the front porch of their hotel. Only a few late diners remained in the room, perhaps hankering for a piece of pie. Beth and Em sat in the comfortable lobby, not ready to retreat to their small room and retire.

"I wonder how my parents knew you were going?" Beth chewed on her nails.

"Yeah, it's not like my father or the step-woman were friendly to anyone in town, even your parents."

J.D. came from the dining room where he had been sweeping the floor. "Where you girls headed?"

Beth tugged down the sleeve of her jacket. "Marshall area."

"Glad to have you stay with us," he said.

"It looks busy around here."

"We have railroad workers hereabouts. There are extra men at the livery, plus construction everywhere, so we hired more gals to help us here." He resumed sweeping, then rearranged chairs around the tables. When he came back into the lobby, he said, "I live in the hotel, so if you young lasses need anything, let me know."

"Thank you, sir." Beth caught glimpses of other workers finishing up for the night.

When it grew late, they visited the necessary and retired to their room. Em slipped a match from the metal box on the nightstand and lit a lamp set in the wall. Beth cleaned her teeth and used the pitcher and basin to wash up. After she changed into her nightgown, she set the chair under the doorknob. Em arranged her clothing on the hooks provided and blew out the lamp.

Beth said, "Do you think we're going to relatives, or just someone they found for us to work for?"

"I don't know, but it seems suspicious." Em's quiet response surprised Beth, but her next comment sent a chill down her spine. "I think something's wrong."

"What?"

Em turned her back and said nothing more.

Beth pondered her last comment, and a few others throughout the day that hung in the air like drifting cobwebs. What did Em know? Beth hadn't been given a choice on this trip, so she had to trust her parents. But the accumulating evidence didn't bode well. Beth's parents had hurriedly whisked her away.

Before long, Em's gentle breathing indicated she'd fallen asleep. Despite her earlier walk, Beth couldn't sleep and had never shared a bed with someone. She clung to her side of the mattress, struggling not to roll into the sunken middle caused by sagging ropes. Stale scents of flowers and straw wafted around her, and the mattress rustled each time she moved—not like her feather bed back home.

Smoke drifted in through thin walls too. She had grown up with her mother's constant fear of fire, and her warnings nagged, keeping her awake and vigilant.

Much later, she still lay awake. The chair she'd wedged under the door handle, its front legs suspended in midair, cast a weird shadow against the wall. She crept to the room's one window and raised the sash as quietly as she could. Clean, crisp air seeped in.

She sat on the floor. Arms splayed on the window frame, her head on her hands, she breathed in the clean, fresh scent. Below her, evident in the bright moonlight, the delivery lot at the back of the hotel stood empty but for two parked wagons. Nothing else was visible this time of night, but stars. Wishing for home, her room, and her bed, she sat until the cold drove her back to the warmth of the blankets.

Beth jolted awake, her heart hammering in her chest. She searched the room, trying to determine where she was and what woke her. Golden moonlight highlighted the contents of the room, and all appeared as it should be. When the noise came again, she shivered and held her breath. Was someone talking to her?

"We ... keep moving." The man's whispered words trailed off and she strained to hear.

Another man spoke, his accent southern. "Ya, let's get shut of this place."

The first man spoke again. "Smith, you explain the operation and show him around." The voice sounded forceful but authoritative. It also sounded familiar, but she couldn't place it.

The voices were coming from outside—right outside her window. She hurried out of bed and crawled to the opening.

"... work the outlying areas." She could only hear part of a conversation. "Take what livestock we can sell and get out."

Beth shivered. What did he mean? Were these men talking about theft? She rose on her knees to peer over the windowsill and look down. Three men gathered in the delivery lot below her window. One of them stood off by himself, while the other two huddled together over a pinpoint of fire. The flame flickered then went dark. Someone whispered. Beth could not make out the comment, but she understood the response when it came.

"I ain't afraid of the law, Smith," the raspy, nasal voice snapped.

"Watch your mouth," said the small man who spoke with the southern accent. "They got a boss man in charge of this whole shee-bang." His hat shadowed his face, but when he inhaled, light glowed for a moment, revealing round, boyish features. "No one gets to meet him but Badger."

"What's he afraid of?" the round man with a nasal voice whined. "Don't want to associate with the likes of us?"

Smith said, "He's a rich fellow. Badger's always sayin' the boss man this and the boss man that." He tilted his head back and blew a smoke ring.

Beth peered closer. The third man hadn't spoken since she'd been watching, and his face stayed in shadow. Could he be the one whose voice woke her?

"I don't get it," the man with the nasal voice spoke again, slapping his gloves against his chaps.

"He knows where the money is 'cause of his folks, they say." Smith flicked his cigarette butt away. The arc of light landed, and he toed it out.

"I don't trust no Jack born with a silver spoon. That's what I says," the round man said, his nasal voice rising in pitch. "He'll get us all hung." He cleared his throat and spat.

Smith pulled the makings from his pocket to roll another cigarette. "They got a slough they keep 'em in. It's a big one, all right, but has an island of high ground smack dab in the middle."

"You'd play hob if a fire got going." The nasal-voiced man tugged at his bandana, turning it to tighten the knot.

"Or if those sod-busters start cutting it." Smith upended the tobacco pouch over the paper and tapped it.

"Time you two got outta here." The third man stepped forward out of the shadows.

Beth bent forward to see him better. Was he the leader?

Loose gravel rattled behind the men. Two of them crouched and backed out of sight. The third man glanced up, right at her window!

Beth sank and ducked her head. Her throat burned. The roar in her ears sounded like someone charging up the stairs. She shivered and watched the door, ready to scream if it moved.

When she could stand the cold no longer, she took a cautious peek out the window. Only an empty yard shown in the moonlight. She crawled back to bed and huddled under the covers on her edge of the mattress. Tremors shook her body, but it wasn't only from cold. She lay awake in the night, recalling that voice. No one else had the gravelly voice of John Bader.

CHAPTER FIVE

The light of early dawn spilled through the window. Beth turned and twisted to loosen muscles stiff from a cramped train ride and the attempt to stay on her edge of the bed. When her bare feet hit the cold floor, she suppressed a cry. Doing her best not to wake Em, she donned the traveling costume from the day before, pulling up the skirt and fastening the waistband over her chemise. She put on the bodice, hooked it up the front, and smoothed the bottom pleats. After attaching the ruffles, she sat in the chair and listened to birds sing their morning song. Her companion still slept, lying in the middle of the bed, snuggled under all the blankets.

Beth checked the watch pinned to her dress. "Come on, Em. Time to get up."

Her friend groaned and rolled over.

"Emileah, I mean it. You need to get up now. My things are packed, so I'll meet you downstairs." Beth jerked the quilt. "Do you hear me?"

"Sure." The girl threw back the covers.

Beth left the room, went downstairs, and sat at the table they had used the night before, positioned to watch the doorway. She scrutinized each patron, hoping and dreading recognition from the encounter a few hours ago. A sleepless night had brought reason—the voice couldn't be John's, and outlaws did not talk outside the open window of a hotel.

When Em joined her, one of the servers brought the meal, a plate of eggs, potatoes, and ham.

"Mm, this is wonderful," Beth helped herself to a bite of ham. "How did you sleep?"

"Great." Em speared a forkful of fried potatoes.

"I see you put on a different dress this morning."

Her friend's snort wasn't ladylike. "You bet. I refuse to wear *that thing* again."

"I'm sure you'll be more comfortable."

"That's for sure." Em took another bite. "Mm, I haven't had anything like this unless Mrs. Henry cooked it for me. Do you know how long that's been?"

Beth glanced around the room. Suddenly, she spotted a man hidden in the shadows at the far corner of the room. He seemed to be looking straight at her. She ducked her head as her mouth went dry and nodded to her companion, pretending to be listening to her prattle.

"Even if Father's new wife could cook, she would never eat this ... or allow me to."

"What does your father eat?" Beth lifted her head to check the corner of the room. The man's hat was pulled low to cover his face.

Em shrugged. "He eats at the hotel."

Beth checked the watch pinned to her bodice. "We need to go soon."

"Already? I just started."

"Well, hurry then." Beth lifted her cup and studied the room over the rim. The workers scurried around as more customers were seated. She set her cup down and selected another bite from her plate. When she checked the corner again, it was empty.

Em scraped up the last of her eggs with a bit of ham and shoved them in her mouth. "I'm ready," she said with a mouth full of food as she pushed back her chair.

Beth jumped at the sudden announcement, and her fork clattered to the floor. She left the fork and hurried after her friend. They retrieved their bags, turned in the key, and walked to the depot. The station agent had already loaded her trunk. Beth rushed to find empty seats in the front of the train where she could watch the rest of the car. Once seated and her bag tucked out of the way, she was free to study train preparations and people.

Who was the man at the hotel, and did his gaze focus on her? Her stomach churned. This train would take her further from home, away from security and away from help.

The pandemonium of passengers and yelling porters finally died down.

"All aboard!" was called, and the train began to move. The town disappeared, and the open prairie stretched before her. Her persistent headache returned, and the overheard conversation played over in her mind. What unlucky family lost stock during the night?

She leaned back against the seat. Even if the end of this trip meant living with a woman she'd never met and a place she didn't want to visit, she hoped today would pass quickly. She yearned to be outside, walking through the tall plants, feeling the stems run through her fingers like water. She would hide in the grass as she had as a child. The wind, plants, and trees were her only friends back then. She fancied they talked to her, and it eased her loneliness.

A sweet child's voice broke through her reverie. Across the narrow aisle, a woman near Beth's age smiled at her. She shared a seat with a young boy and a girl. The siblings each had straight, brown hair, high cheekbones, and lanky frames.

The youngest girl tugged at her mother's skirt. "Are they watching Evie?"

"Yes, Malinda."

The boy asked, "Will I have to share my room?" Beth noticed a peculiar hunch to his back where it rested against his mother.

"I don't know, Son." The mother tucked a lock of hair into the bun at the nape of her neck. Her black dress stretched over a full bust. The fabric, dotted with small circles, was like the selection stocked at her parent's store.

"Do I have to help milk cows?"

"Mother, make him stop asking those questions." The oldest girl gestured to her offending sibling. "He's asked everything hundreds of times already." The young woman faced her younger brother. "Yes, Jimmy, we still have cows. Nothing has changed. We're still living on a farm, just somewhere else."

"Oh, Ester!" The boy turned to her, pulled out the corners of his mouth, stuck out his tongue, and crossed his eyes.

Ester patted him on his rounded back and laughed.

When the young woman looked around, she and Beth exchanged a smile. Beth envied the family—being together for this adventure. A pang seared through her at the dire situation that brought her here. Would this estrangement from her parents ever be restored?

"My, I like the men on this train," Em said. "There's one behind you. My goodness, he's more handsome than your John."

Without thinking, Beth turned. The man sat but a few rows behind her. Their glances met and held for a heart-stopping moment. She struggled to breathe and drag her eyes away.

Oh, my! She turned back around, a flush heated her neck and spread up over her face. Her ears were sure to be red beacons on the side of her head. She patted her hair, checking its chignon, and poked a finger under her velvet choker necklace.

"I told you. But don't forget, I saw him first," Em taunted. "Besides, you have John."

Beth had no intention of replacing her beau, but why this feeling of breathlessness? Young men did not make her tingle and feel warm. John didn't make her blush or leave her with a sensation of weakness, but this stranger left her wanting to take another look.

She must put him out of her mind. A glance out the window brought a small lake gleaming into her vision. Its brilliant blue water invited her to cool her heated body.

The hollow clank of the wheels over a trestle bridge woke Beth. Bright sunshine, the first she'd seen in days, brought all shades of green to life in the valley below. Beth admired the blue-green and yellow green of spring. The damp tree trunks stood out blunt and bold against those thin spots of color.

Em was not in her seat, but her distinctive, flirty voice twittered from behind. Beth turned in her place and saw her companion sitting next to the man she'd pointed out earlier. When Em's gaze fell on Beth, she jumped up, wiggled her fingers at the man, and rushed back to her seat. She plunked down next to Beth.

"Emileah, what possessed you to talk to a total stranger?" Beth nudged her with an elbow. "How long have you been talking to him anyway?" She glanced over her shoulder. The man walked away toward the rear door of the car, his broad back filling the aisle. He ducked his head to keep from bumping the ceiling and disappeared through the door.

"Don't be such a gooseberry. He lives in the town we're going to and told me all about it. He knows your aunt or whatever she is, and even the place where I'm going. He said there are several children, and it's a good God-fearing family."

"That's good, isn't it?"

"God hasn't done me any favors so far," her companion said. "I won't count on help from him."

"Emileah!"

"Well, it's true. I prayed and prayed, like the man at church always said, but Mamma died anyway. I needed her. I still need her, not like when I was little, but I want ... well, someone who loves me."

"We all do." Beth picked up her basket and moved to sit across the seat.

Em slapped her carry bag into place on the seat Beth had just vacated. "Going to a better place, the man said. Sure thing, maybe she did, but where did that leave me?"

"I'm sorry. All of us struggle to understand these things."

Her friend snorted. "That preacher didn't win me over at Mamma's funeral. I don't care to hear such jargon anymore."

"Remember, preachers are people, like the rest of us. Some things we don't understand." When Em frowned and crossed her arms, Beth changed the subject. "What else did the man say about the town?"

"Oh, he said lots. He said it's a fine, growing town, and we'll like it. I told him you wouldn't be staying because of your gorgeous John."

"How could you?" Beth shuddered. The conversation likely hadn't been flattering.

"It isn't a secret, is it?"

"I'm not in the habit of having my life gossiped about," Beth said.

Em snorted. "Alice brought up your name often enough. She said you were spoiled and proud and not good enough for John."

"I didn't know." Beth clenched her teeth. It hurt to know her few friends whispered unkind things behind her back. Though she and Em had gone to school together, Alice had arrived at their town only recently. They barely knew each other.

"I suppose you didn't get together with the girls much." She flipped her hair. "The woman Father married wouldn't allow it, and of course Father agreed. I wasn't there often. I didn't care for those snippy girls. On the part of Alice, it was plain sour grapes. She chased John all the time and promised him way more than she should."

"Emileah!"

"Well, it's true. I don't know any more about men than you do, but I can see when a girl is throwing herself at a man." She swung her arm wide. "I saw it plenty with that woman my father married."

Beth smoothed her hand down the skirt of her ensemble and clenched her jaw. She'd been packed up and put on a train like a disobedient child. Now another girl had her eyes on John. And where did her schoolmate come into this? Her interest seemed more than the casual inquisitiveness of someone from the same town.

"If you ask me, Alice is the one not good enough for John." Em shifted in her seat. "John should have a woman who can rise to the social status his life will have."

Beth pressed her lips together. She had seen the way Alice looked at John when they'd encountered her in town, and she had seen other girls acting coy. Flirting was something Beth had never figured out how to do, but it was part of Alice and Em's whole demeanor. And the men seemed to like it.

John was a man, and she supposed he, like all the others, preferred flirty girls better than simple, unsophisticated girls like her. She thought again of the stranger Em had talked to earlier. Would he be the same? Depression settled like a cloak over her. She rested her face in her hands—she better get a hold of herself. It appeared John wasn't who she thought he was, but she needn't be thinking of other men. Maybe she'd better resign herself to life as an old maid.

CHAPTER SIX

A whistle and the change in the clank and rattle of the train woke Beth. How could she sleep so much? Last night she'd lain awake for hours, but here on the train she slept and slept. She glanced out the window. They were pulling to a stop at yet another small town.

"Do you get homesick?" her traveling companion asked, as if she'd been waiting for Beth to wake up.

Beth turned her head and stretched. "Me?"

"You know, do you ever feel homesick?" Em's brow furrowed.

"I haven't been away from my parents, ever, and I don't plan on staying long this time." She sat up and stretched her back, but the anxiety of being away from her parents stung her again. "I suppose I will be homesick, you know, for my folks and my life."

"You've always had your mother and father beside you," Em said. "I miss Mamma, and I wish for the way things were. Her humming and talking to me, or Mamma brushing my hair. I want my life back the way it was."

"So do I." Beth turned to the window as the train got going again. She wasn't missing a mother who died, but this split from her parents had cast her adrift from the only life she knew. "I'll be lonely for my parents," she said, "and the routine of my life."

"You don't understand." The girl twirled a lock of hair. "I miss her smell and the sound of her around the house. I get homesick for it all, and I took it for granted." She shrugged. "I don't think I'll ever go back."

Twisting her back, Beth tried to relieve the ache. "Why?"

"I must be like Mamma, and Father doesn't want the reminder."

"You think your father is making you leave because you look like your mother? That's crazy. I mean, you do remind me of her, and you have her beautiful complexion, but I would think he would cherish that."

"She was Mamma." Em wrapped her arms around herself. "She held me and loved to sing. Mamma laughed a lot and loved me. I mean it." She jumped forward and grabbed Beth's arm, peering at her like she needed her to understand. "She loved me. It wasn't duty or anything." She leaned back in her seat and crossed her arms. "Yesterday when I left, Father said goodbye to me as if to say, 'We knew each other once, but times have changed.' He doesn't want me around."

"Were you and your father close? You know, before ... before your mother died?"

"I don't know. Father did everything with Mamma and me because Mamma spent her time with me. If we went on a picnic, he sat with her and held her hand. I don't recall him holding me."

Beth rested her chin on her folded hands. The naked pain in her friend's voice held no pretense. In truth, Em's father made Beth nervous. He hung over his current wife like his next breath depended on it. How would a child fit into such a situation?

Beth couldn't imagine life without her parents, no matter how upset she felt right now. Her dear papa doted on her, at least until recently. Could her predicament be the same as Em's? Did her parents not want her around? No, that was impossible.

She straightened and searched out the window for a horseman watching the train. He wasn't there, but maybe the men had ridden off to another town. Was this mystery why she was sent away? A shiver ran down her spine, and she rubbed the back of her neck.

"I've decided to go by Leah here." Her traveling companion brought Beth's thoughts back to the present. "That was Mamma's name, you know. Father wouldn't let me, and of course *she* completely agreed with him. But they aren't here. Though I could never be as good as Mamma, somehow that might ..." Em swiped at the tears pooling in her eyes, her usual perfect complexion blotchy and red from suppressed emotion.

"I've always liked your name." Beth turned to the window to give her friend time to compose herself. "I forgot that Leah was your mother's name."

"I hate my name, but Mamma was Leah, and my grandmother was Emily."

The train blasted its whistle, and Beth craned her neck to see around the heads in front of her. Everyone seemed on edge. Maybe it had something to do with the rumors of a gang. This time, there was nothing to fear as several horses galloped away from the tracks to the safety of a nearby barn. She scanned the horizon.

Em made another abrupt change of subject. "Do you think you'll miss John?"

Beth flinched. How did they get back on that subject? Had her old classmate always been so obsessed with the man? She twisted her reticule back and forth in her hands. She faced her, ready to question her preoccupation with John, when Em interrupted her.

"I just wondered. We don't know each other ... I mean we didn't hang out together, but it might be nice to have a friend in town."

Beth sighed, suddenly understanding that her traveling companion was unsure of her future too. "Sure, but I don't think I'll stay long. A month or two at the most. My parents will need my help with the store over the summer. Mom says she's going to do more, but she gets tired these days."

"Which side of the family is this aunt or whoever you're going to see? Mr. Randall didn't know of any relatives she had except her children and another lady in town."

"Is that his name?" Beth's stomach flipped. "Why did you talk to him about me?"

"We're going to the same area, and he asked," she said. "How are you related to that woman anyway?"

"She's my aunt, I guess, but I'm not sure how exactly."

Just then, a gentleman's voice spoke over Beth's shoulder, startling her. "May I sit for a moment, ladies?"

Beth glanced back. Her eyes met Mr. Randall's brown ones for the second time. Her mouth went dry, and her face heated.

Em grabbed her carry bag off the seat and moved to sit beside Beth. The man sat down on the aisle seat, facing them.

Beth's glance skittered in his direction, and again their eyes met. A tingle feathered through her body. She looked away to focus on the wall beyond him, willing her pounding heart to behave.

When he glanced away, she studied his face. He had a kind but stern countenance, tanned from outside work. He turned back to her, catching her look.

"You're Beth Townsend, I believe." The warm, soothing timbre of his voice vibrated from deep in his chest.

A peculiar feeling thrummed in Beth's midsection.

Em spoke before she had the chance. "Yes, Beth. Remember? I told you."

"You're Nora's niece?" he asked. "You look remarkably like her daughter, Lynn."

"I didn't know she had a daughter." Beth winced at how stupid her comment sounded.

"Really? Yes, older than you, I would say. She's married and has moved away."

"Oh." Beth twisted her fingers, then abruptly dropped her hands in her lap and willed them to be still. She didn't want the man to know he made her nervous.

"She has a brother too," he said.

"What?" Beth's brows creased. Did this man delight in bringing up people she didn't know?

"I just told you, your aunt has children," Em said. "Weren't you listening?"

"Nora Durand?" the man said. "That's who you're going to see?"

Beth nodded, still trying to digest this news. Why hadn't her parents told her about anyone besides this Nora woman? Truthfully, once they'd decided she must go, she'd focused all her efforts on changing their minds, not finding out details. Now she appeared dull and uncaring in front of this man from her aunt's hometown.

When Mr. Randall turned away, Beth covertly studied him. His collarless print shirt looked like those stocked in any general store. He removed his hat, revealing longish brown hair curling over the neckband of his shirt.

He turned to the family across the aisle. "Ma'am, I'm Stuart Randall. I met your boys back in the car with your livestock. It seems you're heading to the town where I live."

"Oh, Mr. Randall, nice to meet you," said the mother. "This is Ester and Jimmy and Malinda. Oh, and I'm Mrs. Osgood." She laughed. "How are my boys doing back there?"

"Fine, ma'am. They're capable young lads—respectful and responsible. They care for the livestock like good drovers, especially Caleb."

"Why, thank you, Mr. Randall."

Ester smiled. "Do you know the farm Papa bought for us, Mr. Randall?"

"Yes, miss. I know the place your brothers described. I haven't seen it in some time, though, as it's on the other side of town."

"What's the house like, sir?" Mrs. Osgood asked.

He paused, appearing to choose his words carefully. After a study of the walls of the train and then a glance outside, he answered. "Well, ma'am, to be honest, last time I saw it, the place wasn't much, but I'm sure your husband has it patched up fine by now."

Beth hid a smile behind her hand. She liked that Mr. Randall tried to put the apparently dilapidated homestead in a good light.

Mrs. Osgood glanced at her oldest daughter, a look passing between them, then squared her shoulders. After a glance at her other children, she lifted her chin. "I see."

Mr. Randall's voice softened. "The outbuildings are good, though, and there are several. You'll have someplace for those sheep, and I gather that's important." He smiled at the little girl.

Malinda grinned back, revealing missing front teeth. She turned to her mother. "A place for Evie and the lambs, Ma."

"You'll also have a place for that crate of chickens," Mr. Randall said. "The previous owner had a good sod coop last time I saw it."

"A sod coop?" Mrs. Osgood sat back in her seat, brushed a hand over her brow, and turned to the window.

Ester asked, "What's the town like? I hear it's getting quite settled."

"I don't know if you could call it settled, but we're working on it."

Mrs. Osgood turned from her study out the window. "What do you mean?"

"The town has anything you would generally need, and if you can't find it, you can always order supplies from New Ulm or Mankato."

"Schools and such?"

"Oh yes, ma'am. We've had a school here since the beginning—a good one too."

Mrs. Osgood poked a hairpin into a loose lock of hair. "Churches?"

"Yes, ma'am, although we don't always have a preacher." Mr. Randall glanced at Em and Beth to include them in the answer.

"Which direction did you say we was living?" Mrs. Osgood asked.

"The old Benson place is northward." Mr. Randall shifted in the seat, his knees accidentally bumping Beth.

She jumped, but he seemed unaware of the encounter. She pushed herself back into her seat so she had no more contact with his long legs. What was wrong with her? Reacting like a schoolgirl—to a mere man.

"What direction do you live, Mr. Randall?" Ester asked.

"I have a farm south. We had a shanty at first and built a house as soon as we could."

"You said 'we,' Mr. Randall ... you're married, then?" Mrs. Osgood asked.

Beth turned to catch his answer—not that she cared. She had a beau, and a handsome one too.

"No, ma'am." His glance met Beth's then slid away. "I came with my parents and uncles originally. My uncles moved west, and my parents passed on."

"Oh, I'm sorry. You're alone in the world, then?" Mrs. Osgood asked.

"No, ma'am, I'm not alone."

Mr. Randall turned in the seat and continued visiting with the family. The noise level on the train grew louder, so Beth couldn't hear much of what he said—something about watching livestock at the back of the train.

His broad back nearly faced her, the muscles evident through his shirt and vest. Her father would call him a man's man. Confident, gentle ... a man in every way. Beth saw many farmers and workers that shopped at their store, but never a man who looked like this.

She studied Mr. Randall. He idly pulled a pair of gloves through one hand while he talked, telling the Osgoods about their farm. His hands were strong, and his pulled back shirtsleeves revealed wrists and forearms rigid with muscle and sinew. John didn't look like this, and since he didn't work hard at anything the way this man did, he never would.

Mr. Randall turned toward Beth. She looked away, her breathing jerky. What if he could tell that she'd been admiring his broad back and muscular arms?

"Nora didn't mention she had a visitor coming," he said.

Beth had no idea how to answer him. His statement seemed one more indication that this trip was sudden but was also none of his concern.

"They just decided. Beth and I are going to help relatives." Em took over and talked, not giving him a chance to get a word in edgewise.

Beth forced her mind away from the man across from her. She thought back to her parents and the last tumultuous week. Her anger over this banishment had blazed hot, but she would like to take back some of the mean and childish things she'd said and done. What had possessed her to be so rude?

In the distance, a squat soddie faced them, its chimney jutting out of a hill. A garden fence held the wash of a woman, several children, and a man. Would Beth be strong enough to live like that if she married a man who farmed—someone like Mr. Randall? She'd heard of women who went by themselves to homestead. She admired them but doubted her inner strength to survive. Even with a husband and children, it would be a lonely existence.

Someone spoke the name John, snagging her attention. She looked around. There were many Johns, but Em and Stuart Randall were looking at her.

"What?" Beth faced the man across from her.

"You must have been daydreaming," Em said. "We've been talking to you, silly."

Beth glanced back at the soddie, reluctant to let go of her daydream about a place of her own, with a man of her own.

"I asked if you were missing your beau already." Mr. Randall's deep voice sang along her nerves.

What about this man left her so unsettled? She lifted her chin and turned away. Her beau was none of his business.

Her traveling companion answered for her again. "Of course, she's missing John."

Beth's gaze skimmed the train. Travelers in family groups conversed, slept, or peered out the window, studying this new land. Across the aisle, Jimmy leaned against his mother and played with a piece of string while Malinda stared out the window. Ester glanced at her and smiled. Beth grinned back.

"Time for me to head back, ma'am."

"Thank you for stopping, Mr. Randall," Mrs. Osgood said.

"You're welcome, ma'am, and please call me Stuart." He stood, tilting his head to keep from hitting the ceiling of the railroad car. He nodded to Ester. "See you soon."

He turned back to their side of the train, and Beth met his eyes. She swallowed the longing his look sent through her. He tipped his head to her. To her friend, he said, "I'll see you again soon, I hope, Leah."

She watched him walk up the center of the car. She shouldn't be interested in him.

CHAPTER SEVEN

Beth squinted out the window as a town came into view. From a distance, it looked like a child's abandoned play area—squares, rectangles, and triangles left in a heap on a bare plain. As the train drew closer and the village rose from the prairie, individual buildings became distinguishable. They approached a lumber station, coal sheds, and the depot itself. Distant trees, likely alongside a stream, provided a perfect backdrop for other buildings sprawled over the land.

As they pulled into the depot, Beth scanned the waiting crowd, her heart skipping in a hopeful flutter, but the boardwalk held no one she knew.

The Osgood family collected their possessions, and the little girl called Malinda pulled on her mother's arm. "Mother, will the boys get the trunks and sheep?"

"Yes, dear, that has been arranged, and your father is waiting for us too."

Beth's heart twisted as she watched the siblings respond to their mother's comment. Malinda turned to her younger brother. "Did you hear, Jimmy?"

"Yes." His face warmed with a huge smile. "Papa will be here."

Beth met Ester's eyes and nodded. Both were embarking on a new chapter of life, but Ester's adventure included her parents and siblings—the whole family facing their challenges together.

She piled her possessions together as tears threatened. She forced them away. It was childish to cry but lately it seemed that's all she did.

Em gathered her belongings. "It'll be grand, won't it?"

Beth swallowed the painful lump in her throat. "I don't want a grand or new life. I liked my old one."

Em's eyes closed, and her shoulders drooped.

Beth chewed on her lip. Her travel mate was trying to move on with bravado, and she had just slapped it back. "I'm sorry, Leah," she said, using the new name Em had chosen in hopes of repairing the damage. "Yes, this will be a wonderful, grand adventure. It will change our lives for the better, starting now."

Leah's mouth pursed as she twisted and untwisted the handle of her bag.

The brakes whooshed their final stop, and the porter shouted. Beth and Leah picked up their bags and baskets and followed the Osgoods to the nearest door.

Beth stepped off the train but kept walking to make room for those coming after her, tightening her grip on the handle of her bag. Her heart hammered as she waited. All around her, families greeted loved ones. The Osgoods were each lovingly enfolded in the arms of a strong, sturdy man in handmade work clothing.

"You must be Beth," said a female voice.

She turned. A woman about her mother's age, perhaps a bit older, stood before her.

"I would know you anywhere," the woman said.

Beth stared at her. *She* didn't know this woman, and if there was a relation to her mother, she saw no evidence of it.

The woman's blue eyes smiled up at Beth. "I'm your Aunt Elnora, but folks generally call me Nora."

Beth's mouth had grown desert dry. "Yes, ma'am," she managed to choke out. The last hope that somehow Nora wouldn't be a stranger left her in a flash.

"Let's get your belongings." The woman called to a man waiting beside a nearby wagon. "Michael, would you get the rest of her things?"

He tore a battered straw hat from his head. "Yes, ma'am."

Turning back to Beth, she asked, "Do you have a check ticket, dear?"

Beth searched her reticule for the small square and then handed her aunt the ticket.

Nora examined it and said, "Michael, can you get everything loaded into the wagon? We'll meet you there."

The man put his hat back on, pulled it down till it hid his face, and turned away.

Beth watched him weave through the crowd to retrieve her things. Her trunk had been part of the argument she had with her mother. Beth insisted she wouldn't be staying long enough to need it, but her mother disagreed.

She looked around for Em—Leah—and found her talking with a woman who held a crying child. The woman handed the toddler to Leah and walked away. Her schoolmate followed, holding the screaming youngster away from her body as if the child had fleas. Poor Leah. She didn't know any more about children than Beth did.

"Maude may appear a little harsh," Nora said, "or shall we say, insensitive, but that girl will be fine. Did you come together?"

Beth nodded. "Her name is Leah."

"I see," Nora said. "Follow me."

Beth followed Nora through the thinning crowd to the wagon where Michael and another man loaded the trunk. The train huffed and belched steam while passengers boarded again. The noise of protesting animals and shouting men also reached them from further down the track.

Eager to be away from the chaos, Beth climbed up the wheel and into the wagon. The moment she took a seat beside her aunt, Michael picked up the reins and set them in motion.

Nora began a running commentary, perhaps understanding Beth's discomfort. "I'll take you on a real tour later." She studied Beth, peeking at her from under her bonnet. "I'm sure you're exhausted with traveling. Let's have something to eat and get you settled."

"Yes, ma'am."

"Oh! There's Stuart." Nora gestured to the end of the train.

Could it be the same man? Beth turned to see whom her aunt meant. She'd acted such a fool when she met him on the train, but sure enough, there he stood, waving at them.

"We'll see him around town." Aunt Nora waved. "He helps me out from time to time."

"Great," Beth muttered as she studied Stuart Randall from the corner of her eye. He moved with assurance though the huge animal beside him looked powerful.

"I see he picked up the Percheron stallion he and his neighbors bought from a horse farm out east," Nora said.

He handled the draft horse efficiently, his tall, well-built form taking control like one used to such animals. Beth forced her gaze away.

"I fear the neighbors take advantage of him." Nora folded her gloved hands in her lap. "There were others who could have made this trip. Stuart isn't married, so the other farmers use that as an excuse to get him to do their work."

Beth glanced back to see him effortlessly lead the horse away from the chaos of the train. He seemed to be doing fine as far as she could see.

Michael left the depot area and drove slowly through the heart of town. Beth studied the mercantile and another building labeled Zacks General Store as they passed. They drove by a livery, several small businesses, and a land office. On the other side of the street, beside a few small stores, a large, boarding house or hotel was being constructed. A bell tower rose above the other buildings on the far edge of town.

Michael stopped the wagon in front of a compact, immaculately kept farm. Bushes, possibly gooseberry or currant, created a hedge along the road. Over the opening in the center, vines climbed an arched trellis large enough for visitors to pass through. The trellis held green shoots at the bottom this early in the year, but the remains of last year's growth still clung to lattice along the structure. In no time at all, the arch would be green and charming.

After Michael helped Beth to the ground, she stood beside the wagon and sucked in a deep breath. The odors of damp earth and fragrant blossoms filled her nostrils. When Nora walked to the house, Beth followed her through the archway into the yard. Herbs lined the footpath made of flat stones set flush with the ground. Trees planted near the house were still small, but someday would be an imposing sight. A solid, wood fence swept away from the house toward the left.

They stepped up onto a wide front porch. The generous roof protected two homemade chairs and a porch swing.

Beth's aunt pushed open the door into the house. "Put your bag down here, and we'll stop for a glass of tea," she said. "Michael, would you see to getting the trunk into the first bedroom on the left?"

"I'll see if I can find someone to help me."

"All right, Michael." Aunt Nora went into the house. "That's a rather large trunk."

Beth followed Nora into her home. "Mother packed it. I don't even know what she put in there." She wasn't going to take the blame for the massive trunk. The woman would think her vain to need all that for a visit.

"I see. Come on in." The woman gestured around. Wide logs, shaved flat with an adze or ax, faced the inside of the one-room cabin. Low windows provided light at the front and side of the house. Deep sills, made from slabs of wood, gleamed beneath each window.

Beth moved to the middle of the room where a kitchen worktable stood ready to do multiple duties. A bench sat along one side and two, well-made chairs on the other. An embroidered muslin cloth, depicting whimsical children dancing in a circle, covered the table. A saltcellar, sugar box, and vase with spring flowers occupied its center.

Nora untied her bonnet and slipped it off her head. She patted her hair in place. "Set your gloves and hat aside for now, dear," she said. "How about we have something to drink, and I'll show you the other boarders around here."

"Boarders?" Beth startled in alarm.

"Oh, my animals, dear."

Beth blew out a breath and sat. A breeze puffed the bright yellow curtains into the room, though the long porch on the front of the house shaded the open windows.

Michael and another man carried the trunk through the house and disappeared behind a curtain.

"Thank you, Dale and Michael," Nora called. She turned back to Beth. "Now, try your tea. It's a recipe of my own. I use plants grown around here, but you'll like it, I'm sure."

"Yes, ma'am." Beth sipped. "My mother makes clover tea too."

"I forgot. Of course, your mother would make this."

Beth scrunched her nose at the puzzling comment but drank down her tea. She hadn't realized how thirsty she was.

Aunt Nora said, "Get yourself settled and change into something more comfortable. You look lovely, but now you have arrived, so you'll want to be in a serviceable dress." Nora picked up their cups and set them in a wash pan. "I'm going to lie down for half an hour myself. Do the same or sit out on the porch. I won't be long, but it helps me. Then, we will visit the characters in the barn," she said. "Now, let me show you where you'll sleep."

They passed through the doorway to Beth's left and faced a curtained-off area. Two rooms took up that side of the house.

"I'll leave you to get settled." Nora gestured to the room Beth would use.

She nodded, puzzled that the woman needed to nap. Aunt Nora appeared well, but maybe her health was the reason Beth had been sent here.

After retrieving her reticule, she returned to her room and looked around. Not as luxurious as her room back home for sure, but right now, she didn't care one whit. Beth set her brush and other toiletries on a small bureau. The single window, its white curtains edged in purple, allowed a breeze. The quilt on the bed—done up in yellow, purple, and green appliqué—looked to be a variation of the Wandering Foot design her mother made.

She pulled the key from her reticule and knelt to unlock her truck. Smells assailed her, and she closed her eyes, remembering the mood at home when she left. The heavenly scent of lavender strong—her mother always grew the fragrant herb. Beth picked out one of her day dresses and brought it to her face. It smelled of home— the mercantile. The worry about leaving home, coming to stay with a stranger, and anger at her parents had left her exhausted. For the hundredth time she asked herself the question: *Why did they make me go away?*

Beth laid the outfit she'd worn for two days over her trunk to sponge out later. Her dresses went on hooks across from the bed, and personal items she would need immediately went into the small bureau. Then, too tired to search the trunk further, she loosened her corset, pulled back the quilt, and lay down on the bed.

CHAPTER EIGHT

Beth woke suddenly and rubbed her eyes. Where was she and why was she sleeping in the middle of the day?

A noise from the other room brought her back with a jolt. She dressed and rushed from the room to find Aunt Nora sitting at the table, a cup of tea in her hand.

"Ah, did I wake you?" Aunt Nora poured Beth some tea. "Come and sit." Aunt Nora nodded toward a plate of sliced bread, jam, and cheese. "Have something. And tell me how your mother is."

Unsure of this woman's exact connection to her mother, Beth said, "Mom is well, and Papa." Her voice faltered. How could she talk to this stranger about the pain of her sudden banishment? "They seemed sad to see me go."

"I'm sure they were, dear."

"Then why did they send me away?" Beth blurted out before she could stop herself. Struggling with having to leave home, she took a slice of bread she didn't want, and folded it over some cheese.

Aunt Nora tipped her head, studying her. "You're a lovely girl."

Beth almost choked. No one told her those things. Her mother's frequent saying, "Pretty is as pretty does," led Beth to believe it wasn't proper to be pretty. She drew an unsteady breath. "Thank you."

"Did you want to tell me why you're here?"

"There isn't anything to tell. I don't understand why my parents sent me away." Her sullen voice portrayed her frustration and anger. She pressed her lips together.

"Did you and your mother have a talk before you left?"

"How do you mean?" Beth's mother had tried to talk to her, but it had come out in irregular, disjointed spurts. She'd made no sense.

Aunt Nora selected a piece of cheese. "Just wondering if you had time for a good heart-to-heart."

"No." Beth scrunched her brow. "Mom and I don't have heart-to-heart talks." Why had her mother always held herself aloof? Watching Ester and Mrs. Osgood on the train had reawakened Beth's longing for that kind of mother-daughter relationship. But it seemed Beth messed up her mother's tidy routine, so Beth retreated to the mercantile, where she could be useful and necessary.

"I see," Nora said, but her expression showed otherwise.

Did this woman know more about the situation than Beth did? Maybe Nora had some answers for her. "Mom and Papa have been upset the last few weeks."

"I'm sorry." Nora's brows pulled together, and her lips pursed. "Let's see the rest of the house."

Beth rose and followed her.

"You saw my room right next to yours." Nora pulled aside the curtain that served as a door. "I love to be able to sleep in here now that the weather is warm again. It's more like a shed attached to the main house and far too cold in winter, but it stays cool in summer with the breeze blowing through."

For the first time, Beth noticed the milled lumber walls in this part of the house were different. The section of the roof attached to the cabin peaked high over her head and slanted down toward short walls.

"These rooms only have a tar paper covering on the outside. Stuart, Howard, and some of the boys move me back to the main room in fall." Nora went to the window and adjusted the curtain.

"It's nice." Beth turned in a small circle, admiring the homey room.

Nora walked away from her bedroom. "We moved here when my husband started slowing down. Before that, we lived in a claim shack."

"A claim shack, on a farm?" Beth followed her aunt to the front part of the house. "Near here?"

"West of here." Nora stopped by the table. "The shack wasn't much but it satisfied the homestead requirements for a dwelling. We were there five years and it was proved up. We had tar paper on the shanty by then."

A rocking chair and an overstuffed chair sat together by the front window. It would be an ideal place to read or do handwork. Beth spent each day at the mercantile, but in the evening, she would read to her parents or do mending. What were they doing right now?

"This is perfect for me." Nora gestured to the street. "I can afford it, and it's right on the edge of town, so I walk anywhere I need to go."

"Yes, ma'am."

"I hope you like your room," Nora said. "Lynn—that's my youngest—she loved having a place of her own. There's a loft above the main part of the house where Evan slept." She indicated the steep stairway toward the end of the room. "It has a window in each gable end, but we never got around to making it into two rooms."

"I see," Beth muttered, needing to say *something*.

Her aunt led her to the far end of the room. "This is the back entrance. I store overflow from my kitchen out here, but mostly wood. The room helps keep critters who want to live in my wood box out of the main part of the house." Nora bent to pick up a grey-striped barn cat that demanded their attention. "Speaking of mice, this here is Toes."

Beth stroked the feline's white, six-toed paw. "I like cats." The animal tucked its head into her hand and purred. "She's nice."

Aunt Nora bent toward the animal and caressed its head. "Of course, you are, aren't you?"

The cat thrust its nose forward to greet her, purring loudly.

"Thank you for having me here," Beth got the words out in a hurry. They were awkward but needed to be said for politeness's sake.

"Don't mention it, dear." Nora held Toes so she could smell Beth. "I'm happy you came, and I love the opportunity to know you."

The cat climbed into Beth's arms. She snuggled her close and hid her face in the cat's fur.

Nora walked through the door into the bright sunshine. "Ready to see the back, then?"

"Yes, ma'am." Beth carried the cat out past a bench and wash-up area. She followed Nora down a path beside a vegetable garden, through an open gate, and into an animal yard beyond. To their left, a windmill and watering tank stood beside the house. Near the fence lay the remains of a hay pile, with a goose sitting on a nest and the gander keeping watch nearby. Beth drew back when the geese set up a tremendous fuss at their approach.

"I have two pair of geese. They're busy setting on nests," Nora said. "They have the run of the place and keep the area mowed too."

The gander advanced toward Beth. She backed away from the animal. "They don't like me."

"Shoo." Aunt Nora flapped her apron at the gander. "I sell or trade the goslings when they're young. With the sheep, cow, pigs, and chickens, I keep busy." Nora leaned on the pasture fence. "Lynn says I get more and more animals, but I like them. It's important to be needed, and they keep me company. You know, it's easy for people my age to become lethargic—not getting up at a regular time or having a good meal or getting dressed proper. That's not for me. I keep active and take time each day to read the Bible and pray too."

Beth leaned on the fence next to the woman. Nora had an interesting way of looking at being alone. Beth knew of some from her town who complained about their lot in life—with no one to care for them. Maybe if they had someone or something that needed their attention they would be happier.

"Now, Beth," Nora said, "you can call me Aunt or plain Nora if you like. Would that be all right?"

"Yes, ma'am."

Her aunt laughed. "I guess that's all right too." She turned away from the fence. "Let's sit on the porch—my favorite place."

Beth followed as they walked around the garden, coming to the house from the front. She stepped up on the porch and sat on the swing.

Aunt Nora picked up her knitting. "How is everything at the store?"

"Good, I think," Beth said. "I work there with Papa. Mom has a hired girl coming to the house every few days and no longer works at the store."

Aunt Nora glanced up from her knitting. "Your mother is fine, though?"

"Oh, yes, just slowing down a little. I think she would rather be piecing or knitting. She's good at that."

Aunt Nora nodded. "Yes, she is, and truthfully, I would rather she sew too. I get some of her needlework now and then."

"You do?" Beth rubbed her forehead. Why had she never heard about this woman?

"Yes, indeed."

"Do you suppose I can work at a general store here in town?" If Beth worked at something she knew, maybe this visit wouldn't seem so awkward. She felt lost without her job at the store.

"We can see. I don't know if anyone here needs help, but we have several suitable stores. It's more likely you can help some overworked country mother like your friend is doing. I thought you could take time to get settled, and then perhaps, we can make inquiries."

"I suppose I can wait, but I don't want to be a burden." Beth clenched her teeth and gulped. "I'm not sure when I can go home." Her mother couldn't expect her to stay for six months. "I haven't been trained in cooking or taking care of children."

Her aunt let her knitting needles rest and glanced at her. "Maybe it's time you learn."

"I would not be able to do the kind of work Em—Leah is doing." Beth could not cook for a family or chase after children with more cooking and cleaning. No, she would not do it no matter how much this woman pushed. She sighed. "Will Leah work very hard, do you think?"

Nora nodded. "I'm sure she will work hard, but for the most part, it will be enjoyable. Did your friend know the family she would be working for?"

"She didn't know the woman, but she knew what she would be doing." Beth laid her head back to watch swallows weaving their way around the tree branches. "She talked about what an adventure this would be. Her new stepmother doesn't want her, so Leah's father sent her away."

"I don't believe they'll mistreat her, if you're worried about that." Nora resumed her knitting. "Maude is pretty much at the end of her rope, and it's good your friend is staying the summer. Are they related?"

"I think she said the woman is related to her stepmother."

"Oh." Beth's aunt changed the subject. "How was the train ride?"

"Busy. We heard various languages as peoples from all over are coming to settle. Plus, we met travelers, like a boy named Lucas, going to the goldfields."

"Many new settlers are coming into this area now." Nora bent her head to focus on her work. "Not all of them have good intentions."

Beth thought of the conversation she'd heard last night. In the light of day, she believed the talk was her imagination. It was ridiculous to think she had overheard the workings of a gang.

Aunt Nora unrolled more yarn and began the next row. "You met Stuart, then?"

Why the question about the man? "Yes." She hoped she didn't sound breathless.

"What did you think?" Nora paused her knitting to study Beth.

Beth fixed her eyes on a robin sitting on its nest atop a porch post. "About what, ma'am?"

"Oh, Stuart."

Beth sensed that Nora and Stuart Randall were friends. Maybe Nora wanted Beth to be his friend too. "I don't believe I care for his type."

Aunt Nora's brow creased, and she studied Beth with a worried air. "What type is that?"

"I don't know him, but he appeared to be one of those men who wrestle a bear if he has a mind to but thinks women should be handled with kid gloves."

Nora threw back her head and laughed. "Had a lot of experience with that kind of man, have you?"

"Well, no, not much." Beth hadn't planned to be funny. She lifted her chin. "I prefer a more refined man."

"Humph." Nora pulled yarn from a ball at her feet and continued knitting. "I've known Stuart for years and his family, too, though his mother and father are now gone. He's a fine young man."

Beth crossed her arms. Nora could choose her friends, but Beth would not be part of it. She would not be taken in by a handsome face, an infectious smile, or even warm brown eyes.

"His farm is outside of town a bit. He helps me with work around here. The sheep and my cow, Daisy, are from his farm." Nora faced Beth. "Now, tell me about your young man."

"I don't know what to think about him," she murmured.

"You are seeing someone though," Aunt Nora said.

Beth gave the swing a shove. "He's been coming around for some time, but ..."

"How does he behave, child? Does he care for you?"

How should she answer that? Her parents had argued about this point. "My parents object to John because they say he's not living as he should."

Her aunt tapped her chin, appearing to give Beth's statement careful thought. "Do you think he's living as a Christian man should?"

"I don't know, ma'am." Beth kicked the swing into motion again. Deep down, she knew the answer to that question. John endeavored to keep his behavior in front of her upstanding, but she was learning differently. He didn't continue it when he wasn't with her.

Aunt Nora studied her face. "What's missing?"

Beth shrugged. "I can't talk to him about family or God, but he's a good man."

Aunt Nora nodded. "Remember, we aren't born again because of what we do, no matter how good he or you think he is."

"But Aunt, he might turn to God, and I love him." Beth bowed her head. "At least, I think I do. I don't think it's right for my parents to make me leave. Surely it's my decision whom I marry."

Aunt Nora counted the threads along her needle. "Has he asked you to marry him?"

"Well, no." Beth had dreams, but she and John had never talked about marriage. She dreamed of having children—lots of them. She didn't want her children to grow up alone. "He's been calling for some time. I'm here because my parents ordered it, but I'm not going to stay away the six months mother wanted." Beth turned to face her aunt. "That's just too long."

"Worried he might forget you?" Aunt Nora asked.

Beth could not hold Nora's steady gaze and she turned away. She wasn't sure about John or if he even cared for her, but her parents forcing her to leave seemed drastic for such a little thing.

"Perhaps we can talk about this again," Nora said. "For now, let's take a short walk around this side of town. My pets will be hungry, and it's getting on time to milk."

CHAPTER NINE

As they walked, Nora explained the history of the town. "The first settlers were Scots, English, and Irish," she said. "Many have moved on already, but some hardy souls have stayed." Aunt Nora pulled her shawl closer. "That is, if one can outlast the winters, the shortage of money and supplies, and family ups and downs."

Beth nodded. "Yes, we saw that too."

They passed several new homes, bright with fresh lumber, sitting small and insignificant in the middle of a town lot. Cows, horses, and chickens scattered about waiting for accommodations.

"You can see we mostly dig up trees from the river bottom to transplant around the houses. We have oaks and maples and those pesky cottonwoods." Nora laughed. "I planted cottonwoods in front of my house. They grow fast, so I might get to see them reach a good height before I die."

Beth turned to study her. Aunt Nora seemed spry for someone who was dying. Is that why she'd been sent here? They circled back to the pasture. Beth watched Nora do chores and rubbed the knotty head of a small lamb before the skittish animal dashed off to hide in the corner of the pen.

"I do earn a nice sum each summer selling eggs," Aunt Nora said. "There are a few families in town who don't have chickens, plus the hotel restaurant and Simon at Mama's Eatery use all I can produce. Many young immigrants are working in or around town who live at the hotel too. Those railroad workers can eat a lot of eggs."

Beth brushed the dust off her hands. She didn't mind doing chores. She fed their chickens when she was home, though her father usually milked the cow.

"I sell butter, too, and sometimes milk." Nora showed Beth where to find feed, pails, and other supplies. "Keeps me busy."

The geese put up a fuss again when they walked near. Beth's nose wrinkled. "I don't think I like geese. They're messy and so noisy."

Her aunt chuckled. "That's why I like them. It's lonesome here with everyone gone. They talk to me and are good warning animals too. They protect all of us, including the sheep and chickens."

Beth didn't bother to hide her sneer as she picked up her skirts. She had better learn to watch where she walked because the geese left droppings everywhere.

Nora smiled at her. "Besides, there is something special about a big, fat Christmas goose."

Beth turned away. Her parents had a Christmas goose, but someone else raised it.

After the evening meal, Aunt Nora handed Beth a full bowl of dried beans. "Can you sort these while I do dishes and straighten up the room?"

"Yes, ma'am." Beth dutifully sifted dried beans through her hands, removing dark or wrinkly ones. Aunt Nora worked on dishes, speaking rarely. Perhaps they were both tired. When she finished sorting, she washed the beans and added them to a pot Aunt Nora filled with water.

"Put them here on the back of the stove overnight," Nora directed. "Now we can retire to the porch for the evening." Beth wrapped her shawl around her shoulders and followed Aunt Nora. She sat in one of the chairs and rested her head against the back.

Nora already had her knitting needles out and clicking away. "Would you like to read to me?" she asked.

Beth preferred to rest, but maybe Aunt Nora had a paper she hadn't seen. She roused herself. "I read to Mom and Papa quite often."

Her aunt laid aside her work and went inside. She returned with a well-worn book and placed it in her hands. "I've been reading in Exodus."

Beth's mood fell. Surely the woman didn't expect her to read the Bible. Her lips pressed tight together.

"Start in chapter thirty-one." Aunt Nora resumed her knitting.

Beth sighed and began reading. When she came to the end of that chapter, she stopped. "Do you want me to go on?"

"Yes, please."

"Chapter thirty-two ... and when the people saw that Moses delayed to come down ..." Beth put her finger in the book to mark her place. She had heard these passages preached before and had several questions. She didn't expect Aunt Nora to have the answers, but it might be fun to test her. "Why a golden calf?"

"There are all kinds of golden calves, dear."

Beth hadn't heard anyone say that before. "How do you mean?"

"Some people have a golden calf of money. It can be children or a spouse—sometimes their land or business. It's the prime focus in their lives. All else will come second."

Beth pondered the answer. Leah's father seemed to fit that description. She shook her head. "I suppose I know people who have that trouble."

"Most of us have to deal with our worship at some point or other. Here, it's often the self-reliance people forge from just surviving—when the maker of the universe should be worshiped. Read on a little more ... say, verse twenty-one."

"And Moses said unto Aaron, What did this people unto thee, that thou hast brought so great a sin upon them? And Aaron said, Let not the anger of my lord wax hot: thou knowest the people, that they are set on mischief."

Aunt Nora explained. "You see, the leader needs to be responsible, even if it isn't popular."

Beth watched the robin come back to the nest with a wiggly worn. Had Aunt Nora chosen this Scripture for her? Her parents had asked her to stop seeing John. When she didn't comply, they acted in this outrageous manner and sent her away. "Why did they get into mischief, as it says?"

"There's no simple answer—fear, lack of dedication, no respect for God."

Beth voiced her thoughts before she could stop herself. "They didn't know how to behave themselves, but wouldn't listen to those who tried to teach them?"

"Precisely," Nora said. "I don't know why we humans are like that, but often we are."

Beth gritted her teeth. "But this says the leader is responsible for teaching, even if people don't like it. It says Aaron is the one who brought the sin upon them."

"Yes." Nora's knitting stopped, and she faced her. "You see, they did it. They can't back out of their part and make him responsible for their sin, but if he had truly loved them, he wouldn't have had any part in it. I suspect Aaron did it because he thought they would honor him because he made their idol for them."

Beth mulled that over, her jaw tight. Her aunt's choice of Scripture rankled. Her parents insisted they were acting in her best interest. They said they were responsible as long as she was under their roof. She pressed her lips tight together and closed the book with a slam. Her parents might think they knew what was best for her, but she wasn't a child.

"I think that's enough for tonight, dear." Nora flipped the yarn with her finger. "I have much to talk to God about."

"Yes, ma'am." Beth pushed uncomfortable recollections of her willful and rude behavior toward her parents' authority out of her mind. "I think I'll turn in early."

"Certainly." Aunt Nora looked up from her work. "Can you remember where everything is?"

"Yes, thank you."

As she walked away, her aunt offered a last comment. "Beth?"

She paused, her hand on the door.

"I want you to know ..." Nora's tone was gentle. "... it's nice having you here, and God will help you sort this out."

Tears rushed to Beth's eyes, and she could only nod. Maybe Aunt Nora knew how alone she felt, but her comment struck a chord. Someone needed to help her sort this out, though she doubted it would be God.

After Beth put on her nightgown, she got out pen and paper. She would write to her mother and let her know she had arrived. Beth chewed on her cheek and finally penned a brief note about her trip. It would have to be enough for now as rebellion burned in her.

With that chore done, she climbed in bed. She curled on her side, drew her gown to her face, and inhaled the scent of home.

CHAPTER TEN

Beth shifted in the narrow bed. Noises she wasn't accustomed to kept her awake. She stared into the blackness, trying to see what creatures lurked beyond the thin walls of the room. When the geese put up a clamor, she bolted up in bed. She clutched her blankets to her chest, waiting for an intruder. Had the gang she'd overheard last night come to rob her aunt? When the geese quieted, she relaxed. If the geese were quiet, she must be safe. She lay back down. Maybe those noisy fowl weren't so bad after all.

Later, the crowing of a rooster shook her awake. A rooster in the house?

One look around brought her location back. She pulled the covers over her head. *Mom, why did you do this to me?* She dreamt of being home again, having breakfast with her father before they went to open the store for business.

A slight noise from the other room motivated her to move. She threw back the blankets. After dressing, she went into the central part of the house. Water boiled on the cookstove, and Aunt Nora sat at the bench reading.

"Well, good morning, dear," Nora said. "How did you sleep?"

"Fine," Beth snapped. She would be home right now if her parents hadn't been so difficult.

"If I may say so"—Nora's eyes narrowed as she studied her—"it doesn't sound like it."

"I dreamt I was home."

"I see." Nora poured them each a hot cup of tea. "Sit down with me before we begin our work for the day. This might help."

Beth did as the woman asked but doubted anything would take away the cloud pressing her down.

"Let's begin in Psalms this morning." Nora paged through her book. "I feel like praising God. I have some favorites—let's start with those."

Beth's brows drew down, her nose wrinkling. That wasn't what she wanted to hear. Her parents read the Bible, and, from time to time, her father talked about the principles he learned but much of the time it meant nothing to her. She clamped her jaw tight and crossed her arms. Was this woman going to talk about God every chance she got?

Aunt Nora read verse after verse while Beth's mind wandered to John. Wondering again why a man who loved attention like he did came to call on someone so boring. People flocked to him and, by association, to her. Seeing him hadn't been without problems though. They rarely agreed and she disliked the disruption his presence made in her life. So why had she persisted in seeing him? She drew a deep breath and closed her eyes. Was it his questionable reputation?

Aunt Nora started another Psalm. She read like poetry, and Beth began to listen. "Bless the Lord, O my soul: and all that is within me, bless his holy name."

Beth smiled inwardly. Her mother liked that Psalm too. Inside, she recited the next verse. *And forget not all his benefits: Who forgiveth all thy iniquities; who healeth all thy diseases; who redeemeth thy life from destruction.*

"Now, I think we're ready to face the day." Aunt Nora closed the book. "Let's feed those impatient boarders and have our breakfast."

They walked to the barn together. This time, Aunt Nora gave Beth specific tasks. Clearly, the woman expected her to do chores. She carried the bucket of milk to the house. Nora strained it.

"This can go in the well house," Nora said. "Bring the cold milk from last night back with you. We'll have that with our breakfast."

Beth took the jug outside and placed it in the well house. Then, she brought in the jar from yesterday's milking, relieved to be finally eating. She usually ate hours ago. Would every morning be like this—hours reading the Bible, then chores, and finally a meal?

"After we eat, I think we should walk again." Nora skimmed off the thick cream at the top of the jar of milk. "That way, you can get your bearings." She turned and smiled. "I walk everywhere and enjoy the time to commune with the Lord."

Beth gritted her teeth as she returned the cream to the well-house. She didn't need to get her bearings around town. She wouldn't be here that long.

Bowls of cornmeal mush waited on the table. Aunt Nora finished cooking the scrambled eggs with chunks of something green. Beth ate the strange meal, but inside her emotions were ready to boil over. Aunt Nora finished eating and washed her dishes, leaving the wash water for Beth.

"Here you go." Aunt Nora handed her a basket when she finished her dishes and took one herself. Beth had little choice but to follow as her aunt strolled down the road and out onto the unfenced prairie.

"This is the best time of day to gather greens," Nora said. "There are many plants that few people around here use. It's a shame, but new immigrants don't know about our plants."

Beth's mouth turned down. Only the poor or eccentric used pasture plants for their food. Though her mother dried some herbs, they were grown in her garden, not gleaned from someone's pasture.

They continued toward the river while Aunt Nora paused to pluck a leaf here and there. "We've circled around to the back of my farm. This stream is on the backside of my pasture. It's my favorite place." Aunt Nora knelt in the grass, inspecting plants. "I love the sound of water." She picked a leaf and handed it to Beth. "This is catmint. I won't harvest this today, but maybe later. I keep it on hand as a remedy for colds and cough."

Beth chewed on the mint leaf Nora gave her and watched the birds. A perky red-winged blackbird, in his black coat with red trim, sang for them. The piercing cry of a blue jay let everyone know strangers were in their midst. Out of the corner of her eye, Beth saw movement on the other side of the stream and rose to her feet. "Aunt Nora, how far does your land go?" Her heart raced.

"To the river here. Why?"

"There's someone watching us." Beth clenched her hands.

Aunt Nora called out. "Is that you, Timothy?"

Beth glanced from Nora to the brush. "Who's Timothy?"

"A little boy from here abouts." Nora called, "Timothy, come meet Beth. She wants to know you."

Beth waited but no little boy showed himself. "I think we scared whoever it was."

"Timothy is a waif. He's recently come to live with his aunt, and she has trouble keeping him home."

"His aunt?"

"His mother and father died when he was quite young and after that he has lived with his grandfather." Aunt Nora wiped away the sweat beading on her forehead. "His grandfather passed on a short time ago and now his mother's sister is caring for him. He's a shadow—what they used to call a fey child." Aunt Nora continued to collect plants, and leaves. "I'm sure you'll meet him eventually."

Beth glanced toward the woods, then joined her aunt as they wandered toward the house. Beth's basket filled as they walked. She began to enjoy her time outside. It had been years since she rested in the afternoon. The plants and flowers hidden in the grasses fascinated her, and Aunt Nora knew so much about them.

"Beth, if you fetch a pail of water, you can wash these for me," Nora said as they reached the house. She dropped her basket on the table. "Fetch a few towels too."

Beth brought the requested items, curious to know what Aunt Nora would do with all they had collected.

"Now then, we need to strip the leaves from the stems and wash them," Aunt Nora said. "Be sure to check for bugs too."

"This wild mint smells good." Beth brought a stem to her nose and inhaled deeply. "Are you going to dry all of it?"

"No, let's keep some fresh. The wild mint is nice to add to cold tea and so is the spearmint I have in the garden. Maybe we will harvest that tomorrow. The rest you can take to the loft. I have racks suspended there." Aunt Nora piled more greens on the table for Beth to wash.

"Mother uses a spare bedroom for drying." Beth swished leaves in the water, shook them well, and placed them on a towel.

"The loft is perfect for me," Aunt Nora said. "It's warm-up there, with good air circulation, so they dry and don't mold."

Beth took the towel full of wet leaves and climbed to the loft. She arranged the herbs on wood racks draped with a thin cloth. The collection of plants smelled like the fields.

"I'll take these scraps to the chickens if you would empty the pail of water onto the trees out front." Nora picked up a cloth full of the discarded foliage.

"Yes, ma'am." Beth carried the pail outside and emptied it onto the cottonwood trees. Movement behind the barn attracted her attention—a boy ran and hid. A tiny memory of the farm where she lived as a child flashed across her mind. She squinted to see back in her recollection, and a faraway memory came back. She'd had a friend there.

She returned to the house. "Aunt Nora, that boy is still around. He's hiding behind the barn."

Nora went to the door. "Timothy, are you hungry?" She smiled at Beth. "Sometimes that does the trick."

They waited but no one appeared. "He must have gone home," Nora said. "Now tell me, Beth, do you sew and knit?"

"I sew but haven't learned to knit."

"You may need to know how to knit socks and will certainly need to darn them. I suppose you have quilts saved already?"

"Yes, quite a few."

"I think I'll spread out my scraps and see what I have." Nora brought a basket to the table.

"You're working on a quilt?" Beth studied the scraps spread out before them.

"I finished a quilt late last winter. I'm at odds with myself until I get a new one going," Nora said. "My mind needs to be working a problem, blending colors and the like."

Beth piled the similar pinks together. "You have some pretty pinks, and I love the gray and browns you have."

"I don't know, dear." Nora laid out different colors next to each other, squinting at them. "Nothing jumps out at me. I think I'll let these sit and see if a pattern makes itself known. If not, I could buy two or three pieces and make an Irish Chain." She laughed. "I'm getting quite a collection. It might be time to start a Broken Dishes quilt."

"Aunt Nora, do you know if my parents lived on a farm where I played with a little boy like Timothy?"

Nora pushed aside the fabric and folded her hands. "What makes you wonder?"

"When Timothy was running away, it's like I saw a flashback to another little boy—a playmate, I think."

"You did live on a farm," Nora said.

"I remember a little about it." Beth rested her head in her hand, trying to bring up the image from her memory.

Nora rose from her seat. "I'll start lunch."

Beth lifted her head and glanced at Aunt Nora. Was Aunt Nora so uncaring that she didn't want to hear Beth's memory?

CHAPTER ELEVEN

The next morning after chores and breakfast, Beth helped Nora finish dishes. She planned to suggest she go into town to look for work. "What are we doing today?"

"Let's work on the garden before the weather changes."

Beth closed her eyes and pressed her lips together. Her aunt planned to get all the work from her she could. She followed her aunt to the garden and sat down at her assigned row. Her thoughts turned to John as she picked at the weeds. What if he could see her now? He would laugh at her.

"Did you have a letter to mail?" Nora asked after some time.

"Yes, ma'am." Beth finished her row and stood up.

"Let's do that now before it starts to rain." Nora brushed her hands off and washed up at the basin outside.

Beth washed off the garden dirt, checked her hair, and retrieved her letter.

"The dry goods store has the mail contract. We'll stop there first." Nora picked up a basket, and they strolled into town.

They opened the door to a busy store that had been left in shambles. Shovels had fallen to the floor near the door, blocking the aisle. Beth itched to pick them up, but the tangle included the rakes, so she stepped over them. She looked around, but no one gave attention to the danger.

Beth had to step around barrels left in the aisle and a jumble of harnesses fallen off the wall. Everywhere she turned, merchandise needed to be restored to order.

"You can mail your letter there." Nora pointed to the counter where a line of ladies waited already. "I'm going to look at fabric."

Men gathered around in the far corner, talking and laughing, while the women attended to their shopping and trading. The busy woman behind the counter cast frequent glances toward the men as she rushed here and there filling orders.

"What can I help you with, miss?" the frazzled shopkeeper asked when Beth reached the counter.

"I have a letter to mail, ma'am."

"Yes, miss." The woman named the price, barely speaking above a whisper.

Beth paid for a stamp, then rejoined Aunt Nora who was ready to leave the store.

"I'll stop and see you in a few days, Clara, when you aren't so busy," Nora called to the woman behind the counter.

"Thank you, Nora," Clara replied softly.

"I can't believe it," Beth burst out once they were outside. "Was that her husband? Doing nothing while his wife rushed around like a chicken with its head cut off?"

"Her husband isn't known to be a hard worker in the best of times." Aunt Nora pulled her shawl up onto her head. "I think we have a spell of rain coming. We'd better hurry along."

"All the more reason to keep things in order," Beth said. "The place is a hazard. My father would never allow such a mess. I can't imagine how they stay in business."

"A whole passel of loyal relatives," Nora muttered. She picked up their pace, but not soon enough.

A loud clap of thunder sounded almost on top of them, and the heavy skies opened. Cold raindrops pelted their faces. Beth ducked her head and hurried beside Aunt Nora to their next stop.

She couldn't see two steps ahead, though in truth, she wasn't looking, her head bent to keep her bonnet on in the wind. The loud beat of rain drowned out all other sound. A shape came around the corner and ... *oomph* ... ran right into her—or she ran into him, more likely. The man gripped her arms, preventing her fall.

"Oh, Stuart," her aunt said from somewhere nearby.

He clutched Beth in an apparent effort to keep them both upright, and she felt as if she couldn't speak nor hardly breathe. When he pulled her secure against his chest, protected from the rain, she rested there with her head buried under his chin. At another boom of thunder, she pushed away. He stepped back and let her go.

"Miss." He opened his mouth to say more, but the downpour cut off his words, and they rushed down the boardwalk in different directions.

Beth followed Nora into The General Store and Merchandise, its sign advertised. Though crowded like the dry goods store had been, this one's interior shown bright, cheerful, and organized.

A girl about Beth's age came from the back with arms laden for a waiting customer and nodded to them. "Hello, Mrs. Durand." She tsked in sympathy at their damp clothing. "It looks like you got caught in the shower. Come over by the stove and hang your shawls and hats."

"Sally, I'd like you to meet Beth," Nora said. "I'm showing her the town. She's staying with me this summer." She shook out her shawl. "I wanted to check out some fabric for a quilt. My scraps aren't coming together."

Sally nodded to Beth and laughed. "I'm sure you'll find something here, Mrs. Durand."

Beth said, "You have a beautiful store."

"Thank you. Let me know when you need help."

Aunt Nora hung her shawl with the others near the stove and immediately began searching through the fabric. Beth sifted through the shelves, curious to see if this store carried the same dress goods as their store at home.

"This blue would go well with your pinks if you do an Indian Hatchet pattern," she said. "These yellows will add light color if you make a Broken Dishes design. We don't have any like this at our store."

"You might have something there, and a few yellows would brighten up the rest of my scraps," Nora said, tipping her head to the side.

Beth left Nora searching and walked around the store. Her mind wandered to the encounter in the street just moments ago. John had never held her like that. Indeed, such an embrace would not have been proper.

Why had Stuart clutched her so firmly? She supposed they were both off balance, catching each other by surprise like they had. The sensation of warmth and protection had been like a hug from her father, but so ... different.

Suddenly, the subject of her thoughts blew through the door. The men in the store teased him as he shook hands all around.

Beth watched them from her position across the room. Her father believed he could tell a lot about a man by the quality of men he drew to his circle of friends. He usually meant John when he made such a reference. Mr. Randall moved toward the stove and spoke to those lounging there. She saw several lean in to hear what he said. She turned away. Maybe her father would like Stuart Randall, but she would not.

When Aunt Nora finished her search, they hurried home during a break in the rain. Nora pointed out other businesses along the way. "There is Polly's Millinery and Glove Pavilion." She gestured to the quaint shop with blooming window boxes facing the street.

"Papa often commented how it thrilled him when he saw a new business spring up so quickly." Beth glanced at the flowers, colored fabrics, and ribbons on display as they sped past. "And that someone had an idea and opened a store."

"We find ways to earn extra money," Nora said. "Local women sell eggs, butter, cheese, or meat like I do, and some wash and iron for the many single men around, especially the railroad workers."

Nora passed through her gate, stepped onto the porch, and then into the house. "How about we sit and have a cup of hot tea to warm us? I could use the rest."

"I'll get it." Beth noticed that her aunt had become breathless as they hurried home. Beth poured two cups of tea, then refilled the kettle and set it back on the stove.

Beth brought the cups to the chairs situated in front of the window and set a cup beside Nora. "I love all the display cases. That last store has more than we do. Papa says they're expensive, and we do fine without."

"Thank you, dear." Nora sat back and wrapped her hands around the hot cup. "He's right. Until a store is paying for itself, that's the best way."

"That's what Papa says." Beth sat back in her chair. "He says store owners need to plan their money right from the beginning."

"Your father has better business sense than some."

"Yes, Papa is good at managing, and he likes the work." Beth tested her hot brew. "I miss it too."

"I'm sure you do, but life is full of changes." Nora inhaled the contents of her cup. "You might not understand how many changes you'll live through until you're my age, but it seems I get used to one thing, and then life changes, and I have to learn to deal with something new."

"I suppose," Beth grudgingly agreed. In her short life, there had been many such changes, but she didn't like it one bit. Even the feelings she had for John had changed. In its place was a lonely, homesick longing for her family. Would she ever fall in love if her mind kept changing? To marry someone and find out it was a mistake would be unbearable.

Nora set down her cup and rose from her chair. "Let's do chores before it starts to rain again."

"Would you like to rest while I do them?" Beth hurried to offer.

"Nonsense, dear." Nora headed toward the back door.

Beth took a hasty sip of tea and followed. She gathered eggs while Nora milked the cow. The geese made a fuss but didn't chase her this time. They must be getting used to her. She realized she had begun to enjoy doing the work and tending to the farmstock. What was happening to her?

"I'm amazed how fast the chores get done," Nora said as they walked to the house. "One forgets how nice it is having someone to share the work."

"How long ago did your children leave?" Beth placed the egg basket in the cool house and shut the door.

"Well, now, let's see. Lynn married a little over a year ago."

"You mentioned a son?" Beth asked.

"Evan? Yes, he moved away just before that." Nora handed Beth the pail of milk. "Can you strain this?"

"Yes, ma'am." Beth took the milk pail inside. After it was strained, she poured the milk in jugs and set them away.

"It's turning out to be a beautiful evening. Let's make supper, and if it stays pleasant, we can sit on the porch tonight."

Beth wondered at the change of subject. Had it been on purpose? She shrugged. Maybe Aunt Nora had secrets she wasn't ready to share with her. Everyone seemed to have secrets. Her parents kept secrets, Em had secrets, and John had many secrets. Her mind wandered to Stuart. Did he have secrets too?

After breakfast and morning chores, Nora lifted a large crockery bowl from a lower shelf and set it on the table. "It's cool again today. Would you like to bake?"

"Fine, as long as you give me directions." Beth hated to admit how inadequate her cooking skills were. Hopefully, Aunt Nora would overlook her ignorance.

"Here is the first recipe." Aunt Nora handed Beth a piece of yellowed paper. "Let me know if you have questions. The ingredients are here." Aunt Nora pulled out a bowl.

Beth became absorbed in the work and didn't notice how quickly the morning passed until the geese set up a fuss.

"Now, I wonder who's here." Nora pulled a towel from a hook by the door and dried her hands. "And coming to the back door."

Beth glanced out the window and saw Stuart Randall striding toward them. He'd seen her, or she would have gone to her room. For some reason, this visitor made her want to run the other way. Instead, she plastered a smile on her face and opened the door for him.

He stepped inside. "You look mighty nice today."

Warmth spread over her face, down her neck, and back over her ears. Had she looked that bad before?

"What I mean to say ... I think this place agrees with you." He turned to Aunt Nora.

Beth glanced in the small mirror by the back door, wincing at her rosy appearance. If only she blushed an exquisite shade of pink like the heroine in some book. Instead, her face mottled red with white blotches.

"Smells mighty good in here," Mr. Randall spoke behind her.

"We're baking up a storm." Nora smeared lard on a baking sheet. "Stuart, you met Beth?"

"Yes, ma'am." He nodded in Beth's direction.

Beth met his gaze then turned away and slipped out the back door to splash water from the basin on her heated face. A slight breeze cooled her skin, and she waited to gain her composure. But she had work to finish, so squaring her shoulders, she went inside, and returned to her task of rolling out dough.

"I heard some interesting news in town today." Mr. Randall took a bite of warm cookie. "The sheriff from Marshall spoke to the proprietor of the hotel, the hostler, and a few others. It seems there's a gang operating around here, and he thinks someone in town might be helping them."

Beth bit her lip, bent her chin down toward her chest, and kept rolling dough.

"Who would do such a thing?" Nora asked.

"Maybe the sheriff's making a wild guess." Mr. Randall leaned back against the table like he had plenty of time. "Still, I've heard farmers mention losses in livestock, and it's more widespread than everyone thought at first." He grinned at Beth and took another warm cookie from the rack. "Is everything all right here?" He took another bite. "Mmm, these are good."

"We're fine here." Nora wiped her hands on her apron.

"Good to hear. I'll leave you to your work and head home. Thanks for the cookies." He grinned at Beth as he made for the door. "I can't remember when I tasted anything so good."

Beth watched him go. How could a few simple cookies leave her with a warm glow all over?

CHAPTER TWELVE

Beth looked forward to church. Maybe she would see Leah, or even Stuart. The morning rush to do chores and get ready left her frazzled though. The sheep had zigged when she zagged, and she'd gotten soaked. Once she finished dressing, she found her aunt serenely waiting for her. Nora's pose had become familiar to Beth—her head bent in prayer and meditation.

Just then, Nora glanced up. "Ready?" she asked. "Stuart is out front." At Beth's look, she explained. "He offered to give us a ride this morning."

"Yes, ma'am." Beth poked her hair in place, her pulse picking up. "How do I look? I feel a fright after rushing like that." Her question annoyed her, but she wanted Mr. Stuart Randall to think well of her.

Her aunt chuckled. "You look lovely, like always."

Beth's cheeks grew warm. "Aunt, I'll sit in the back, so you're not crowded."

"Nonsense. There is plenty of room up front. Besides, it will mess your pretty dress."

"Well, I just thought ..." Beth's mouth went dry. The prospect of sitting close to Stuart Randall took the words right out of her mouth. She followed Nora to the wagon, but hung back, waiting for Mr. Randall to assist Aunt Nora. But her aunt stepped aside and motioned Beth to go first. Stuart turned to assist her in climbing aboard. Her face heated, but it would be silly to make a scene. With a glance at Aunt Nora, Beth allowed Mr. Randall to help her into the conveyance.

After Nora was seated beside her, the wagon shifted with his weight, and Stuart sat down on her other side. He picked up the reins, a smile on his face.

Beth glanced around. He appeared to be enjoying *something* immensely. With her back stiff, she stared straight ahead, careful not to let any part of her arm touch his when the wagon jostled.

The Osgood family arrived at the same time they did. Ester waved and waited for them. Stuart Randall pulled the horses to a fence and climbed down. He walked around and helped Aunt Nora, but Beth wasn't about to let him help her again. She climbed down the opposite side and hurried to meet Ester.

Aunt Nora joined them, and Beth introduced the girl. "Aunt Nora, this is Ester Osgood. I told you about the family I saw on the train?"

"Oh yes, Ester, it's nice to meet you." Aunt Nora lowered her voice as they reached the open door.

The service began soon after. Beth watched for Leah, but the family she worked for did not come. The congregation sang, and one of the men in the community read from the Bible and they sang again.

When the service ended, Aunt Nora took Beth's arm. "There is someone I want you to meet."

Nora brought her to a family waiting in the shade. The mother's body rounded with a child on the way. She looked strained and tired as she wiped perspiration from her red face and then flung herself into Nora's arms. "Oh, Aunt Nora!"

Nora patted her back and spoke over her head to the man standing behind her. "How goes it, Martin?"

"Coming along."

"And you, Fanny?" She leaned back to look at the woman in her arms.

"I'm tired. The service plumb wore me out."

Nora released the woman and patted Beth's arm. "Fanny, Martin, this is Beth."

"Oh, Beth, I thought it must be." Fanny took her hand. "You are lovely."

Beth's face warmed. She'd never had so many people tell her she looked well.

"Stuart," Nora called, "I think we'll walk home. It's beautiful out, and you're busy."

"That sounds good." He stepped closer to them so he wouldn't have to yell. "Martin wants me to come to their place today." He shook hands with another man but turned back to them. "See you later, Aunt Nora, Beth." Their eyes met and he smiled.

Beth's heart did a skip, and then he turned away. The trip next to him had been thrilling, but she must stop this silliness. She ran her finger under her suddenly tight collar and turned with Aunt Nora to meet other church members.

Finally, Nora was ready to go home. "It was a nice morning, wasn't it?" Nora took her hand as they walked.

"Yes, ma'am."

"We'll eat when we get back to the house. I generally have a day of reading and sewing on Sunday. How does that sound?"

"Yes, ma'am." The warm sunny day would mean a drive with John if she'd been home. She paused. If he drove up right now, would she ride with him? Her hesitancy surprised her. He had seemed perfect for her but being away from him brought to mind how he treated her. He accused her of being jealous if she asked him questions about why he was gone. If he drove up now, maybe she would go. She would test him one last time. Her thoughts flashed back to Mr. Randall, a scene in her mind of them side by side on a wagon seat, his teasing grin and warm eyes turned to her.

The next morning after breakfast, Nora said, "Let's go visiting and take the treats we made. I know we have washing to do, but I'm in the mood to go." She slipped a basket from a hook by the door and began to fill it. "Sophie, for sure, and possibly Dixie."

"I think I remember Dixie, but have I met Sophie?"

"No, she wasn't at church yesterday, which is unusual. I'm concerned, so let's see how she's doing."

"Where does she live?" Beth helped pack Nora's basket with eggs, cookies, and cornbread.

"The other side of town, but we can walk it easily."

They discussed herbs Aunt Nora used as they walked, but before long, she stopped at a gate in front of a small residence.

Beth's aunt knocked and called out. "Sophie?" She waited, then called again. When there was no answer, Nora opened the door, calling the woman's name.

They walked through a front room and into a tiny sitting room where an older woman sat by a window. When she saw them, she jumped up, quick as a girl, her small figure dressed in a bright, print dress, her hair tied with a scarf.

"Nora, I didn't hear you."

"Sophie," Nora raised her voice, "I have Beth with me today."

"Beth?" She frowned but gestured to them. "Come in, come in and sit. Nora, is church today? I've been waiting for someone to pick me up."

"Church was yesterday," Nora said. "I brought you eggs and some leftovers."

"Well, land sakes!" Sophie said. "Let me get you something then." She rushed off to another room.

"Is she deaf?" Beth surveyed the tiny sitting area. Two chairs crowded together in front of a window and a minuscule table with a lamp stood along one wall of the small room.

"Pretty close," Nora said, "and she can't see well either."

Sophie returned with cups and handed them out. "I thought I needed to be somewhere today."

"Beth will put the food we brought away for you, Sophie."

"Oh, that's fine then, miss." Sophie's white head bobbed as she talked, setting her scarf tails bouncing. "Thank you, Nora. You know how I appreciate it."

"I'm sorry you missed church." Beth heard Aunt Nora tell the older woman about the service while she put away her supplies.

After bringing out cookies for their tea, Beth selected a chair from the kitchen for herself. Beth studied the older woman. As she knit, Beth noticed how fast her fingers moved.

"I'm sorry I forgot." Sophie said. "I'll be sure to make the next one."

"You feeling blue, then?" Nora asked.

"No, just a little tuckered."

They talked on, and Beth's mind wandered. Maybe she should stop at the mercantile and ask for a job. Her emotions were in a quandary though. She should be working, yet Aunt Nora kept her busy. Is that why her parents had sent her here?

"Time for us to get home," Aunt Nora said at last.

"Is she all right?" Beth asked once they were outside.

"She's able to care for herself, as you can see," Nora said. "Shopping is getting more difficult, and she relies on her knitting to bring in money. She doesn't need much for supplies, and many of the townsfolk bring wood and other necessities to help her out."

"Is it enough?" The wind picked up strands of Beth's hair and blew it across her face. "She's ... sweet." She tucked the hair behind her ears. "She reminds me of Eva, one of our customers. Father usually delivers her supplies." She missed the customers at the store—they were her family.

Nora shrugged. "I bring contributions when I can. This winter, I couldn't get around much. We had a lot of snow, but others did the visiting for me."

Beth dodged around a hole in the path. "How long do you think she'll be able to knit?"

"That's hard to say." Nora held onto her bonnet in the wind. "She knows her house inside and out, so as long as she can knit and get help from time to time, she's able to live by herself."

"Her home is well cared for."

"Several of her children come." Nora brushed a hair back in place. "But she doesn't want to live with them. She and I could combine houses, if necessary. I would need a little work done, but we could manage if things get worse for either of us."

"Oh." Beth couldn't imagine Aunt Nora having to give up her home. It seemed perfect for her.

"Everyone gets on in years," Nora said, as if sensing Beth's mood. "That's the way of life."

"I don't think of my parents as old, but with me gone, they're alone."

Aunt Nora stopped walking and turned her back to the wind to catch her breath. "It happens to us all."

"I always wanted to be with them, helping in the store." Beth shifted to glance back at Sophie's house. "When I was small, we lived on a farm. The memories are coming back to me since I've been here. I liked it, but I don't think my father did. He used to say he wondered how some farmers knew whether to cut hay one day or wait a few days. He felt he chose the wrong time to do everything, while others did better."

Aunt Nora resumed walking.

Beth fell into step beside her. They passed a young boy holding onto a rope tethered to a cow that grazed along the road.

"At the store, it was better." Beth smiled at the boy. "They didn't want me there, but I finally convinced Mom I could help."

Her aunt said, "Perhaps your father didn't have a feel for the land. My dad was a farmer because he wanted to be, not because that's what his father did." Nora tightened her shawl against the brisk wind. "He loved the land, and it responded. It is a spiritual relationship, I think. I can feel it myself."

As they crossed Main Street, Beth glanced around. One of the wagons seemed familiar to her.

"When you're part of the land, it's hard to leave it." Nora changed course and turned toward the mercantile. "I decided to do what I could do. I dig in the dirt, and I care for my livestock. I may be an old lady, but I'm a farmer. It's what I am."

Beth nodded. "My papa is good at running a store, and you're good at what you do."

A man walked from the store, a drooping sack over his shoulder. Aunt Nora said, "Stuart, what brings you in town today?"

Beth's head jerked around.

"Hello, there, Aunt Nora, Beth. Just picking up supplies for Martin. He didn't have time." He placed the bag in his wagon. "What are you ladies up to today?"

Beth's heart sang at this unexpected opportunity to see Stuart. She tried to remind herself she wasn't interested in this man.

"Visiting Sophie," Aunt Nora said. "But it's past time for us to get back to work."

"Bye, then." He tipped his hat. "See you, ladies."

Beth forced her gaze away and hurried to follow her aunt.

"Stuart is a busy man. I'm grateful he's able to help Martin and Fanny," Nora said as Beth walked up to her. "But once he's married, he won't have this much time."

Beth wondered why Aunt Nora kept referring to Stuart and marriage. "Is he seeing someone?"

"Not that I know of. At least right now." Aunt Nora slowed to catch her breath. "Now, as I was saying, the gospels tell us to be good stewards of the land. There is also great importance put on the land God gave the Israelites. Someday, they will get their land back."

As they walked closer to Nora's house, she said, "For those of us called to the land, I believe God wants us to love it. We must also ask for wisdom to manage everything God has given us."

Beth turned to look back just before they rounded the corner off the main street. Stuart stood by the wagon watching them.

Later that week, someone knocked at the door. Beth dropped her project to answer the knock.

"Howdy, miss." A nice-looking boy about her age waited on the porch. "Is your ... is Mrs. Durand home?"

Beth stepped away as her aunt came to the door.

"Hello there, Steven," Nora greeted the smiling visitor. "What can I help you with?"

"Oh, ma'am"—he eyed Beth—"do you have any chores that might be needin' done?" When Nora didn't answer immediately, he went on quickly. "I'm not looking for pay, ma'am, just being neighborly." His face took on a rosy hue, and he shifted his weight from one foot to the other.

"Well, Steven, I believe I have some work on the chicken coop enclosure. Let me show you." Nora turned. "Beth, would you like to come too?"

Beth followed, though she knew nothing about the chicken coop. However, Steven was rather cute.

Nora showed Steven the loose area on her chicken enclosure and where the tools were for completing the job. "Steven, Beth will bring you something to eat later."

He glanced at Beth, then away. "Yes, ma'am."

When they got back to the house, Aunt Nora asked, "Beth, did this ever happen to you at home?"

"What do you mean?" Beth took up the sewing again. "Did what happen?"

"I think that young man out there is trying to get your attention." Nora went back to scrubbing potatoes.

Beth's face heated. "Why would he do that?"

"Honey, you must have noticed—you're a lovely young lady."

Beth shook her head, but later, when her aunt asked her to take the hard-working boy some cold milk and cheese wrapped in bread, she obliged. Though it wouldn't do to encourage him, he did deserve thoughtful consideration.

"Nice day," he said, reaching for the dipper of water. He drank it down and swiped his arm across his mouth.

She took the dipper back and handed him his lunch. "Yes, isn't it?" She glanced up at the blue sky.

He took a bite. "You like our town?"

"Seems nice," she said. After an awkward silence, she asked, "Do you live close by?"

"Oh, we live about four miles out of town, my parents and us, of course. I don't get in town often, but saw you the other day and …" He paused, apparently not able to think of any words to finish the sentence.

"I see … that's nice," Beth said.

As she turned to go, he made one last try. "Maybe I could take you for a ride sometime?"

Just a few days ago, she longed to go for a ride with someone, but this boy was not the one she pictured. "Thank you," she said. "Nice job you're doing."

"Thanks." He grinned.

"I'll let you finish." She turned toward the house.

"Thanks for lunch," he called after her.

She waved. "You're welcome."

Later, Steven came to the door and returned the empty milk container. "All finished, ma'am."

"Thank you, Steven," Nora said. "I appreciate your thoughtfulness."

Beth quickly added, "Yes, thank you for your help, Steven. I enjoyed meeting you."

Steven grinned. Beth liked his friendly smile. "Be seein' ya." He tipped his hat and went on his way.

"Did you like Steven?" Nora asked after he'd left.

"He's a hard worker, has a pleasant disposition, and a nice smile," Beth said. "He seems nice."

"I think you're right not to form attachments right away," Nora said. "You have a situation at home unresolved. I'd better come up with a few more jobs though."

"Why ever for?"

"I think Steven is just the beginning. Once the other young men have heard he paid a visit, they'll all want to come meet you."

CHAPTER THIRTEEN

True to Nora's prediction, a man came to their porch a few nights later while Beth and her aunt were enjoying the spring evening.

"Nora, ma'am," he said. "How are you this pleasant evening?"

"Chipper as a young squirrel, Mr. Graystone. How are you?"

"Oh, I'm feelin' mighty good myself. How about I sit a spell and visit with you ladies?" He sat down on the edge of the porch. "And who do we have here?"

"This is Beth from over Rochester way," Nora said. "She's visiting—"

"Howdy, girl," he interrupted Aunt Nora and went right into his speech as if he needed to get it said before he forgot the words. "You look right strong and healthy. You got you a man?"

Beth gasped.

"Now, George." Nora straightened in her chair. "You're a trifle forward with this young lady. She isn't attached, but she has plenty of time."

"No harm in trying, ma'am, no harm a-tall." He adjusted his position on the edge of the porch, lit a pipe, and leaned back against the support post like he had all evening.

Beth ducked her head to side-glance at Aunt Nora out of the corner of her eye. Nora raised her brows, then went back to sewing.

Beth concentrated on the towel she'd started hemming a few days ago, but her mind wandered as the man talked on about his livestock, his children, and his farm.

They listened for what seemed like hours before Aunt Nora folded up her work. Beth quickly followed, putting away the towel and thread. She prepared to go in the house, relieved to have this night over when Mr. Graystone came toward her.

"Well, what do you think?" he asked.

Beth backed away from him and peeked at Aunt Nora. She and Mr. Graystone were both looking at her. "About what?" Beth hadn't been listening to the man's prattle.

"About what I just told you," he said.

"Oh!" Beth felt her cheeks grow warm. "Well, that's nice, I'm sure."

"You like it then?" He stepped closer.

Beth backed up, coming against the porch door. "Like what?"

"I think the girl will need more time to think about it, George," Nora said, coming to her rescue.

"I'd like to have an answer now. I ain't visited the girl that come with you yet." He cleared his throat and spat into the darkness.

Beth shuddered. "Leah?"

"That her name?" he asked. "She looked mighty pert. I seen her helping out at Ornsbys. I hear she's learning to cook but doing fine. I like pies, now and then, myself."

Toes rubbed herself against Beth's legs. She bent and picked up the cat, hiding her face in the cat's fur. She waited for her aunt to help her out of this mess, unclear what Mr. Grayson wanted from her.

He knocked out his pipe and continued speaking. "I did hear of a widow woman over Amiret way. I could visit her, but this would save me a trip."

"If you mean Widow Westamann"—Nora moved to Beth's side—"I think it would be good to visit her, George. You'd better hurry before someone else snaps her up."

"You think so?" He tucked his pipe into a shirt pocket. "You may be right. Thank you, ladies. Be seeing you." With that, he strolled off into the darkening night.

"What was that all about?" Beth stepped through the door and held it open for her aunt.

"That, dear girl, was a proposal."

"For heaven's sake, he must be at least twenty years older than me, and he spits and ..." Beth shuddered.

Aunt Nora set aside her sewing basket.

"No love, or courting, or anything?" Not that she wanted the man to court her. The very idea made her skin crawl. She rubbed her hands up and down her arms to brush away the feeling.

"George maybe thinks he's beyond all that."

Beth followed Aunt Nora to the kitchen area to set it aright for the night. She picked up a dishtowel and folded it with a snap. "So, get my mind made up quick and save him a trip?"

"George doesn't have the time to waste," Aunt Nora said, filling herself a cup of water.

"What happened to his wife?"

"Hilde died over the winter and the new baby with her. George has eight children with no mother. At least he's thinking of getting help for his children."

"Well, for heaven's sake." Beth untied her apron and hung it up behind the stove.

"His children are wonderful," Nora said, checking the stove for coals. "Actually, Hilde and George were a nice couple and very close." Nora wrapped the bread cooling on the table in a clean cloth and set it inside the breadbox. "George would be better off with a woman more his age, and Edith Westamann would suit him. She has several children, and they need a father too."

Beth knew older people sometimes married for convenience, but this was the first time anyone had asked her. Would any girl her age be desperate enough to consider such a thing?

"This cold-hearted planning of marriages—no love at all?"

"Love grows, but that isn't something for you, anyway. You're young and should have plenty of time to decide who you want to settle down with." Nora strained the tea that had been steeping in the sun. "George and Edith have families to support, and they're looking at survival. I've had proposals, even at my age."

"You have?" The words came out before Beth could stop herself.

Aunt Nora laughed. "Yes, dear ... me, at my age. I can still cook and clean."

Beth blew out her breath, relived that Nora hadn't taken offense. "Why haven't you accepted, then?"

"I haven't needed to, and maybe now it's too late." Nora pulled her knitted shawl close around her shoulders in the cooling evening.

"Is there a family you could live with or your children?" Beth walked toward her bedroom, still able to see in the dim light coming through the windows.

"I don't want to be a burden to my children," Nora said. "That may be a silly sentiment, I know, but I have my ways, and so have they." She paused by her bedroom. "Besides, I like this town. My oldest daughter, Lottie, married and settled in Wisconsin before we moved here. Carl went on west with Stuart's uncles and has settled there."

"Oh?" Beth's heart sped up. Here was an opportunity to find out more.

"Goodnight, dear." Nora disappeared behind the curtain door of her room.

"Goodnight, ma'am." Disappointment needled her. Aunt Nora seemed willing to share certain things, but for some reason, she held back when it came to her family.

Later, as Beth lay in bed, she pondered the visits from Steven and Mr. Graystone. She lay in the dark, and the handsome face of Stuart Randall imposed itself over the others. Warmth flowed over her, and she buried her face in her pillow. Would he come by like the others had?

"Let's go for a walk." Aunt Nora had been quiet this morning but now started to gather things to set out for town. "I think I'm ready to pick up some fabric, and we can check for mail."

"I'll finish setting the milk." Beth was used to every day the same, but Aunt Nora seemed to like variety in her days. "Do we take the eggs and butter too?" Excitement surged through her. Maybe they would bump into Stuart again.

"Yes, but perhaps I'll keep some back so that we can do more baking."

They first stopped for mail. This time the store was clean and in better condition than the last time they'd been there.

"Hello, Clara. Any mail for us today?"

No men loitered in the corner this time while Clara and an adolescent boy served customers.

"No, Nora. If something comes in, I can have Judd here deliver it."

Beth glanced at the boy when he looked up from his work. He was about twelve. Beth could well imagine how he loved to get away from the store and deliver mail.

"No need, Clara. I like the walk." Aunt Nora turned to the boy as if she understood how she had disappointed him. "Judd, you can come by with a bag of lime later if you have time."

He grinned, straightening his shoulders. "Sure thing, Mrs. Durand."

They left and walked to the mercantile where Sally greeted them the moment they came through the door. "Good morning, Aunt Nora, Beth. How can I help you today?"

"I've made up my mind about the fabric I want," Nora said.

Sally tucked a pencil in her blond hair. "What pattern have you chosen?"

"I'm in the mood to do Broken Dishes."

"That will use up your scraps. What colors do you need?"

Their conversation faded into the background as Beth became lost in memories of the smells and sounds of home. She straightened the display of jacks by the children's toys, adjusted the dress on a doll, and pulled the books on a shelf forward to line up perfectly.

She wandered back to Nora, who finished picking out fabric and traded the eggs and butter they brought. Aunt Nora ordered salt pork, flour, and molasses to be delivered as well, plus dried beans and apples.

"Do you want me to have the fabric delivered along with this?" Sally asked.

"Oh, dear me, no." Nora set her basket on the counter. "I've decided, and now I want to get started. Beth and I will begin cutting today."

Sally chuckled. "I thought so."

Soon afterward, Nora and Beth left the store with a bundle of fabric.

"It looks like you bought more fabric than you needed for one quilt." Beth stepped aside for a lady to pass on the boardwalk.

"Just an idea. You'll see."

Beth hoped to stop at a few other stores, and perhaps wander around town a little, but Aunt Nora seemed to have a goal in mind and hurried them on toward home.

"Now let's have a quick bite, and then we can wash this fabric and hang it out to dry. Would you like to weed or bake this afternoon?"

"It's still windy and not real hot so either job would be good for today. What do we need?" Beth had no practice planning for the day when so many possibilities were laid out before her.

"I'll have water heating to wash these pieces so you might as well bake. Later you could weed at least enough to feed the chickens and pigs."

"I'll go to the cold house." Beth brought leftover mush and salt pork and then filled pots of water and set them on the stove to heat. "My mother always did certain things each day—wash on Monday, iron on Tuesday—and like that."

Aunt Nora set a fry pan on the cook stove. "I followed it when I had a family to care for, but I don't need to anymore. My wash hardly takes any time, and the same with most of the other household tasks, but it's a guide. Some women look at their week, and the work they must do, and it overwhelms them. When you have a family, with much cooking and washing, it helps to have a set task for each day. The rest of the work can be added around the one big task."

"I can see that." The aroma of leftover mush and strips of salt pork reminded Beth how hungry she was. "There are peas that I picked yesterday."

"Yes, let's have those too." Aunt Nora turned the pork. "A woman who has a garden to take care of needs to do that in the cool of the day, or at least a day where it isn't rainy."

Later, Beth baked and then worked in the garden. She knelt in the row, daydreaming of doing this for a husband and children. Her potential husband's face lay in shadow though.

Her throat went dry, and she forced those thoughts away. Time to face reality. She might never have such a family.

After supper, Beth finished dishes while Aunt Nora spread her scraps and new purchases.

"My old templates are getting so ragged around the edges I don't trust their accuracy anymore. It's time I made new ones." Aunt Nora gathered her basket of supplies.

Beth thought of her mother as Nora drew her design on brown paper. Her mother had an extensive collection of patterns, and they started this way too.

Nora drew the design she wanted, using the straight edge of a piece of wood. When the triangle pattern met Nora's satisfaction, she traced it on the cardboard of a saved cracker box.

Aunt Nora made two extra sets of triangles and put the duplicates away in her sewing basket. "You never know when one of these might go missing."

Beth finished the dishes and hung the towel to dry on a bar behind the cookstove. "Should I heat the flat irons tonight?"

"Yes, please."

Beth pressed a pile of fabric pieces, then sat down and began tracing around the Broken Dishes template with a pencil. She cut out the pieces, leaving an extra quarter inch seam allowance. After threading a needle and tying one end of the thread into a big knot, she impaled each light-colored quilt piece onto the needle and pulled it down to form a stack. She made a different pile for the darks.

Before long, Aunt Nora started sewing. She creased the seam with her fingernail and laid it out to admire her work. "I do like this patch."

"It's satisfying somehow." Beth squinted at the small patch, picturing a whole quilt.

"It changes the look when it's pieced random like we're doing." Nora picked up two triangles and began to sew. "You can also make it more structured with only a few fabrics."

"I love the wildness of all those colors but held in discipline by rows." Beth covered her mouth to stifle a yawn.

Aunt Nora laughed. "It's like people you know."

"What?"

"Go on to bed, dear. I couldn't stop now if I wanted to."

"All right then. Goodnight, Aunt."

Beth contemplated her aunt's comment as she lay in bed. The wildness inside needed to be disciplined. She thought of people she knew, her parents, regular customers, and others. Likely everyone struggled in some area of their lives. The thought struck her hard. John was undisciplined, and since she started seeing him, she had become that way too.

CHAPTER FOURTEEN

Several days later, Beth walked to the store where Sally worked, taking butter and eggs for trade.

"How's the sewing going?" Sally asked from behind the counter.

"I do the cutting. Aunt Nora is the sewer."

"You likin' things here?" Sally counted out the eggs and placed them in the display basket the mercantile used.

"I like Aunt Nora."

"Oh, everyone does. She's good to people here. Why, a few winters ago, she had my father take the credit on her account and use it to give beans, flour, and salt pork to a new family that wasn't doing well."

Beth pursed her lips. "Sounds like her."

Sally added the tally to the account book. "I don't know how she does it. She has feed and supplies, even when others are struggling."

"I thought she had plenty of credit."

"That's what I mean." Sally called to a shopper who came in the door. "Hello, Mrs. Caden." She turned back to Beth. "Your aunt is blessed with plenty when others are in want. Papa says she's the perfect example of a godly woman." Sally closed her account book and whispered, "The young people hope to organize a day to get together sometime before the summer gets away from us."

Beth blinked at the sudden change of conversation. "Do you usually do that?" She hadn't planned on socializing.

Sally placed her ledger under the counter. "Yes, we do. It's about the only way the young people ever get to spend time together." She handed Beth her basket. "I'll let you know when we get it organized. Would you come?"

Beth didn't want to be rude, and she liked Sally. "I guess so, if I can get there."

"Let me take care of that. See you soon."

Another young man stopped by Aunt Nora's the next day. "Mrs. Durand," he said, "I thought to see if you needed anything done here."

"Howard, that's right nice of you." Aunt Nora walked with him to the barn.

After a bit, Beth thought she heard someone whistling. She looked out to see what her aunt had found for Howard to do. In the open barn, Howard bent over a pitchfork, cleaning out the winter accumulation of manure. His melodic, happy whistle sounded akin to birds singing.

Beth brought him a dipper of water. "You're a good sport to be doing such a job." She leaned back on a fence post and brushed away a pesky fly.

He took off his hat, brought his arm across his face, and wiped the sweat accumulating there. "No trouble, miss. Needs doing."

Beth handed him the dipper. "What I mean to say is ... well, you don't seem to mind."

"Hard work is good for a man." He tilted the dipper and drank. "I've been taught to do it willingly."

Beth accepted the dipper back from him. "Thank you again, Howard. We both appreciate it."

"Sure thing."

Beth returned to her duties but thought of John. He would not have done physical labor to impress a girl, at least not her.

Later, she hung clothes on the line and scrubbed the floor. Then she took a cloth-wrapped packet of food to Howard. The pungent odor of fresh manure stung her nose and eyes.

"Can't stay longer," he said, "but got the inside cleaned out. Later in the fall, I'll come back and work this into the garden and spread it in the field with Stuart's manure spreader. Be best to let it cure some first."

"Thank you." Beth handed him the bundle. "Aunt Nora put some bread in here for you, and I made cookies." She liked Howard and his happy attitude.

"Thank you." Howard put away the pitchfork. "I thought I would see Timothy today."

"Nora thinks he's afraid of me," Beth said.

Howard smiled. "Why would he be afraid of you? I bet he thinks you're pretty and he's shy."

Beth felt her cheeks warming. Howard thought she was pretty?

"I better get on home. Thanks for the vittles." He tucked the parcel into his shirt.

Beth watched as he headed down the street with a bounce to his stride and a tune on his lips. Now why hadn't she met a man like that in her town? Maybe she would never have gotten involved with John, and she and her parents would not have argued.

One evening several days later, Beth finished washing up, pleased to be clean after a hard day in the garden. Just when she emerged from her room to empty the tub, a knock shook the back door.

"My goodness, aunt!" Beth cried, "I haven't combed out my hair. Could I go out on the porch, and you talk to whoever it is?"

"Yes, go." Nora made sweeping motions with her hands.

Beth sat in the middle of the swing and began the tedious task of combing out her long hair. Holding her comb out from her head, she marveled as the last rays of sunlight shone through the strands. When it pulled free, her hair fell in waves and curls. Then the hair on the back of her neck prickled and she glanced up.

Stuart leaned against the doorjamb, watching her.

"What are you doing here?" She turned her back on him, her face heated like a summer day at high noon.

"I thought I'd stop by to see how you two were getting along."

"Oh, we're fine." She stared straight ahead, her breath coming in short gasps.

"So I hear," he said. "Nora tells me you've had a steady stream of visitors."

She pressed her hand to her chest, needing to still the hammering of her heart. "Not that many."

"I can't blame them," he said, his voice light, as if he might be smiling. "And it seems Nora is getting some difficult jobs done."

"Yes." Beth smiled. "Howard did a fine job." She had wondered if Stuart might come. Now that he stood so near, she had no idea what to say to him.

Silence stretched between them for a time, then he spoke. "Your hair smells good."

"I just finished washing it." Her hand flew to her mouth. What a thing to say! For some reason, she wanted to impress him, but ended up sounding silly.

"I know. I emptied the water for you."

"Oh, no!" She ducked her head, letting a wave of hair hide her face.

He laughed. "Hardly anything improper about that, is there, Beth?"

"It's embarrassing." His use of her first name affected her to the pit of her stomach.

He laughed again. "It's hard to hide, besides, wash water means a day of work, and that's a worthy thing."

Beth resumed combing her hair. Doing so in front of him might not be proper, but if her hair dried in tangles, it would be impossible to manage.

"I do like your hair," he said, "but I would also enjoy seeing your face."

Beth snapped around to look at him. "You're rather forward, aren't you?"

"Yes, I suppose I am." He met her eyes. "I decided I'd better—with all the boys in town stepping up to meet you."

She turned away to hide from his look. "They don't know me at all."

"Of course, but this is the way it begins. They can get to know you by stopping by." He paused, and she turned to look at him again. "And Nora can get an idea of how willing they are to work." He grinned.

Beth turned away. What did he mean—this is the way it begins? Did he want to start something? Heat rushed to her face again. "Well, the barn is clean."

He laughed and stepped forward. "Mind if I sit down?"

She glanced up, meeting his eyes and warming to his grin. Beth moved down to one end. His grin was the intimate smile of a friend. Could she be considered his friend or maybe something more?

The swing sank a little and creaked with his added weight. He set it in motion. A breeze brought the scents of sun, hay, and man to her nose. The warmth of his body radiated to her, even though they weren't touching at all.

She moved on the seat and turned to look at him.

He kept his gaze straight ahead but rubbed his forehead.

"It's a nice night, isn't it?" He turned to her.

She glanced around at her surroundings. "Did you see the robin's nest?" She resumed combing her hair.

Stuart shifted in his seat.

"Yes." His answer was more like a croak. He cleared his throat. "Yes, I hear her scolding."

"Much of the time, the adults go back and forth to the nest without a peep," she said, "but they must not like a stranger here."

Stuart loosened his collar and shifted on the swing. "That seems likely." He gave the swing a push.

"I enjoy the birds around here so much. There are swallows in the barn too."

"So, what did you think of Howard?"

Beth pulled her hair aside to see him. "He's nice and not afraid of work." She grinned. "And he whistles when he works. I'm impressed."

Stuart seemed to sag and turned to look back over the yard. "Yes. Howard helps me out from time to time. He's a good man." He rose from his seat. "Time I got going." Without ceremony or farewell, he ran from her, through the arched trellis and onto the road.

Beth's voice called out to him. "Thank you."

"No trouble," he yelled, pulling his hat on.

Beth shook her head. What did Stuart have on his mind? He seemed anxious to be away from her.

CHAPTER FIFTEEN

When they finished chores a few days later, Aunt Nora asked Beth, "Is there something you want to learn? Later, we can work on the quilt, but you wanted to learn to knit, yes?"

"Mother says I'm hopeless."

"Merin could be too impatient," Nora said. "Every woman should know how to knit. There are socks, scarves, mittens, and other things you'll need. Your mother won't always be around to make them for you."

Beth shrugged. Would she ever have a home of her own where socks, scarves, and mittens would be needed? Would she be making such things for a husband and children? She shivered. "I'd like to learn."

Nora rose from her chair. "Well, then, I have needles of all sizes in my trunk. Let's start you on a practice piece, something straight and plain. Then, we can add stitches as you perfect each one."

"I can start," Beth said. "I learned that much—as long as you'll help me after that."

Aunt Nora gave her the needles and yarn, and Beth began the cast-on process. She decided to use this time to ask the questions that had been on her mind. "Aunt Nora, how long has your husband been gone?"

"Oh, dear me," Nora said. "It's almost three years now."

"You moved here after that?"

"No, we moved just before. He was slowing down, and I thought that's all it was. I wasn't prepared for him to go."

"I'm sorry. You must miss him." Beth struggled to thread the yarn through her fingers as her aunt did.

Aunt Nora nodded. "More than you can imagine."

"I don't understand why you and mother live so far apart." Beth inserted a knitting needle next to the one holding the knitting, wrapped the yarn, and pulled it onto the new needle.

"It's a long story." Nora moved closer. "Here, Beth, let me show you the next step." She pulled out a length of yarn. "Now that you have the cast on, let's do the garter stitch. Then you'll be ready to learn the purl stitch. You will make the stockinette stitch by doing the purl stitch one row and the regular knit stitch for the next row."

Beth worked on the stitch Nora taught her. She poked one knitting needle in, trying to hang onto both needles while she brought the yarn around the first one. She then pulled the new stitch through and pushed it off onto the second needle.

"When it's uniform and smooth, you can rip it out and make something usable." Nora went back to her own knitting.

"If that ever happens," Beth muttered. She twisted her neck to stretch the kinks already forming. Her hands cramped around the needle as she began another row.

"Is it supposed to be this hard?" Beth asked.

"The tension is not right," her aunt said.

"I can tell the tension isn't right," Beth wailed, reaching over her shoulder to massage her back and neck. "I hurt like crazy."

"I think it's time to do something else," Nora said. "You'll get it figured out over time."

Beth threw her project onto the swing. "Yes, please, let's do something else. I'm hopeless, like Mom says."

"Nonsense, anyone can accomplish new things if they have patience and take the time to learn properly."

"Who's hopeless?" Stuart called from the street before he walked under the trellis and up to the porch.

"Stuart, I wasn't expecting you." Aunt Nora laid her knitting on her lap and tugged it straight.

"Can't stay long." He turned to Beth. "So what are you hiding?"

She lifted her chin. "Nothing that would interest you in the least." Her face heated at the feisty remark.

He laughed. "Aunt Nora, Fanny asked me to tell you the food you sent was greatly appreciated. I'll be going there in a few days if you want to send something again."

"Thank you, Stuart. I will have something ready, and Beth can bake again."

Stuart turned back to her. "The hopeless thing must not be your cooking then."

Beth had a childish desire to stick her tongue out at him. Aunt Nora came to her rescue. "Beth is a fine cook and bakes well too."

Stuart jumped off the edge of the porch. "I'll leave you to your hopeless project then. See you later." He laughed and stepped through the trellis.

Beth bit her lip to hide her smile as she watched his back as he strolled down the street. It wasn't fair that he came and then left without giving her time ... time for *what*?

When Beth and Aunt Nora came through the pasture after their walk a few days later, Stuart was mending the fence.

After greeting him, Beth stopped in the garden to work a bit while her aunt rested her arms over the fence and leaned on it.

"I forgot to tell you about Tad," Stuart said. "Fanny sent word that she needed help."

"Yes?" Aunt Nora pulled her bonnet forward to cover her face against the sun.

"It seems Tad thought he'd found a way to shorten his chores."

"What happened?" Aunt Nora asked.

"He decided to take the chickens to the feed bin." Stuart pushed his hat back, revealing a tan line on his forehead.

"I see."

"He apparently filled the bin with chickens and let the lid close." Stuart moved to rest against the fence beside Aunt Nora. "Most of them got out somehow, but by the time Fanny found them, she couldn't save two."

"Mm." Aunt Nora's brows made a lump between her eyes. "Tad should be old enough to know better."

"I don't know about that. Sometimes I wonder how I was at his age."

"You were a serious and completely wonderful little boy."

He scratched his head, knocking his hat askew. "And how would you be knowin' that?"

"Your mother, of course." Nora smiled up at him.

He laughed. "She might not have remembered everything. I distinctly recollect putting my brother and sister up to helping me paint the house with leftover paint. We did one wide strip all the way around. Bright red, I believe it was."

Beth and Aunt Nora laughed.

Stuart removed his hat and ran his hand through his hair, laughing with them.

Beth melted inside, picturing him as a little boy.

"Fanny didn't want to waste any of the meat." Stuart pulled on his hat and adjusted it low over his eyes. "But she couldn't handle cleaning them. So, she sent word to me."

"You had chicken for supper, I presume," Aunt Nora said.

Stuart threw back his head in laughter, revealing a strong, tanned throat and broad shoulders. "We did, indeed."

While Aunt Nora and Stuart talked on, Beth went back to weeding. Her mind wandered to John and his behavior compared to Stuart's. She loved it when John brought her gifts, yet he seemed to expect more than a thank you. She pressed her lips together. She couldn't imagine Stuart expecting such a thing. He was a generous person, freely helping her aunt, Fanny and even his neighbors.

"Beth?" Nora called to her.

"Oh, I'm sorry," she said. "Did you say something? My thoughts were elsewhere."

"I need to be going." Stuart turned his gaze on her.

Beth got up from her knees. "See you later, Stuart." His intense look as he walked away sent a shiver to the pit of her stomach.

"Beth and I will have baking for you next time you go out there," Nora called to him. Then she turned to Beth. "Come in and have something cool to drink before we make supper."

Beth wiped her hands on her apron and joined Aunt Nora on the porch. What could be on her mind?

Aunt Nora sat and patted the spot beside her. "You remember that Fanny's husband is working for the railroad to earn extra money? She may need someone to help with the children."

"I don't know anything about children," Beth blurted before her aunt had a chance to ask. Three rambunctious children—putting chickens in a bin? What would they think of next?

"Oh, that's not a problem," Nora said. "You would do fine. Children are easy, but we can think about it."

Beth helped with chores, and they ate a small meal on the porch. Later Aunt Nora brought out her sewing and yardage lengths of muslin.

"Here is the fabric I bought the other day. Would you hem these towels and embroider them?" She held up the fabric to show Beth. "I think you need a break from the knitting."

"I agree." Beth laughed and picked up a length of toweling and threaded a needle. "I enjoy embroidery and it reminds me of home. It's Papa's birthday at the end of the week." She dropped her handwork into her lap and turned to Nora. "I miss them. I still don't understand why my parents did this."

Nora picked up her knitting. "But dear, they are your parents, your elders. They have the authority and the responsibility to do what they believe is the right thing for you."

Beth rolled the edge of toweling in her fingers and took a stitch. "They just don't like John." She sounded petulant but the whole situation still frustrated her. She wasn't sure she wanted to see John again, but she hated being forced from home like a child.

"Beth, from what you've told me, you have serious concerns about him yourself."

"I do, but couldn't they have talked to me about it instead of sending me away?" Beth bent over her work. Her parents had made their reprimand so public, humiliating.

"Did you listen when they tried?"

Beth threw her handwork onto the swing. "No, I didn't stop seeing him." She jumped to her feet and paced the porch. "I had no other prospects. And yes, maybe I had a dream that he was something he was not."

"That happens more often than you realize." Nora swung her arm wide as she pulled more yarn from the ball at her feet while the cat chased it across the floor. "You could have found yourself married to an unsuitable man before you woke from that dream."

"He might have changed." She cringed at the inane comment. It was a childish thing to say.

"Come, sit." Aunt Nora put down her work. "You know that's not the basis for a marriage. Your parents are concerned about your relationship with God too."

Beth plopped down by Nora. She no longer resented the woman like she did at first, but she didn't want to hear a lecture either.

"If you're unequally yoked, you disobey a clear warning from God. There are always serious consequences for disobeying him."

Beth crossed her arms and pressed her lips together. She looked at the colors of the setting sun, and at the bats feeding as evening darkened. Before her, the beauty of nature functioned in peace and harmony—something her last few months had not.

"You want to be careful not to be rebellious, dear," Nora warned, taking her hand.

Anger at her parents, this woman, and John surged through Beth. Maybe she did want to hold onto her rage, but Nora had no right to call her rebellious. The accusation hurt. She stared at the sky as dark descended, the silhouetted trees resembling black, crippled apparitions in the waning daylight.

"I know you were raised to be a kind and considerate girl." Aunt Nora released her hand. "An attitude that does not allow you to submit to authority is a dangerous thing."

Beth jumped up from her seat, keeping her back to Aunt Nora.

"Beth, I want you to know, all of us struggle," Nora said. "There is difficulty in life you'll understand soon enough."

Aunt Nora paused, and Beth clamped her teeth. It wasn't how she pictured this conversation. Aunt Nora had become her friend, and anyone could see that her parents were unreasonable to require her to leave. She'd believed Aunt Nora would say her parents were wrong.

"We can't prevent everything bad from coming," Nora said, "but when we obey God, we keep some of it from ever showing at our door. Marriage to an unsaved person would bring much loneliness, misery, and pain, and it's not God's best for you. Talk to God, dear. Pray, and he will help you sort it out."

Beth fled to her room so Aunt Nora wouldn't see her cry. As she readied for bed she thought about what her aunt had said. Kneeling by the bed, her head in her hands, she bent over and sobbed.

Exhausted, she rested her upper body on the bed, still kneeling on the floor. Closing her eyes, she thought of John and then about the boys she'd met here. Any one of them would be a better choice. They were courteous, kind, hardworking men. Had she been so childish as to choose someone her parents disapproved of only because they objected?

She buried her face in the quilt. "Oh, Lord, I don't understand," she whispered. "But I'm tired of this. I'm sorry I hurt my parents. I love them, and I miss them, and I hate the wall between us."

As she sobbed into her blankets, the choice came to her with sudden, surprising clarity. She could either stop being rebellious or refuse and become hard. Pride wanted to hold out, but the fight had exhausted her. It reminded her of the Scripture someone had read at church recently—choose life.

The comments she'd made to her parents came to mind and brought shame. Never, before John, would she have said such things to them. She did not want to admit it, but her parents were right. Tears burst forth again, and she covered her face. She hated being wrong in this, but life with John would be constant turmoil, and when she faced the truth, it would be lonely and painful as well. He didn't care for her in the way she desired. Maybe he didn't care for her at all.

She let go of the anger at being forced to leave. The choice hadn't been hers, and she resented it. But now, she accepted what she knew deep inside.

An uncontrollable shivering began in her stomach and took over her whole body. She climbed into bed, pulled the covers over her head, and curled into a ball. The pain and loneliness of separation from her family shook her. What if she never had a chance to make amends? Lonely and hurting, she cried out to God.

His peace came through her tears, and the truth of his goodness soothed her soul.

The next morning, Aunt Nora asked, "Are you all right, Beth?"

A lump formed in her throat. "Yes, ma'am."

"I'm sending a letter to your mother. Would you like to enclose a note?"

"Yes, thank you," Beth said. "After breakfast?"

"Yes, dear." Aunt Nora gestured to the table. "Sit down. I have our mush cooked already."

Later Beth wrote, asking her mother and father for forgiveness. Though her family did not talk much about love, she told them she loved them. Peace flowed over her as she signed her name.

Aunt Nora added the note to her envelope, and they walked to the store together.

Beth reveled in the bright sunshine. The summer colors filled her with joy. If it didn't cause stares, she would have thrown her hands up and danced.

"I'm proud of you, Beth," Nora said.

"Why?"

She waved to a woman working in her garden as they passed. "You made a very grown-up choice."

"Beautiful flowers," Beth called to the woman then turned back to her aunt. "How do you know what choice I've made?"

"My dear, it's evident on your face. If you'd chosen to remain hard, it would show. Today, you are radiant. That's the kind of glow only God and his forgiveness can give."

Beth grinned. "I can't believe how much difference a simple decision can make."

Aunt Nora patted her arm. "As time goes on, I believe you'll realize it wasn't a simple decision at all. You were at a crossroads."

CHAPTER SIXTEEN

Beth woke early after recurrent nightmares left her shaky and afraid. In one, she'd been trapped in a small bed. She'd cried, but no one came. An even worse dream had followed—the one in which she ran down the road to a house, but when she reached the top of a hill, the way grew longer. As she ran, the house at the end grew close, then another hill in the road would snatch it away.

Yawning, she grabbed her Bible and went out onto the porch. A little later, Aunt Nora brought out their breakfast.

"What has you up early today?" She set the bowl of hot oatmeal close to Beth's chair.

"Nightmares." Beth's depressed tone brought Aunt Nora to sit down next to her.

"We need to throw those back out of your head." She clutched Beth's hands. "Just like Satan to attack you right after you made a godly decision yesterday." She bowed her head and immediately went into prayer.

Beth closed her eyes, hearing the words, silently adding her petitions to God, and thanking him.

When Aunt Nora finished, she moved to a nearby chair and took up her bowl. "Now that we've taken care of that, I want to talk about our plan for the day." She paused, then clasped her hands and closed her eyes briefly.

Beth watched, puzzled by her behavior.

Aunt Nora went on as if she'd never stopped. "But first, let me invite you to tell me when you are under such an attack. I would like the opportunity to pray with you. Would that be all right?"

"Yes, ma'am. I would appreciate it very much." She shuddered as the last vestiges of terror left her. It would be an amazing relief to get rid of the nightmares.

Aunt Nora smiled, the wrinkles in her face seemed to melt away. "Thank you, Beth. Now onto my question. I asked Stuart to come by next time he goes to see Fanny. I'm thinking of doing some baking after we have our time in the Word. What do you think of that?"

"What does Fanny need?"

"Nora!" a man yelled, cutting off her response. "Mrs. Durand?"

Beth and her aunt turned to see a man riding down the street toward the house.

"Yes?" Nora called out to him. "What is it?"

"My wife ..." He stopped and slid from the animal. "Her time has come, and they can't find Dr. Charlie. Maria's there, but they want you too."

Nora sprang to her feet. "Of course. I'll be ready in a minute." She motioned for Beth to follow her inside. "Now, Beth, can you do chores this morning, and if I'm late, tonight too?"

"Yes, ma'am."

Nora nodded, gathering her things. "Skip the baking and visit Sophie if you like." With a shawl around her shoulders and a parcel tucked under her arm, she hurried out to the porch.

"Ready, ma'am?"

"Yes, Mr. Ornsby," Nora said. She handed him her bundle. "I'll walk."

Mr. Ornsby? Beth resisted the urge to stop him. That was the family name where Leah worked.

Aunt Nora headed down the street. Beth turned away to do chores. When she finished, she paced, hating the uncertainty. She decided to have an early lunch and run her errands. A visit to Sally at the store might help, and then a trip to see Sophie. She ate quickly and packed a basket.

At the store, Sally leaned over and whispered to Beth, "We heard about Mrs. Ornsby. The neighbor ladies are attending her—along with Dr. Charlie's mother. They want your aunt there too."

"She hasn't been called to a birth while I've been here."

Sally cupped her hand on one side of her mouth. "Mrs. Durand has tended many hereabouts. We have a doctor in town now, but she has more knowledge than most."

"I didn't know."

"Oh, yes, the town relies on her."

"I'd better get going," Beth said. "I'm planning to see Sophie."

"Would you take this to Sophie?" Sally held a package in her hand. "It's yarn she wanted, and I know she keeps herself busy knitting."

Beth hurried toward Sophie's house, intent on completing her errand and getting back home. She caught sight of a man stepping from the alley down the street and stumbled in her effort to keep him in view. Though the rough, country clothing, low hat, and bandana wasn't his usual attire, the man looked like John. But something wasn't right. He cast furtive looks from side to side under the low brim of his hat, then ducked behind a store. What was he doing here in this small town?

When she reached the spot where he'd disappeared, she peered around the corner. A man's back was visible for a moment before moving behind another building. Was he trying to lure her into following him?

She looked around the streets and alley. A carpenter working nearby raised a brow and tipped his hat to her. Pulling her basket securely to herself, she hurried on to visit Sophie.

"Oh, you dear girl." Sophie pulled her into the house. "How nice of you to visit. Come in, come in and sit."

"Ma'am, did I disturb you? Were you going out? I brought you—"

"It's lovely of you to visit me." Sophie clutched her arm.

Beth almost laughed. Apparently, Sophie needed a visit today. "I have something for you."

"Put them on the table then and come and sit. Tea will be ready in a minute."

Beth laid the food on the table, then held out the yarn. "Sally sent this for you."

Sophie reached for the package and undid the string. After pulling off the heavy paper she caressed the skein against her face. "I remember this from my childhood. The green-blue of the sea—when it's rolling and the sun shining." Sophie grew silent as she stared at the yarn, but then abruptly turned to Beth and grasped her arm. "This is not the color of the sea in a storm."

Beth flinched at her intensity. "No, ma'am."

"That is a color one never forgets—the blue is overshadowed by gray and black." She stroked the yarn against her cheek. "It draws you with its power, but I never wanted to be anywhere but on solid land. My father—oh, I adored him. My father loved the sea."

The kettle on the stove whistled and Beth rose, but just then Sophie heard and rushed to the boiling pot.

"Our tea is ready." Sophie returned with hot tea and a plate of shortbread cakes. "Here now. I wasn't sure why I made these, but now I know. I was to have a visitor today."

Beth took a small bite of the crisp wedge-shaped cookie, its buttery sweetness filling her mouth.

Sophie took the skein of yarn, and again stroked it against her face. She turned to Beth. "Have you seen the sea then, dear?"

"No, ma'am."

"Ahh ... well, it's been a long time for me too, but one never forgets the sea and its colors and moods." She closed her eyes and drew a slow deep breath as if she could smell it right at this moment.

Beth sipped her tea and waited. Sophie's history was unknown to her, but she used certain words often, like ayuh, to answer in the affirmative.

"My mother didn't though," Sophie said. "Love the sea, I mean. My mother hated the sea, and she hated everyday Father went out. The neighbors used to say to her, 'Myra'—mother's name was Myra—they'd say, 'Myra, you better learn to love the sea like he does, or it will kill you.'"

Sophie sipped her tea and peered off in the distance. "The sea will kill you they said," she repeated.

Beth pursed her lips, wondering if Sophie had more story to come. "Yes, ma'am."

Sophie fingered the yarn and looked out the window. "In the end, it did. Kill her, I mean. She just couldn't or wouldn't let it be."

Beth gulped her tea, her mouth suddenly dry.

"I was the oldest. The others didn't know what happened, but one day she just walked right into it."

"What?" Beth couldn't stop the outburst, but Sophie didn't notice.

"Father was late. There had been a storm out to sea. We watched it from shore. The wall of cloud was gray and black and fearsome looking." Sophie shivered, gathered the ends of her shawl, and crisscrossed them over her heart. "The boats drifted in day by day, but not Father. Stories were that some ships had capsized, and some of the seamen were lost."

"I'm sorry, ma'am."

"Mother said she couldn't take it." Sophie plucked at the dangling fringes of her shawl. "Old Mr. Earl that lived near the wharf saw what happened but couldn't get to her. He said she walked into the sea."

Beth slapped her hand over her mouth. She didn't want Sophie to stop her story now, but she couldn't mean her mother had died.

Sophie continued, still caught in her memory. "Father did come home—the very next day. I remember the sound of his cry when they told him. It was not a human sound. The hurt and pain, oh, the anguish in that cry. I cannot forget it." Tears rolled down wrinkled cheeks and shimmered in the woman's almost blind blue eyes. "He kept saying, 'Why couldn't she wait for me. Why couldn't she believe in me?'" She turned to Beth, appealing to her.

"I'm sorry," Beth whispered, fearing to say more and end the story.

"Father went back to fishing after a time. It was all he knew how to do, he said. I took over the family as best I could." Sophie rewrapped her shawl, bringing the ends in front and tying them. "The neighbor women helped for a time, but we weren't their ... responsibility. Father changed, and I felt bad I couldn't do better."

The old woman gazed straight ahead at nothing. Perhaps she saw some distant picture of this day in her mind. "Finally, Father saw how things were and hired a spinster that lived down the coast. She was nice. My brothers took advantage of her, not knowing children and all, but she did right by us. When my father married her, I left."

Beth waited, but when Sophie stayed quiet, she asked, "What happened?"

"Oh, Beth, I forgot you were here." The blue eyes pierced her, and at that moment Beth doubted they were dim at all. "I wanted to be far away from the sea. I didn't want my mother's life. Oh, boys wanted to court me, but I became frightened I would be like Mother. I answered an ad in the paper. 'Someone needing a woman to help' it said."

Beth nibbled on the shortbread and sipped her tea.

"I helped Mr. Monroe, and then he married the schoolteacher. I like children, so I was hired to help another family. Eventually I worked for Mrs. Dudly. They had two sets of twins and four other children. They had a house full. In a few years, I married their hired hand, and we both stayed on for a bit, then Richard and I moved onto our own place."

"Where was that, ma'am?"

"That was in Ohio. The cusp of the new frontier they said." Sophie smiled, her hands relaxed and resting in her lap. "Times were often difficult, but we were happy."

"Yes, ma'am."

"We raised our young'uns, and we lived a full life, he and I."

Beth said, "Where do your children live now?"

Sophie seemed not to hear or chose not to respond. "Well now, Beth, I've kept you long enough. Better get back to Nora, and I'll get on with my work."

Beth stood. "Goodbye, ma'am."

"Goodbye, dear." She walked Beth to the door. "Thank you for coming and thank Nora too."

"Yes, ma'am, I will, and thank you for the cookie."

"My yes! I was thinking of my mother. She used to make them. They were one of her favorites."

"They taste good." Beth stepped to the door.

"Today is the day."

Beth turned back to Sophie. "What day, ma'am?"

"Today is my birthday."

"Oh, well, happy birthday, ma'am."

"I don't celebrate it. It was always so painful, but for some reason ... for some reason I wanted to make my shortbread today."

"I've never made shortbread, but I like it. Maybe Aunt Nora has a recipe."

"Today was the day."

"The day, ma'am?" Beth frowned, wondering why Sophie kept saying this phrase. Was this painful memory causing Sophie to have trouble with her mind? She'd heard of such problems with older folks.

"The day mother walked into the sea." She spoke softly like a small child. "Why does it seem just like yesterday?"

Sophie wandered back to her chair like a sleepwalker and sat down, leaving Beth at the door. "I made shortcakes, Mama."

Beth hesitated at the door, unsure of what to do.

"Mama, come sit and have one. Father will be back. You wait and see. Please, Mama." She begged like a child desperately trying to change the inevitable.

Beth could do no more. With tears pouring down her cheeks, she left and softly closed the door. Beth walked toward home, surprised to see a piece of shortcake still clutched in her hand.

A horse whinnied down the street, and Beth wiped her tears, shaking off the melancholy of Sophie's story. She popped the last of the sweet into her mouth and checked her surroundings. She needed to pay attention on the way home, the incident from earlier back on her mind. Her skin prickled, and she shivered as she passed the alley where the figure appeared last time. In her imagination, someone followed her. She was almost running and out of breath when she reached home. Slamming both doors shut, she locked them. Then looked under the beds and searched the house.

Beth checked out the loft windows, going to the front and then to the window in back. Her apron twisted in her hands, she chewed on her thumbnail and tried to reason what to do. John had appeared under her window at the hotel and now in the town where she lived. What was he up to?

Finally, her aunt strolled down the lane.

Beth rushed downstairs to open the doors. "What happened?"

"I'm happy to say, we had a good outcome," Nora said. "Mother and baby are doing fine."

"Yes?"

"Maude Ornsby is exhausted, but if she has the grit in her I think she does, she'll come through fine. It's good she has help."

Beth took her aunt's bundle. "How is Leah?"

"Let me sit, dear." Aunt Nora sank in her chair. She leaned back and closed her eyes.

Beth fetched them both a cold drink. "Did you eat?"

"Oh, my, yes. Your friend has learned to cook splendidly, and she loves to bake. She has mastered the cookstove too."

"I'm happy for her." Beth fidgeted with her fingers. "Is the baby all right?"

"He came folded in half with his little bottom presenting first," Aunt Nora said. "Maude did well, but the baby was tired and not ready to nurse. Sometimes, we can be hasty. I'll go back tomorrow to make sure he's still progressing."

"I see," Beth said, but she didn't see at all. She had no idea what a normal delivery looked like.

"Chores went all right?"

Beth hadn't realized it was so late. She'd gotten so caught up in watching she didn't realize. "I'm just heading out."

"Do you mind doing them while I rest?"

"Not a bit. Can I get you anything before I go out?"

"No, dear, I'll just rest."

Beth practically ran through chores, all the while feeling as if eyes watched her. She peered off into the trees that surrounded the farm. In her haste, she missed setting the chicken coop door and it popped open when she walked away. Her hands pressed against her head, she chastised herself.

"No ... I must get a hold of myself."

She latched the chicken coop and then retraced her steps, checking the latches for the pigs, sheep, and cow.

Taking the pail of milk into the house, she returned to put the strained milk in the cold house. Only then did she notice footprints not hers in the garden path.

CHAPTER SEVENTEEN

The next morning, Aunt Nora asked, "Beth, would you be able to do chores? I want to rest before I see Mrs. Ornsby again."

"Yes, ma'am."

When Beth stepped outside, Stuart was bent over patching the fence. Her shoulders relaxed, and she sighed, grateful to have someone around. She took extra time, hopefully making up for the hasty job of last evening. She was headed to the cold house with the basket of eggs when Stuart stopped her.

"Is Nora all right?" he asked.

"Just tired." Beth brushed hair out of her eyes. "It was a long day for her yesterday."

"What about you?"

Beth had tossed and turned all night, playing the scene from yesterday over in her mind. She must look a fright. "I'm fine." She turned away.

Stuart called at the back door. "Aunt Nora, I have to pick up a few things in town. Do you need anything?"

"No," Aunt Nora called back, "but I'll walk part way with you. I want to check on Maude yet this morning."

Beth closed the cold house door and almost groaned aloud. Why were they conspiring to leave her alone? Surely Stuart could find more fences to fix. She folded her hands in her apron and entered the house. There was nothing to do about it, so she kept busy, cleaning but checking the view from the loft windows often. She decided to bake. She wasn't Leah, but she could at least bake bread.

Beating the dough gave her great satisfaction, and she put her whole effort into the task. While the dough rested, she made another trip to the loft. No one passed in the street. Back down in the kitchen, she did the kneading—press-pushing and lifting—turning over and over, until she had a soft, elastic dough. Later, while she cleaned up the work area, Aunt Nora's distinctive footsteps creaked on the porch.

"Can I fix you something to eat, Aunt?" Beth asked as soon as she came in the room.

"My gracious, no." Nora took off her shawl and set her basket away. "Leah made us a big breakfast this morning."

Aunt Nora put her feet up while Beth brought her a drink and sat down, waiting to talk with her.

"My, you've been busy today," Aunt Nora said.

"Yes, ma'am," Beth said. "How is Leah?"

"The only thing I would say is that the girl is in desperate need of some suitable dresses."

"Her stepmother didn't allow her to have much." Beth picked up her embroidery, then set it back down, unable to sit still. "Do you know if Mrs. Ornsby can sew?"

Aunt Nora laid her head back and closed her eyes. "I'm not sure. Why are you wondering?"

"Would we be able to get the yard goods? I can pay for them. Maybe someone can sew them for her."

"I don't know. Leah hasn't learned?"

"I don't believe so."

"What's this world coming to?" Nora said. "Girls not learning to sew or cook or keep house? What do they plan to do when they have a home and family of their own to care for?"

Beth ducked her head. She was one of those girls.

"I guess you'll learn," Nora said. "I do believe Mrs. Ornsby can sew, but I don't know if she would do that for a hired girl. Maybe I can find out."

Beth headed back to the worktable, shaped her dough into loaves and let her aunt rest. She finished cleaning while the bread rose—moving barrels around and sweeping and scrubbing the floor before she put them back. When the bread was ready to bake, she built up the fire and put the loaves in the oven. The fresh bread would be a perfect complement to their vegetable soup.

Aunt Nora nodded to her. "Beth, you're a good worker."

"Thank you."

"Is there something wrong?" Nora asked.

Yes. Her imagination took facts and turned them into nightmares. She massaged her temples with her fingertips. "Just tired." That part was honest. She'd run up and downstairs for two days, checking windows and doors.

That night, after Beth washed and put on her gown, she knelt by the bed. "Lord, help me to know what to do," she prayed. "Am I seeing things? What's happening?"

She climbed into bed, curled on her side, then brought the sleeve of her gown to her face and drew in a big breath. It no longer smelled like home.

Beth sat on the porch the next afternoon, watching and waiting for Nora to come back from the Ornsbys. When she saw her aunt coming, she hurried to meet her.

"Do you want tea? I have water hot."

"My goodness, dear. Yes, I'll sit and have a cup."

Beth brought the cups to the porch and set one down next to Nora. "How was everything today?"

Aunt Nora said, "I talked to Maude. She says Leah needs clothes. She'll make the girl a dress or two while she's taking it easy, and she'll teach Leah how to sew."

"Really? I think that will make Leah happy."

"I should hope so. Maude has the goods and will make them as part of Leah's pay for the summer." Aunt Nora sipped her tea. "We talked about what she had in mind, and I think she'll do nicely for the girl."

"Maybe that's why I haven't seen Leah this summer," Beth said. "She didn't have suitable clothes."

"Could be. Although I can see that she's been busy as well." She blew her nose and tucked her handkerchief in her pocket. "Though Maude is concerned about a man that has come to call."

"Mr. Graystone?" Beth felt sorry for Leah if Mr. Graystone had called.

"No, Maude says this is a young man from her hometown." Aunt Nora leaned back in her chair and closed her eyes.

Beth's blood chilled and she licked her lips. "What does he look like?"

"I heard no description." Aunt Nora sat up and studied her face. "What's going on?"

Beth shrugged but wondered what boy would be here in this town except John?

"Did Leah have a beau?" Aunt Nora leaned forward and put her hand on Beth's knee.

"Not that I know of."

Aunt Nora's forehead wrinkled as she peered at Beth. "Other than the boy, Maude says Leah is a great help. She's hoping to convince Leah to stay on past the summer and continue to work for them. It seems the whole family is quite fond of her." Nora reached over the arm of her chair and picked up her knitting. "I hope this boy doesn't mess things up for her. She would have a family."

It seemed Leah had found a home where people cared for her, and she would not have to go back to her stepmother. Beth felt no jealousy, only worry that John would use Leah's infatuation for his benefit. The reality of such understanding stunned her. Had John been using her?

"That's it, Beth." Nora dropped her knitting in her lap. "Tell me what's on your mind."

"I thought I saw John," she blurted out. She could not hold back.

"When? Today?"

"The other day when I walked to see Sophie. A man came out of an alley right in front of me. He turned so I couldn't see his face and he wore work clothing, including boots and a low hat. I've never seen John dressed like that, but from the side and back ... I'm sure it was him."

"Are you worried about what he might do?"

Beth chewed on a fingernail. "It doesn't make sense, and now I wonder if he's the man who has come to call on Leah."

Nora stared at her.

"Aunt, I felt like he was trying to draw me off the street and into the backstreet."

"Would he hurt you?"

Beth stared at her aunt, the answer shocking her. "I don't know."

"I think we should go, Beth," Nora said on Sunday morning. "The circuit preacher won't be there, but everyone will get together to sing and read Scriptures. There will be people around us the whole time, and I like to get out."

Beth thought of how busy Aunt Nora had been all week but let her excuse pass. "Fine, we'll go."

By the time they left church, the weather had changed. The air held so much moisture it almost dripped off Beth's face. Sally's father offered them a ride home.

"Not sure when, Nora, but I feel a storm brewing," he said as he dropped them off. "Might be a good idea to get chores done right away and pick up anything that will blow. Likely there will be wind with it."

As the afternoon wore on, Beth and Aunt Nora sat wherever they could find relief from the stifling heat. On the porch part of the time, under the trees in back when there was a breeze. When Beth went to pick ripe vegetables and complete chores, a boy waited for her.

She stopped, not wanting to scare him. "You must be Timothy. Does your mother know you're here?"

He dug in the dirt with his bare toes.

Beth moved into the barn and went about her chores, talking to him as if he answered. "Time for me to milk the cow." She picked up the stool and milk pail. "This is Daisy. Daisy, I would like you to meet Timothy. He came over to visit today."

He ducked his head, but Beth saw the corner of a smile at her humor.

She milked and talked, telling him about her garden, the church service, and the quilt Aunt Nora was making. When she finished, she turned the cow back into the pasture, and took the pail of milk to the house. "Aunt Nora, Timothy has come for a visit but doesn't talk." She glanced out the window to make sure he was still waiting for her. "Is that normal or is he afraid of me?"

"I'll come out. With a storm brewing he should be at home."

Beth returned outside. "Well, Timothy, the milk is strained." She headed to the chicken enclosure. "The chickens are hot today. Hope they laid some eggs for us."

Timothy followed and leaned up against the chicken fence. His dark eyes watched her every move.

Aunt Nora came from the house with a slice of bread smeared with jam and came to stand beside the chicken pen. "Hello, Timothy. I have an extra slice of bread I can't eat. Do you know anyone who can help me?"

"Maybe I could."

"You, Timothy?" Aunt Nora handed him the slice. "Thank you for helping me out."

The boy finished the treat by the time Beth finished gathering eggs and came to the door.

Aunt Nora said, "Now, Timothy, you know Beth, right?"

He nodded.

"Hello, Timothy." Beth squatted down to be on his level.

He tucked his chin close to his chest but kept her in sight.

She lifted his hand. "Thank you for watching out for me."

He curled his lips together.

"Timothy, I think it's time for you to go home. Your aunt will be worried about you with a storm coming." Aunt Nora brushed her hands together.

Timothy turned, his head down, and walked away.

"Bye, Timothy. Thank you for visiting me," Beth called to him. He made no indication that he heard her. They watched him go through the pasture and out of sight at the crick. "Is he going to be fine?"

Aunt Nora shrugged. "He manages to cope. He has been through a lot and is shy of new people."

Beth wondered if he would ever talk to her.

"Let's have our supper now. Will you walk through the garden and make sure you have everything picked that needed it?" She reached for the basket of eggs.

"Sure, I'll be right in."

They ate a light supper of hard-boiled eggs and vegetables from the garden. The wind picked up, and the rumble of thunder in the distance signaled the coming storm.

"How about we pray for safety through this weather?" Nora put the rest of the dishes away. "That we get the needed rain but no damage?"

"Yes, please. I'd like that."

They bent their heads in prayer, thanking God for the rain and his protection over them. Aunt Nora prayed the blood of protection over area homes, buildings, and crops. Beth had never heard anyone pray such a thing, but when Aunt Nora also prayed the Scripture—whatever you ask in my name I will do it—she understood.

"In Jesus's name, amen."

Beth opened her eyes and lifted her head as lightning flashed.

"I believe the power of a storm is a little like the power God used to create the world." Nora opened her Bible.

Beth paced from the windows overlooking the street to the windows in back. "It's amazing. I can feel the power, all beautiful and exciting, as long as a person is safe inside."

"Remember, God's power raised Jesus from the dead," Aunt Nora said.

Beth mused on that truth as she watched the storm. The wind bent the two cottonwood trees almost to the ground. Twigs, branches, and leaves blew across the fields and down the street. Thunder shook the house, and rain and debris pelted the windows. Aunt Nora burned a small candle on the table and recited the ninety-first Psalm. Beth thought of home—her mother didn't like storms.

When Beth retired for the night, Stuart was on her mind. She prayed his farm was safe, and she wondered when she would see him again. She shivered and fell asleep with the sound of a gentle rain tapping on the thin roof.

CHAPTER EIGHTEEN

The next morning, Beth woke with a start at the sound of a man's voice.

"Morning, Stuart," she heard her aunt say, "What do you have on your mind today?"

"Checking storm damage. Saw a few downed trees on my way here, but mostly just a nice bit of rain."

"I'm having breakfast. Would you like some?"

Beth rushed from the bed and scrambled to put on her dress.

"Sounds good. Beth doing chores? I didn't see her."

It felt odd to hear him ask about her, but her heart skipped a beat just the same.

"Noisy last night, and she's still sleeping. I thought I'd let her be."

Beth rushed from her room. "Oh, Stuart!" She slowed her step and walked to the table in a more sedate pace, but her face flushed. "Aunt, I'm sorry to be late."

"That's fine, dear," Nora said. "Would you like some breakfast?"

Beth tucked loose strands of hair behind her ear and patted it in place. She turned to Stuart. "You're here early."

"Checking on storm damage," he said.

She met his look and a jolt like lightning jarred her. She turned away from him and stepped to the stove where her aunt was frying eggs. "Aunt, I can fix breakfast."

"I have it ready, dear. Sit down."

She sat at the table, directly across from him.

"Everything all right in the barn?" Beth asked.

He nodded. "Looks okay as far as I noticed. Will check the fences before I leave. A cow or sheep would find a weak spot, for sure."

"I see."

Aunt Nora placed a heaping plate of eggs, pancakes, and spinach in front of him. "Here you go, Stuart. Beth, what would you like?"

She looked at his plate and laughed. "Half that, Aunt. I wouldn't be able to move if I ate all that."

He attended to eating his breakfast.

When Aunt Nora set a plate in front of Beth, she closed her eyes and said a quick silent prayer.

He finished his meal and rose. "Thank you, Aunt Nora. That was the best meal I've had since the last time you fed me."

"I reckon it was, Stuart. Come by anytime, though breakfast is the biggest meal we eat around here." Aunt Nora sat down at the table with her own plate of eggs.

"Thanks again. I'll head out and check the fences." He glanced at Beth.

"I'll be out in a minute to do chores and help check fences."

He put his hat on as he walked out the door. She heard him whistle as he walked away.

Beth shoveled in her food and then put herself together for the day. When she walked to the barn, he was bracing a corner post.

"Everything look good?"

He straightened. "Should be soon. I'm working on this loose post."

"Good. I'll just get to chores." She moved through the usual routine, thinking about Stuart and the easy way he worked. He gave attention to detail yet wasn't impatient if he was interrupted. She sat down at the milking stool, the pail at her feet. "Easy, Daisy." She patted the cow's flank to settle her down.

Her mind wandered to her father. She loved being with him at the mercantile. He was easy to work next to, leaving the tasks she was good at to her and sharing the ones she didn't care for.

She turned Daisy into the pasture and emerged from the barn, carrying the milk pail. When she reached Stuart's position by the fence, he leaped over it, using one arm as a prop, and landed close beside her.

She jerked back.

"I'm sorry. I didn't mean to startle you." He peered at her from the corner of his eyes.

"You didn't. I'm fine."

He turned and their eyes met. She shuttered her eyes from him. "Are you happy here, Beth?"

Her eyes widened and she looked away from his intense scrutiny. "What a question. I'll be going back home soon."

"I was thinking ... some people have trouble trying to figure out what makes them happy." He leaned on the fence. "My uncles keep searching. They're off now, going further west to find their fortunes or the perfect piece of land." He glanced at her then went back to leaning on the fence. "Your parents, now, are they content with their store?"

"Yes. Papa is organized and knows what farmers need."

"Maybe it's good for people to try different things," Stuart said. "I like farming and will farm all my life, but I want a wife and children too."

She raised her eyebrows but didn't reply.

"I suppose women don't have a problem trying to figure out what they want."

"What makes you think that? I know girls who don't want the lives their mothers have."

He faced her. "What do they want?"

"Some might want to run a store or business. Some girls think their mother's lives are boring. They dream of a different life."

"I understand that." He removed his hat. "What does your beau do?"

Beth pressed her lips together and turned her back on him.

Stuart went on. "I meant that you and he must be talking about your dreams for the future."

"No." She began to walk toward the house.

He settled in step beside her. "No, he doesn't work, or no, he isn't your beau?"

Beth whirled to face him, and their gazes locked. She searched his eyes, her brows pulled together. "Just no."

He opened the door and touched her back as she went into the house. "All done. See you later, Aunt Nora," he called.

Nora came to the door. "Thank you for all your help. Goodbye, Stuart."

"Bye, ma'am. And you, too, miss!" he called.

"Bye." Beth watched him disappear down the street. "Aunt Nora, how are you acquainted with Mother? I don't remember her mentioning you, but you know all about us."

Nora resumed her seat and turned her attention to her reading.

"I suppose there were letters," Beth said, sitting on the footstool. "Mother handled the mail, so I never paid attention to it. Did she write back and forth to you often?"

"Yes, we had a good correspondence. She knew the children, too, of course."

"I didn't know that."

Aunt Nora looked up. "Chores all done?"

"Yes. I put the milk away." Toes rubbed against Beth's legs, so she picked her up. "Stuart was asking me about what people do for a living where I'm from. My mother must have a life similar to her mom, but my father is living quite different, I guess. They don't talk about dreams and the like." She rubbed her face against the cat's fur.

"How do you know?"

"Well, I've never heard them." The cat purred as she stroked its soft fur. "I suppose they are old now."

"Hopes and dreams are important, no matter a person's age."

Beth stilled her petting. Tipping her head, she considered Nora's comment. Would her parents have dreams that didn't include her?

Aunt Nora put a marker in her book, then closed it. "It's hard, sometimes, to keep a bright hope for the future when situations happen that are difficult and painful. I believe God never stops talking to us about dreams."

Beth scratched the cat's ears. "Stuart thinks women don't have trouble deciding what they want to do."

"Do you agree?" Nora asked.

The cat struggled, so Beth set her down. "No, I don't. How can he think we all want to be the same? Men don't."

"Maybe Stuart meant something else." Nora opened her book again. "You might have to ask him."

The thought of asking Stuart filled her with anticipation. He would look at her with those eyes that made it hard for her to think.

Aunt Nora made her think too. Beth supposed a person could be learning and not even be aware of it.

"You're always teaching, Aunt. Did you know that?" In the time she'd spent with Nora, she'd learned about herbs, God, herself, and more.

"Yes, I've been told that." Nora leaned her head back on her chair and rocked.

"Is that something you try to do?"

"Oh, dear me, no. It's become a part of me. Not everyone appreciates it, but it's the way God has shaped me as I've gotten older."

Beth wound a loose tendril of hair around her finger. "God has shaped you?"

"Yes."

Could God be shaping her? Did she have dreams? Yes. Hidden desires she wouldn't talk about, especially to Stuart. She jumped to her feet, unable to be still a moment longer.

"Do you suppose I could help Sophie with her garden?"

"I'm sure she would be happy for the company."

Vigorous work at Sophie's was just the thing to get her mind off Stuart. She hesitated. Would it be safe to walk across town, so near the place where she'd seen John? It was silly to worry. She and John had been close, after all—friends. She had nothing to fear from him.

After putting on an old dress, Beth set out, but checked the alley where she had seen him, relieved to find it empty.

Sophie answered the door at her first knock. "Oh, Beth, come in, come in. I prayed you would stop by."

Beth laughed. "Do you have something special you'd like done today?"

"The kitchen, dear. I can't see, but something got spilled. I feel it sticking."

Beth pulled her apron from the basket she brought. "I understand. Here are a few things Aunt Nora sent."

Beth got busy, moved a table, and scrubbed Sophie's floor. Then, she went on to clean the entry and pull some weeds in the garden.

"Sophie, I'm heading back home," she called a few hours later from the doorway. "Did you empty the basket?"

"Here it is." Sophie handed her Aunt Nora's basket. "Thank you."

"You're welcome. Now I need to weed our garden." Beth rubbed dirt off her hands.

"Thank you, my dear. My kitchen floor is clean again."

"You're welcome. Bye, ma'am." Beth headed for home, fatigued, but at least Stuart hadn't been on her mind. Well, not much.

She walked across town, breathing deep of the rain-washed air, happier than she dreamed this visit with Aunt Nora could be. She stepped up on the porch.

"You missed Timothy, and he talked a blue streak," Aunt Nora said. "I think he's in awe of you."

"I see him peeking at me from time to time." Beth drank a dipper of water.

"I told him he could come again when you're here." Aunt Nora returned to her sewing. "So be prepared for him to appear out of the blue."

After the evening meal, Beth took her favorite spot in the swing then held up the woven blanket lying there. "Aunt Nora, is this new? Did you get this from someone around here?"

"I brought it out today. I should use it." Nora closed the book in her lap and set it aside. "Dixie made it."

"Dixie?" Beth studied the pattern. It had a beige and brown stripe warp with multicolored weft. "It's beautiful."

"Yes, you remember her from church? She sits by Sophie and helps her."

"Oh, yes, the lady with ..." Beth waved a hand in front of her mouth.

"Yes," Nora said. "Dixie is just about toothless. She supports herself by weaving. She wove the rugs in my house from rags I sewed together. The throw you have there, she also made. She often uses wool from my sheep too—colored with natural dyes. Walnut hulls made that brown color."

"This is gorgeous and so soft." Beth brought the piece to her cheek and caressed the silky fiber.

"She makes lovely tapestries too." Nora pulled a stool over and put up her feet. "I use them in winter to cover the door, but blankets and rugs are the items she sells most."

"I'd like to see them."

"We should visit her. She has several looms and enjoys showing her work. It's stimulating for my creative juices to see what she's working on."

"She isn't a relative?" Beth did want to visit Dixie and her looms, but she wanted to find out more about her family.

"No, she's a friend." Aunt Nora stared at Beth. "What else do you have on your mind?"

Beth twisted her hands. "How are you related to my mother? You don't look like each other."

"Your mother took after her father, and I look more like my mother."

"What? Grandma was married twice?"

"Yes, didn't your mother tell you?"

"No." Beth pulled out the hairpins holding her bun. "You're sisters, though?"

"Yes and no."

"What do you mean?" It seemed to be taking so long to learn about her family and trying to get answers from Nora was like playing hide and seek with a ghost.

Nora stared off into the waning evening. "We are sisters only by marriage and weren't raised together. I was grown and married before my mother married again. Merin's father was a widower."

"You mean you had different fathers and mothers?" Beth did not know her mother's people, though she knew all about her father's family. The absence of information from her mother puzzled her.

Aunt Nora nodded and snuggled her shawl tighter around herself. "My mother and her father didn't marry until we were older."

Beth continued piling hairpins in her lap. "You have brothers and sisters?"

"I have several of each. Some have passed on, but most still live in Missouri."

"Do you have family here?" Locks of hair began to fall around Beth's shoulders, and she finger-combed it away from her scalp.

Aunt Nora picked up her basket of mending. "One of my sisters was Fanny's mother."

"What? Fanny is your niece? You never told me that. They don't call you aunt."

"Yes, they do," Nora said.

"Well, everyone does. I didn't know they were related. I mean ... it's so peculiar."

Aunt Nora picked up her mending and rolled a wooden ball to the heel of a sock.

"There's family right here," Beth whispered. "I must be related to them somehow. I never had relatives close by." She gathered her pile of pins together on her lap. "Mother must have been an only child?"

"No, she had several siblings. A brother killed in the war, some brothers and sisters in Wisconsin."

"Oh, yes, that's right. I do remember aunts in Wisconsin." Nora nodded.

Beth threaded her fingers in her hair and drew it out in long strokes. "Mother didn't talk about them much. I wonder why?"

"Merin had difficulty at family gatherings. Her nerves were on edge. I found I couldn't live near her, so we moved here."

Beth knew her mother struggled with large gatherings and avoided people, even at the mercantile. "I don't remember you living close to us." Her childhood seemed a vague, shadowy recollection.

"It was some time ago, but we did." Nora threaded a darning needle with yarn the same color as the sock she prepared to mend.

Beth struggled to sort out the timeline. "Was this before we moved to Minnesota?"

"That's right. Our family lived near you in Missouri."

Beth braided her hair for the night, pulling it forward over her shoulder to finish the long tail. "Did we see you often?"

"No."

"Oh, maybe that's why I can't remember. Why didn't we? See you, I mean."

"That," Nora said with a sigh, "we'll have to talk about later, my dear."

"But—"

Nora's look of censure silenced Beth. She forced herself to sit calmly for a moment then took a deep breath, smoothed her skirt, and changed the question.

"Were you surprised when Mom asked if I could come?"

"Yes, Beth, but never think I don't like having you here." She put her work in her lap, reached forward, and took her hand. "The differences between your mother and me have nothing to do with you, and I love having the opportunity to know you."

Beth pressed her lips together, pushing away tears. She still didn't understand. "Your son, Evan? Why don't I hear about him?"

Nora picked up her work again. "That's a long story for another time."

"Does he live around here?" Beth couldn't help pushing for more information.

Aunt Nora bent over her work of weaving in the sock's heel. "No, he went west."

"I'm sorry." Beth brought her clenched hands to her mouth and chewed on a finger. "It must be hard to have him gone. Is he all right?"

"I sincerely believe so."

Beth went back to an earlier comment her aunt made. Perhaps it would be a safer subject. "Who moved from Missouri first?"

"William and I did. He had heard of good farmland to the north, and the children were old enough to be of help, so we packed up and left. That was before the war, of course, but I think he saw the writing on the wall, as they say."

Beth watched as several bats swooped and flew nearby. "Did you come to Minnesota right away?"

"No, we settled in Wisconsin."

"Oh, yes, that's right."

"That's when we met Stuart and his family. Your family came later." Aunt Nora turned her sock and wove crossways. "We came here right after the unrest started. Will thought it would be a good place, and, indeed, he was right."

"It's nice." Beth turned her head to listen to the forlorn call of a mourning dove.

"Yes," Aunt Nora said, bending over her mending. "This area was slow to settle, but it's making up for lost time."

The mourning dove called again, and a melancholy response came from nearby. Beth sighed. Why had her parents stayed in Missouri? They'd farmed, but her father didn't like it. When they moved to Minnesota, they ran the mercantile. Why had there been no more children? She'd never heard of her mother losing a baby like Leah's mother had.

"Now, I think I'll turn in." Aunt Nora set aside her work. "Goodnight, Beth."

"Goodnight, ma'am."

CHAPTER NINETEEN

Beth greeted Stuart at the door in answer to his knock. Her pulse picked up tempo. "Hello, Stuart. Come in."

"Beth." He removed his hat and followed her inside.

"Hello, Stuart, what's on your mind today?" Nora asked. "You look upset about something."

"Aunt Nora, I'm a sight worried about the situation out at Fanny's."

"How is she?" Nora asked.

"The children are running wild. Just the other day, when I took her the food you prepared, I found the boys playing in the wash water Fanny set out warming for their baths. I guess they'd played in the dirt and felt they needed to wash up. They kept adding dirt to the water." He shook his head. "It looked like they'd been wallowing with the pigs."

"How did Fanny take it?" Nora moved back to the table where she had her quilt project laid out.

Stuart followed and sat down on the bench. "I suspect she was napping with Mandy at the time. When I caught them, I refilled the tub with clean water and cleaned them up. The water was straight from the well and cold, but I figured they had it coming."

Nora's brow furrowed as she stopped sewing and looked at him. "Are those children getting enough supervision, what with Fanny not feeling well?"

"Martin asked me to stop in as much as I can during the week." Stuart shrugged. "As long as they don't take it in their heads to play in the pond …"

Aunt Nora sighed. "I might have a solution for her. Meantime, when you go again, stop by here first, and I'll send more meals."

"I can do that. I'm going out there anyway." He walked to the door. "I've got chores awaiting me."

"Thank you for coming by, Stuart," Nora said. "I appreciate knowing about Fanny."

"I knew you would want to know." He glanced at Beth, their eyes met and when he smiled, she grinned back like a little kid at Christmas. Good grief, had she no decorum at all?

"Martha is having a get-together this Saturday night for the young people in the area." He shifted his feet. "Would you like to go?"

"Oh, yes." Beth's immediate smile soon died. "I mean, I don't know how I'd get there."

"I'd be happy to pick you up." Stuart seemed nervous as he twisted his hat. "Sally will be there, and you'll get to know Martha."

Beth smiled. "Well, in that case …" Her chest tightened so she could hardly breathe. "Yes, I would like to go. Thank you."

"See you Saturday then."

The day of the party, Beth couldn't decide what to wear. "What do you think of this one?" She twirled for Aunt Nora.

"The other girls won't have anything fancy, and you might feel out of place if you dress beyond what girls here can afford."

"They must have at least one good dress."

"Some do, but this is just a get-together." Aunt Nora resumed her stirring of the cheese she was making. She wiped a bit of sweat from her brow with the back of her hand before saying, "You'll make candy or ice cream and play a few games. They won't wear their best. Don't trouble yourself about clothes."

"Oh." Beth chewed on her fingernail. Would the girls here actually play games? She couldn't imagine.

"We washed that blue dress with the yellow-and-white inset. I think it would survive a few games, and it's charming on you."

"I do like that dress though it is rather worn in places." Beth began to unbutton the dress she was wearing.

"No matter. It will look fine." Aunt Nora lifted a spoonful of curds to examine the cheese.

Stuart arrived a few hours later as promised. He loaded the food Beth and her aunt were contributing, then helped her into the wagon.

"You look nice, Beth," he said in an offhand tone, as if offering an emotionless courtesy.

She fingered a bow at her throat. "Thank you."

He flicked the reins and started the matched team of bays into motion.

Beth glanced at his shirt and string tie. He sat relaxed, with his arms on his knees. Her breath came in short bursts. She jerked her eyes away from those hands. "You have a beautiful team."

"My father trained them. They mean a lot to me."

"They look like they could be twins." She settled back in the seat willing her heart into a steady beat.

"Yes, we foaled one and bought the other from a farmer near us."

She felt him glance at her and resisted the urge to smooth the bodice of her dress. Did he like what he saw when he looked at her?

As they cleared the last house and barn at the edge of town, Beth grasped for something to say. Etiquette for young ladies suggested conversation about the weather, nothing personal. The whole uncertain evening set her on edge.

"Don't worry about tonight," Stuart said as if sensing her tension. "Everyone is friendly."

She straightened the sleeve of her dress. "I'm still nervous."

"You'll see Sally."

"I'm looking forward to that. I liked Sally right away." Beth pushed herself to relax.

"You'll like Martha too. Some days are hard for her with her fiancé gone." Stuart snapped the reins to hurry the lagging team along. "Tonight will be a good diversion."

"I've met Martha at church." She licked her dry lips, feeling like her responses seemed stupid and inane.

"You and John were close, I imagine," Stuart said.

"What?" Beth reared back to look him full in the face. "Why are you bringing him up?"

"He's your beau, isn't he?"

"No!" She glanced around to see if anyone had heard her outburst and then straightened her sash. "He's not my beau. We weren't close either."

Stuart cast another glance at her. "But I thought you'd been seeing him for some time."

"I don't think I really knew him." Beth hated to admit the truth that she had considered pledging herself to a man she didn't know.

"Sometimes, it doesn't take long to know a person," Stuart said, waving to a family in a passing wagon.

Beth smiled and nodded to the couple in the other wagon but inside a deep sadness pulled her spirits down.

"I've heard that, you know, in books, but I can't imagine it." She wanted to make Stuart understand. "Maybe I held back. He wanted to kiss me, and I refused." She gasped. What had come over her, rambling like Stuart was one of her girlfriends?

"Oh?" This time, he shifted in his seat to look at her full-on.

Beth cringed. How could she get out of this conversation? She wanted to be honest, as she wanted him to be honest with her.

"He said we would be married soon, so one little kiss wouldn't hurt."

"I didn't realize he'd proposed marriage." He snapped the reins, and the horses surged forward, forcing her to grab onto the seat.

"No, he hadn't." She looked around them, wondering why he'd set the horses almost to racing. The road seemed deserted.

"Did you want to kiss him?" Stuart asked, emphasizing the word *you*, like it was Beth's fault.

"No, of course not. Well, not much." Now he had her dander up.

His next words sounded hoarse. "Not much?"

"I was a little curious, I suppose." She'd never been kissed, and she was curious—no different than any other girl.

"I suppose." His jaw tightened, and a twitch moved his cheek muscles.

"The thought is completely disgusting," she said, "and I surely shouldn't be having such a conversation with you." She pulled her bonnet forward. "Mother and Aunt would be horrified." She clutched the seat again. "Can you slow down?"

She glanced at Stuart. He was scowling at the road, but he let the team slow.

"I wouldn't kiss a man I was not married to." She straightened her dress, hoping to regain her composure. "It would be improper."

"No doubt," he said.

The rest of the trip passed in silence. Beth had messed up her only time to talk to him. Some girls said their beau was an instant friend. She and Stuart were not friends today, but he wasn't her beau either.

They rounded a corner. "Here we are."

"Oh, already?"

They pulled to a stop, and he set the brake and jumped down. Then, he lifted her right off the seat with his hands at her waist. She gripped his muscled shoulders as he swung her around and set her on her feet, his face close.

Martha ran up to them. "Beth, I'm so glad you came. Let me introduce you to everyone."

Beth's heart pounded against her ribs and shortened her breath. Stuart's mouth, as he bent to set her down, had been so close. The warm imprint of his hands at her waist lingered. Martha pulled her away, and she resisted the urge to turn back and look at him.

Most everyone was already there. A makeshift table of planks propped on sawhorses and covered with a sheet, held an assortment of food.

"Oh, I forgot," Beth said. "Aunt Nora sent food."

When she turned back to get it, though, Stuart and Ester were carrying the food to the table. Her heart jumped. Were Stuart and Ester together? Had he only picked Beth up to be nice?

"You've met everyone, Ester?" Martha asked.

"I believe so." Ester set a basket of rolls down in an open space.

Sally came up, wrapped Beth in a hug, and whispered in her ear, "Your friend from home is here."

"Who? Leah? Oh, where is she?"

"Here she comes," Sally said. "Lookout."

"Yikes, Beth, I didn't think you'd be here," Leah said in a rush. "What with a beau at home and all. Did you hear the news? Good thing your parents got you out of town. Father says John got Alice pregnant and refused to marry her."

Beth's jaw dropped as she stared at Leah, blushing at the twitters from others who had heard the juicy bit of gossip.

"Ha!" Leah said. "Could have been you instead of Alice." Laughing, she flipped her hair and flounced away.

Beth stared at her back. First, the girl tells her a former beau has gotten someone pregnant and then announces that it could be her? Beth went hot then cold.

"Who's ready for hide and seek?" someone called.

Sally gripped Beth's hands. "Some friend. Forget her. Let's have fun."

"I shouldn't have come." Beth glanced around as the others wandered off in pairs or trios. "I was nervous enough before, but what will everyone think of me?"

"You're here to have fun," Sally said. "Most people will not let such talk influence them."

"Yes, they will." Beth allowed herself to be lead away from the food tables. "I'm here now. Only tell me you don't play hide and seek."

"No, we don't. Albert was kidding." She laughed. "They are doing races, though."

"Races?"

"I hope you'll join us," Sally said. "Some of the girls won't run, but a few of us are pretty fast. It won't be long before we're all married and can't do this anymore."

Beth shook her head. "I don't know everyone."

Sally squeezed her arm. "Come on. I'll introduce you."

From the middle of a cleared space in the yard, Martha called. "We're getting ready for the races. Follow Mom and Dad at the ends of the field."

Martha's father shouted directions. "Just pay attention to the markers we put along the side!"

The younger boys pushed to the starting line as Martha's father called, "Go!" The group surged forward.

Sally grabbed Beth and pulled her toward the starting line. "Beth meet Hugh, Steven, and Albert."

"Hello." Beth leaned over to acknowledge them. "Hi, Steven, it's nice to see you." She hadn't run a race in a long time, but since her mother wasn't watching to tell her it wasn't proper, she stepped forward.

"There's Laura, Jane, and you know Ester." Sally took her arm as Martha took Ester's hand and pulled her to the line. Stuart stepped up beside them.

"The rest of you will have to wait until next race," Martha's father yelled. "Ready, set, go!"

Beth cheered when Ester picked up her skirt and ran. Her lean frame was built to run, and she finished first. The next race set up quickly, runners elbowing their way into the line. Albert, Martha's brother and sister, and Steven took positions.

"Come on, Beth," Martha's father said. "You going to give it a go?"

"I guess so."

"Well, step up, then." He gestured with a swing of his arm.

Beth stepped to the line with Sally and the other runners. Something happened to her when he yelled, "Go." She took off like she was fourteen again. She picked up her skirt and raced in the darkening day toward Martha's mother.

Laughing and breathing hard, she and Sally fell against each other when the race ended.

"My goodness," Sally said. "I need to do this more than once or twice a summer. Beth, you've been holding out on us."

Beth laughed. "That was fun." She felt embarrassed though. Maybe she should have followed the advice her mother would have given.

"The winners have to run!" Martha cried.

Sally shouted, "We get a minute to rest, don't we?"

"I'll give you five minutes."

When Martha's father called for the Winners Race, Sally caught Beth's arm and grabbed Ester by the hand. She led them to the starting line.

"All right, now, we'll show you boys." She laughed. "We're the fastest girls."

Martha's father teased the boys as he prepared to start the race. Then, with a suddenness that startled them all, he yelled, "Go!" and they took off. Howard's barefoot stride took him across the finish line well ahead of the rest of them. Ester finished second, Beth and Albert tied for third, with Sally only a hair behind.

"That was close," Martha said.

"We got us a bunch of runners, for sure." Her father slapped his leg. "Always good to see."

"Let's eat," Martha's mother called.

The boys ran to the tables, jostling each other with good-natured pushes and nudges.

Sally took Beth's arm and pulled her to the line. "Don't let these boys intimidate you."

They dished up, then moved to sit on stools and benches randomly placed around a fire burning in a bare patch of ground. Beth and Sally sat together, and Hugh, Steven, and Ester joined them.

"How are you settling in, Beth?" Ester said.

"Good. How about you and your family?" Beth tucked her hair back with a pin. "Is your new place nice?"

"Pretty nice. Mother was worried when we talked to Stuart on the train, but Father had fixed up so much before we got there."

Beth turned to Sally. "You should have seen Stuart try to answer questions about their farm without making it sound bad."

Ester laughed. "He didn't do a good job, though. Mother peppered Father with questions as we drove to the farm." She turned to wave at Stuart. "Dad finally asked who she'd been talking to."

Sally leaned back to talk to Stuart as he dished up his food. "Stuart, I hear you almost scared Ester's family into leaving before they got here."

He came over and sat beside Ester. "I made a mess of it for sure."

Ester smiled at him and bumped his shoulder with hers. "Only for a moment. We like the place fine, and Father says the land is good."

"How is your brother?" Beth asked.

"Oh, Jimmy? He complains about chores. I think it's painful for him, but Mother and Father require everyone to help."

"I don't mean to pry, but was he injured?" Sally whispered.

"When he was little." Ester shook her head. "He was thrown from the buggy when the team spooked."

"Oh, I'm sorry." Beth covered her open mouth with her hand.

"He did better in the beginning, but as he has grown, there is something wrong in his back and shoulders and they are not growing right." Ester broke a small piece off her biscuit. "Mother still gets upset about it, and I suppose

Father too, but there's nothing they can do. They feel lucky he wasn't killed."

"He's a cute little boy," Beth said.

"Don't let him hear you say that." She picked up a piece of chicken. "We won't be able to live with him."

Beth studied Ester's smiling face. That she adored her little brother was obvious. What would it have been like to have siblings?

"Aunt Nora has a neighbor boy, about your brother's age, that visits sometimes. Timothy ... but he's afraid of me."

"Awe, Beth, did you scare the poor kid?" Hugh said.

She blushed. "I don't think so."

Sally stood up for her. "Don't tease her. Timothy is more likely in awe of someone so pretty."

Howard laughed. "That's for sure. What guy around here isn't struck speechless when they see Beth?"

Someone said, "That's for sure." It sounded like Steven.

Beth wanted to sink into the ground. Why had they singled her out?

Everyone laughed as Sally bumped her shoulder and whispered, "It's true, you know."

Later, as darkness descended, the guests came together and collected around the fire, bringing stools and benches to sit on. Some boys lay on the grass, making room for everyone, and the talk soon turned sinister as fantastic tales were shared. Stories took on tension and trepidation as the flames burned low and cast faces in shadow. Beth shuddered, clutching her arms with each tale of mystery and murder. Ester snuggled closer to Stuart and Beth's heart sank. She didn't need a new beau, so why did she long for something more?

"Let's sing," someone called, and Beth relaxed.

Sally led the singing, though Jane and Ester had strong voices too. They harmonized songs from church like "What a Friend We Have in Jesus," and "Jesus Paid It All." They sang the haunting melody "The Cruel War" and the rousing "Battle Hymn of the Republic." Beth hadn't heard some of the verses of "Comin' Thro' the Rye" and "Jimmy Crack Corn." they sang, and a few people led songs from certain countries only one or two in the group knew like "My Highland Mary," but those were fun to learn too.

Before Beth wanted to go, Martha's father called, "Time to head home."

Sally began "Auld Lang Syne" and everyone joined in to help with clean up, packing leftover food, and putting out the fire.

During the ride home, Beth sat rigid in the wagon, watching the horse's heads bob up and down and reliving the evening in her mind. She and Stuart were alone, but she couldn't think of anything to say. Stuart only took her home from duty anyway. It was clear that he would rather be with Ester. The air had turned chilly, with a slight breeze scented with flowers, hay, and corn.

Stuart flicked the reins. "You are a surprise. I can see you've done some running in your past."

She laughed, but it came out a nervous gurgle. "I usually won the races at school."

"You should have warned me."

"I haven't run in ages. I wasn't even sure I could anymore." Beth wrapped her shawl tighter and glanced at him out of the corner of her eye. "I had such a good time, Stuart. Thank you for taking me."

"No trouble at all."

Beth turned back to watching the shadows cast by the light mounted above their seat. "I could do without the stories."

"Scary stories are part of young people getting together, at least if boys are present," he said.

"I love the singing. Sally and Martha sound good together. I could listen to them all night. Oh, and everyone's voices blending—it sounded like a choir."

"I noticed that. The hymns sounded better tonight than they do in church sometimes."

"It was wonderful."

Stuart asked, "Were you upset about the news from Leah?"

"It hurts how she blabbed it, and I'm sorry for Alice and her family."

"What about *your beau*?" He stressed the last two words.

She bristled. "He's not my beau, and I surely will not trust a man like that again."

Stuart pulled on the reins. "Whoa."

"Oh, I didn't see we were home." Beth straightened. "Thank you again for driving me."

He lifted her down from the wagon but released her as soon as her feet touched the ground. She wobbled sleepily for a moment before getting her bearings. Stuart climbed back into his wagon and picked up the reins.

"Goodnight, Beth." Then he turned and drove away.

Beth walked into the house. The food, the races, the singing, and getting to know some of the young people in the area all combined to make it the perfect evening.

She cleaned her teeth and got down on her knees. "Lord," she whispered, "help me understand, and don't let Stuart judge me because of John."

She climbed into bed, huddled into the blankets. Would Stuart have preferred driving Ester?

The words from "Jesus Paid it All" rang in her head ... *change the leper's spots and melt the heart of stone.* "Lord, thank you for changing me," she whispered. "My heart felt like a rock within me when I came here. I may not understand much, but I've learned that you are my Shepherd, and you will never leave me or forsake me."

CHAPTER TWENTY

"Aunt Nora," Beth called through the back door, "do you have any idea where I can find Daisy?"

"Oh, dear me! Where could that wretched thing have gone to?"

"How does one go about finding a lost cow?"

Aunt Nora gazed off into the empty pasture. "You better start toward the river. Take a rope with you."

Beth headed through the pasture. The gaping hole in the fence was easy to spot. She didn't need the matted grass and cow pie Daisy left as evidence. The meandering path headed toward the river, so she traversed there, hoping to spot the wayward animal.

Seeing nothing, she sat down to ponder the situation. She should have eaten breakfast but hadn't expected this to take all morning. Looking around from her position on the ground, she spied the errant animal, its backend facing her. Water surged around Daisy's belly from the creek. And judging by the hoof prints at the water's edge, the mud was deep.

Now what? Who could she call? Aunt Nora shouldn't be climbing the ravines along the creek or wading in mud. Beth didn't know the neighbors, and Timothy didn't seem to be spying today. She looked back at Daisy who stared ahead and let out a melancholy lowing.

Beth took off her stockings and boots, and then tucked her dress into the waist of her apron. Thus garbed, she grasped the rope and eased toward the animal.

Cold, gluey mud oozed around her feet and squeezed between her toes. "Yuck." She shuddered. Musty, dank smells wafted around her. She cringed at what the muck might contain—leeches, spiders, or snakes. Every step she took, she sunk further. What if she got stuck too?

Rethinking the situation, she went back for a long branch, each step ponderous. Stories from her childhood when boys tried to scare her, came to mind. Could there be quicksand?

She picked up a branch to use as a walking stick and leaned on it to balance herself. When she reached the place where water covered mud, she took extra care, unable to see what lurked under the water. By the time Beth got to the cow, the water had risen to her knees.

She soothed Daisy with nonsense words as she began to secure the rope around her neck. Beth tugged. The cow stretched her neck, revealing the whites of her eyes, but her legs didn't move.

Beth tried coaxing and pulling, prodding, and cajoling. "Aw, come on, Daisy, please?"

But the cow wouldn't budge.

Beth sighed. She needed to push instead of pull.

The stick she'd used was now floating downstream, so holding the rope in one hand, she went to the back end of the cow and leaned hard against it. Daisy bellowed and took a lunging step. Beth pushed harder. When the cow took another step, Beth's feet didn't move, though her body went forward. She screamed, but a mouthful of cold, murky water cut off the sound. Her falling body brushed the hindquarters of the cow. That sudden movement and her scream must have been the substance of whatever terrorized the mind of a cow because the frightened animal lunged forward another step, barely missing Beth's head with a hoof.

Beth stood, sputtering water, and gasping for air. She struggled to the far shore since it was closest, then sat on a log, resting her head in her hand. Muddy water dripped off her hair onto her dress and ran in rivulets down her legs. Mud, with leaves and grass pressed in, stuck to her feet.

The cow stared at her from its position in the creek, the rope now dangling downstream.

"I should leave you there, Daisy," Beth grumbled, "since you were the one that got yourself into this predicament."

With her head in her hand, Beth glared at the animal. Finally, she pushed off her knees and stood. "I will not be defeated by a cow."

She waded back in, picked up the rope, and pulled. The annoying animal looked pitifully back at her. Beth pulled harder, the rope drew tight, the cow stretched its neck until it looked like its head would come off, but it didn't move an inch.

"Looks like you have a problem there."

Stuart came down to the edge of the stream, not bothering to hide his enjoyment of the situation.

Of all the luck! She'd almost gotten the cow out. Now he decided to come and help? Why couldn't he have shown up sooner, or better yet, why couldn't the man stay home?

Beth didn't need to cover her legs for modesty's sake. Her dress and apron had come undone, but they hung heavy with water and mud.

Stuart snared the rope, wrapped it around his hand, and pulled. The cow stretched her neck and rolled her eyes but didn't move.

Beth squinted at him. "I tried that."

He grinned. "Since you're already wet, would you like to push?"

"What? She almost knocked me senseless with a hoof last time."

"It appears she's stuck for good unless someone pushes, and someone pulls."

Beth scrutinized the situation and regarded the grinning man. "I about got *myself* stuck."

"I'll pull you out." He grinned some more, and she watched how his eyes danced. A little part of her brain wanted to smile with him, but she felt too miserable.

Instead, she glared back, her words slow and measured so he wouldn't miss one of them. "Are you telling me, I have to go back and push that stupid animal from behind?"

"I wouldn't malign Daisy. She might hear you."

"Oh, for goodness' sake." Beth's hands clenched, but Stuart was already moving to the tree.

He took a turn around a tree, giving him leverage to pull, and he waited for her, his brow raised.

"Argh!" She stomped back behind the animal, hanging onto Daisy to keep from falling. Once in position, she called, "I'm ready."

"Okay, push."

"Okay, push," Beth muttered.

The mud made a sucking sound and finally gave, one hoof pulled free, then another. After more straining and heaving on the humans' part, the cow took several steps, and then, with a bellow, the animal charged out of the stream, spraying water with each step. Once on the bank, Daisy stood with full udders swinging, dripping and muddy, bellowing at them like it was all their fault.

Beth trudged after her, but the rocks were slippery under her feet. With a sudden lurch and shriek, she fell once more. She thrust her hands out and down, trying to keep her face above water, but the move caused a wave to splash into her face. Her mouth, open to scream, filled.

Hands yanked her, arms flailing from the depths as Stuart pulled her to shore. Beth swayed like grass in the wind, dizzy and breathless, pushing hair and water out of her eyes.

Stuart said, "Of course, the cow is on the wrong side of the stream, but there's a better crossing down this way."

Beth dropped down on a log. Her dress dripped with gray water. Her feet had several painful scrapes.

Stuart came back to her side. "I tied Daisy up. You coming?"

Beth's head rested in her hand. She did not respond.

"Now, Beth, it isn't so bad, is—"

She threw up her hand, palm facing him. "Don't say it."

He walked away.

Beth was tired, wet, and completely unconcerned that she looked worse than a street urchin—an almost drowned one. It was a miracle she had survived. Then, her stomach growled again, reminding her that Daisy needed to be milked. Sighing, she rose from her log. Movement out of the corner of her eye pulled her to look in that direction. Timothy stood on the bank watching her. Now she understood. The boy had come to her rescue in the only way he knew how.

"Thank you, Timothy," she called. "I could hug you for your help." He ducked his head. "But you wouldn't want to get all wet."

He turned around and ran as she trudged toward the crossing where Stuart waited.

He untied the cow and walked next to Beth, gripping her elbow to give her balance as they crossed the rock-strewn ford and then back up onto the prairie. When they reached the spot where she'd left her boots, she sat down and looked at her feet.

Going back to that monstrous creek to wash her feet seemed beyond consideration. Putting the boots on over her messy feet would ruin them. After picking up the socks and boots, she grabbed Daisy's rope and limped toward the barn.

Behind her, Stuart called out, "Don't forget to milk her."

He laughed, but Beth was beyond caring. With luck, he would go away and fall in the creek.

How could the cow endure the full udder that heaved from side to side as she walked? Maybe she couldn't. She mooed all the way home.

Beth's aunt met her halfway to the barn. "What on earth?"

There were no words to describe the ordeal. She just held out the rope. Aunt Nora took the cow and headed to the barn without another word. As far as Beth was concerned, Nora could take that beast anywhere. The further away, the better.

After filling a pail of water, Beth stopped at the lean-to, wrapped her hair in a cloth, and removed her dress. The wash water was cold, but her one desire was to be clean and free of critters.

A short time later, in her room, she finished cleaning up by tossing all her garments in a pail. After Beth had dressed in fresh, dry clothes, had her hair washed and wrapped in a towel, she mopped the floor, washed her clothes, and hung them on the line. Then she retreated to the porch to comb out her hair.

"Dear, here is something to eat," Aunt Nora said, holding out a plate of biscuit and boiled egg. "You must be famished."

"I guess I am."

"I'm sorry. Daisy gets a notion once in a great while."

Beth shrugged. "Stuart helped me ... eventually. I think Timothy went to get him. I saw the boy after Stuart arrived."

"That doesn't surprise me. Timothy is special." Nora turned to go back in the house. "I have some vegetables for

Sophie. After you've finished eating and doing your hair, would you like to take them to her?"

"As long as it has nothing to do with a cow, water, or mud."

CHAPTER TWENTY-ONE

"Come and sit now, Beth," Sophie greeted her at the door.

"I have some garden produce Aunt Nora sent."

"Thank you so much." Sophie set them in the kitchen. "I'll put them away later." The old woman took her arm and led her to the chairs by the window. "Tell me what's been going on."

Beth laughed. "You want to know? Today hasn't been the best day." She told Sophie about the cow. "I guess it's funny now, but I wasn't laughing earlier."

"That reminds me of something Mrs. Watson did," Sophie said. "That was a place I worked for a time. Mr. Watson raised and sold horses, so we often had horse buyers at the farm. Mr. Watson believed we should feed them a meal. One day, we had no prospective buyers scheduled, so Mrs. Watson decided to try a new kind of concoction she'd read about in a lady's magazine. It was to clear her skin, remove age spots and her gardening tan—lard and nettle leaves, or some such mixture. I tied up her hair and smeared the stuff all over her face and hands."

"What happened?" Beth asked.

"I went to milk cows and didn't know a horse buyer had shown up after all. He came to the house with Mr. Watson. I don't know why Mrs. Watson had gone outside—must have been helping one of the children ... Anyway, Mr. Watson and the buyer were coming so she looked for a place to hide. Her hands were slippery, and she couldn't open the door. She figured to climb in the open window, but she got stuck. Her skirts plugged that window right up."

"My goodness." Beth laughed. "What happened?"

Sophie's eyes danced as she continued her story. "Mr. Watson pulled her out of the window like she was one of the children. He opened the door for her and continued to talk to the horse buyer without batting an eye. I served them dinner and she never showed her face again while the buyer was there."

The pair continued to chat for a bit more until Beth said, "I should be getting back."

As Beth headed for home, she rehearsed Sophie's story so she would remember to tell Aunt Nora. She laughed to herself, picturing the woman stuck in the window with only her feet and petticoats poking out, surely kicking in frustration.

Without warning, hands grabbed her arm and yanked her off the path.

"Hey!" she screamed, clawing her attacker. "Stop, let me go!"

A grimy hand covered her mouth, and the grip tightened. She struggled harder and tried to yell, but the sound stopped in her throat. She could see the alley as it tilted and lurched past her. The hand slipped and she screamed and fought to keep her feet. She twisted and saw her attacker's face.

"John? What are you doing?"

"I want to talk to you." He glanced around.

"What do you mean by grabbing me?" Her voice rose to a hysterical pitch. "Let me go!" She thrashed to pull away. "You're hurting me, John ... let go." She opened her mouth to scream.

He gripped her by the arms and shook her until her hair came loose. "Listen to me."

"John, please." She shuddered, dizzy, and disoriented. "You're scaring me. Why are you here?"

He bent his face to hers, leaving mere inches between them. She flinched from the crazed look in his eyes. Here was something far worse than she'd imagined.

"I want to talk to you." He yanked her arm and shook her again.

"If you wanted to talk to me," she stammered, "you could come to the door like a decent man." She gulped a breath. "What's going on?"

She must be strong and not let him see her fear. Red hot anger rose in her—anger at John, this situation, and her stupidity. She had been forced from home because of this man.

"Your parents want a better man for their darling?" He seethed into her face. "What ... a banker's son, not good enough for you?"

"John, what's gotten into you?" Maybe she could reason with him. "If you're in trouble or something, turn yourself in."

"Maybe if you'd believed in me, Beth." He shook her again, surely leaving bruises. "If you'd stayed ..."

"Wh–what's that supposed to mean?" she stammered.

His speech slurred through his next words. "You are good and decent. I'm none of those things, but if you'd stuck with me, I might have changed."

"Don't put that on me!" He couldn't have gotten more of a reaction if he'd held a snake in her face. "Behave yourself like a decent man. Quit skulking around." She pulled against his grip. "Whatever you've become is not my fault."

He shook her again, then looked around. "I suppose you're right, but Beth, don't think ill of me when you hear the rumors. I'm not all bad."

"John, please stop this." She had to try to change his mind. "You can start over."

"It's too late." He spat the words through gritted teeth.

"John, please. Go home and take care of Alice. Stop using everyone and stand up …" She struggled to pull her arms free.

"I can't!" He flung her away from him.

She lost her balance, falling into weeds along the path. Half crawling and stumbling, she got to her feet, but pain shot up her leg. Stickers impaled her hands, her ankle hurt, and tears blinded her. When gravel crunched behind her, panic burned like hot pepper in the back of her throat. Staggering on shaking legs, she had no thought but to get away and home. She stumbled but lunged forward.

"Beth, what are you doing?" a man called to her from across the street.

Her ears rang. She stumbled again, crying out when her hands and knees hit the ground, but then someone was pulling her to her feet.

She struggled. "No, let me go!"

"Hey, I've got you." Stuart wrapped his arms around her and held her steady for a moment. "Don't fret. I'm here. What happened to you?"

"Home. Please."

"All right, let's get you to Aunt Nora."

He murmured comfort while his strong arm around her waist kept her on her feet. She hung on the best she could and let him lead her home. Her hands hurt, and so did her ankle, but mostly she ached inside. She had never been treated like this. What terrible thing was John doing?

"You're doing fine," Stuart said. "Not much further, and you'll be home to Aunt Nora."

He helped her to the swing on the porch and sat beside her.

Aunt Nora came from the house. "My goodness, Beth, what happened?" She pulled a chair close and sat in front of them.

Beth swiped her hair out of her face. When her aunt took her hands, she winced.

"Nora," Stuart said, "we'd better remove her shoe and check her foot."

Beth's body began to shake uncontrollably. Nausea rose in her stomach, and endless tears coursed down her face. "I fell," she said. "No, I was pushed. I saw John—I mean he grabbed me. He's here. He's into something bad."

Aunt Nora checked Beth's ankle and foot. "Appears, you twisted it," she said. "Let me wash those hands. Stuart, can you get her inside?"

Stuart carried her into the house and placed her in a chair with her foot propped on a stool. He retrieved a quilt from the rack and wrapped it around her. Her shivering had worsened, and her teeth chattered.

Aunt Nora brought a cloth and a bowl of water. "Stuart, can you put the kettle on? I'll pull as many of these stickers as I can, but she needs a wash and bed."

Stuart fetched water then stoked up the stove as Beth told Nora what had happened.

"He was dressed in farmer's clothing and had a wild look in his eyes. Aunt Nora, he frightened me. He'd been drinking, and he said maybe if I'd believed in him, he would have turned out different."

"My goodness," Nora said. "We need to send for the sheriff right away."

"I don't have anything to tell him," Beth whispered. "I mean, I don't know what he's doing. Well, not really."

"Nonsense, girl, let the sheriff be the judge of that. He needs to know these things." Nora finished with Beth's hands. "Do you know more than you're telling me? Do you know what he's up to, Beth?"

"I might."

"What is it, Beth?" Nora asked, her voice stern.

"I thought I saw him from my window at the hotel."

"What ... when?"

"When Leah and I came out here. I couldn't sleep and thought I heard something. I snuck to the window and listened. Some men were talking about stealing cattle and horses."

"What makes you think he was part of it?"

"I saw him." Beth trembled.

"Are you sure?"

"I wasn't." She clutched her arms close to her side. "I mean, it seemed so preposterous. I thought I must've been dreaming, but now I'm sure he was one of the men."

Stuart interrupted. "I'm going for the sheriff. I only wish I'd been down that street sooner."

"I'm scared," Beth said, her trembling voice stopping him before he reached the door. "I can't think what he must be up to."

Stuart turned to study her before saying, "I'm riding for the sheriff."

CHAPTER TWENTY-TWO

Beth hobbled to a chair at the back of the house to watch the sunrise. A bright slice of orange light illuminated the sky. Then, streaks of pink and yellow, colors no man could reproduce, gleamed into day.

Aunt Nora set a chair beside her and interrupted her musing. "How did you sleep?"

"Not well. I kept going over what happened, and my ankle hurt when I moved." She shifted in her chair. "It's stiff this morning."

"You picked a good place to sit."

"I wasn't sleeping anyway, so I thought I'd enjoy the view." She turned back to the sky, trying to imprint the colors in her mind.

"I've been wakeful too." Aunt Nora sat down next to her. "Thinking about this situation, yours, and Fanny's. I believe you might be able to help each other."

"You want me to stay with her, don't you?" Beth wrapped her arms around her middle, clutching herself tight. She knew Aunt Nora worried about Fanny. "What if it's not safe at their farm?"

"I believe it will be." Aunt Nora took her hand. "John seems to be working his outlawry right here. Everything in town is terrifying to you now. I think you'll be safer and happier away from here." She paused for a moment.

"Besides, the Cantwells are a hard-working couple who could use your help."

"Mr. Cantwell isn't home much?" Beth approached this new experience like someone testing thin ice. She didn't want to do it.

"Martin is working on the spur line, so he's only home on Saturday and Sunday."

Beth watched the geese in the pasture, pulling grass and catching bugs. How could she leave now?

"Fanny would be fine out there by herself, but with a baby coming and all ..." Nora patted Beth's hand. "Fanny needs help, and I think you're the answer. You're a good, strong girl. You can take after those three little ones without any trouble, I'm thinking."

"What about my ankle?" Beth protested. "And I'm not good with children."

"You'll learn, and the ankle will heal. Besides, I think this is the best place for you right now."

"Do you *want* me to go?" The way Aunt Nora pushed felt just like when her parents had sent her away.

"Bless you, dear, I love having you here, but Fanny needs the support. I'll rest easier if you two have each other."

"I'm afraid to do this," Beth whispered. She didn't want more new situations, or new people or more loneliness.

"Change is like that," Nora said. "If you agree, Martin can pick you up when he comes through town. I'll send a message, and we can pack some of your dresses right away." Nora stood to go back to the house.

"What about my sewing?"

"Take it with you. Fanny might have time to help with it. You'll enjoy her immensely, you'll see." Aunt Nora chuckled. "You'll love the children too."

"It feels like you're shipping me off the way my parents did." Beth fought back tears.

"My goodness, dear." Nora sat back down next to her again and put her hand on Beth's shoulder. "Please don't think such a thing. I'm worried about Fanny, and now, with this happening to you, well ... I want you safe."

Beth pondered Nora's words. Would it be fun to be with the children and spend time with Fanny? She turned to Aunt Nora. "You think I can be of help to her?"

Aunt Nora patted Beth's hands where they lay twisted in her lap. "You know how much I love having company?"

Beth nodded.

"Think of Fanny, all alone with the children, and waiting to have a baby. If nothing else, you will be company to her, but believe me, you will be of immense help."

Beth nodded. "All right, I'll go." The words were out before she could stop herself.

Aunt Nora bent down and hugged her. "I'm glad, dear. Now I'll take the eggs and butter into town. You rest your ankle. I'll be right back."

Beth could not sit still though. She hobbled around fixing breakfast, but soon, her ankle throbbed. How was she going to watch children when they could move faster than she could?

Aunt Nora came back soon afterward and hastened to spread her packages on the table. "I found a piece for another large apron for you," she said with a wide grin. "Believe me—you'll need it."

"Great," Beth muttered.

"Let's eat and then I can show you," Nora said.

Nora talked more than usual while she ate breakfast. "I think we should get more meals made up, so you won't have to cook much the first few days."

Beth frowned. Why was Aunt Nora so excited to have her leave?

Later, Nora unwrapped her package and revealed a bundle of fabric. She unfolded a yardage of white muslin with dainty flower motifs scattered throughout. "This will make a lovely apron. Functional too."

"How long do you think I'll be there?" Beth asked.

"Well, certainly until the baby comes in the fall."

Beth closed her eyes and rested her head in her hands. "Not that long. I need to go home before then." The reality of what she had agreed to hit her like a bucket of cold water right in the face.

"We'll see, dear, we'll see."

Nora put the package away and went to the barn to start chores while Beth returned to her chair and tried to fathom spending a whole day with children. As the day wore on, Beth tried her best to help with chores and meals but had to sit often as her ankle throbbed.

That night, they sat on the front porch and read again about the children of Israel while a bundle of clover smoked to keep the mosquitoes away.

After Beth finished reading, she picked up her knitting. "How did you fix this? It was so tight. I kept trying to loosen it, but I only made it tighter."

Aunt Nora laughed, laying the apron she was hemming in her lap. "Yes, it was tight. Try to relax and keep your tension looser this time."

"Thank you. It looks so pretty." Beth examined her project. "I'm not sure I can do this justice. Your knitting is beautiful."

"You'll get there."

Beth yawned.

"You've had a long day and hobbling around is sure to have tired you out." Aunt Nora rose. "I'll put out the fire and come in myself."

Beth folded up her work. She did feel sleepy, and her eyes drooped like a hound dog's face. "Goodnight, Aunt."

"Goodnight, dear."

After she prepared for bed, Beth prayed and thought about the stubborn children of Israel and her own stubbornness. She hadn't thought of herself as stubborn or rebellious, but when her parents insisted she obey, it had been for her good. They choose to be responsible—even though it went against her wishes.

Beth rose early on Sunday morning. Sleep had eluded her again and it was no use trying now. She dressed for chores and hobbled around feeding the livestock.

"My, you were up early," Nora said as Beth returned inside.

"I couldn't sleep," Beth grumbled.

"I'm sorry to hear that, dear. Go change for church and then we'll have breakfast."

Beth limped to her room. As she pulled off the skirt of her chore clothes her sore ankle caught in the hem, and she almost fell. Then, as she pulled on her church dress, a ripping sound filled the room. Plopping down on the bed, she gave in to the tears. "I can't do this," she muttered. "I don't *want* to do this." Before long, she sobbed into her pillow.

"Now then, dear, it will be all right." Aunt Nora walked into the room and pulled Beth into her arms. "Let it out. It's time you let it all out."

Beth cried out her terror and anger from the attack and the worry and fear of the unknown. She cried because she felt homesick and had bottled up her feelings. The time was well past for a release.

With the tears spent, she sat up. "I'm sorry your dress is soaked." She dabbed at Nora's shoulder.

Nora laughed. "Nothing to worry about, dear. I'll change it. You get dressed." She took the ripped dress and handed Beth another dress from off the hook. "Come on out when you're finished. We'll talk."

"I'm sorry, we'll be late for church."

Nora shook her head. "We might miss church, but we need to talk."

When Beth moved in her unsteady gait from the bedroom, Nora sat at the table. "Come and eat."

While Beth ate, Nora read to her from Psalm 91. "I will say of the LORD, He is my refuge and my fortress: my God; in him will I trust." Beth felt better when she finished eating but was embarrassed to have lost control. She'd acted like a child.

"Do you want me to tell Martin you can't help them?"

No condemnation flashed in her aunt's eyes, only concern.

Beth shook her head. "No, I'll go."

Nora studied her, then reached out and took her hand. "You're a strong girl."

"What? How can you say that?" Beth pressed her hands on the table to stand up, then banged her ankle. "Ouch."

"My dear, sit. Take it easy." Nora brought Beth a glass of water and sat across from her again. "Beth, you've had a horrendous week and, after all that, you're ready to take on more new and unknown experiences. As I said, you're strong. I'm proud of you."

"After I carried on this morning?"

"God never asked us to go through life without emotion. It's what makes us human."

"I feel silly." Beth didn't cry often. Her life usually rolled along safe and stable—at least until lately. "But I should pack a few things." She struggled to stand.

"Why don't you let me do that for you?" Nora helped her stand. "Come, sit by the window where you can put your foot up and rest." She propped Beth's foot on a stool and covered her with a blanket.

Beth lay back and closed her eyes.

CHAPTER TWENTY-THREE

Beth woke at a knock on the door.

Aunt Nora called, "Come on in, Martin."

The man stepped inside and nodded to Beth. "Miss, Aunt Nora."

"Hello," Beth said as she rose from her chair and hobbled to her room.

"I have a box to send out with you, Martin, and Beth can be ready in a few minutes. Would you like something to eat?"

"No, ma'am," Martin said. "I need to get home."

"I understand. I have preserves packed—maybe they'll perk Fanny up a bit."

"Thank you, Aunt Nora, and for lending me your young lady." Beth carried her valise from the bedroom. Mr. Cantwell turned to her and took the bag from her hand. "We appreciate it more than we can say."

"I believe she'll be a great help to you, Martin." Aunt Nora hugged Beth tightly. "I'll see you soon."

Beth returned the hug. She hadn't known this woman long but had found acceptance and even love from her.

Aunt Nora's eyes were damp. "I'll be praying for you all, dear. You'll be fine—you'll see."

Beth sat beside Mr. Cantwell on the wagon seat. She curled and uncurled the edge of her dress between her fingers as he drove the wagon from town.

"It's not going to be that bad." Mr. Cantwell nodded toward her rumpled dress.

Beth untangled her fingers and smoothed the fabric. "What are the names and ages of your children, Mr. Cantwell?"

"Call me Martin. Our oldest is Tad. He's almost nine and my big helper. He's a responsible boy for his age." He pulled his hat lower over his eyes. "The next is Sam. He's six and full of mischief and often in trouble, I'm sorry to say. He doesn't talk much, so it comes as a surprise, at least to me."

Beth's stomach tightened. How would she keep ahead of such a child?

"Mandy is next, and she'll be three. She follows her brothers. Her constant wail is 'wait for me.'" He laughed and shook his head. "They leave her behind because she's slow and a girl, but in a year or two, they won't get away with that."

"I see," Beth said, because it seemed right to say something.

"Now, my wife," Mr. Cantwell said, "is tough and willing to do all she can, but there's no reason she should tire herself needlessly when there's a strong, young girl willing to help out."

They passed another wagon on the road, and Martin waved to the occupants.

"You be knowing a lot about a mercantile and figuring and such," Martin said, "but this here's a different situation altogether. Still, Fanny figured if you was related to Aunt Nora, you'd do fine."

"How did you know I worked in a mercantile?" Beth gripped the seat as they passed over a chunk of rough road. "Does everyone here know my business?"

He leaned back and turned toward her. "Why, girl, you was spotted right off the train. You and that pretty friend of yours." He faced the road again and snapped the reins. "We ain't exactly gossiping, but we married men want to get the single boys hitched, and so do our wives."

Beth knew how these small towns functioned, but this news seemed an affront to her pride.

"Now, don't be mad at us, girl." Martin flicked a glance her way. "You being such a pretty thing and all, you'll be snatched up before you know it, and we want you to get the best man. Course, the right fella to us may not be the gent you're looking for."

"What if I don't want anyone here?"

"Why, girl, that's fine too. It makes us no never mind, but we butt in now and then in spite of ourselves." He flipped the reins. "Come on Jack, Jane."

Beth glanced at him. His sparkling eyes were almost hidden by the brim of his wide hat.

"Course, Aunt Nora talked to us too." He ran his hand around the back of his neck. "She was some worried about the kids while Fanny was resting. That's my blind spot, I suppose. I should've seen how tuckered she is most days. We coulda had you out a long time ago."

Beth kept her disagreement to herself.

"'Course, with the new situation, we think it's the best place for you in the long run. So, no harm done. We're getting ya now, and though I can't pay much, we do need your help."

Beth hadn't thought about pay. She'd only spent a small amount of the money she'd brought with her, so she still had her train money to get back home. "I don't need much," she said.

Mr. Cantwell nodded. "That's what Aunt Nora said. She said you were a kind girl who liked to be useful."

Beth bit the corner of her lip and raised an eyebrow. Aunt Nora gave her credit she didn't deserve.

"We be knowin' you need to rest and heal that ankle too. What with the extra food Aunt Nora sent, we should be fixed for today."

Beth listened while Mr. Cantwell talked about the farms they passed, pointing out the benefits or the problems with a particular property. One farm had good drainage, another had large hills, while another had too many rocks.

"Look there." He pointed to a piece of land that, to her, looked like all the rest. "I would say it's about perfect—not as good as our special place, but mighty nice."

"It's pretty," she said.

"Well, girl, it might be pretty, but look how nice those fields are—flat with good, black dirt."

Beth studied the abandoned building site. Weeds grew around the buildings, and the fence of a corral lay broken and haphazard. A twinge of sadness coursed through her. Someone's dream lay in ruin.

"I was telling Hugh about this place a while back," Mr. Cantwell said. "I hope he or Howard might be able to get it. The young men around here are going to have a hard time buying their own places, things been pretty rough."

She thought of Howard and this place. He would be able to fix it up fine. "Back home, we saw farmers head back east many a time."

"Some can't take the backbreaking work," Mr. Cantwell said. "Or the storms and blizzards. Add to that the shortage of money and just plain hard times, and it's tough for folks. If the men are willing, sometimes the women ain't."

Mr. Cantwell threw his arm wide. "Still, this is perfect country, to my way of thinking. We have flat land around here, but with easy, rolling hills to make it interesting. Sloughs full of ducks and geese, creeks, and plenty of rainfall." He pointed. "We're here."

Pride colored his voice, but when Beth turned to where he pointed, their place looked like every other farm they'd passed. Just a house, a barn, and a few outbuildings—bare and lonesome like all the rest.

"It looks right nice," she said, not wishing to offend on the first day.

Mr. Cantwell laughed. "That's okay, girl. It ain't much to see, I guess, but it's our little place, and we sure are proud of it."

Two children and a barking dog ran to meet them as they drove up the drive. Mr. Cantwell pulled up in front of the house and jumped down as the children lined up beside the porch and stared at Beth. Mr. Cantwell helped her down and she grabbed the side of the wagon to maintain her balance.

"Now, children, this is Beth." Mr. Cantwell picked up her valise from the back of the wagon. "Don't both of you talk at once, now."

Beth studied the boys as they stared up at her. Tad, tall like his dad, swept thick, brown hair out of his eyes. Sam's blond head gleamed in the sun.

"Let's be gittin' in the house now." Martin headed up the stairs onto the porch. "And git acquainted with the missus."

"Ma, Ma, she's here!" the boys shouted as they ran into the house, each trying to outdo the other. "Pa's home, and she's here."

Martin shrugged. "I guess they found their voices." He left her valise on the porch and came back to help her up the steps, through the porch, and into the house.

"I'm in here, Martin," a woman called to them.

Beth glimpsed the kitchen. A large table dominated the room with a cookstove off to the right. She gripped the chairs for support as she limped after Mr. Cantwell.

In the next room, Mr. Cantwell said, "Fanny, is everything all right?"

"Yes, just resting," she called. "Come in here, Beth. I've been trying to get a space cleaned for you to sleep. I may have overdone it slightly."

"I'm sorry." Beth hobbled into the room. "I'm sure I can sleep anywhere."

"Not if you want any rest." Fanny brushed back strands of hair that had fallen across her brow. "It was either the kitchen or put you in with Mandy. You might not sleep as well back there with her, but I couldn't see putting you in the kitchen when we have workers and company coming by from time to time." She sighed. "Thankfully, we're putting on a wing later this summer. We need it."

"I see."

"I'm sorry, Beth." Fanny's small, pixie features showed strain, and sweat dampened her hair. "I'm tired and not much at conversation. I need to lie down. This isn't fair, your first night, but you can follow Martin around to get the lay of the land."

Fanny hoisted herself off the chair, her husband helping her gain her balance. She glanced over with a tired smile, and Beth noticed her bare feet poked out from under her skirt. Her over-blouse draped over the girth of her belly.

Beth limped back to the kitchen and found the children sitting at the table. Three sets of eyes stared at her. When Martin came back into the room, she asked, "Can I help?"

"Let's get these youngsters fed," he said. "I retrieved the things Aunt Nora sent. There's plenty for tonight. It's a nice evening, so we'll go outside and let Fanny rest. Sam, carry this to the table, please."

Beth helped where she could. After the meal, she washed dishes while Mr. Cantwell took the children outside. With no one to watch her, she felt more comfortable looking into cupboards to locate supplies.

When she joined them outside, the little girl in her rumpled dress reached for her hand. Beth limped along while Tad and Sam kept up a running commentary.

"Here's the garden," Tad said. "But we got to keep the chickens out. Pa said we mustn't go in the pasture with the cows and horses, but we can go where the sheep are."

"We can't go to the creek by ourselves, but we can go with you, Pa says," Sam added.

Martin went to check on Fanny, and Beth lowered herself onto the grass to rest. She winced when Mandy bumped into her sore foot while trying to sit in her lap. The boys got louder and more animated as they related stories of importance.

"We found a nest in the grass by the cornfield," Sam said. "Pa says we got to stay away, and we found a nest by the pond on a willow branch."

Tad gave his little brother a little shove and said, "There's a robin nest in the bush by the garden too."

Even Mandy had a lot to say. The child leaned her face close to Beth's and told her a long story, none of which Beth understood.

"Kids, bath time," Mr. Cantwell called.

He bathed Mandy in the washtub of sun-warmed water, and then, Beth took her into the house to dress for bed. When Tad and Sam finished their baths, the children gathered around Martin for stories on the porch. Mandy and Sam were on his lap while Tad hung over his shoulder.

Afterward, Martin tucked the children in for the night, showed Beth the pantry, explained the children's chore routine, and gave general information about the neighborhood.

"I'm sorry the only place we have for you is to share with Mandy," he said. "It might not be so restful, but maybe we can come up with something else later."

"I'm sure it will do."

She wasn't sure at all. This situation was opposite to anything she'd ever experienced. At home, she'd had a bed all to herself, alone in her room. There were responsibilities at the mercantile, but nothing like this. The awkward, misfit feeling she was experiencing left her with no appetite, but somehow, she had to cope—there was no getting away from it.

Beth entered her room now and noticed Mandy was used to her own space too. The girl had sprawled completely across the small bed. Beth moved her as delicately as she could and then climbed in beside, positioning her sore ankle opposite the sleeping child. For a long time, she lay wide awake. The bed was narrow, and Mandy a restless sleeper. The sounds of Tad and Sam tossing and turning disturbed her too. How would she get used to sleeping with a little girl and sharing a room with two boys?

Later, Beth woke in the dark and lay for a moment, needing to identify her surroundings. She came fully awake when Mandy's arm hit her in the face. She removed the appendage and noticed dim light streaming through the window. A door banged closed somewhere. Mr. Cantwell must be leaving for the week. She closed her eyes and tried to sleep again. At least the memory of the attack hadn't bothered her this night.

When Beth awoke again, light streamed into the room. After dressing, she hobbled to the kitchen, her ankle stiff and sore from the activity of the previous day. She filled the kettle and added wood to the stove. Then she sat down, propped her foot on another chair, and waited. Was Fanny all right? Should she go to her room and see? Beth chewed on her fingernail and waited.

Fanny stepped into the kitchen when the water began to boil. "Beth, I'm sorry I wasn't very sociable yesterday." She went to the stove, checked the fuel chamber, and noted the full kettle of water. "You've started water. Thank you." Fanny added a large pot to the stove and poured water from the kettle into it. "I feel better this morning, and this cool day is welcome. Did Martin show you around?"

"Yes, I saw most everything."

"Good. If you can oversee chores when you're better—just check on Tad and Sam." She sat down on a kitchen chair and looked at Beth's ankle. "Oh my, that foot is quite swollen. Yesterday was a hard day for you too, I see." She sat back and propped up her feet. "We'll take it easy today so you can rest it."

"Did you hear why I came?" Beth knotted her hands in her lap.

"You're going to help me—and, yes, we know the rest." Fanny pulled pins from her apron pocket and pinned up her hair. "I'm sorry you went through such a terrifying experience."

"Will I be safe here?"

"I'm counting on it." Fanny rose, measured cornmeal from a container in the cupboard, poured it into the boiling water, and then used a wooden paddle to stir the mush. "If you aren't safe here, we aren't safe here. We've never had any trouble and we have wonderful neighbors."

"Yes, ma'am."

The older woman laughed. "Please call me Fanny." She stirred a bit more and then called. "Boys! Tad and Sam."

A few minutes later, both boys staggered into the room, their hair mussed and their eyes bleary. They both smiled as soon as they spied Beth.

"Get done with your visit to the outhouse and wash up. We're almost ready to eat."

Beth made to get up and find some way to help, but Fanny waved her away. "Sit. I'll bring you a bowl. You'll be out and about soon enough. Rest now."

Beth ate her mush like they did, with molasses and butter. Maybe this visit wouldn't be so bad after all.

CHAPTER TWENTY-FOUR

After a few weeks, Beth got around with only a limp, but fell into bed each night exhausted. Each morning she hastened to start anew, and she felt surprised to be surviving this new experience and settling into the family routine. She'd tried a bit of cooking at Aunt Nora's and now Fanny encouraged her to try new things.

One morning, she had an idea.

"Fanny, do you think I could make donuts? I've never made them, and I'm not sure about the recipe."

"I like them out of sweetened bread dough, and it's certainly warm enough for them to rise quickly," Fanny said.

"You think it's all right then?"

"It's a good idea." Fanny sat back with her feet in a tub of cold water. "Make dough for rolls, and I'll help you with the rest."

Beth mixed and kneaded. Before long, the dough sat resting.

"Tad and Sam," she called, "how about we each weed a row in the garden while the dough is rising."

The children finished their rows with astounding speed, but Beth decided not to check their work. She washed up, rolled the dough, and let it rest again.

After the dough had risen a second time, she cut it into rounds. She let them rise again while the lard heated.

Fanny shooed the children out of the kitchen. "This is hot, and I can't have you in the way," she said. "Listen to me, or you'll have to stay outside." When they were slow to move, she added, "Now, out."

They went—as far as the other side of the table, where they lined up to watch the proceedings.

When the fat grew hot enough, Beth began dropping the dough rounds into the pot. The satisfaction of seeing the dough spring into big circles and brown to a mouthwatering color was a pleasure like the first warm day of spring.

Once the donuts browned on one side, Beth turned them with a long-handled fork. When the other side had cooked, she removed them from the hot fat and dropped them in the dishpan. She marveled at the beauty of the row of fragrant donuts laid out in the pan.

While the donuts were still warm, Fanny sent each of the children to the porch to eat one.

Tad came right back in. "Ma, Howard is here."

Beth kept at her job of dropping in and taking out donuts as Howard came into the house. "Smelled them, did you," she teased.

Howard took the warm donut Fanny handed him. "Must have."

"Ma, can we have another one?" Sam asked.

"No, you've had enough," Fanny stacked the warm ones. "You eat any more, you'll spoil your dinner."

Howard tousled each of the boys' hair and picked up Mandy. "Why don't you show me how you've been doing on your chores?" He winked at Fanny, then led the way outside.

"What was that all about?" Beth asked.

"He knows the boys will be much happier doing chores if someone notices," Fanny said. "Their mother's attention may be appreciated, but a visitor's is better."

Beth could well imagine the chatter and commentary as they showed Howard around. When he came in to say goodbye, Fanny asked him if he wanted to stay and eat with them.

"Please stay," Tad begged.

"Sorry, but I need to get home." Howard set Mandy back on her feet. "I'm working with Stuart tomorrow, and I need to be helping my father with chores tonight. Just wanted to let you know, Stuart talked to the sheriff. Aunt Nora told him all she knew too. He said he would come by if he has any questions for you, Beth." He gestured to the bundle of donuts Fanny had given him. "And thanks for these."

"You're welcome, Howard." Fanny handed him another package. "Would you mind taking these to Stuart? Both of you have been doing so much for me this summer. I appreciate it."

"Sure thing." He grinned before turning out the door.

Beth swallowed. Stuart would be eating the donuts she made. She hadn't seen him since she came to the farm. Maybe the donuts would remind him that she was still around.

Tad and Sam worked hard on the corn patch all week, astounding Beth with how much a child could do. They might be rather young to understand how important the crop was to the family, but they were old enough to take pride in the accomplishment of a job well done.

Beth kept busy from sunrise to sunset with family chores, each day similar to the one before. There was no time to worry or wonder what was going on in the rest of the world. She made donuts again on Friday as a treat for when Martin came home. A carnival-like atmosphere filled the house, with everyone excited for the chance to surprise him.

Tad watched out the window. "Ma, when will he come?"

"Soon, dear," Fanny said, but worry lines creased her face.

"How about we take a walk," Beth said. "Surely, we'll see him."

Beth took the children out along the driveway toward a patch of scrub brush that lay between it and the road. Part of the enormous slough in the next section of land, the brush protected the farm and house from road dust. It also provided privacy. They walked back and forth until they grew tired.

Carrying Mandy, Beth led them back to the house. "I'm sorry, Fanny," she said, glancing at the boys' sad faces. "Maybe I made it worse."

Fanny shrugged. "Time to wash up for bed, all of you."

"Aw, Ma, we want to wait for Pa," Sam said.

"You can see him in the morning." Fanny rubbed her back. "Goodnight."

"I'm tired, too, so I'll see you in the morning," Beth said.

Much later, the sound of heavy footsteps woke Beth. Martin's deep voice and Fanny's soft one murmured in the room across the hall. Beth's entire body relaxed. Everything was all right now that he was home. She rolled over and fell back asleep.

Saturday was hectic with chores, and Martin cut grain late into the evening. The next day dawned clear and crisp, so Beth and the children went with Martin to church while Fanny stayed home to rest.

The circuit preacher preached on grace. "Trust in the Lord and lean on him completely," he said, "not your own understanding. We're not saved by works, lest any man should boast."

Beth shifted in her seat and glanced around at the rest of the congregation. The head of a man in front of her bobbed, and several women spoke quiet "Amens" at the truth of the preacher's words. Was she the only one confused? Not long ago, this same man had told the congregation that faith without works was dead.

Finally, the stanzas of "I Love to Tell the Story" filled the air, and the church dismissed.

Sally rushed to Beth. "How's it going with the children? And how's my darling girl?" She kissed Mandy on the cheek, and the little girl giggled.

"We're doing well," Beth said. "The children are fun, and Fanny and Martin are great."

"I knew you'd like it there," Martha said, coming up behind Beth.

"It's a fine thing for her to do, and she gets to play with this darling every day." Sally took Mandy from Beth's arms. "Let's go and see my mom, honey."

Martha gestured to Beth's feet. "It looks like your ankle healed fine. How are you?"

"We're doing great. Thank you for asking, Martha."

Just then, Aunt Nora came and wrapped Beth in an embrace. "How's it going?"

Beth savored the comfort of those arms around her. Though there were many hugs from the children, she missed Aunt Nora's habit of hugging.

"Good. I love the children, and they seem to like me. I'm cooking a lot." She smiled at Martha and Aunt Nora. "At least, I'm getting lots of practice. The children will eat the same thing every day, but Fanny doesn't have much of an appetite." She turned to Aunt Nora. "Do you think that's because of my cooking?"

"I'm sure your cooking is fine," Aunt Nora said.

Beth shook her head. "It doesn't seem she's eating like she should. I mean, I know she doesn't have to eat for two, but most of the time she isn't even eating for one."

Martha laughed and put her hand on Beth's arm. "You're doing fine. It's not your fault. My mother had difficulty with pregnancy in the summer. If Fanny isn't doing it already, soak her feet in cold water. That will help her whole body cool off." She turned toward the door. "I should go. Good to see you, Beth, Aunt Nora."

"Thank you, Martha," Aunt Nora called.

Beth waved. "Thanks, Martha."

"She's right," Aunt Nora said. "Have Fanny soak her feet, and put a cool cloth on her head, and around her neck. That'll cool her down. Try to get as much fresh food straight from the garden as you can too."

"That I can do." Beth removed her hat and fanned her face. The air movement blew wisps of hair loose. "I've never been close to anyone who was expecting. We're alone with the children so much, and I worry about her."

"Fanny will know, child." Aunt Nora patted her shoulder. "Don't worry about it. I'm praying for you."

Sally brought Mandy back over to them just as Martin walked up.

"We need to be going, now," he said. "Thank you again, Aunt Nora. Beth's more help than I can say."

"Bye, Sally," Beth said, fighting back the urge to cry. "I miss you." Often, she longed for the carefree days at her parents' store, working at the mercantile like Sally did.

"I miss seeing you too," Sally said. "Come and visit when you're in town."

"I will, for sure, thank you."

Aunt Nora said, "I'll try to think of something special to send this week that might perk up Fanny's appetite."

"Thank you so much, Aunt." Beth hugged her.

Aunt Nora blinked away a tear. "Well, my dear, I do like that."

After they arrived home, Beth put Mandy down for a nap and excused herself from the family to spend some time alone. She walked to the creek and sat on one of the large rocks Martin had positioned there. Willows provided mottled shade, and birds sang. Whenever she had an extra moment, she escaped here. It had become her favorite place. She could think here, pray, and dream.

This time, Beth intended to read. She was curious to discover what the Bible said about the relationship between men and women. Aunt Nora had read those words to her, and Beth found them again in 2 Corinthians 6:14. "Be ye not unequally yoked together with unbelievers." Aunt Nora had said that meant light and dark. Jesus was the light—anything else was the dark.

Aunt Nora said Beth had no idea what she would be letting herself in for if she married a man who did not believe as she did.

"Light and dark," Beth whispered. Before the attack, the dark in John had shown itself in veiled criticism or slant humor. Then the anger of his attack brought out the darkness he'd let into his life. She shuddered. Nothing would entice her to be a part of that again.

Beth read on and found other verses she now understood. She read that Paul told the Corinthians something they didn't want to hear. The truth was painful to them, but it caused them to change. So, Paul rejoiced that his comments, though they disturbed the people for a season, lead them to repent and change.

Beth accepted and now appreciated what her parents had done. They'd hurt her for a short time, but it had forced a change. The adjustment she made was good and necessary. She was happier than before. Their actions might have saved her life in many ways.

The crunch of a stick broke her concentration. She jumped to her feet and whirled around in alarm. She'd thought she was alone.

"Stuart," she said in a rush of air. "What are you doing here?"

He walked up to her. "I'm sorry, Beth. I didn't mean to startle you."

"I didn't hear you approach." Her legs shook. Just thinking of John and her narrow escape apparently left her more on edge than she'd thought. "What are you doing here?" She sat back down.

"I came to talk to Martin," he said. "He asked me to stop by."

"He needs help, did he tell you?" She tucked her bare feet under her skirt.

"He asked me who might be able to help him get the grain harvested," Stuart said. He picked a piece of dry grass, broke off the stem, and chewed on it. "There are several men and boys who don't yet have their own places that can help out here and there."

"I'm glad. Martin needs these crops."

"We all need to get our crops harvested and we help each other as much as possible." He rested a foot on one of the big rocks and leaned on his bent knee.

"Good. I don't know much about what needs to be done, but I'm happy you help each other."

He gestured to the book in her lap. "Looks like you found some good reading for today. What did you think of the sermon this morning?"

"I do wonder about the preacher's comments on grace." She shrugged, unable to explain her confusion. "I keep thinking I have to do a good job to win God's approval."

"I know what you mean. I've talked to Aunt Nora about that very subject." Stuart threw the grass stem on the ground. "How has it been to be out here?"

"Good. I never expected it to be like this, but I'm enjoying the kids, Fanny, and even the work."

"Far different than what you were used to?"

"Yes and no. We certainly worked hard at the mercantile, but here it is constant. There are always hungry people, gardens, chores, washing—it never stops, but there is also a feeling of accomplishment." She closed the Bible over her fingers.

"Some people can't take the constant work." He picked another grass stem and put it in his mouth.

"It has seasons, I think. In winter, there won't be gardens, but the wash is harder."

"That is true. And cooking and baking warm the house in a good way. Coming in from the cold with the scent of baking ... mmm, one of the things I like about winter."

Beth smiled. "I guess my mother did bake more in winter. Papa and I liked it for sure."

He removed his foot from the rock and threw the grass stem he'd been chewing on. "I'd like to stay, but I need to get going. I wanted to say goodbye before I left, though."

"Yes, thank you, Stuart. I wanted to ask you though—is everything good for you and your farm?"

"Yes. I picked up the lambs Aunt Nora had. I left her the ewes as usual but put the lambs with my flock. Had a new calf last week. Crops are doing well." He lifted a shoulder.

"That's good to hear." She laughed. "All conversations around here are about farming, so I wondered. Thanks."

He turned to go. "I'm glad you asked." With a wave he was gone.

"Bye." Beth clasped her hands together and watched him walk away. He had spent time just talking to her. She opened her Bible to reread the verses they had covered that morning, the grin still on her face.

CHAPTER TWENTY-FIVE

The day dawned heavy with humidity. The children were cranky during breakfast because their dad had gone to work again. Fanny, too, was irritable and snapped at Beth.

"Come on. Let's get the milking done and let your mother rest." Beth brought Mandy with her and helped the boys with milking, scrubbing all the pails, and getting everyone as wet as possible to cool off. After she pitched out manure, they gave the horses a brushing.

Beth gathered up the hoes and walked with Tad and Sam to the field. She had Mandy play in the shade while they each hoed a row. Today the flies buzzed around Beth's ears and into her eyes and face. "Kids, my father says flies swarm and bite before a storm. We might get rain tonight, so let's do an extra row today."

"Aw." The boys whined. "It's hot."

"I know, but in a minute, we'll rest in the shade, and I'll read to you."

"I want to play ball." Sam kicked at the dirt.

"No stories or ball until you get those rows done, Sam." Beth moved over to help Tad finish his row. "Tad will dump this pile of weeds for the chickens while you finish."

"Aw."

"I mean it, Sam." Beth helped Tad gather a pile and he walked away, his arms full. "If you want to rest, finish that row. Stop stalling. We did those rows once already and they should be easy. You make them harder by your attitude."

Finally, Sam finished, and Beth called a break. She read aloud while they rested in the shade, but Sam grew restless. "I want to play ball."

"Sam, it's much too hot to play ball."

"You promised."

Beth shook her head, but she had promised. "All right. Do you know where the ball and bat are?"

Sam ran off but was soon back with the collected supplies. They stepped off bases and Beth pitched.

After they grew tired, they talked her into batting. When she hit an errant ball, it flew over her head and almost broke a window.

"That's it," she said. "No more. I won't be responsible for breaking any windows."

"We can move farther from the house. Please," Tad begged.

"We better move way back, then."

They moved out by the barn so the large structure would stop any wayward balls. That worked well until Beth swung hard at her next at bat. The connection vibrated through her hands, all the way up her arms.

"Wow!" she exclaimed, watching the ball soar. And then, "Oh, no!"

The ball just missed the barn as it sailed by the corral and into the field beyond.

The boys raced to the field. Careful not to damage the corn, they searched up and down the rows, crawling on hands and knees for a long time, until Sam finally found the ball. They put everything away, sober at the prospect of losing their only ball.

A half hour later, Beth scooped cooked eggs with garden vegetables onto everyone's plates for supper as they watched the clouds and storm move in.

"I'm sorry I was so difficult this morning," Fanny said.

Beth nodded. She understood. The humidity had zapped everyone's reserves.

Fanny sighed. "I hope we get the needed rain but no damage."

"Aunt Nora prays over storms," Beth said.

"You're right," Fanny said. "Let's pray right now."

They joined hands and Fanny bent her head.

"Lord, we need the life-giving rain you have for us. We thank you for the nourishment for our crops, and we pray safety over our friends and neighbors too. We plead the blood of Jesus over Martin, our home, and our crops, in Jesus's name."

The loud "Amen" almost drowned the first crack of thunder, but not quite.

Mandy cried, so Fanny took her into bed with her as the boys clung close to Beth.

"Why don't I read to you?" she offered.

The boys agreed in unison.

She brought out a tattered book—*Old Mother Mitten and Her Funny Kitten*. When they tired of hearing that story, she told stories from the Bible. From time to time, they jumped when the thunder hit close to the house.

After a particularly loud boom, Fanny came from her room. "Mandy's asleep. We're getting it now, aren't we?"

"Yes, there's some wind but a nice bit of rain, mostly." Beth watched the sheets of rain blown by the wind. "I love how storms wash everything clean."

Sam fell asleep, and Beth carried him to bed then sent Tad off too. The worst part of the storm passed over. Fanny and Beth opened the house where they could, thankful for the porch that covered the windows in the front.

"I love the front porch," Fanny said, "and have decided I want one on the back when Martin adds the addition. We may not use it much, but it would shield the windows from the sun and cover them when it rains."

The next week Martin stayed home. They were planning to take the family to the town's Founder's Day celebration which would correlate with an Independence Day observance.

"The mayor will be giving a speech," Martin told them. "I'd like to hear what he has to say about law enforcement."

"I can't say I'm looking forward to the day with the humidity we've been having," Fanny said. "But everyone comes, so you'll be able to spend time with the young people." She wiped her face and neck with a wet cloth. "Usually, the festivities center along the river near town. Those who care to can go wading."

Beth packed the basket with fried chicken and added bread, a pot of beans, and skillet cornbread. She'd used a small amount of sugar and a few lemons to make up several jugs of lemonade too.

Fanny got together plates and silverware. "Martin is making sure we have trees to sit under."

"Do you gather with a certain group?" Beth asked.

"Aunt Nora, of course, plus Stuart, maybe Lynn and Bernard and our neighbors."

"Oh, does Lynn live that close?" Beth asked.

"They're not close now. She has come the once since she married. Bernard enlisted and wants to go farther west. He may get a chance, yet, with the unrest out there."

"It must worry Aunt Nora." Beth wrapped the dishware in towels and packed them in the basket along with the food. Aunt Nora hadn't talked much about her daughter, but she seemed to be always on Aunt Nora's mind. Maybe this was part of the secret Aunt Nora didn't want to share.

"Pa's ready," Tad said, hopping from one foot to another. "Can we leave? We don't want to be late."

"Yes, dear, we're ready to go," Fanny said. "Beth, please take that pile of blankets. I may go to Nora's and nap."

After several trips from the house with blankets and food, and a last-minute change of clothing for Mandy, Beth climbed into the wagon. Martin's riding horse, tethered behind, tossed its head, and Tad rode his horse beside them.

"Do you have horse races here?" Beth asked.

"Yes, Martin said he would allow Tad to race this time. He's been such a help with his dad gone, and he's growing up so fast." Fanny smiled at her boy and then turned back to Beth. "Martin says it's a boy's reward. It can be dangerous, but Martin says he'll be fine."

"He seems pretty excited." Beth was happy for Tad. The boy was serious beyond his years, and sometimes reminded her of herself when he took on more responsibility to lighten the load for his parents.

Martin drove the wagon to a spot under the trees then helped Fanny get down. Mrs. Morrison was already there with Sophie and Aunt Nora. Stuart helped Martin unload the wagon.

Martin set up the rocker he'd brought for his wife and then took the boys while Beth watched Mandy. She listened to them discuss the possible tornado, Sophie's collapsed porch, and other damage in the area.

Stuart was leading the team of horses off to graze but stopped when he saw Beth. "Why aren't you with Sally and Martha?"

"I didn't see them, and I'm watching Mandy." She hoped to get away from chores, but Fanny wasn't paying attention and Martin had left with the boys.

"I'll show you where they are." He turned to Fanny. "I'm going with Beth to find the other girls."

"Oh, yes, Beth, I'm sorry," Fanny said. "We'll watch Mandy."

Beth hoped she and Stuart would have time to talk, but they had to take Mandy back to their blanket twice before one of the women held onto her. The child fussed and cried out for *her Beth*.

"That girl has grown rather attached to you." Stuart glanced back as they walked away again.

"I don't know how it happened. At first, it was overwhelming to be with Fanny. I knew next to nothing about children, farms, cooking, or anything."

"You're a big part of their lives now."

"Yes, and I love the kids, but it'll be nice to have some time away too." Beth shrugged, not able to explain how confined she felt some days.

Sally ran up to her. "Beth! I thought I saw Martin with the boys. Can you sit with us? We girls have a place by the creek."

Beth glanced at Stuart, feeling torn. She wished to spend time with him, but she also wanted to see the girls.

Stuart stepped back. "I have to take this team to the corral. How about I show you around after the races."

Beth's middle did a flip. She'd hardly seen him since she'd gone to the Cantwells. "I would like that."

"See you later then," Stuart said.

Sally took her arm. "Come on, we're over here." She side hugged Beth. "I think Stuart is interested in you."

Beth shrugged. "I don't know how you can tell."

"I've known Stuart a long time."

They reached the group, Beth sat down on a blanket, her skirts spread over her lap. "I can stay awhile," she told Sally. "Fanny promised to watch Mandy, and I hope that girl doesn't get away from her. Mandy moves a lot faster than Fanny can."

Sally laughed. "I bet she does."

Beth glanced around and spotted Leah off in the distance with two older boys she'd seen at church. When Ester sat down beside Sally and Jane, Beth turned away from watching Leah and smiled at her. She had immediately liked the girl when they saw each other on the train. "It seems like ages since I last saw you."

"I know. The summer is going way too fast." Ester brushed her hair away from her face. "I miss seeing everyone."

"Martha, how is your beau?" Jane asked.

"Granger is well," Martha said. "I receive regular letters from him ... well, when he has time."

"I haven't met him yet. When will he be back?" Ester asked.

"Another year, maybe." Martha absently pulled up tufts of grass. "He would like to apprentice with a doctor in New York. They see many more medical situations there, he tells me."

"That's a long time. I can't imagine being away from Davey that long," Jane said.

"I miss him, but he'll experience more in a year there than he could learn in five years here." Martha brushed at a fly. "He's so dedicated to being a doctor. I wouldn't be happy if he didn't realize his dream."

Beth studied Martha. Her smile seemed sad, and her face had a haggard look no girl her age should have. Beth had never felt that deeply for someone, especially not John, and she realized how the absence had taken its toll on her friend. She reached forward and squeezed Martha's hand.

Martha's eyes glistened, and she ducked her head.

Beth glanced around, wondering where Stuart had gone, and spotted Leah between the crowd. Just then a man walked up to her. Leah turned to him, and Beth saw his face. She gasped.

Sally leaned in and whispered, "What is it?"

"John!" Beth whispered in Sally's ear. "He and Leah are over there." She pointed to the pair with their heads close together. Why was John here? Was it more than a day to relax with their neighbors? Considering the gang he was part of, his presence here most likely wasn't good.

Her view of them disappeared when a cluster of people walked by. She shifted, waiting for them to pass. When they had finally moved on, Leah and John were nowhere in sight.

"They're gone," Sally said.

Beth nodded.

"When is Fanny due?" Ester asked.

Beth had only been half listening but looked around at the mention of Fanny's name. "What? Oh, Fanny? The end of summer, I think."

Ester shook a bug off her skirt. "Are you going to help her when the baby comes?"

"I don't know anything about babies." They were tiny, fragile, and cried—loud. She had never even held one.

Sally laughed. "You didn't know anything about children either. Now look at you."

Beth glanced around the circle at the other girls. "I'm excited about a new baby, but nervous too."

"You'll do fine," Sally said.

"Yes," Martha agreed. "Everyone loves a baby."

Ester waved to someone. "Beth, I think Martin is looking for you."

Martin came up to the group of girls. "We're eating now, Beth, if you're hungry."

Beth rose and waved to her friends. "Be back later." As Beth walked beside Martin, she said, "I saw John."

"Where?" He spun around as if the man were lurking right behind them.

"That's the strange thing." Beth glanced back, but the crowd was thick. "I saw him talking to Leah. Mrs. Ornsby told Aunt Nora that someone from Leah's hometown had come to call, and I feared it was John." Beth turned, looking for them again. "He must be up to something."

"Keep your eye out," Martin said. "I'd like to know what that no-account looks like."

When they reached the family blanket, now with several others sitting around, Beth sat beside Mandy to help her eat. Aunt Nora brought a young woman and a man in uniform over. Finally, Beth would meet the girl who, she'd been told, looked like her.

"Bernard, have you met Martin, Fanny's husband, and Virgil, the owner of the mercantile?" Stuart said.

After shaking hands with Sally's father and Martin, then acknowledging others around the circle, the couple turned to Beth. Lynn's complexion was flushed and blotchy from the heat and her hair was scraped back with no style at all as she held tight to her burgeoning belly.

"Hello, Beth," she said. "I'm Lynn. This is my husband, Bernard."

Beth nodded. She couldn't do more right now. If this woman was supposed to be related somehow, Beth couldn't see it. Nothing seemed similar. She didn't know what she expected from this meeting—a best friend, a kindred spirit, or a cousin that might replace the sister she'd always wanted.

"Howdy, Miss." Bernard offered a charming and infectious smile.

"Hello, nice to meet you." For some reason, he reminded Beth of John.

Lynn adjusted herself, moving to find a place for her belly as she shifted on the blanket.

Beth shot a questioning look at her aunt, but Nora watched her daughter. Had Nora mentioned a baby coming? Surely Beth would have remembered such a thing.

"You goin' out west, for sure?" Martin asked Bernard.

Bernard nodded, his blond hair gleaming in the sun. "I have my papers." He patted the pocket of his shirt. "We have a little time to see family. Last week, we visited my parents. After we spend a few days here, we'll be off to the post."

"How long you plan to stay in?" Stuart asked.

"The enlistment is for five years." He shifted his feet and straightened his shoulders. "I'd like to see the west and maybe get some land there."

Beth watched Lynn as she pressed her lips together and shifted on the blanket.

"Where will you live?" Fanny asked. "Lynn can't do washing, or the kind of work required on the post."

Bernard stiffened, his chin lifting. "There is housing outside the fort. We'll be able to stay there."

"That's crazy!" Martin exploded, his shout loud in the quiet gathering. "That housing isn't in the best location."

"Full of brothels and saloons." Sally's father snorted. "And not fit neighbors for our Lynn and her baby."

Martin whipped off his hat and beat it against his leg. "Life there is dangerous for a young woman. I thought you were better fixed than that."

"I prefer to make my own way," Bernard snapped.

"Have you thought about leaving Lynn here until after the baby comes?" Aunt Nora asked.

"That's a splendid idea," Fanny said.

Bernard's harsh voice cut through their talk. "We'll manage fine." Gone was his grin, replaced by a forbidding set to his jaw and hard glint in his eye.

Beth watched as Lynn's shoulders sagged. She brushed away loose hair from her damp brow. As if sensing Beth's gaze, she turned.

For a heart-stopping moment, Beth stared into eyes filled with naked pain—then they were shuttered. Beth did not know this woman, but she'd seen into her soul—seen her despair and regret—and there was nothing she could do to help.

"Bernard." Martin's voice was rough and impatient. "What will you do about midwives and such?"

Beth glanced at Martin as his brows pulled together and his face turned red. Perhaps because his wife was in the same situation, his protectiveness overrode his usual non-combative nature.

Bernard glared at Martin, then perused the rest of the assembled crowd with a haughty demeanor. Beth found his arrogance almost funny, except that his wife suffered for it.

Martin ignored the "stay out of my business" look. "Those sawbones know about bullet wounds, dysentery, and setting limbs, but not about birthing."

"I'm sure we'll be fine." Bernard squared his shoulders, a petulant look marring his handsome face. He thrust out his chest and stood to his full height, which was far below that of six-foot, four-inch Martin.

His blustering of superiority didn't faze Martin. He gathered a breath, as if to begin another line of protest.

Fanny interrupted. "Martin, I'm going to Aunt Nora's to lie down. Can you help me?"

Martin rushed to help his wife struggle to her feet, Bernard and his problems seemingly forgotten.

"I'll take Mandy with me, and she can nap too," Fanny said.

Sally came up behind Beth and tugged on her arm. "Can you come with us?"

Beth rose to her feet and joined Martha and Sally.

"Is that Lynn?" Martha asked once they were out of earshot.

"Yes." Beth glanced back. Bernard stood off by himself, the others ignoring him as they gave his wife all the support they could.

"I didn't know she was going to have a baby." Sally waved to her dad as he talked to Stuart.

"Me either," Beth said, "and I don't think Aunt Nora knew. At least, I don't remember her saying anything."

Martha ducked her head as they passed under a tree. "That's odd. They were always close."

"I know it's been some time since Aunt Nora's seen her," Beth said. "They're going west."

"Now?" Martha turned in front of Beth, facing her square on and stopping their progress.

"In a few days, Bernard said. They were all trying to talk him into letting Lynn stay here until she has the baby, but he wouldn't hear of it."

"I thought it seemed rather uncomfortable around there," Martha said.

"Bernard is downright hostile—no matter what anyone said. I mean, wouldn't a man, a husband, want his wife safe? He seems the opposite—purposely taking her into danger."

"Poor Lynn!" Martha turned, and the trio continued walking. "Bernard might be a nice man, but there was always that about him."

"What?" Beth tucked back a lock of hair.

Martha's mouth pressed into a tight line, her brow furrowed. "Stubborn."

"Oh?" Beth doubted the man's love for his wife and child, and his arrogant stance seemed laughable in front of Martin's strength. In the end, Lynn would have to do what her husband decreed. "Martin seemed to think Bernard could afford to do things differently."

"Yes, I seem to remember that his family is wealthy," Martha said. "I'll try to see Lynn later. I didn't know Bernard well. He wasn't around here long, but Lynn and I used to talk some. She hated how unyielding he was. His opinion was the only opinion, but I guess she decided she could live with it."

The three girls arrived at the group along the river where Jane and Laura were giving support to those turning the handle to make ice cream.

"Wherever did you get enough ice?" Beth asked.

"We hope we have enough. Mr. Givens said we could take the bits and pieces, but they don't last long in this heat," Andrew said.

The boys were taking turns at the handle when Beth spotted Leah. She stood with the Ornsby family, holding the baby. She had on what looked to be a new dress. It must be the one Mrs. Ornsby made for her. The two little girls of the family twirled around her in matching dresses—made from the dress Leah wore on the train.

CHAPTER TWENTY-SIX

When Stuart didn't come, Beth, Sally, and Martha toured the food contests and sampled pies and cakes. They watched races and saw Tad compete in a horse race with other young boys, then they waded in the river. Beth told them about her adventure with the cow, and they laughed until tears rolled down their faces.

"You two are so easy to talk to." Beth wiped her eyes. "It's like I've known you forever."

Sally kicked at the water. "That means you can't leave us."

Beth laughed. It felt good to be wanted. "I don't know. I'll have to be going home soon."

"Maybe, and maybe not," Martha said.

Sally locked arms with Beth and Martha and pulled them toward the shore. They climbed up the bank and began putting on their discarded shoes and stockings.

Beth stood, brushing leaves off her dress. "I'd better be getting back. I should be helping." She pulled Sally to her feet and then Martha. When she turned, Stuart was walking toward them.

Martha called, "Looking for us?"

"Yes," he said, then turned to Beth. "Do you want to walk around before everything closes?"

"Sure," Beth said. "But we saw some of the races."

"I think you should take all of us, Stuart," Martha teased. She walked on ahead with Sally running to catch up with her, leaving Beth with Stuart.

"I saw John," she whispered.

"You did? Where?" He turned to the crowd. "Is he still around?"

Beth turned forward and kept walking. "He disappeared."

Stuart blew out a breath and smacked his fist in an open palm. "I wish I knew why he's here. I heard there was a farm robbery on the other side of town last week. They pistol-whipped the farmer."

She looked over her shoulder and moved closer to Stuart. "It's getting worse, isn't it?"

"Someone needs to get to the bottom of this."

Beth shivered. What if someone stopped by Fanny and Martin's place when Martin was gone?

"I wanted to let you know, Aunt Nora is getting ready to go home," Stuart said.

"Oh, I want to say goodbye."

When they reached the family, Beth hurried to Aunt Nora. "Are you tired?"

"Yes, it's been a long day. I need to do chores and be in my own home." Nora wrapped Beth in her arms. "So glad you could take time with the other girls today. You've been working hard."

"It was fun."

"Now, Sally," Aunt Nora said. "Your father is taking me home, so I'll be riding with you."

"Oh, I didn't know we were leaving." Sally turned to Martha. "Come see me." And then she faced Beth, her lip in a pout. "When you're in town you know what to do."

"Bye, Sally." Beth pursed her lips. The day had gone way too fast.

Martin picked up the lunch basket. "Fanny would like to go home now too, Beth. I'll stay with the boys, but I have the wagon hitched."

Beth glanced at Stuart, and he shrugged. This was her job, right now, to do what Fanny and Martin decided. She turned to Martha, "Thank you for such a nice afternoon. I enjoyed myself so much."

"Me too, Beth." Martha hugged her. "I needed that today."

Stuart picked up the rest of the blankets they'd brought, shook them and, after they were folded, piled them in her arms. Their eyes met and her heartbeat picked up. Then he held her arm and assisted her onto the wagon seat.

"I'll see you soon," he whispered close to her ear. The intimate comment thrummed along her nerves and relieved some of her disappointment.

Martin finished loading blankets and a chair and then Mandy and Fanny. Beth picked up the reins, setting the horses in motion and maneuvering them through the waning crowd toward the road. She waved at Stuart as he watched them leave. Sometimes he acted as if they had an understanding, but they'd never talked about their relationship status. She sighed.

"What did you think of Lynn?" Fanny asked once they were clear of town.

"Surprised."

"It was a surprise," Fanny said. "We didn't know about the baby and all. I can't figure why she didn't tell her mother."

Beth shook her head, but she knew nothing about what Lynn was going through. "It seems odd."

"We women are upset about Bernard taking her away. It doesn't seem necessary to make this time so difficult for her." Fanny shifted in her seat.

Beth pulled another blanket from the back for her to sit on.

"I would rather it wasn't her first," Fanny said, resettling herself on the extra padding. "Bernard doesn't seem to be the kind to help much. There will be other women at the post, but wives of officers often don't mix with the wife of an enlisted man."

Beth gasped and twisted to look at Fanny, checking if she was serious. "I didn't know that. They won't help her?"

"Some might." Fanny shrugged. "When you have your first baby and don't know what's happening, it's frightening."

"Oh," Beth whispered. If the look Lynn had given her was any indication, Aunt Nora's daughter was afraid too. "Maybe some of the women will take pity on her."

"I pray they will." Fanny cupped her belly. "You'll be with me this time, and of course, Aunt Nora will be there."

"Giddyap," Beth called to the team as she remembered Stuart had mentioned the attacks were getting more violent. She and Fanny were alone, and they needed to be home before dark.

Fanny said, "Lynn might know what to expect if she's helped her mother with births over the years."

Beth eyed a grove of trees they had to pass, hoping no one lurked. "Do you know if they are staying with Aunt Nora?"

"No, that's another curious thing. They're camping along the river outside of town. Why would Bernard choose the uncomfortable ground when they could have a bed?"

"Maybe they thought I was still there."

"Maybe."

When they arrived home, Beth cleaned out the wagon while Fanny readied Mandy for bed. The two cows waited at the gate, so Beth fed and milked them. Who would have thought she'd enjoy this—a cow's warm coat beneath her face and the rhythm of milk pouring into the bucket?

She strained the milk and set it in the milk house, shut the chickens in for the night, and checked the rest of the stock. The night had grown quite dark by then, and a breeze teased the balmy air. Beth deemed it too beautiful to retire inside, so she settled down to churn butter on the porch and listen to the night.

When the flashes from the fireworks reached the farm, Fanny and Mandy joined her. They strained to see the faint bursts rise above the trees, Mandy oohing and aahing over each one.

"You're getting to be a regular farm wife," Fanny said.

Beth lifted and dropped the dasher on the churn. "I was thinking about that earlier. It's a big change for me."

"Do you regret it?"

"Oh no! I never thought about it much, but I like the work, and I've always enjoyed caring for livestock." She was reminded of the soddie they passed on the train. Her dream needed a man, but she was learning more each day about how to care for a family.

"I can see that you do." Fanny sighed. "Mandy Miss, it is time for you to be in bed."

Beth checked the cream in her churn and found it liberally sprinkled with chunks of butter. She strained out the buttermilk and, using the butter paddle, pressed out all the buttermilk she could. While she worked, she wondered who Stuart was watching the fireworks with.

CHAPTER TWENTY-SEVEN

On Monday, Martin went to work, and Fanny charged into activity with enthusiasm. Or, at least, she directed Beth and the children to the projects she wanted done.

Tad's face drooped as Fanny assigned first one task and then another, so Beth put her arm around him. "We'll work together."

"But I want to go play."

"Maybe later, Tad."

Beth had curtains to add to the regular week's wash, and Sam beat blankets and rugs. Fanny insisted they deep clean every room in the house, fill all the mattresses with new hay, and scrub walls and floors. When the week ended, the house was clean and organized, but they'd had their fill of Fanny's cleaning spree.

Friday afternoon, Stuart came to the farm and asked Beth to walk with him. They meandered toward the pond as Beth waited to hear what he'd come to say.

"Nora says she heard from Lynn." He slapped the gloves he was holding against his leg. "It seems Lynn still has some of her gumption left. She refused to go out west. I guess Bernard's parents completely agreed with her and are keeping her with them."

"I'm glad Lynn pulled rank and refused to go."

Stuart laughed and gave her shoulder a playful shove. "Oh, that was bad, very bad."

Beth grinned back, loving this side of him. "What is it with a person who won't let anyone give him a suggestion?"

"Like your parents did to you?"

Beth stopped walking, hands-on-hips, and glared at him. "Yes, like my parents did to me, if you must know."

"Do tell." He grinned.

"No, I didn't like their decision, and I behaved badly." She started walking again and picked up her pace. "But they kept me from making a big mistake."

He hurried to catch up with her. "Really? What would you do if you found yourself married to a man with a bad temper or worse?"

"I'm not sure." She faced him again. "I would hope I'd make a better choice." She had put herself in the position to do just that until her parents forced her to leave. If John had asked her to marry him, she would have said yes.

"Did your beau have a temper?"

"Stop calling him my beau." She flailed her arms and started walking.

"Okay, *John*." Stuart grabbed her hand and slowed her down. "He either does, or he doesn't."

"I don't think his temper is any worse than most people's." Beth knew her answer wasn't being truthful. She'd been the target of his temper recently, as Stuart well knew.

"Does your father have a temper?"

"The very idea!" she snapped. "My father is a lovable man, and rarely have I seen him in a temper."

"How about you?" Stuart taunted with a smile.

She turned to him with her hands clenched in fists. "I have quite a nasty temper, to be truthful, and I can feel it rising."

Stuart grinned. "Tell me more."

"Maybe another time. How about you, Mr. Charming Stuart?"

He pressed his hand to his chest with an angelic air. "I'm the picture of a perfectly modulated temperament."

Beth snorted. "My, my—never a temper and humble too."

Stuart smiled and took her hand as they walked along. "I'm concerned about Lynn, though."

"Why?"

"I don't know what's going on with Bernard." He stopped walking and gazed off into the distance. "Beth, can you promise not to tell Aunt Nora what I'm about to say?"

Beth studied his face. He wouldn't meet her eyes, and his forehead creased with worry lines.

"I don't think I can do that," she said.

"Then, I won't tell you."

"It's about Lynn and Bernard?"

"Yes." He nodded, his lips a compressed line.

Beth sighed. She would not be able to keep whatever he knew from Aunt Nora or even Fanny. "No, you'd better not tell me."

He turned to walk to his horse, his shoulders drooping. She ran to catch up.

"Stuart, is she going to be all right?"

"I don't know. I hope so." With a distracted wave, he rode away.

Beth walked back to the house, chewing on her lip and twirling a lock of hair over her finger. Poor Aunt Nora! It must be hard to know her daughter was in an untenable situation. Beth hugged her arms against her middle. She had almost done the same thing. When had she gotten on the path to be taken in by such a man?

After settling in the kitchen with a tub of beans to snap for supper, she mentioned to Fanny what Stuart had said.

"He knows something?" Fanny asked.

"Apparently." Beth tossed a bean into the bowl.

"The best thing to do is put it out of your mind," Fanny said. "We should pray for them often, though. Life will be tough for her with a man like that."

"Mandy, don't run in the house," Beth called out, then turned back to the beans in her lap. "Aunt Nora is as close to being a mind reader as I've ever seen. If there's something to know, she knows it. God tells her or something."

"Bernard's behavior was hard to miss, at least to everyone but Lynn," Fanny said, filling a pot with water. "She was blind, and I'm not sure it was love."

Beth brushed a lock of hair off her face with the back of her hand. "What do you mean?"

"Do you think you were in love with John?" Fanny asked as she added cucumbers to the bowl of water and rubbed them clean in her hands. "Is that why you didn't see the true John?"

Beth had tried to understand why she had been deceived. "No, I guess not."

"People say love is blind, but it isn't true. Real love opens people's eyes. I remember when I was thinking about marrying Martin. He's sometimes thoughtless and exaggerates." Fanny began filling jars with the clean cucumbers. "In the end, I made my decision on how kind, faithful, and solid he is. We talked about our commitment to the Lord too."

Beth rinsed the beans, put them in a pot with a little water, and added a chunk of salt pork. She sensed she might be falling in love with Stuart but had an open mind about him and tried to see the whole man, human and imperfect as he was. Fanny's comments made her realize she had not been truthful with herself about John.

"My parents felt it would be a good match too," Fanny said, "and I valued their opinion. A person should be better with the one they're marrying."

Beth removed biscuits from the oven and set the hot pan on the table. "What do you mean?"

"Well, marriage makes two people become one, right?"

"Yes, I guess the Bible says so."

"Let me tell you, it's true. I look at it this way. The two of us, Martin and I, should be better as a couple then either of us is separately."

Beth took out a skillet to fry ham but stopped to consider Fanny's idea. She had not been better with John. "I never thought about it that way. It makes sense, though. Two together is more powerful than one."

"Oh, yes," Fanny said as she lined up the now full jars. "When you're with the right person, you'll be more moral, not less so, more of a servant, more considerate of everyone, kinder, happier, and less selfish. When I see someone choose a mate that brings conflict into a family, I wonder why they think it'll be better once they're married."

"Like me?" Beth asked. Just then Sam entered, and Beth instructed him to wash up and set the table for supper.

"You were teachable, Beth. That's a good thing in your favor." She drew her shoulders up and rubbed her back as she glared at her motionless son. "Sam, what did Auntie Beth say? Now get moving. Tad and Mandy, you two wash up and be quick about it."

Thank God Beth had seen the truth in time, but only when she'd put distance between them—as if John's influence had overpowered her good sense. She shook her head and set the plates down so Sam could reach them.

"Here you go, Sam." She tousled his hair.

"Remember, with God all things are possible." Fanny snipped sprigs of dill into each jar. "I didn't think it was possible, but Martin and I get closer all the time."

Beth admired Stuart's strengths as a man and his commitment to help others. He was a man she could honor and respect. He didn't bring conflict into her life either.

"All families go through hard times. Has Stuart told you about his?" Fanny asked.

Beth swung around to give Fanny her full attention. "No. What should I know about Stuart's family?"

"I'm sure he'll tell you in time. All families have secrets, I guess. Yours, mine, Stuart's—everybody I know has some story they hide for whatever reason. Sometimes it's because it's shameful, but other times the pain is still so great—so raw." She took the plate of ham and set it on the table. "All right, let's pray."

"I wonder what he wants," Fanny said as she looked out the window.

Beth joined her and saw the sheriff and Martin walking toward the house.

Fanny went to the porch, but Beth kept washing dishes, her mind replaying the attack. Why was the sheriff here now after all this time? She had managed to forget her terror and didn't want to talk about it.

Martin called, "Beth, can you come out here?"

She stepped outside, glad to have both Fanny and Martin with her. "Yes?"

"This is Sheriff Long from Marshall," Martin said. "He has a few questions for you." Martin gestured to the sheriff to step onto the porch.

Beth sank into a chair, clutching at her apron. Fanny shooed the children off to play, then sat with her.

The sheriff loomed over her. "I understand you know John Bader?"

"Yes." Beth squinted to look up at him.

"How long have you known him?"

She didn't like how he fired the question, as if she were part of whatever John had fallen into.

"A little while—ever since his family came to the town I'm from."

"Did you help him there too?" he barked, shaking a finger at her and almost forcing her to answer without thinking.

"Help him? With what?" Beth looked at Martin and Fanny. Just because she had been John's friend, this man focused suspicion on her?

"See here, Sheriff," Martin interrupted. "You got no call to talk to her like that. She's a young lady, helping us out and minding her own business. I won't stand for any such accusations, not in my house, I won't."

The sheriff turned to Martin. "I can't figure this thing out. The trouble seems to be a gang of men who are mostly stealing family livestock, but last night, a girl was attacked."

"No!" Martin said. "Was she hurt?"

"Shook up pretty bad." The sheriff pinched the bridge of his nose then turned to Beth. "I'm sorry, miss. I should have taken the report you sent through Mr. Randall more serious."

"Have a seat, Sheriff," Martin said, pulling out chairs for them. "How can we help?"

"It could be someone's helping the gang, at least that's the rumor." He turned to Beth. "I got no idea how much credence I should give to them. How about you tell me what you know?"

"John and I saw each other." She tapped her toes on the floor. "At least, he came by my house from time to time. My parents didn't approve of him, so they sent me to stay here with Aunt Nora."

"Here in town?" he asked as he wrote in a small notebook.

"Yes, sir. I thought I saw John and a group of men outside my hotel on the way here but wasn't sure. He wasn't in the town clothes he usually wore, and it was dark."

The sheriff struck the arm of his chair with his hand. "You sure?"

"No, sir. I thought I must be imagining things, but then I thought I saw him on the street in town." Beth shivered.

"When was that?"

"About a month after I got here. The man didn't show his face, but it looked like John."

The sheriff rubbed his forehead. "Anything else?"

"Just a few weeks later, he grabbed me while I was walking home from Sophie's place."

"Grabbed you? Did he hurt you?"

Fanny interrupted, "She had a twisted ankle, and you should have seen the bruises on her arms."

"That was the time we tried to get a message to you," Beth said.

"Yes, I'm sorry." He rose from his chair. "Anything more?"

Beth hesitated. Should she mention Leah? "No, sir."

"Okay." He shrugged and slapped the small notebook on his wrist.

"Hey, wait a minute, Beth. Didn't you wonder if Leah was mixed up with him?" Martin asked. "You saw them together on the Fourth of July."

Beth shrugged. "I don't know anything for sure."

"Leah? Her name came up before. I hear she's working at Ornsbys. I'll check into it." The sheriff picked up his hat. "Your report didn't sound like much at the time, but now … well, now it's serious. Now, we believe the gang you're talking about is the same one stealing livestock."

"That's serious," Martin said.

"You bet." He tipped his hat at Beth and Fanny. "Ma'am, miss, I'll let you know if I have more questions."

Martin walked with the sheriff to his horse.

His comments made the puzzle more worrisome. In the beginning, it sounded to Beth like John was the leader but hiding his identity. It appeared more violent men had taken over now.

On Sunday, the family and Beth attended church without Fanny. When they returned, Beth decided to walk barefoot through the unplowed fields around the farm that were used for hay.

She breathed deep, the scent of curing grass filling her nostrils. Walking by the willows and young cottonwoods at the pond, she inhaled the intoxicating perfume of wet plants and blooming flowers.

Martin had told her about the pond. "There was only a seep here, but I did some digging the first few dry years we were here. I kept at it and cleaned out the spring, and a beautiful, clear pond was born. I dug it deep enough, in those dry years, and added rocks we cleared from the fields."

Beth walked on, past the pond to the fields beyond. She let her hands skim through the grasses. The sunbaked smell reminded her of baking bread.

An ancient lakebed, the same slough from across the road, left a discernible bank visible from the knoll on which she stood. She shivered as a flock of red-winged blackbirds flared away from the slough. When crows lifted from the same general area, protesting loudly, she watched for a long time but saw nothing further.

A gold and black butterfly danced around her head when she sank into the grass, and a sparrow, perched on a nearby stem, sang to her. Near her face, a triangle-shaped stinkbug made its way down a stem. She removed her apron and folded it beneath her head, then lay back. The grass filtered the sun, but its rays penetrated her body with warmth. She closed her eyes.

Moments later, Beth's nose tickled, and she brushed it away. She opened her eyes, but sunlight blinded her until a dark shape moved to hang over her. She screamed.

"Hey," Stuart said putting his hand to her shoulder. "It's just me. What's the matter?"

She pressed her hand to her throat, willing the panic to subside. "What are you doing here?"

"I came to talk to Martin, and he worried because you've been gone for hours. He asked me to make sure you were all right."

Her heart raced and sweat popped out on her face. She'd had a nightmare. She charged to her feet, snapped up her apron, and faced him.

Stuart touched her on the arm, his touch warm and comforting. "What's the matter?"

She swallowed, allowing the warmth of his hand to wipe away the residual terror. "I'm fine."

"Let's go to the pond. Your face got a little pink in the sun." He took her hand and they walked back the way she had come.

The flowers seemed brighter, the bird song sweeter, and the butterflies more delicate. She tried to think of something witty or smart or profound to say, but the comfort of his hand as it sent warmth up her arm filled her body. The terror left. She sighed.

"That's better."

She glanced at him. "What?"

"You looked anxious when you woke up. I'm sorry to have frightened you."

They reached the shade and then the stones around the pond. She let go of his hand and hopped up on one of the big rocks. "I have bad dreams sometimes."

"I understand." He nodded.

She sat down, pulled her knees up, tucked her skirt around herself, and hid her bare feet. She rested her chin on her knees. "For some reason, they've gotten worse lately. I don't understand why. Aunt Nora is wonderful. I miss my folks, but I love it here with Fanny and everyone ..."

Stuart sat down near her. He stretched his legs out and crossed his arms.

She lifted her head and looked at him. "What are you doing?"

"What do you mean? I'm sitting here, enjoying your company on this nice summer day."

She jerked her head back, almost tipping herself into the pond. "Why?"

He steadied her until she stopped wobbling. "Why is that strange?"

"Most people I've been around do all the talking." John hadn't been interested in listening to her. If he did, he corrected her and told her how she *should* think. She had learned to keep silent because she felt like she was losing herself.

"I try not to be like that." He got up from his position and pulled up a piece of grass. "What have you been studying lately?"

She tipped her head and regarded him. Could she tell him? Might as well try. If he turned out to be like the others, then she needed to know now. "Growth."

"Growth? In what way?" He pulled the grass from his mouth and lifted a brow.

"You know how babies and children work to grow? I haven't seen babies much, but I do know they work over and over to crawl and then stand and walk. Mandy is determined to learn how to make her letters. Fanny has her practicing, and her effort is inspiring." She turned and let her feet dangle in the pond. "I find myself thinking how much more I would know about God if I worked as hard on it as children work to grow."

"I never thought of it that way, but you're right." He rocked back and forth on his heels. "In what way has that changed your growth?"

"I look for God's lessons more. Children can't grow up if they don't learn lessons. How to treat people, how to talk proper, their numbers, learning to read—everything. I have lessons to learn too, and now that I'm learning to see Jesus in everything, I think I am growing." She didn't want to make it sound like she was some paragon of virtue or smarter than others. Would Stuart think she was boasting?

When he was silent, she turned. "Stuart, I don't mean to say ..." Out of the corner of her eye, she saw something swimming in the pond. She screamed and pulled up her feet. She backed away and started to fall over backward.

Stuart grabbed her and pulled to her feet. Looking over her shoulder at the pond, she giggled in relief to see a frog swim away. He still held her by the shoulders. She turned to face him and met his eyes.

The beginnings of a grin flitted across his face and when he laughed his brown eyes fairly danced with light.

His face was red from exertion, making the tanned skin browner, harder, and more masculine.

Her breath caught in her throat, then whooshed out of her like someone had socked her in the belly. Her eyes fastened on his mouth—the wide, full, firm lips and straight, white teeth. She couldn't take her eyes off his mouth, and she realized he was no longer laughing.

Beth turned, and he let her go. She walked away, struggling for breath in the airless vacuum his nearness had created.

CHAPTER TWENTY-EIGHT

"I'm so glad Stuart brought you out for a few days, Aunt Nora," Fanny said, lounging with Nora in the shade. "It's hard having Martin gone again."

"I am too." Aunt Nora set aside the soaker she was knitting for the baby to reach for the tea Beth offered. "Thank you. It's nice to be waited on."

Beth turned and poured Fanny a glass. "No trouble."

"You deserve it," Fanny said. "Stuart brings you out here, and we put you to work immediately."

"We didn't do bad, though," Nora said. "The wash is drying on the line as we sit here and rest."

"You keep resting, Aunt Nora," Fanny said. "I'm wanting the baby clothes down from the attic. I was going to ask Stuart while he was here but forgot." She massaged her round belly. "Beth, do you mind? I have clothing we've outgrown to put away too."

"Sure," Beth said, gathering up the tea things.

Beth went inside with Fanny and grabbed a broom.

"If you open the end windows and get a breeze going first thing, it should be bearable."

"All right. A few spiders and cobwebs won't hurt me any." Beth couldn't hide her shudder though. "I'll start with emptying and cleaning." She covered her head with a scarf and ascended the ladder.

Fanny laughed. "I'm not sure you have to worry about critters. Nothing could survive such heat, I'm thinking."

Beth poked her head through the hole in the attic floor. The area covered the whole house but tapered down at the edges. Twin windows gave the space its only light, ample this time of day. The chimney ran through the floor near the middle of the room.

"It's not real hot up here. Is it safe to walk everywhere on this floor?" she called down to Fanny.

"Yes, but don't knock yourself out on the rafters."

Beth advanced farther up the ladder and climbed onto the floor. She used the broom to sweep down dusty cobwebs, and flung open the windows, allowing much-needed fresh air to blow through. "Fanny, you want this bassinet down, don't you?"

"Yes, but I think we'll have to wait for help."

Beth couldn't climb down with it, and it wouldn't be good for Fanny or Aunt Nora to reach up and catch it either. "I suppose you're right."

She turned to the trunk Fanny mentioned. Burying her revulsion at crawly creatures, she moved a pile of items from atop the lid and brushed it off. She snapped open the latches, then, like opening treasure, she lifted the lid.

A tray divided into compartments and holding photographs and papers sat on grooves near the top. She slipped her fingers into holes on the ends and lifted the tray aside. Underneath rested a layer of kids clothing. When she moved them aside, she found the baby things stacked at one end. Beth held up a gown, so tiny it looked like doll clothing.

She collected the layette and bundled it in a large blanket. Then, she descended the ladder and laid the blanket out on the kitchen table.

Fanny wept at the sight of the little gowns, shirts, and booties. Beth filled a bucket and went back upstairs, leaving Fanny to relive her memories.

After more dusting and scrubbing the attic, she rearranged until the space resembled a room. She shook out the clothes waiting to be packed and fit them inside. When she was done repacking, she set the tray back, but found it difficult to get the lid closed. Moving aside pictures and mementos, she rearranged the overflowing space.

One photo slid out through a small crack. She attempted to push it back and then tried to pull, but the photograph wouldn't budge. Being gentle with the old pieces, she removed everything from the tray to dislodge whatever was keeping the photo from moving. The obstruction turned out to be a family portrait. She tilted it toward the window to get a better look.

The image depicted two adults—the woman sat in a woven, cane chair, holding a child on her lap. The man stood beside her, a boy in front of him, all solemnly staring at the camera.

A shiver raced down Beth's back as she studied the subjects in the portrait, wondering why the photo wasn't on display. She set the picture aside to take downstairs. Maybe the photo would get Fanny out of her crying mood. If Fanny didn't know who the people were, surely Aunt Nora would. She finished her work and descended the ladder.

"Aunt Nora is outside, already giving the clothes you unpacked a light wash," Fanny said.

"I can hang them to dry. I'll get to it right away." Beth held out the portrait. "Do you know these people?"

Fanny looked at the depiction and then at her. "Don't you?"

"What?" Beth glanced again at the image in her hand. The shiver returned. Had she missed something?

"I thought you would know them," Fanny said.

"No, why would I?"

"Oh, I just thought—"

"Ma, Ma, Sam is caught in the haymow!" Tad yelled, running in from the barn.

"What is it, now?" Fanny exclaimed.

"He's hanging—"

Beth didn't wait to hear the rest of Tad's report. She ran for the barn, used to Sam's antics by now. He habitually tried all kinds of adventures, without any consideration for the consequences. She'd rescued him more than once.

"He's hanging in the air!" Tad yelled as he trailed after her.

Beth used the mounted handholds and steps to ascend into the haymow and saw Sam hanging near the wall, in midair, caught on something. "What on earth?" Time for questions later. "Tad, a ladder," she yelled. "Hang on, Sam. We'll get you down."

"What if the ladder isn't long enough?" Tad said.

"Let's get it anyway."

Tad dropped down to the barn floor and, despite his size, managed to drag the heavy ladder to the hole in the loft floor. Beth helped him maneuver it up through the opening and place it under Sam.

Fanny and Aunt Nora stood under the hole in the haymow floor, each panting from their exertions.

"He's in the air and needs to be pushed up I think," Beth spoke to them from above. "It looks like his shirt caught on something, and his weight is keeping him hooked there."

Fanny covered her mouth. "The shirt will rip and give way!"

"I can't reach," Sam's voice squeaked.

"Tad, what can we put the ladder on?" Beth asked, searching for a solution, hoping Sam's shirt would hold a bit longer.

"Some barrels, maybe?"

"That will be wobbly," Fanny yelled up to them.

"My fingers can't hold much longer!" Sam squealed.

Even with her bulk Fanny managed to step up enough to stick her head through the hole in the haymow floor to see what was going on. "We don't have time. Beth, you'll have to catch him!"

"I'm going to lose my hands," Sam wailed.

"I haven't done this in a long time," Beth said, scrambling up the ladder under Sam so fast, she set it bouncing. "Tad, hold the ladder."

"Sam, Beth will hold your legs, and you let go. But be careful," Fanny instructed.

"Do it slowly, Sam," Aunt Nora said, her head poking through the haymow floor beside Fanny's.

Beth reached the top of the ladder, but to reach Sam, she had to climb beyond the two upright supports. She dug her fingernails into the rough studs of the wall with all her strength and stepped onto the top rung, her knees quivering. Her mind told her she wasn't safe, but she fought down the panic. Sam's feet were about to her waist, but she couldn't let go to hold onto him.

Sam's body relaxed slightly and sagged against her. She clung to the wall until her fingers were white. Then, the shirt tore away, and he sank, sitting on her shoulder.

"Please, God," she prayed. How was she going to keep this child on her shoulder? Beth's throat went dry. "Sam, I'm going to take a step down. Hang on to the wall."

Her vision blurred. She closed her eyes and rested her head against the wall taking a breath. Then, opening her eyes, she moved one hand down, then one foot. Sam moved his hands with her.

"Sam, you got it?" she asked, barely breathing.

"Ya."

She moved her other hand and foot down, then repeated the process. It seemed ages before she had the sides of the ladder to hang onto again.

"Sam, you hang onto the ladder now, and let Beth come down," Aunt Nora said.

Beth glanced at Sam, who now had his feet and hands on the ladder. She was lightheaded, her fingers ached, and her legs trembled as she descended.

"That's the way," Aunt Nora said.

"Now, Sam," Fanny said, "it's your turn, but come slow. I mean, slow!" She emphasized the word as the ladder shuddered under the force of his descent.

Each step he took vibrated down the ladder and through Beth's hands. Once she reached the haymow floor, she picked slivers from under her nails and flexed her fingers to get the circulation back.

"Sam, you come here, this instant," Fanny ordered when he reached the haymow floor.

"Tad, let's put the ladder away," Beth said. She had to keep going or her shaky legs would collapse right on the spot. They put the ladder to rest where Martin kept it, in the lower part of the barn. Then she sat on the nearby milking stool, her legs no longer willing to hold her, her quivering arms resting on her knees. She trembled all over, and tears filled her lashes.

Aunt Nora and Tad helped her rise and, together, the three walked to the house, leaving Fanny with Sam.

"Is Ma going to yell at him?" Tad asked.

"I would," Beth said, taking a shuddering breath. "I'd like to yell and paddle him myself. What were you two playing at?"

He looked away. "He said he could climb the barn walls."

"You're the older one, Tad, you know better," Aunt Nora said.

"Just because I'm older doesn't mean I can stop Sam."

Beth and Aunt Nora glanced at each other. Nora's eyebrow rose. "I know, Tad. Sam is old enough to know better himself."

Tad ran ahead and disappeared into his climbing bush where the children like to play.

When Beth returned to the house and sat down, her arms still shaking from her death-grip on the wall. Aunt Nora went to check on Mandy, asleep in the other room through the whole thing.

Fanny came in and sat down. "My gracious, that boy. I left him cleaning up the woodpile." She sighed and wrapped a cool cloth around the back of her neck. "What am I going to do with him?"

"He'd better learn some wisdom and quick," Beth said, none too happy to put her own life in peril to rescue the boy. Farm accidents happened, but children knew about such dangers at an early age. Why did some children pay attention and others not?

The day Stuart came to take Aunt Nora home, he asked, "Did you have something you wanted me to do before I left, Fanny?"

"Yes, Stuart. If you could help Beth bring down the bassinet for me? Martin hasn't had time, and one never knows when I'll need it."

Beth and Stuart both turned to look at her.

"Don't worry," Fanny said. "I'm fine, but I would like to be ready, just the same."

Beth followed Stuart into the other room and ascended the ladder after him. He surveyed the attic. "Looks like you've been cleaning."

"Fanny's been on a cleaning binge. In other words, Tad and I have been cleaning up a storm."

He laughed. "The rockers won't come off. I think I'll go down first, and you maneuver it through the hole to me. We could get Tad if you think you need him to help you."

"I'm sure I can do it." Beth ducked her head so she wouldn't hit the rafters. "You'll be doing the hard part."

"Shouldn't be any trouble."

Beth helped him move the bassinet right to the edge of the hole in the floor. While he backed down, she lay on the floor, and helped maneuver the piece to him. When he set it on the floor, the children crowded around.

"Did I fit in that?" Sam asked.

"Of course," Fanny said as she ran her hand slowly back and forth along a rail.

Stuart dusted while Beth brought a pail of water.

Mandy squealed. "Did I sleep in it too?"

"Tell me about when I was a baby," Sam said.

Getting ready for the baby in their special way, the children had called upon Fanny to retell their baby stories many times in the last month. They were precious stories, and Beth enjoyed hearing them too.

After they'd cleaned up the bassinet, Stuart and Aunt Nora made for the wagon.

Beth gave Aunt Nora a long hug. "I'm glad you came. It's been long, at times, with Martin gone so much. Fanny and I both needed your company."

"I can see you did," Nora said. "Maybe we can do it again soon. I enjoyed it myself."

"That would be wonderful." Beth had learned to appreciate Aunt Nora and her gentle ways. "I miss our times of walking through the fields."

"Me too, dear, and did I tell you Timothy was worried when he didn't see you?"

"Really?"

"He came to the barn while I did chores and asked."

Stuart laughed. "Sounds like another male has fallen for the lovely Beth." He squeezed her hand, then helped Nora climb into his wagon.

Beth pondered his comment, warmed by the compliment. She thought him a handsome man, and he seemed to like her—a plain girl with no unique talent or distinguishing ability. She could barely sew, hardly cook, and knew little about God.

Stuart turned back to her and pulled her aside. "I'm helping out the Morrison's. When we finish there, we'll be working at Martin's."

"What for?"

"Martin has grain ripe and ready to be cut. Haven't you noticed?"

She nodded.

"I wanted to ask you if ... I mean, I would like to show you my house and farm."

"Really?" Her heart did a flip-flop. "Yes, I would like that." She often wondered what his farm was like. "Thank you for asking me."

"Good." He smiled at her. "I better get Nora back."

Beth watched him go and wondered if he was as nervous as she felt.

CHAPTER TWENTY-NINE

Martin left on Monday morning, saying he would work a short week then be back to put up hay. When the children grew irritable over his absence, Beth took them to the pond so Fanny could rest.

Tad fashioned a boat to float but Sam played in the water—pushing and pulling his hands apart.

"What are you doing, Sam?" Beth asked.

"I'm parting the Red Sea."

"Oh?" She'd been reading to them from the Bible, making it as understandable as she could. It seemed Sam had been paying attention after all.

Tad smirked. "That's stupid."

"Tad, please, no talking like that," Beth said.

"The water would be high." Sam opened his hands in an expansive gesture above his head.

Tad said, "What if it came back while you were there?"

"I don't think it would." Beth's brows scrunched together. "The Bible says it stayed open all night so the wind could dry the bottom." What a strange conversation to be having with children.

"Yeah, I bet the bottom had fish bones and stuff." Sam spotted a frog and went after it.

"I suppose so." Beth grabbed Mandy before she could topple headfirst into the pond. "I guess there would be sea plants too."

"Yeah," Sam said, watching his frog disappear in the rocks. "Maybe whale bones."

Tad snorted. "There are no whales in the sea, stupid."

"Tad!" Beth shot him a quelling look.

Sam ignored his brother as usual and said, "Big fish and parts of boats, I bet."

"You might be right." Beth pictured her version of how the Red Sea must have appeared. "There might have been fish bones, rocks covered with snails, and plants."

"I think God moved the snails too," Tad said, "just like he moved the fish."

"That's an interesting idea." She tapped her chin with a finger. "The Bible says God cares about the sparrow."

"Yes." Mandy nodded, setting her curls to bouncing.

Sam crouched, staring at a water bug. "The people would crush them."

"They probably walked on plants and around rocks, and I suppose, stepped on bones and other things on the bottom," Beth said as she bounced Mandy on her lap.

"We learned about scavengers once," Tad said. "Buzzards and crows and animals like that. The teacher said there are scavengers everywhere—in water too." He screwed up his face as he thought, the peppering of freckles over his nose blending as one.

"I want to go first." Sam made swooping motions with his hands. "So I can see the shells. If I came later, they would get walked on."

"I wanna go wit you," Mandy said as she splashed, covering Beth with water.

"Maybe the animals went first," Sam said.

"No." Tad threw a stick into the water. "They would leave poop, and then everyone would have to walk on the poop."

Mandy pouted. "No poop."

Beth laughed, squeezing Mandy. "So, the animals didn't go first. Who first walked down the bank, saw weird plants, and stepped onto the shells and sand on the bottom?"

"Me!" Sam shouted. "I want to go. I want to touch the sides."

"You can't!" Tad yelled, throwing another stick. "The sides would break, and the water would come down."

Beth startled at Tad's outburst and noticed his ashen face. This whole story was making him afraid.

"But Tad," she said, attempting to reassure him, "God would make provision for that because cattle or donkeys might accidentally touch the sides."

"Cows would be scared. You know how stupid cows are." He slapped the surface of the pond, sending a plume of water into the air.

Beth grabbed Mandy and turned them out of the way of the splash. "Goodness, Tad."

He hung his head. "Sorry."

Beth pushed wet tendrils of hair out of Mandy's eyes. "To answer your question, cattle and donkeys push each other. We don't hear of anything breaking the sides and making water come down. Moses had to point down his staff to force the waters to return."

Tad leaned back, holding his boat as water dripped down his arm and ran into his shirtsleeves. "I bet they made the boys go first."

"Why do you think so?" Beth asked.

"They do it all the time. Adults make us kids go first, like at church."

"I think the boys would be in the back with the animals." Beth pulled her feet from the water. "Mothers and little children would be in the middle. That leaves the men. I think they must have gone first."

"The boys get stuck with the animals." Sam lunged for a grasshopper. "We gotta walk in the poop."

Beth released Mandy to play but hung onto her dress. "I think boys usually had the job of watching animals, don't you? Like David, the shepherd boy. He wasn't old enough to fight, but he could take care of animals."

Sam snorted as he cupped his hand around a grasshopper. "Any kid can take care of animals. What's so hard about that?"

"Well, exactly," Beth said. "They were experts at handling the livestock."

"I want to be in the front," Tad said. "Of the animals."

"I want to look at the fish swimming." Sam opened and closed his mouth, making gaping movements.

"Me, me! I walk!" Mandy squealed, sticking her chin out.

"Aw, you're just a baby," Tad said.

"Am not!" she yelled.

"Enough of that!" Beth scolded. "Mandy, you would walk as much as you could, and then they ... I mean, if it were us, then *I* would carry you awhile until you could walk again."

Sam's grasshopper got away, but he looked up with a sudden gleam in his eye. "I know! They had carts."

Beth's forehead wrinkled. She'd read the story more than once but had no recollection of carts. "Maybe ..."

"They *had* carts!" he said. "There was a picture in our book. It had carts."

"Maybe," Beth said again. "The Egyptians had chariots which were two-wheeled carts. They could have had two-wheeled carts, each pulled by a man or an animal." She improvised the best she could to keep up with the wild, creative minds of the children.

Mandy backed up and plopped into Beth's lap, the little girl's wet skirt soaking through onto hers. "I ride."

"I think that would work admirably." Beth kissed her wet cheek.

"I bet it echoed," Sam whispered to Tad.

Tad's face relaxed for the first time. "Yeah, I bet—like in the haymow when it's empty. I bet the cows were making noise, and you know what goats and sheep are like."

"But it was so strange, maybe they were all quiet," Beth whispered.

"Not donkeys," Sam said. "Nobody can keep donkeys quiet."

Tad nodded. "Stupid donkeys."

"That's it," Beth said, tired of Tad's comments. "Time to put effort into the garden."

"Aw!" Sam scowled and slapped his hands against the water once more before climbing out.

She pushed the children along to the garden. "Tad, why don't you help me check for any late strawberries while Sam weeds the potatoes."

He shrugged but moved to obey.

Once they started working out of Sam's earshot, she asked, "Tad, is something bothering you?"

He hung his head, his lower lip in a pout.

"Are you worried about something?"

He slumped over in his spot, his back to her. She gave him some time to respond but when he didn't, she pressed further.

"What's wrong?"

"Nothing." Tad's voice rasped like he was trying to hide emotion.

Beth thought back over the last few weeks, trying to figure out what might be going through his mind. "It'll be exciting for you to have a new brother or sister."

"Ya." Tad slouched over the strawberry patch but didn't seem excited or bothered at her comment.

Beth pursed her lips. "Sam's working hard."

Tad snorted, then suddenly scooped his hands, making a hole in the dirt.

Beth crawled closer. "Come on, what's wrong?"

"He gets all the attention." Tad continued digging his hands into the dirt, lifting, and letting it run back to the ground. The wind blew it into Beth's eyes.

"That's blowing in my face."

"Oh." He stopped digging. "Sorry."

"What do you mean, Sam gets all the attention?"

Tad shrugged. "He does bad things, and I get in trouble because I'm the oldest. He gets to do things with Pa."

"I see." Beth wasn't the parent here, but she had been guilty too. "I'm sorry we blamed you. I don't think your mother and father intended such a thing. Let's find more strawberries and have a snack."

Tad dutifully obeyed once more, and Beth wondered how she'd bring this up with Fanny.

After lunch, Fanny sent the children off to play and Beth decided to tell Fanny about their conversation.

"We had an interesting discussion about the parting of the Red Sea earlier. Did you know it echoed?"

Fanny turned to look at her, dropping her sewing in her lap. "What do you mean?"

Beth told her about their exchange.

"Did the children ever consider the parting of the Red Sea might not have happened?"

"No," Beth said. "There's something about picturing real people that makes it all come to life. We know some of their names and events in their lives before and after."

Fanny went back to sewing. "I see what you mean."

"And with the kids talking, I could see it—the noise of livestock, the echo, and the family groups moving between the walls." Beth tied on a dry apron. "Little boys like Sam would walk along the sides, looking for shells and staring at the fish swimming around."

Fanny laughed. "Yes, I can picture it."

"And you get to ride in a cart."

Fanny turned to her, eyebrows raised.

Beth laughed. "Sam saw a cart pictured in a book somewhere and is sure the people had those. Who am I to argue?" She paused, wondering how best to bring up Tad's demeanor and comments. "And I found out something else."

Fanny looked up again from her sewing. "What?"

"Tad and I talked."

"Tad?"

"He says Sam gets him in trouble all the time, and then Sam gets extra privileges."

"How do you mean?"

Beth explained the conversation they'd had.

"My goodness, he's right." She shook her head. "I didn't see that. Tad is level-headed for a boy his age and ... my goodness. Martin and I will have to make some changes in the way we do things."

CHAPTER THIRTY

"Martin is going to be home to cut our grain. Some of the neighbors are already cutting theirs," Fanny said as she sat at the kitchen table while Beth washed breakfast dishes.

"Stuart will be at the Morrison's." Beth dipped a plate into the rinse water. "Will we have a lot of people to feed?"

"A half dozen or so. I think you can handle it easily," Fanny said.

"Thanks a lot."

"You're already doing it in small increments."

Beth nodded and picked up another plate to dry. "But children don't mind if I get something done early. They're ready to eat before the rest is finished anyway."

Fanny laughed. "Hungry men don't mind either. How about I ask Aunt Nora to come?"

"Oh, yes, please."

"I think Stuart could pick her up and take her back home like he did before. She would be tired, but I think she would enjoy it. Aunt Nora still has a lot of spunk."

"Yes, she does." Beth set the plates away and dried her hands on a towel.

"We could also ask Lydia Sandsure," Fanny said. "She's older, but she would love the visit."

"All right. When is all this to start?"

"In a day or two. They will be cutting at Bob Billinger's in the next section and Jack Fritz's place. There might be more. They will move onto the other fields, so you'll only need to cook one day."

A day later, Aunt Nora arrived with Stuart. He let his team loose in the corral and helped Aunt Nora bring her bundles to the house.

Stuart stepped inside the kitchen. "Fanny, I see sawhorses here. Did Martin want a table set up on the porch?"

"Yes, please. I didn't realize he hadn't gotten it done." Fanny grabbed Mandy as she raced by, before she tripped Aunt Nora. "We can bring chairs from inside if we need more."

Aunt Nora unloaded her supplies at the table and Lydia Sandsure arrived with a pan of baked gingerbread. She set it on the table too.

"Now, miss, it's nice to meet you. I can sit right down to snapping beans. I'm guessing you have beans aplenty?" She pulled an apron from her bag and tied it on.

"Yes, ma'am. Thank you for helping."

"Happy to do it. Fanny, how are you feeling?" Mrs. Sandsure took the beans Beth hadn't strung yet and sat down to work. She bent over her task—the coils of her bun sat in the middle of her riotous curls like roses in a nosegay.

"I'm feeling fine, though a summer baby is a challenge. Aunt Nora, I'll peel potatoes if you can help Beth with the chicken you brought." Fanny shifted herself to a more comfortable position.

"Please help. I have no idea how to cut up a chicken." Beth spread her hands in appeal.

"You want to learn?" Aunt Nora asked.

"Do you think I can?"

"Why certainly. Let's begin by cutting off the wing. I'll do one and you can do one." Aunt Nora showed how the wing was loose from the body of the chicken and then she cut between the joint. "Now you do the next one."

Beth cut each piece as Nora directed. Her mother usually did these kinds of chores, but Beth was anxious to learn. Amazing how she had acquired so much knowledge this summer. "All done?"

"You can do the next one by yourself. I will be right here."

"How much time do we have?" Beth looked at the bird.

"I'll get the first batch going while you cut." Aunt Nora said.

Beth sliced and cut with some promptings from Aunt Nora on where to place her knife. "They look a little ragged." She said holding up a thigh with scraggly skin hanging.

"They fry up the same. Fanny, do you want us to boil up the necks and backs and wing tips?"

"Thank you, Nora. Beth can make dumplings from it later in the week."

"It's a good thing I'm around you good cooks because I need all the help I can get," Beth said.

"You're doing fine." Aunt Nora washed her hands and started mixing cornbread. "If you fry the rest of the chicken, I'll bake the cornbread. The cookstove will be hot anyway."

"The beans are finished. What do we need next?" Lydia Sandsure washed the vegetables.

"Set the table, I think." Fanny sat up. "I can direct you to the plates."

Beth floured and fried the chicken, fitting the pieces in the large fry pan around those already in there. Then she set the pieces in the warming oven. She made gravy, brought pickles and sauerkraut from the cellar, and helped Lydia move chairs from inside the house. Her ability to care for a family had doubled while being with Fanny and so had her confidence. The mercantile used to be the only place she felt comfortable, but here she felt competent.

Tad burst into the house. "Ma, Pa said they'd be in soon."

"My goodness," Aunt Nora said. "Let's get this out to the table."

"Everything done?" Beth filled a platter with pieces of chicken and added the plate to the table while Aunt Nora brought a pot of baked beans. Then they added potatoes, gravy, green beans, and pickles to the fare.

"All set." Aunt Nora rubbed her hands together. "I set places for Tad and Sam to sit with the men."

"Yes, they've been working hard," Fanny said.

The pump squeaked outside, and the sound of water splashing on the washstand reached Beth's ears. She hurried to finish the last of the preparations. Aunt Nora and Lydia attended the table outside, while Beth called Mandy to the kitchen to be out of the way while she cleaned up the meal preparation dishes.

When the men voiced their appreciation, and returned to work, Beth put their used dishes to soak, and refilled the bowls while Aunt Nora set the table so the rest of them could eat.

"I hate to see you work so hard, Aunt Nora," Fanny said.

"Nonsense, I'm enjoying it." Aunt Nora took extra chicken and potatoes from their warming spot in the oven and set the platter on the table. "I learned a long time ago, a table full of men will eat until the food is gone."

Fanny sat in her rocking chair. "That's for sure."

Beth put Mandy's doll away and set a plate in front of her. At last, she, too, sat down and helped herself to a piece of chicken.

"This day is just practice for when they're here for threshing," Lydia said.

"Will it take days?" Beth asked, pouring gravy over her potatoes.

"We'll have a slightly larger crew here when our grain has dried," Fanny said.

"I'll come and help again," Aunt Nora said. "I enjoyed this."

"I will too," Lydia said. "Please include me."

Beth took a spoonful of potatoes. "You're a big help, and it appears your gingerbread was a hit." She lifted a corner of the empty pan and frowned at the crumbs left in the bottom.

"I'm happy, I am, to do it. I do know what men like to eat. Next time, I might dig into my recipes and find another favorite. I don't get to do this often."

"I would've liked to taste your gingerbread." Beth shrugged. "I should have saved us a slice."

Aunt Nora grinned and tilted her head toward the cupboard. "Like I said ... I've learned a little over the years."

When they were ready for dessert, Beth brought the plate from the cupboard. She tasted her square of ginger-seasoned cake. "Oh, this is delicious. Do you think I could make this?"

"Oh, my, yes! You would have all the ingredients around, I'm sure. I can write the recipe down if you like." The older woman gestured with her hands.

"Yes, please." Beth heaved a great sigh and rose from the table. "I guess it's time for the cleanup."

"If you two wash and dry, I'll put away and straighten up. We'll be done in no time," Lydia said. She rose to her feet and began clearing the table.

"Fanny, if you want to take Mandy off for her nap, I'll help do dishes. You go rest," Aunt Nora directed. She added hot water to the pan of soaking dishes.

"Thank you, ladies." Fanny rose. "Miss Mandy come with me."

The three of them cleaned, washed, and put away until the kitchen was in order again. Beth wondered why this situation was so different from the mercantile. She liked her work and the people, but she had never been included there. In this place she was treated as an equal.

After Beth saw Nora and Lydia off, and the men went home, she strode to the field as Martin was tying the last of the bundles into shocks.

"Would you like to try it?" he asked.

"Sure, if you show me what to do."

"Well now, you see where we dropped the bundles off the cradle?" He gestured to the piles of cut grain lying in the stubble. "Some places call these bundles a stook, but around here the word is shock."

Beth nodded.

"Now, pick up a heap you can manage and prop it under your arm." He picked up an armload to show her. "Take some pieces of straw and wrap them around the middle of your bundle."

Martin wrapped the sheaf, twisted the ends of straw, tucked them under the band, and laid the shock down. Beth did her best to follow what he had done. The process was awkward, but she finally finished and picked up another.

Martin brought more sheaves to where she labored. "Now, we set the stubble ends down and prop the head ends together in a kind of triangle."

He set them down, and Beth added her two bundles to the shock.

"We want five or six here," he said, "and that's enough. These are pretty big." He picked up a loose pile waiting to be tied and deftly twisted a few straws together to secure the sheaf. "Now, we take this bundle and spread it out as much as possible. It lays on the top for a thatch type roof to shed rain."

"I see."

"This is a good-sized shock," he said, "so let's put two bundles on top. If these would be sitting awhile, we would make sure the heads are facing away from the prevailing wind, but we will be thrashing soon."

Beth tied another sheaf and spread it on top of the pile, then she moved down the field and continued helping until all the cut bundles were tied and shocked.

"We'll finish this field in a few hours tomorrow and move on to Bob's," Martin said as they walked out of the field. When he reached the edge, he stopped and looked back. "That's a good feeling."

Beth turned to look. The setting sun cast the shocks in deep shadow as they stood in uneven rows all over the cut portion of his field. The uncut grain shone in the waning light, as it swayed in the breeze.

"Yes," she whispered. "It is beautiful."

"That's why we farm." He slapped dust off his hat, turned his back on the field, and walked toward the house.

Beth stood a moment, absorbing the beauty of the scene in front of her. She had helped. She was part of this harvest. Martin's parting statement resonated in her soul. *That's why we farm.* Would she ever have that kind of accomplishment—maybe with Stuart? She longed to tell him she had done this. For some reason, she wanted him to be proud of her.

Two days later, Beth was feeding the chickens when Stuart rode up. He slipped from his horse and walked straight to her.

"How are you today, Beth?"

"Well, Mr. Randall."

"Care to walk with me?"

Beth set down the pail and closed the door of the chicken enclosure, her insides quivering. Stuart had been stopping to see her more often. "Sure."

She walked beside him as he headed toward a field road behind the barn. Fanny's voice reached her, calling the children back to the house.

"Beth," Stuart said, "I've been rather awkward about this, but I want to ask if I can court you."

She turned to stare at him, her mouth open.

He laughed. "You must know I'm interested. I come by all the time to see you."

"I thought ..." She forced herself to stop the words. "Yes, I would like to know you better."

"I've been praying about us," he said, reaching and taking her hand.

He stroked the back of her hand with his work-roughened thumb, sending a tingle up her arm.

Beth gazed at him, studying his face. She prayed to understand Stuart, but never thought to pray about a relationship with him. "You're right. I will pray."

"I still want to show you my farm, but we're cutting wheat today, and there are many other farmers needing help." He squeezed her hand.

"Did you get your crops cut?"

"My fields aren't quite ready. I think next week the grain will be dry and then we'll be able to cut. I'd better go." He shrugged and let go of her hand.

"So soon?"

"They won't wait dinner for me." He grinned.

"By all means. Go and eat. I wouldn't want to be responsible for you starving." She laughed when he pressed his stomach as if he were hungry. Then she waved when he mounted his horse. Beth waited until he rode from sight, then finished her chores and put the pail away. She sighed as she entered the kitchen and plopped down by Fanny who rested with her feet up and a cold cloth on her forehead.

"Fanny, why can't things be simple?"

"Depends on what you're talking about." Fanny removed the cloth on her face. "Some things are straightforward, and we make them complicated. What's the problem?"

"Stuart and I can hardly find time to get to know each other." She longed to be near him.

"I noticed he'd come by." She laughed. "Beth, you are my entertainment around here."

Beth smiled. "That bad, is it?" She didn't mind letting Fanny know some things, but she wasn't willing to admit how much she cared for Stuart.

Fanny sat up and looked at Beth. "Not really, but it's funny to those of us old folks who've been through this already."

"I thought Stuart was interested in Ester."

"What makes you think so?" Fanny waved a fan made from a postal card.

"He picked her to sit beside, and they talk together … like friends." Beth got up to fold laundry.

"Friends is good."

"Did Stuart spend time with any particular girl before?"

"No, nothing serious," Fanny said. "There were one or two, but they're married now. He spent considerable time with Lynn, but in the end, none seemed to be right for him."

"How will I know what God is saying about this?" Beth asked.

"Give it time," Fanny said. "I've found if I can't hear anything from God, I'm usually saying I don't like what I'm hearing, and maybe if I keep asking, the answer will change." She chuckled. "God's answer isn't going to be contrary to the Word either. You need to look for the kind of man God wants. That's always the best way."

Beth placed a shirt on the stack.

"There is often tension between two people because of an attraction." Fanny lay back with her face covered again. "Of course, if there isn't an attraction, then there's no interest. We have to trust and believe by faith that God will work it out for our good."

"I suppose, but Fanny, I haven't thought of Stuart and I as having a relationship."

"Keep praying and keep being friends. That is the basis of a marriage relationship anyway."

"Does God care who I marry?"

"Beth, dear." Fanny sat up and removed the cloth from her face. "Don't you know that? The Scripture is clear about us looking to God for things like that. Marriage is one of the most important decisions you will ever make, next to getting saved. Why would you even wonder?"

Beth shrugged. This figuring out who was the right man for her was hard work.

CHAPTER THIRTY-ONE

After dinner on Sunday, Beth left the house to give Fanny and Martin time with their family. The need for a drink brought her to the spring and its haven of shade, water, and singing birds. What a summer it had been. She'd left her parents in early spring and now the work of harvest had begun. She felt tired—not from her walk, but from the week of doing more of Fanny's work.

She had left because of John and learned he wasn't the man for her. Now Stuart was becoming exceedingly important to her.

Overhead, a hawk glided through the air and let out a scream. Here and there, meadowlarks flew, and goldfinches and robins stole down to the water's edge to take a drink. A chipping sparrow sang from its hiding place while Beth soaked up the warmth of the day. It wouldn't be long, and these birds would be leaving for the winter.

Later, the crunch of footsteps approached. Beth turned and smiled as Stuart walked toward her. She studied his face, wondering what he was thinking. He sat next to her and, when he removed his hat, the hat line across his forehead made her smile.

"You've been working hard," he said.

She smiled and nodded. He had noticed.

"Quite a farm wife you'll make."

Warmth flowed through her. Did he mean she would make *him* a farm wife? She glanced at him, but he was studying the ground.

He picked up a stone and tossed it up and down in his hand. "Albert is buying a farm near here."

"Oh, that's terrific. Is he getting married?"

Stuart shrugged. "Maybe Laura, though I hope he reconsiders."

Beth plopped her hands in her lap. "Stuart, people fall in love."

"What do you mean? Do you think who you fall in love with isn't your decision?" He turned to her, a frown bunching his forehead. "Surely, you don't think a person just walks through this world, and if they happen to get hit with cupid's arrow, they fall in love, and that's it?"

"Well, no. You make it sound stupid." She dangled her hand in the water, embarrassed to try to explain. "Are you saying you choose who you fall in love with?"

"I'm saying ... I'm saying I wouldn't fall in love with someone unsuitable."

She raised her eyebrows. "Oh, and please tell me, how do you expect to keep from falling in love with someone ... unsuitable?" She wrinkled her nose.

"Beth, I'm a man. I do notice pretty girls. I'm not blind, and I'm not dead."

Beth's face heated at his implication. She kept her head down and let her fingers dance in the water.

Stuart twisted his hat in his hands. "As a responsible man, I'm looking for a person to be a partner. A pretty face can come with selfishness, cruelty, or greed."

Beth rested her chin in her hands and wrinkled her forehead as she stared off across the pond.

"How responsible would I be to my children if I choose from the characteristics of looks alone?" he said. "The body will change, and so will the face. Sometimes, the deprivation of this life changes people's personalities, too, but I believe the seed is there, if a man prayerfully considers his life partner."

Beth looked around at the trees and water. Finally, she asked, "What about love?"

"What about it?"

"Don't you believe in love?" she asked.

"That depends on how you're defining it."

She met his eyes squarely but remained silent.

He said, "Do you think love is some mushy, gushy feeling?"

Her mouth turned down, and her brow furrowed once more.

"I'm sorry, but I hear girls talk about love in those senseless words. What kind of thing is that to base your entire life on?"

"But shouldn't the person you're with make you feel good?" She yanked a twig from an overhanging branch and pulled off a leaf.

"Of course."

"Well?"

He stood, put one foot on a stone near her, and leaned on his knee. "The question is, why do they make you feel good? You don't throw away your brain when you go looking for a mate."

"I know that." She flung the leaf into the water and stood facing him.

"You should be praying about your mate."

"I do pray," she said, "but, you know, life changes people. There are no guarantees, Stuart. Sometimes people are not what they seem."

Stuart stayed silent. She grew uncomfortable at his scrutiny and yanked another leaf off the branch.

Finally, he answered her. "I agree. I've seen plenty of that myself, but when we pray and ask for guidance, we're going to make a decision based on what God wants, not on what we might be lusting after." He looked off across the pond and then said, "Families are God's plan for his people."

She remained silent, spinning the leaf in her fingers.

"Life hurts, and sometimes, people can't recover from that hurt. If their relationship with God isn't strong, or they don't have one, if their spouse doesn't pray for them, then surviving the vagaries of life is even more difficult. God sent you to a Christian woman who began to teach you about cooking and such." He adjusted his foot on the rock. "And then he sent you to help a mother."

"What makes you think that?"

"You're an only child and weren't being taught about such things. How to raise a family and such."

She planted her hands on her hips and glared at him. "My parents taught me well."

"Indeed, and I'm sure you'll use those skills, but you needed to know other things too. I bet you were frightened of children before coming here."

She shrugged and looked away.

"If I could have read your thoughts when you heard about Tad stuffing the chickens in the grain bin," he said, "I bet you were shocked."

She wrinkled her nose at him, scooped up a handful of water, then threw it in his direction.

He flung his head back and laughed.

"How did we get on that subject?" she asked. She smiled a sweet smile, hoping to bring him closer. Although he challenged her, she appreciated the nudge.

"I don't know," he said. "I think you like to argue with me. You told me, before, you thought young people should be able to take advice from their elders."

"Yes, Methuselah."

"Well, well, the child has a quick wit."

Beth grinned at him and splashed water toward him again. "Well, sir, how old are you, anyway?"

Stuart removed his foot from the rock and stood before her, then took a step closer. "Old enough to stop this slip of a girl from getting me wet. Or perhaps she's looking to get dunked."

She screamed, threw the twig at him, and ran. When she got to the house, she looked back. He waved, but stayed where he was.

She smiled to herself and went in the house.

CHAPTER THIRTY-TWO

Martin finished helping with neighbor harvests and went back to the railroad for another few days. Stuart came by to see Beth and brought a box of baby clothing one of his neighbors had sent for Fanny.

Beth sorted through the box and noticed it contained items for the older children, too, including a darling dress that would fit Mandy.

"Oh, my!" Beth said. "This is lovely. Who gave this box to you?"

Stuart rubbed his hand over his chin. "I don't remember. Mrs. Maynard got it from someone."

She threw up her hands. "You're a big help."

He grinned and pulled her into his arms, clasping his hands around her back. "I am a big help, just you wait and see."

Beth hands landed on his shoulders as she gazed into his eyes. He had never held her like this unless she counted the time when he helped her from the wagon. She savored this look he gave to her alone.

"Ma, Stuart has his arms around Beth," Tad yelled.

Beth flushed and pulled away. She took the bundles to Fanny who set aside the garments the children could wear now, while Stuart took the rest to the attic.

"Thank you, Stuart. I appreciate it," Fanny said. "You've been doing so many favors for me this summer. I'm surprised you get any of your work done."

"I manage." He gave Beth a wink. "But now, I do need to get going."

Beth followed him to his wagon. "Thank you for doing this for us."

"Happy to. As you know, it gives me an excuse to argue with you." He grinned, raising his eyebrows several times in a silly look.

She laughed at his antics. Stuart had a lighthearted sense of humor, and his steady, solid character was something she now craved. This lightheartedness was never something she enjoyed with John.

"I want to take you to my farm this Sunday while Martin is home. Will that work?"

She nodded, pleased that he hadn't forgotten. "I'd like that."

"Good. Tell Fanny goodbye." He leaned forward and kissed her cheek before she could move. "I'll see you Sunday."

Stuart arrived in his wagon on Sunday afternoon. Beth's hand tingled when he grasped it in his, and she thought of his kiss. He helped her reach the seat, then climbed up beside her and set the horses in motion.

They traveled roads Beth hadn't seen before. "How long have you been in this area?"

"More than five years. A few others were here then, but it wasn't much of a town." He pointed to a stream beside the road. "I live along this stream too. It's wider here than by my place."

While he talked about the area, she breathed in the scent of him and pictured them together in this wagon, going to town, to church, his hands competent and steady on the reins.

"My driveway is the fourth one on the left." He pointed, pulling her out of her reverie. The time had gone quickly.

Beth moved to the edge of her seat, eager for her first glimpse of the house. Young trees stood in rows on each side of the long driveway, protecting the buildings from road dust. On the left, a training ring and run-in shed for horses, and then a barn with corrals around it. To the right, the house nestled in a grove of trees.

"Your house is quite large." She hadn't expected a bachelor to have much more than a shack, but this appeared to be a real house. Her heart sang.

"My uncles stayed here, so we added onto it before Uncle Arthur and Uncle Ben left for the last time. They did much of the settling work around here."

He drove past the house, straight ahead to a hitching post.

"Let me show you the outside first," he said, helping her down and offering his arm. "The building in front of us, I use for storing wood." He gestured to the small building, then turned toward the barn. "The barn isn't as big as I would like."

A configuration of pens surrounded the sides and back of the structure.

He walked past the chicken coop and the hens scratching in the dirt, without a second look. "Aunt Nora says I need chickens to clean up the yard and provide eggs, but they're a nuisance."

Beth smiled. That would be his wife's job—taking care of the chickens.

"The barn is my favorite place." Pride filled his words as he swung open the door and led her into the cool interior.

Beth followed him, glancing about. The stalls along one wall stood empty since the horses were in the pasture, but another part of the barn contained a cow and new calf. The milking area was empty and clean, closed off from the outside until milking time.

"I sell milk to neighbors now." He seized a nearby broom and swept the ground between pens. "But some of us are thinking of starting a creamery. We have a man lined up to run it and now need to see about the buildings and a good water supply. We could make a go of it."

Beth was thrilled at his comment. Stuart was just the sort of man to think ahead to the future and include his neighbors in the venture. It pleased her immensely to know he was that kind of man.

He set the broom away and continued their tour. "The pigs, I sell. The creamery might feed pigs, so we have talked about combining the two businesses. Young pigs thrive on the whey leftover from cheesemaking."

They passed black and white sheep grazing in a separate pasture that ran alongside the woods.

"The sheep have shade along the woods." Stuart lifted his arm to gesture. "Some stock—like horses—will destroy the woods if allowed. My father planted those trees. They are thriving now, but it took a lot of work to get them to this state. I wouldn't want anything to happen to those trees."

She walked beside him across the yard toward the house. "I like the way this is laid out."

"My father had definite plans for this farm."

Beth nodded.

"Look at the garden," Stuart said, his voice lighter. "Dad fenced, planted, and maintained it. There is his garden shed. He also planted the herb garden by the back door. I'm ashamed to say, it's some overgrown, but I don't seem to be able to get to it all."

Beth itched to weed it. The plants had been allowed to seed out, and it contained dill and chamomile, as well as catnip and bachelor button. She could imagine it cleaned and orderly.

"My father loved to garden and liked his flowers and herbs," Stuart said. "I learned a lot from him about plants."

"Yes, Aunt has taught me too."

"Aunt Nora is a knowledgeable woman. She and my father helped each other learn about the local plants."

"Aunt Nora is the kind to keep learning."

"That's right, and so was my father. Now watch your step." He stepped up onto the porch and held the door open for her.

They entered a kitchen that took up one end of the house. The room held a table, hutch, a large stove, and shelves. Stuart passed through the kitchen into another room.

"This is the parlor. We didn't finish it, and I couldn't figure out what to do with it after Mother died."

He opened the curtains, and light filtered into the room. She blinked at the sudden bright sunshine. Several relics from the war, including a sword, hung on the wall. A chair and small table, in front of one window, were the only furnishings in the room.

Stuart stepped to a mantel shelf. "Here's Dad's canteen, haversack, and the pistol he found on the battlefield."

Family pictures lined the mantel. One contained a young man in a uniform, smiling and sitting comfortably with his hat on his knee. There was also a portrait of a young couple with three small children. The man was the same. Beth spotted another photo, of the couple—older. One of the man's pants legs was empty from the knee down.

She looked a question at Stuart.

"Dad didn't mind what he gave up in the war until the end." Stuart set the canteen in place again. "He was proud to be part of keeping this country together and fighting for the nation to grow."

Beth nodded and looked again. The man's head was turned away. Had his face suffered too?

"My youngest sister wasn't born when this picture was taken." A spot on his temple pulsed as if he was clenching his teeth. "It was bad in Missouri after Dad left, and my brother and one of my uncles were killed in a raid."

He indicated another photo.

"Mother's uncle and Dad's brother took us out of there. We moved to Wisconsin together. More of the family went to war, my little sister died in an epidemic, and my uncle kept the farm for us."

Beth moved to look at the family photo again. In it, Stuart stood stiff and serious behind his little sister.

"When Dad was wounded, Uncle Arthur traveled to the makeshift hospital set up at Shiloh and brought him home." Stuart took a photo down from the shelf and rubbed his thumb across the frame. "When we came here, my uncles came too. Mother never liked it. She was afraid and depressed much of the time. Some of it might have been because Dad was different, and she was grieving for my brother and sister." He set the photo back and turned away from the shelf. "She died our fourth winter here."

"You have another sister?" Beth wandered to the other corner of the room where a what-not shelf hung.

"I did. She died."

She gasped. "Oh, I'm sorry." How had Stuart coped with so much loss? Beth pressed her lips together and blinked away sudden tears. Her parents were fine, and though she didn't have siblings, she hadn't suffered the loss of them.

"She died in childbirth," he said.

Beth put her hand to her mouth, stifling an outburst. "I'm so sorry. Did she live around here?"

"Yes," he said, then walked out of the room as if dismissing her.

She stifled the hurt. His history was painful and maybe too recent and raw to share. He'd asked to court her, but she couldn't get to know him if he wouldn't talk about his life and family.

She left the depressing room and followed him back into the kitchen. "How long ago did your father die?"

"Just after my mother passed—almost two years ago." Stuart settled the chairs around the table in perfect order. "He made it a long time, by some miracle or just plain desire to live. He got around one way or another. The winters bothered him more and more, though I did my best to keep the house warm. Sometimes he had it so hot I couldn't breathe. In the end, I moved him in here by the stove."

Beth watched his face, trying to understand what he was going through. According to Aunt Nora, Stuart had been a good son, but he seemed to be blaming himself. The loss of his parents, and more recently, his sister must have been hard to bear.

Stuart gestured out the window. "We used the spring for our water from the beginning. Uncle Ben built a spring house over and around it, and the spring's functional all year long. I dug a well closer to the house to have piped water."

Beth looked around, considering the lack of conveniences in the house. It didn't have an indoor pump like Aunt Nora's. This house could do with a few feminine touches.

"Back there is the bedroom my father used," Stuart said. "I still use the one beside his that I moved into when my sister married. I didn't change much after he died. I suppose it's time to do that."

He gestured to a stairway. "There are three bedrooms up. When the uncles lived here, those were full. I only use one bedroom and the kitchen. Mrs. Maynard does the cleaning and washing for me."

The kitchen faced the garden, but Stuart now led her out the other door. They stood on a small porch set into the square formed by the walls of the kitchen and bedroom. Boots, a rug, and wash area revealed this as the porch he used.

"I stack wood here and on the front porch in winter." Stuart shoved his hands in his pockets. "I use corn cobs now for cooking—what little I do."

Beth nodded. "It's nice, Stuart. It must be difficult to keep this up by yourself."

"I have the neighbor boys, Steven or Michael. They help out with farm work." He paused. "I wanted you to see it, but I guess it's time I took you back."

She nodded, somehow disappointed. This had been the sort of tour he might give a neighbor, or someone interested in buying the place. He'd asked to show it to her, but now, he didn't seem to want her here.

"Would you like something to drink before we leave?" he asked.

"Yes, please."

He seated her on the front porch where she could watch the farm site. When he came back, he held out a cup of coffee. "I know you prefer tea, but this is all I have." He sat next to her on the bench with a cup of his own.

When she finished, he set her cup aside. "Shall we, then?"

He helped her into the wagon. On the way back, Beth tried making conversation, but she received only abrupt answers. A depressing weight pushed her down. What had happened? Something or someone stood between them.

CHAPTER THIRTY-THREE

All evening, Beth's mind replayed over the day, but she had no answers. After supper chores and the children put to bed, Beth sat with her Bible, wanting peace and understanding. Martin had gone to sleep so he could start work early the next day. Fanny was up again, restless, and uncomfortable.

Beth put her finger on the page and closed the book over it. "Fanny, Stuart said he had a sister who died in childbirth. Did you know her?"

"Yes, of course."

Beth gazed at her. "What happened?" Maybe Fanny could give her insight into Stuart's odd behavior.

Fanny held her hand to her lower back and closed her eyes. "It's complicated and not my story to tell."

"Whose, then?"

"Stuart."

"But I asked him. He clammed up, and his whole attitude changed."

What was with these people? Her parents kept silent, Aunt Nora wouldn't talk, and now Fanny was saying it wasn't her story.

"Perhaps if you ask Aunt Nora?" Fanny shifted and massaged her round stomach.

"Aunt Nora?" Beth wanted to scream. They were sending her round and round like children playing a game. "I have asked her plenty. She puts me off."

"I think she'll tell you now."

"But ..."

Fanny rose from her chair. "I'm heading to bed. We have a big day tomorrow."

Beth bit her lip and went to bed too, but she couldn't sleep. What had happened to make everyone so secretive?

Noise from the kitchen jerked her awake. She glanced around. It was daylight and she had overslept. She dressed and rushed to the kitchen.

"Ho, Beth. You must be worn out to sleep through the racket this family makes." Martin said. "We're making good progress. Once the new wing is added, we'll double the size of the house." Martin rubbed his hands together as if ready to go. "The lumber is ordered. Beth, how about a trip to town for a visit?"

"Can you spare me?"

"Might as well do it now, girl. Looks like you could do with a few days' rest. Soon, we'll be into harvest, full-swing, and then the new baby ... I would say, take the trip while you can," Martin downed the last of his coffee. "I'll drop you off when I pick up the lumber, if that suits you."

"Stay a few days," Fanny said, shelling late peas. "You can certainly do with a rest from this menagerie."

"I would like to see Aunt Nora and maybe visit Sally. Are you sure?"

"Won't be a better time," Martin said.

When Martin dropped Beth off at Nora's front door a few days later, she hurried through the trellis.

"Aunt Nora, surprise! They sent me to visit for a few days," Beth called.

Aunt Nora met her on the porch and wrapped her in a hug. "Come on in. I have someone here to see you."

Beth passed through the porch and took a step into the house. Her mother rose from a chair.

Beth dropped her valise, her grin melting. "Mother?" Her gaze flicked from Aunt Nora to her mother and back again. "What's going on?"

"My, Beth," her mother said, "you look as if this country agrees with you."

Beth clutched the skirt of her dress, a sudden knot forming in her throat. "How's Papa? Is he unwell?"

"He stayed to mind the store, but he's fine. We've been busy this summer, as usual."

Beth came farther into the room. "I should be there."

"Nonsense!" Mother said. "We have two young men helping, and your father enjoys teaching them. One has a family. He may be able to take over for us."

"Is Papa selling?" Beth dropped into one of the chairs. She rubbed her forehead with cold fingers, pushing away the sudden headache. Did Martin and Fanny send her here because something had happened?

Beth's mother sat beside her. "He's given it some thought."

"I miss the store," Beth said.

"You're obviously happy here, and Nora tells me you're a great deal of help."

"Yes, Fanny does have her hands full." Beth took a breath. "How is everyone?"

"Beth," her mother said in an odd tone, "did you unpack your trunk?"

Beth's brows drew together, her stomach clenching. "What ... my trunk?" She stared at her mother. What was there in her expression—fear, anger? "Not really. I only unpacked what I needed. Why?"

"I'd wondered."

Beth scooted to the edge of her chair to get closer to her mother. "What is it, Mother? What's wrong?"

"Beth, John has left town."

"Yes, I know."

"Alice is ..." Her mother rose and paced the room. "She was reported to be expecting a baby." She paused. "John's baby."

"I know that too." Beth snapped. Her mother was wasting time on mundane things when there was something important to say. Beth could feel it, and she would burst if her mother didn't tell her soon.

Her mother looked out the window, her hands twisting in her apron.

"What else, Mother? Surely, John isn't enough to make you so upset."

"I'm sorry, Beth. Your father and I heard rumors. I hated to say such a thing in a letter. It didn't seem proper."

Beth sat back in her chair again. If that were all this was about, she needn't worry. "Alice did chase him all the time. I'm certainly not hurting over this, Mother, though I'm sorry for her."

Her mother rubbed her hands up and down her arms. "Beth, I need to finish."

Beth stared, the knot tightening in her stomach. There was more, yes, something was wrong. Her throat constricted.

"I have a confession to make." Beth's mother wrapped her arms around herself. "I should have done this long ago. I'm sorry for it to be now, but it's past time."

Beth sagged back in the chair and gripped the armrest. Sweat beaded on her upper lip. "What is it, Mother?" Her heart hammered, the neck of her dress choking her.

"Beth, I—I should have told you." Her mother's chin trembled, and she rocked with her arms clutched into her stomach. "You had a right to know."

Everyone and everything went silent as she waited for the secret to be let loose. A robin broke the quiet with a long melody. How normal—a robin singing in the summer sun, but Beth was losing control.

"Mother!" She could stand the wait no longer.

"There's no easy way to say this, Beth." Her mother took a big quick breath and said in a rush. "Your father and I are not your real parents."

Beth fell back in her chair as if someone slapped her. "What?" She stared at her mother, unable to grasp what she'd heard. She looked for Aunt Nora, but she was in the kitchen, her back to her. The only sound in the room was the roaring in her ears.

Not her parents? She shook her head. Of course, they were her parents. She was their daughter.

Aunt Nora brought her a glass of water and sat next to her.

"Your father and I adopted you when you were a baby." Her mother's words were clipped. "Your parents died, leaving three children. We took you."

The words flew around wildly for Beth to grab and put in some semblance of understanding. Her mother focused on her wedding band, twisting it round and round her finger.

"What? Who?" Beth jumped to her feet, grasping her pounding forehead with both hands. "What three children? I'm adopted? I'm not your daughter? You're not my parents?"

"Of course, we're your parents," her mother snapped.

"What children? What three children?" Beth retreated behind the chair. She pressed her back into the wall, needing something stable and unmoving to hold her world together.

"Well, you see ... Nora took them."

"What?" Beth's loud question rang in her ears. She bent forward over the chair and gaped at her mother. She was talking gibberish, the language of a child.

Beth looked at Aunt Nora for confirmation, but her aunt silently watched her, pity in her gaze.

"Lynn and Evan were ... I mean, are ... your brother and sister." Her mother's lips trembled. "They were older. I felt I couldn't handle three children. Nora had two of her own still at home, closer to their ages, so she took the other two."

Beth stared stupidly at her.

Aunt Nora finally spoke up. "Lynn and Evan *are* your brother and sister."

Until a few months ago, Beth had never heard of Lynn or Evan. Now they were her siblings?

"I was adopted? You passed us out like you would pass out the mail?" Beth grabbed a nearby pillow and slammed it against the chair.

"Don't be absurd," her mother said.

"Why ... why didn't you tell me?" Beth hit the rocking chair, setting it in motion.

"I couldn't bring myself to."

Beth pulled at the neck of her dress, struggling for air. "Why?" she said again, brushing at the tears raining down her face.

"I'm sorry, Beth," her mother whispered.

She collapsed in the chair, her legs no longer supporting her weight. She huddled on the edge, her arms about herself, rocking back and forth. "Why didn't I know this?" The lonely little girl, afraid of being left alone, burst forth.

"I was afraid," her mother said. "Nora and I fought over this frequently, I'm sorry to say. I was afraid when you children spent time together ... I didn't want you to know.

I suppose I feared you'd prefer Nora for a mother, rather than me."

"Why?" Tears ran down Beth's face, her body rocking back and forth. The security of family was gone. She was not who she thought. Her life was a lie.

CHAPTER-THIRTY-FOUR

"I'm sorry, Beth. Your father said I was wrong to feel the way I did, but I wanted a child so badly, and I was afraid to lose you."

"But I look just like Papa. Everyone says so." Beth jumped to her feet and walked about, swinging her arms. "Who am I?"

"You're our daughter. I'm your mother, and Papa's your father. We love you."

Beth leaned back, her hands clutched together at her throat, and let out a breath. "You never told me that before."

"Told you what?" Her mother's tone was sharp, demanding.

"That you love me," Beth whispered.

Her mother hid her face in her handkerchief and sobbed.

Beth stared at her mother's quaking, writhing form but didn't offer support. A nasty grain of satisfaction niggled at her.

"I'm not good at that," her mother moaned into the handkerchief. "Your father and I do love you ... very much."

Beth sighed, growing oddly detached. This was her mother—no, Merin, the woman who had posed as her mother—but it was only make-believe.

"We can't imagine life without you," she said. "We've missed you more than you can know, while you've been here. I've been quite jealous of Nora."

Beth glanced at Aunt Nora, but the woman shook her head. Her mouth pressed in a tight line.

"Why didn't you tell me?"

"I'm sorry, Beth. It wasn't my story to tell," Aunt Nora said.

"That's your answer for staying silent when it was past time for someone to tell me the truth?" Beth yelled. Everyone had been so careful not to step on another's toes. Then they dropped her like a stone in an abyss.

"Beth, you have no call to be rude to Nora," her mother said.

"Why have I no right, *Mother*?" Beth yelled. "You get to unburden yourself, but I'm supposed to simply understand, in a few minutes, something you've known for years?"

Her mother stared at her feet. "I'm sorry. It hurts me too."

"It hurt you to lie to me all these years?" Beth said.

Aunt Nora stepped up to Beth and took her arm—none-too-gently. "It's time for a walk." She pulled Beth from the room.

Beth had to keep her legs moving or land face-first in the dirt. They went out the back door, through the yard, and into the pasture. Nora's grip was strong for a woman her age. She kept a hold on her arm and marched her through the field, keeping up a pace that didn't allow Beth to stop. When they came to the stream, Aunt Nora let her go.

Beth kicked a branch. "What're we doing out here?"

"Finding your manners." Aunt Nora raised an eyebrow at her.

"Manners?" Beth tromped toward the woods. "Who cares about manners?" She picked up a branch, swung around, and whacked it on a tree. She hit the tree over and over until the stick had broken into many pieces. A deep well of tears overflowed, but she continued to swat at everything.

"Stupid." She picked up another stick and pounded the ground, scattering dirt and leaves in all directions. "How stupid can I be?" A groan wrung from the well of pain inside her, and she doubled over and sobbed.

"Come now, Beth. Come on." Nora pulled Beth's head up and wrapped her in an embrace.

Beth clutched at her aunt, grasping at any human warmth to bring her back from the nightmare. Aunt Nora patted her back and murmured into her ear.

After a long time, her tears subsided, and she rested her head in Aunt Nora's lap. Her aunt stroked her hair, starting at the temple and feathering back to the top of her head. The pain eased some.

"Why don't I remember them?" Beth asked. It hurt beyond belief that she didn't know her real family. Somehow, some sixth sense should have revealed her siblings to her.

Aunt Nora smoothed the strands in short strokes. "Lynn and Evan? You were very young."

"What happened to them?"

"You met Lynn."

"But I didn't know I was meeting my sister ... my ... *sister*." She sat up. The last word came out in a yell. "I have a sister!" It was a thrill and a shock to say the word. "I thought I was meeting someone, a cousin, who everyone said looked like me. I didn't see anything about her that was familiar." She beat the ground in time with her words. "How ... could I not ... know?"

Aunt Nora struggled to stand. "Let's walk home now." She turned around. "Timothy is getting concerned."

Beth swung around in a circle. She stopped herself and faced the little boy who stared at her. "Hi, Timothy." She swiped at the tears on her cheeks and forced a smile for him.

He studied her with big wise eyes. "Why is Beth crying?"

She bent down. "I'm all right, Timothy. Thank you for worrying, but I'm fine."

His serious look didn't ease.

"Why don't you go home, Timothy," Aunt Nora said. "You can come back tomorrow when Beth is making cookies."

His eyes lit up, but when he turned away, he kept looking back at her.

Beth stood up and faced Aunt Nora. "I have a feeling he isn't fooled."

Aunt Nora shook her head. "No, I don't think he is." She reached for her hand. "Come. Your mother will be concerned, and she has more to say."

"There's more?" Beth hung back and fastened her eyes on Aunt Nora. "No more," she murmured.

"She'll want to answer your questions."

Beth slouched beside Nora, head down, arms limp. Aunt Nora took her hand and tucked it in her arm.

"Did they care?" Beth asked. "Did they wonder what happened to me?"

"Yes, they did. Evan and Lynn were distraught over the whole situation. They missed you too."

"Do you know how lonely I was, how often I dreamed of having a sister or brother?" Beth drew a shuddering breath. "Do you know how many years I had nightmares of being left in bed to cry myself to sleep?"

Aunt Nora wiped her own tears and hugged Beth's arm. "When you first saw Timothy, remember how he reminded you of another little boy?"

"Yes." Beth stopped walking and turned to her aunt.

"You used to play with Evan and Lynn."

"I did? I don't remember."

"You were young, and you followed Evan around like a puppy," Nora said.

"What happened?"

"Your mother worried you would try to find him and get lost. That's about the time she thought you wanted me for a mother instead of her." Aunt Nora turned to walk again toward the house, her arm in Beth's. "You adored your big brother."

In her mind, Beth changed the memory, from that of some little boy to a big brother.

Her mother walked out to meet them. Without a word, she wrapped Beth in her arms. After a time, she took Beth's hand, and the three of them walked back to the house, Beth in the middle, holding her mother's hand like she'd done when she was a little girl.

When they came to the house and were seated inside, Beth asked, "Where's Evan? Why won't anyone tell me what's happened to him?" She looked from her mother to her aunt. "Did he do something wrong?"

"No, nothing like that," Aunt Nora said in a rush.

"What, then?" Beth asked, taking the cup of water her mother handed her.

Aunt Nora rubbed her hand across her eyes and leaned back against the chair. "Evan was an easy boy to love. He had friends here. After his father died—my husband, William, you know—he became closer and closer to a girl here."

Beth studied Aunt Nora's face. Here was the story Nora had found too painful to tell.

"I didn't object to the girl, but they spent so much time together, leaning on each other more and more. She was lonely, too, because of trouble with her mother, but Evan wouldn't talk to his friends or me. He was going through something with losing another father, and I didn't know how to help him." Nora paused, looking away. "Jean was a delightful girl, and we loved her. She was Stuart's sister."

"What?" Beth cried. How had Stuart become part of this?

Aunt Nora nodded. "Stuart saw his sister falling in love with Evan, but worried about what was happening between them. He didn't know what to do."

"What *was* happening?"

Nora sighed. "Jean was going to have a baby."

Beth licked her lips that had gone dry. "What did they do?"

"We had a wedding, and they were happy. Evan found land with a house on the property. Things were going along fine, then she died."

"In childbirth? Stuart mentioned that."

Aunt Nora nodded. "She and the baby both died. There was nothing anyone could do. Oh, maybe if we'd had a doctor around ... but they can't do much for such things." Aunt Nora brushed her palms over her eyes then rested her forehead in her hand. Her body bowed over, looking small and insignificant.

"You were there?" Beth asked.

"Oh, yes." Aunt Nora lifted her head. "We'd mended our hurts, and I always loved the girl. I'd helped as I could with preparations for the baby, and they were both happy. Evan made a rocking chair for her and finished a cradle. He was working on a bureau too. He's good with wood."

So, this was why Stuart was such a part of her life, past and present. She pushed Aunt Nora to go on. "What happened after ...?"

"I had the responsibility to lay out that young mother and beautiful baby boy." Nora brushed at tears again. "You see, she did finally deliver him, but he was stillborn. It tore her up inside. We couldn't stop the bleeding."

"Oh, how awful." A tearing, ragged sob shook Beth for this woman she would never meet.

"This lovely girl," Nora said. "I had watched her grow into a wonderful, young woman who, under such circumstances, became part of my family. She was a daughter to me ..." Her words trailed off.

After a few moments, Beth asked, "What happened to Evan?"

"He left after the funeral. He was so angry." Nora rubbed her arms. "Angry with himself for the situation he created. Angry, angry! Stuart tries to keep in touch with him, but Evan has resisted. We hear occasional news. He's gone west and found work on a ranch. He's content, I hope. I fear, he continues to run from memories, but who's to say. Maybe he will find peace."

Beth blew her throbbing nose, thinking of the young couple who had begun marriage in such a way. She grieved for the woman and baby she would never know and the brother she did not remember. Stuart must have been angry and hurt too. She was thinking of him when her mother interrupted her thoughts.

"Beth, I'm sorry. It hurt you not knowing your family, but maybe it will work out."

Beth instantly raged inside. Did her mother think it was so simple? Was she just to accept their apologies and move on? Beth had to get away before she said hurtful words she would regret.

"Nora tells me there's a young man I should meet," her mother said.

Beth had moved to the door but turned back to her mother.

"So, when am I going to meet this Stuart I've heard about?"

"Why would you want to meet Stuart?" Beth asked.

"Is there any reason I shouldn't?"

"No." Beth fumed. "It's not up to me, anyway. He's a grown man. He does what he likes. I need to gather eggs and check on the chickens." She rushed out and slammed the door.

Beth walked and walked, crossed over fences, the bridge, the river. Her mind went over and over the news she'd been given. There were more questions, though. Did Stuart know all this, and why had her mother asked about the trunk?

When she arrived back at the barn, she did chores then sat to soak up the warmth of the afternoon sun. She felt cold to the marrow of her bones.

Aunt Nora came and sat beside her.

"How could I be home and not sense these things?" she asked her aunt.

Nora took her time, as usual, to think through her answer. "The family we live in is our family. We don't choose them. We had nothing to do with who our parents are, or our siblings, our neighbors, or our schoolmates. It's our life, and that's the way it is."

Beth pulled up a hunk of grass and tore it apart. "But I didn't even talk to Lynn! I looked at her to see why everyone thought we looked alike, but I didn't *see* her. You know? I didn't see a sister."

Aunt Nora nodded.

"This is hard to take in."

"I know." Her aunt looked away. "I asked Stuart over to supper tonight."

"Why?" The last time she saw Stuart, he had turned silent and unapproachable. She had begun to believe he'd changed his mind about her.

"Your mother wants to meet him, and he's wondering how you're doing," she said. "You must be hungry. I think you missed lunch."

"Does he know all this?" It felt embarrassing to have her family secrets on display.

"Yes, he confronted me a short time ago. He said he acted a fool when he showed you his farm. I told him the whole story, and then I let Merin know she had to do this now."

"I wondered what I did wrong."

"Stuart wants to explain."

CHAPTER THIRTY-FIVE

The women prepared supper together, and it went well, considering the tension from the unexpected revelations. When Stuart arrived, Aunt Nora introduced him to her sister.

Beth's mother shook his hand. "Good to finally meet you, Stuart."

"Ma'am." He looked at Beth.

They ate supper, making stilted small talk. Then, Stuart escorted Beth to the front porch. She went to the swing and wrapped herself in the woven blanket Aunt Nora left there.

"Give me a bit, Beth. I have to ask Aunt Nora something." With that brief comment, Stuart disappeared.

Beth sat in the swing, resting her head back and closing her eyes. She was more weary than a day with Fanny and the children. Even Stuart's presence could not excite her today. If only she could turn back the clock.

Stuart soon returned to the porch and sat down beside her. "I'm sorry you had to find out this way. How are you doing?"

"I'm fine," she lied.

"I have more to tell you."

Beth jumped to her feet and retreated to the other side of the porch, as far away from him as possible. "No more. I'm done for the day."

He came to her. "Beth, I know this is hard." His voice was gentle, coaxing. "But we need to clear up something else, and I think it will give you some peace." He held a photo out to her. "Remember, you asked Fanny about this photo? She said you never got around to talking about it."

She took the pasteboard from his hand and walked to the edge of the porch to catch the waning light. A couple with two children.

She thrust the photo back toward Stuart. "Who are these people? Isn't this Fanny's? Why do you have it?"

"This photo is yours." He handed her another pasteboard, nearly identical to the first.

"What?" She looked at the photo then faced him, hands on her hips. "Mine? What do you mean, mine? I've never seen this before."

"Your mother put it in your trunk."

"Oh. I never looked in the bottom." Her head tilted. "Why would she do that?"

"Beth ... this is your family."

"What?" She seized the picture from him. "Who?"

"Your parents, Lynn, Evan and ... you."

"Me?" Unexpected tears filled her eyes. She swiped at her face and peered at the people in the photo. "How long have you known this?"

Stuart rubbed his hand over his face, and his shoulders drooped. "I came to see Aunt Nora awhile back. I needed to know what this was all about."

Beth nodded. "She mentioned it." She reached for the other photo. "Who is this?"

"The other man is your father's twin brother. They had pictures done at the same time."

"What happened to them?" She gazed at the two families. The men were indeed similar, stern expressions and tall frames.

"Please let me tell you a story. When it's all over, we can discuss everything."

Beth clenched her teeth. She didn't know how many more surprises she could take. It seemed like everyone was baring their souls and getting rid of pent-up pain and dumping it on her. But she had no one to do the same.

"I know your mother and Aunt Nora told you about the adoption," he said, "but there's more."

"I'm done with tales for today, Stuart."

"Just let me ... let me begin at the beginning." He rubbed his hand around the back of his neck. "Families can get complicated. Your mother and Nora weren't raised together."

"She told me that," Beth said, her voice snippy.

Stuart continued, ignoring her tone. "I was puzzled by the similarity between you and Lynn. You have the same coloring and facial structure, and you sound so much like her, if I have my back turned, I can't tell the difference." Stuart thrust his hand in his pocket. "I knew Heat was Lynn's brother of course, but in some ways, you're more like him than Lynn is. I was closer to Heat but saw Lynn all the time."

"Back to that, are we?"

"What?"

"You and Lynn?"

"Beth, I'll get to that, just wait!" He drew a deep breath and let it out slowly before going on. "I know cousins can be similar, but there were other things. Aunt Nora told me it was good for you to be with Fanny and Martin. I knew she had a relationship with them, but I'd never gotten it straight."

Beth put her head in her hands and closed her eyes while she massaged her temples.

"Fanny and Martin have the photo because those were Martin's relatives. The brothers were twins. They married about the same time. When sickness hit one young couple—first the wife and one of the children, and then the husband—everyone figured the remaining children would go to the other twin. But he was unable to take you because of his wife's illness."

Beth came to him and gently lifted the photos from his hand. She studied the faces.

"Other siblings in the family were older and beyond raising more children," Stuart said. "Nora and William had four children of their own, though only two were still at home. They hesitated to take three, and your mother, Mrs. Townsend, that is, wanted a child. The family agreed, even though she wasn't related. They believed you would have a good home." He paused, giving her a keen look. "You did, didn't you?"

"Of course!" she said, sitting down again.

"The only thing that caused a problem," he said, "was that your mother couldn't face anyone knowing."

"I know that now."

"Beth, let me finish." He put his hand on her knee to keep her in her chair. "Aunt Nora was forced to keep things more secret than she wanted. She moved away because your mother couldn't stand to have you all play together. Lynn and Heat remember you, but you would've been too young."

"It was appalling for Mother to keep me from my brother and sister." Beth's voice trembled.

"Yes, but, Beth, you must know your mother, certainly better than I do. Did she mean to be hurtful?"

She rose. "That's easy for you to say. You've no idea." She knew not to blame Stuart, but she didn't care. Anger and hurt vied for supremacy, and someone would hear about it. "Why are you the one talking to me, anyway?" She stomped around, waving her arms. "They told me all this."

Finally, she sat, her face heating, and ducked her head. Her eyes stung, and her nose felt raw, but she would not cry anymore today. Silence reigned while Beth attempted to calm herself. Finally, she answered his question as if the previous raving had never occurred.

"No, I don't think Mother meant to be hurtful." She waited, but Stuart didn't chastise her, so she went on. "Mother was rather ..." She groped for words. "Unsure ... I guess."

Stuart nodded. "I don't think we understand our parents until we've left home. Maybe we don't understand them until we have children of our own."

Beth rested her head in her hand, studying the floor of the porch. There was so much to digest.

"Are you managing all this?"

She shook her head, dabbing at her eyes with a handkerchief. "No, but I guess I have no choice."

"You asked about Lynn and me," he said quietly.

Beth looked up at him, not liking his tone. What other hurtful things did he have to say?

"To others, it may have looked as if Lynn and I were together," he said. "When she married and moved away, I heard speculation of a broken heart." He rubbed his hand over his face.

Beth watched him, wondering if he'd tell her the truth.

"I'm sorry it happened, but Lynn said she was in love with me. I loved her as a sister, but that's all. I thought her affection was just a case of infatuation."

She met his eyes and nodded in answer to the question she saw there. She believed him.

He reached out and took her hand. "Lynn and I worried about your brother and Jean," he said. "We tried to intervene.

When they were together, we made their outings a foursome. We tried everything. In the end, Lynn told me she loved me, but I didn't feel the same, and then Jean died. I don't know but losing Jean and the baby and then Heat left—it was unbearable for her. She acted as if her life were over."

Beth nodded. This man they were talking about was her brother. She could imagine a sister would suffer as he suffered.

"Lynn married Bernard very suddenly." Stuart shrugged. "I worry that I'm to blame, and Aunt Nora is concerned about them too. I've visited with them a few times, and though Bernard is rather unbending, I think he loves Lynn."

"Does she love him?"

He swiped his hand through his hair. "I don't know. Bernard was completely smitten, as they say."

Beth shook her head. "Lynn looked at me with such pain and sadness in her eyes. I didn't understand it. If only we could have talked like real sisters."

Stuart nodded.

"Why do you call Evan, Heat?"

"Don't you know?" Stuart leaned back to look at her, his eyes narrowed.

"What?" It was an innocent question, surely not worthy of the disbelief she saw on his face. "What can be so serious about a nickname?"

"Heaton," Stuart said. "His name is Heaton."

Now Beth reared back, her mouth gaping open. "What do you mean?"

"Evan Heaton," Stuart said. "We call him Heat."

"Heaton? But Aunt Nora's last name is Durand."

He shrugged. "I guess Will and Nora felt it was important for them to keep their family name."

She straightened her back and stretched her neck around to look him full in the face. "My last name was Heaton?"

Stuart nodded.

Beth plopped her head in her hand, rubbing at the furrow between her brows. This was all too much. She glanced at the photo again, her exhausted mind refusing to take everything in.

"There is more family?"

"Let's see. Martin would be your first cousin. Martin's mother and your father were part of a rather large family. There must be cousins all around. Some are in Missouri, Iowa, and Wisconsin, but there are many aunts and uncles." He shrugged. "Fanny is Nora's niece. You'll have to ask Aunt Nora about the rest. I think she's a great one to keep the family history straight."

"At least someone does," Beth murmured.

"When are you going back to Martin's?"

"I don't know—a day or two. I need to talk with Mother again. I don't want to leave until this is mended ...if it can be."

"Would you like me to take you?"

"Thank you." She sighed. "I'm sorry, Stuart. My family has caused you a lot of heartache."

"We do it to each other." He smiled. "How about you stay until Sunday, and I'll pick you up and take you back?"

Beth nodded, wondering if she could sort everything out by then.

Alone in her room, Beth studied the family picture. She longed to have a life-size version so she could look into her parents' eyes. They could not have known that only a few months after they happily posed for this portrait, their family would be ripped apart.

She could see Lynn in the little girl leaning on her mother's knee, and her brother took after his father—*their father*—with the same jawline. Tears fell when she traced her mother's face—a beautiful mother with a kind face. Propping the portrait next to her bed, she blew out the candle, and wrapped herself in quilts against the shivering that shook her body.

CHAPTER THIRTY-SIX

"Beth, I think it's time we talk," her mother said the next morning, as soon as Aunt Nora had gone outside to do chores.

"I thought we were talking, Mother."

"Sit down."

Beth sighed. "Mother, I'm tired. I didn't sleep all that much last night. I planned to help Aunt Nora do chores. Do we have to hash this out again today?"

"Yes, Beth, there's something I want to say. Maybe I'm trying to ease my conscience, but I want to tell you. You can help Nora in a few minutes." She knotted her apron in her hands.

Ice dropped into Beth's stomach. She had no stamina left for further confessions.

Her mother sat on the footstool at Beth's feet. "Nora tells me I keep myself away from everyone. I guess I'm afraid to be hurt. I've always felt I had nothing to offer, and no one would care whether they got to know me or not." She accordion-pleated the edge of her apron. "I was afraid to lose you because I didn't think I deserved a child. You see, I thought I was being punished ... I mean ... because I couldn't have children."

Beth clutched her folded arms tightly to her stomach. Some of what her mother said rang true. Beth often felt that her opinion, and even her existence, didn't matter.

Her mother dabbed her eyes and blew her nose on a handkerchief. "Your father and I finally talked about this last month. I've blamed myself, all these years, for not being able to have children. I'm sorry if it isn't proper to discuss such things with a young girl, but I've made mistakes by not talking for so long." She twisted her fingers together. "The doctor thinks the sickness Grant had, before we got married, left him unable to father children."

Beth watched her mother look out the window and at the ceiling, anywhere but at her. She waited, puzzled by her mother's pain.

"You see, when we got married, we were young. I was afraid of having a baby and afraid I wouldn't know how to care for a baby, so I ... I prayed for us not to have a child right away."

Beth gaped at her.

Her mother wiped her face. "I know it was selfish of me, and Nora tells me it's silly."

Beth agreed with Aunt Nora but kept silent. Who was she to understand what her mother had been like at nineteen? She didn't even understand herself.

"I did other things too," she said. "There was another boy before your father. Oh, Grant knows about him, I told him the whole thing. But you see, I loved Jim, and we planned to marry ... but he was killed. Though I married Grant, I still loved a memory and didn't want children with another man."

Beth stared at her mother, remembering the photo of her and Papa's wedding. She was beautiful, and Papa so handsome. "I'm sorry, Mother. That must have been hard."

She nodded. "Then, time passed, and no baby. I prayed and prayed for one. Over and over, I confessed my sin, but it didn't happen." She twisted the embroidered handkerchief in her hands. "You see, I thought I wasn't supposed to have a child of my own, so I would lose you too. It's a terrifying way to live."

Beth nodded. She well knew the terror of thoughts bombarding the mind over and over—thoughts that wouldn't go away.

"Nora and I talked about the Lord Jesus and the things we heard when we were growing up," her mother said. "Our parents and church meant well, but people thought God was waiting to punish us. If a situation went wrong or was contrary to what we expected, we found something to blame. Life was a constant retribution." She surged from her chair and paced the small space between them. "Nora and I both realize this was foolish—now that we know Jesus as our Savior. We know he loves us and doesn't want to hurt us." She sat again and faced Beth. "It's the decisions we make, not God, that cause the pain in our lives, but he is always with us, guiding us if we will listen."

Beth nodded, then a sudden thought came back to her. "Mother, was I ever left alone in a child's bed?"

"How do you mean?"

"I have a dream, over and over. I'm in a bed—a crib, I think—and left there. I cry and cry, but no one comes." She shuddered and clutched her arms around herself. "I see faces laughing at my tears, and then I can't move. Pain knots in my stomach, like hunger, but worse. It's fear—terror, really—because no one will come."

"I'm so sorry, Beth."

"I had another, where I'm older, and I try, over and over, to run away from danger, but can't move. Maybe everyone has such a dream, but it terrifies me. I was frightened to leave home and come here, to a stranger who might not like me."

Her mother pulled Beth into her arms. "I'm so sorry. I didn't know. You did cry a lot when we got you. We thought you would be missing your mother, so your father and I never left you alone."

Beth sobbed against her mother's shoulder. Here finally, was acceptance and understanding from the woman she called mother.

"It was a terrible time for your family when your parents died." She patted Beth's back. "Evan and Lynn were too young to care for you, so you might have been left—while your mother was sick, and when she died—before we came to get you."

"How old was I?" Beth asked.

"We got you at nine months."

Beth leaned back and faced her mother. "No wonder I don't remember anything."

After they returned from church, the three women prepared a meal. Stuart arrived to take her back to the farm. Beth watched his reactions to her mother. They appeared to get along fine.

After they'd eaten, Beth began to clear away the dishes.

"I'll finish them now, dear," Nora said. "You and Stuart need to get on to Fanny's."

"I'm glad you're with Fanny," her mother said. "Nora tells me she could have the baby any day."

Beth looked at Aunt Nora, who nodded and said, "I expect it soon, but don't worry, Fanny knows what to do."

"You know," her mother said, "more and more, I think this is where we should live."

Nora and Beth stared at her for a moment. Beth barely breathed.

"We have a nice community." Aunt Nora picked up dishes from the table.

"You would move?" Beth asked her mother when she could get the words out.

"Your father and I have given it serious thought."

"I'm sorry to interrupt," Stuart said, "but we'd better get out to the farm."

Beth picked up her bag and hugged her mother. "I love you, Mom. Please tell Papa I love him and miss him."

Tears filled her mother's eyes. "I'm so proud of you. Your father and I love you very much. I'm sorry I didn't do things differently, but ... well, maybe it will be all right despite my mistakes."

"Yes, Mom, it's fine."

Beth and Stuart didn't say much as they started for Fanny's place. She looked around, hardly recognizing where she was, and yet it felt so familiar. So much had changed inside her, she almost expected the scene to change outside.

"Is it all right?" Stuart said. "What you've learned?"

"There's nothing I can do about it," she muttered. "Aunt Nora and I talked this morning. She has such faith, and it gets on me. She says it'll all work out."

"Have you and your mother talked?"

"Several times. She's worried I won't forgive her."

"It looked like you two were getting along nicely."

"I might not have made sense of it all, but there isn't anything to forgive. Mother and Papa gave me a home. They did the best they could, and they're dear to me. I miss Papa more than I would have thought possible, and Mom too, of course. After Fanny has the baby and all is well, I look forward to going back home."

"What if your parents move here?"

"That would be wonderful. I could see Aunt Nora and Fanny all the time." She sighed. "I miss Fanny and the children even after such a short time away."

"I see." After a moment, he continued, "Is there anyone else you might miss?"

She went on as if she hadn't heard. "I know Fanny would like me to stay longer, and I enjoy being with Aunt Nora. I would like to know Lynn better, but I can't since she will be out west after she has the baby, and I've never met Evan. Maybe I never will."

Stuart stopped the horses with a sudden pull to the reins. "Beth, would you leave?"

She studied his face. So much had changed. Was he asking her to stay? "Why would I stay?"

"I thought … I mean." He removed his hat. "You don't want me to come courting?"

She shook her head. "I thought you'd changed your mind." She waited for him to look at her. "What happened at your house? Did I do something wrong?"

"No, no, it's not you." He turned and set the horses in motion again. "I need to tell you about Mother sometime, but for now … well, Mother was unhappy, and her mind settled on terrible dark thoughts. Seeing you standing in her kitchen threw me. It made me anxious that you would be like her. I could not go through that again."

She had no idea he'd experienced such torment because of his mother.

Stuart flicked the reins. "I talked to Aunt Nora about my worry when I came to visit her. You see, I never did talk about what happened back then."

"Stuart," she whispered, "I'm sorry it was so difficult with your mother. I had no idea." She wanted to get this right. "You're a good friend to Aunt Nora. You were a good friend to Lynn too. You're a friend of Evan, my brother. For some reason, you run like a thread through my family. Why is that?"

"I guess I was there."

"Maybe." She glanced down when he took her hand. Stuart filled her thoughts so often. During the day as she worked around the house, she wondered what he would say about this or that. She looked for him to stop and see her—wanted to be near him.

They pulled up in Fanny's yard, and the children burst out of the house with the barking dog and questions. They climbed into the wagon to get closer and clung to her. She met Stuart's eyes, just as Sam was pulling her head down to his for a sloppy kiss.

CHAPTER THIRTY-SEVEN

When the children were in bed for the night, Beth washed dishes while Martin and Fanny—her with her feet in a pan of cool water—rested on the porch. She joined them later and brought Fanny a drink of water. Then she plopped in a chair and leaned back to watch the sky. A pleasant breeze kept the mosquitos away.

"Beth," Fanny murmured, "it's a relief to have you here with us again."

"Thank you, Fanny." Beth marveled how dear they had become to her. "I'm happy too."

"Did you have a good visit with your mother?" Fanny asked.

"I don't know if you would call it good, but I think it was a relief for her to finally tell me." Beth began to take down her hair. "Fanny, I keep wondering about Alice. It's upsetting to think what she's going through on account of John. He proved something my parents suspected. And who knows what would have happened to me if not for their concern. I'm sorry Alice got hurt by John, and I feel stupid I didn't see what he was like."

Martin huffed. "Don't be doing that to yourself now, girl. Men can be sly when they want to be. If they have a bend that way, they'll find ways to trick a gal. Any man that would do such a thing is a lowdown polecat—"

"Now, Martin," Fanny interrupted.

"Well, he *is* a lowdown skunk." Martin huffed again.

Beth smiled. "Thank you."

Fanny sighed as she pulled her swollen feet from the pan of water. "I'm sorry, Beth, but I'm done in. I might not sleep well, but it's time to try."

"It's a nice night," Beth said.

"Yes, thankfully," Fanny said. "The windows are open as wide as I can get them, and the breeze is cooling the air in there."

Martin got up. "Well, honey, let's get you settled."

Fanny reached up for his hands, and her husband helped her to her feet and off to their room.

"Goodnight, Beth," Fanny murmured.

"Yes, goodnight."

Beth savored the coolness of the evening. A baby in just a few weeks, how would they ever be ready?

The next day, Beth dried her hands on a towel and pulled out the large bread bowl. "What else should I bake today?"

"How about a pan of gingerbread, after you get the bread going? We might have neighbors to feed if anyone stops to help with the house," Fanny said.

"Oh, that's perfect." Beth added a scoop of lard to the bowl and stirred it into her sour dough mixture. "You know, Fanny, I've been thinking of something Mom told me about John. I guess his mother complained to her that John had always been a problem, ever since his sister died."

"Really? Did he ever mention a sister to you?"

"Oh, yes, and he loved his sister. He said she was his mother's favorite, though. I guess she was blond like his mother. I know you haven't seen John, but he has darker coloring—dark hair, darker skin—swarthy, I guess they call it."

"Is his father dark?"

"Yes, I would say so."

Fanny paused in her sewing. "What happened to his sister?"

"She drowned." Beth added floor to her bowl and beat it into the mixture. "John was six, and she was eight."

"Did he tell you what happened?"

"He said they were both playing in the water—a stream, I think, that ran near their house." Beth mixed in more flour. "The edge broke away, and they were too deep. He was able to get himself out but couldn't get to her. His mother blamed him for not rescuing her."

Fanny's hands lay unmoving in her lap, and she looked at Beth. "That is so sad. He was six?"

"Yes. John had no idea how he made it." Beth stirred the mixture, scraped down the sides of the bowl and added more flour. "If you'd seen the look on his face when he remembered it, you'd wonder how he's alive today."

"That's a lot to expect from a six-year-old who was trying to rescue himself."

"His parents moved from that place afterward."

Fanny shook her head.

"I felt so bad for him when he told me. He still blames himself." Beth poured the mass of dough onto the table and gave it a smart pat. "The memory of nearly drowning terrifies him, and he avoids water if at all possible."

The clang of a shovel striking stone outside the window interrupted their talk. The children's voices peppered Martin with nonstop questions as he worked on the new wing.

Fanny laughed. "It's a good thing Martin can dig out the foundation and talk at the same time."

"More like listen at the same time. I hear questions, but not many answers." Beth laughed, happy to have someone else the recipient of the children's questions. "Have you any idea when the neighbor men are coming to help?"

"Possibly this afternoon. Martin asked several of them." Fanny picked up her sewing again.

"Good. I only have to provide a lunch." Beth wiped out the bowl and began to knead the bread.

Neighbors stopped to help with the foundation as they found time. Beth made coffee, sandwiches, and cookies and did her best to keep Mandy and Sam out of their way.

Howard arrived with more lumber the next day, and in short order, the men put up the outside walls. The structure started to look like a house when they built the rafters. Stuart came and worked steadily, pounding on the existing house as they attached the new to the old. Beth noticed Stuart had the skills to pitch in wherever it was needed.

The tie-in to the old house happened on one of the hottest days they'd had.

"I hate to ask men to be on the roof in this heat," Martin explained when he took a break to check on Fanny. "When it's done, we can put up siding where the shade is."

The weather continued hot and relentless. The men came to work and connected the two houses and finished the roofing. By afternoon, thunder began to rumble in the distance and the sky looked ominous. Everyone headed home.

"Beth, can you help me cover the window openings?" Martin glanced at the sky. "Boys, get chores done—real quick now."

Beth rushed out to help as the wind rose. Holding onto the boards Martin tacked over the window openings took all her strength.

"This won't be tight but should keep out most of the water." Martin talked around the nails between his lips.

When the windows were covered, Beth searched the farmyard for anything not put away that would blow in a storm. She found a milk pail, a hoe, and more vegetables to bring in. Her apron full of produce, she barely got in the door before driving raindrops began.

"We're in for it now," Martin said as he paced from window to window watching the storm. "We need the rain though."

The next morning brought little relief from the heat and humidity and no one came to assist Martin.

"Beth, with your help, I think we can set the glass in the windows." Martin wiped the perspiration collecting on his forehead. "It's so humid I'm guessing there's going to be rough weather before this heatwave breaks."

"I wish we had our cellar completed," Fanny said.

"We will soon," Martin said.

Another storm passed over, leaving more rain and taking the humidity with it.

Mr. Zick, a neighbor on the east side of them, stopped by the next day. "I was in town this morning and heard they had tornados to the east," he said. "There's litter and parts of trees and houses all over several counties east of here."

After he left, Beth asked Fanny, "Do you suppose my parents had the storm?"

"We need to believe the best and not worry," Fanny said. "We'll hear soon enough, I expect."

The next day, a rider from town brought a message for Beth. Her hands trembled as she opened the telegram.

WE'RE FINE. LOT OF DAMAGE. HOUSE STANDING. LOVE, PAPA.

She brushed away tears. "I should be there."

As she continued her routine work—cooking, cleaning, washing—she thought about what her parents were going through as they assessed damage and cleaned up the mercantile. The lovely brick house her father built because her mother worried about fires was still standing, but was it damaged?

Days later, a letter arrived. Beth tore into it.

Dear Beth,

The house wasn't touched at all, and we are putting up several people. The mercantile is patched, and most of the goods survived. Your father is giving away supplies. I'm not sure if any of them will be able to pay us back, but some of the goods had water damage, so couldn't be kept long.

Families with severely damaged or destroyed homes are in makeshift tents or staying with neighbors, and most hope to rebuild. Some people have been able to recover their possessions as folks bring in items dropped after the tornado dissipated.

John's parents' beautiful home was demolished, and we were told they left and went back east. One of the Johnson children was killed when their house was destroyed, and a wall fell on him. Some farmers lost cows and chickens. Many sod homes and barns sustained damage from the heavy rain. We had some injured, but not as bad as other towns. We are counting our blessings.

Love to all, and love to you, Beth. We're proud of you.

Mother and Papa

Beth waved the letter to Fanny. "They're fine. The house wasn't hurt, and Papa is giving away food and supplies to the people who have nothing."

"That's a relief," Fanny said.

"Mother is putting people up in the house. Can you imagine? She hates having anyone messing up her house."

"It sounds like she's risen to the challenge." Fanny pinned Mandy between her knees and brushed tangles out of the little girl's hair.

"My goodness. I am so relieved." Beth pressed her hand over her racing heart. Her parents were fine.

The next Sunday, after their noon meal, Stuart rode in. "Hello, all."

"Stuart, come see our house," Sam called.

"I've been here almost every day, Sam." Stuart ruffled the boy's hair. "But after I talk to Beth, you can show me around."

"Girls," Sam griped.

Stuart winked at Beth. "We're going for a walk."

Beth wiped her hands on a towel, her body flushed with warmth. She took the hand he held out to her.

The tingle she had come to expect when they touched zipped up her arm. Their hands fit together like they were meant to be. She loved how fear, uncertainty, and rejection fled when he was near.

Beth stepped down the porch steps. "Did you get your haying done before the rain?"

"Yes, thanks to the bout of clear weather. It dried quickly, and I was able to get it put up." They headed toward the pond and the shade of the willows.

"Who helped?" Beth asked.

"Hugh, among others. I like him." Stuart pulled her close once they were behind the willows. "I was thinking of asking him to be one of our witnesses."

Beth smiled. "Witness for what?"

"When we get married."

Beth waited for him to say more, but he did not.

"Stuart Randall, do you consider that a proposal?"

He laughed and stroked her cheek with the back of his hand. "Not so good, huh?"

"I'll say." She pulled back and pretended to move away from him.

"Oh, no, you don't!" Stuart took her by the shoulders and turned her back to him.

He stood close and drew Beth up against his broad chest. Her breath caught when he brushed a tendril of hair off her cheek then followed the line of her jaw, a slightly crooked smile on his lips. She let out a breath and drew another in quickly, bringing his scent into her head.

He searched her eyes. Beth waited, lost in his look, not able to move. She let her heart speak through her eyes.

He took her hand and led her to one of the rocks beside the pond. "Beth, I think there's something you should know. I was interested the first time I saw you, but I wanted to be careful. You know, I take my relationship with the Lord very seriously, and I want a woman who is the same. I've given you a hard time this summer, and I'm sorry." He knelt in front of her and took her hands. "You have an abundant and giving character. I think of you always and want you to be with me. I've prayed about us, and I talked to your mother and Aunt Nora too. I hope and pray you feel the same." He stroked the back of her hand with his thumb. "Beth, will you marry me?"

He thought of her always? Beth forced her wild mind to focus on his question. Was there any doubt in her mind what the answer would be? She'd known for some time that she cared for this man. In truth, she loved him. She didn't know when or how it happened, but she did, and she wanted him to know. She stared into his eyes. He hadn't said anything about love. Should she hold out for the word?

"Yes, Stuart," she said, unable to wait any longer. "I would be honored to marry you."

He stood and pulled her into an embrace, warm and electric. She didn't want it to end.

"I'd like to be married right away." He leaned back to see her face. "But I know Fanny needs you."

"Yes."

"At least, I know you're mine." He stepped back and grabbed her hand. "Let's go tell the others."

Beth didn't move with him, and he turned back to her. "What?"

Beth glanced at their clasped hands. "Yes, Stuart, but I want to say something first."

Stuart turned back to stand close to her again. "What is it?" he whispered.

"I want you to know I ... I love you." She looked at her feet, not sure what his response would be, but she needed this out in the open.

He lifted her hands to his lips. "I wanted to know, but hardly dared to ask." He leaned forward, touching his forehead against hers. "I love you."

CHAPTER THIRTY-EIGHT

A week later, Howard stopped to tell Beth her parents were visiting Aunt Nora, and he could take her there on his way home if she wanted.

"Beth, go while you can," Fanny said.

She rushed through her chores, and when Howard came by later, she rode into town with him. When he dropped her off at Aunt Nora's, she ran into her father's arms.

Her father held her like he never wanted to let go. "I missed you, girl."

"I missed you too. Oh so much."

Her father's eyes twinkled. "You have news for us, I hear?"

"Yes, Papa. I'm going to marry Stuart."

"Good for you. Your mother tells me he's a fine young man."

"I can't wait for you to meet him. You'll like him. He's kind and loves God, and he has a farm, he's smart and ... wait till you meet him!" She took a breath and laughed. "You'll see. Tell me what happened at home?"

"Our house is still standing," he said, "but many people needed a place, and we've been thinking of selling anyway. Some goods were damaged, and I didn't have the heart to start over. The new owner is a young man with a family." He tucked her arm in his and walked with her to the porch.

"They all pitched right in and patched the roof and cleaned and inventoried the store. I'd given so much away, he didn't have a full store to start with, but he couldn't have paid me for the goods right then anyway."

"What will you do?"

"We've decided to move here, so we can all be together. Your mother and I will find a house with a garden to putter in. I can help out some of these young bucks from time to time too."

"This is so unexpected," she whispered. "But I'm glad we can be together."

"I know you've learned some tough information this summer," he said. "I want you to know, we considered ourselves lucky to raise you. You've been our joy and delight these years." He wiped a hand across his face. "Can you forgive us?"

"Papa, there's nothing to forgive. You took care of me, and I'm grateful."

He took her hand in his. "I love you, sweetheart."

Beth wrapped her arms around her father. He smelled of the store. Her heart overflowed. Her parents had raised her to be the kind of woman who could attract a man like Stuart, and they would all be living here now together.

"Who do we have here?" her father asked.

Beth leaned away from her father to see who had come to visit. "Hello, Timothy. I would like you to meet my father. Dad, this is Timothy, my friend."

"Hello, Timothy."

Beth smiled. "Would you like to sit here by us?" She gestured to the swing. The boy stared at her father like he'd seen an angel.

"Dad, what do you think?"

"I think Timothy should come sit by me." He sat down in the middle of the swing and patted the place beside him. Timothy sat right next to him.

Beth pursed her lips and sat down on the other side of her father. Her dad went on with his conversation. "Your mother packed what was left in your room before we let others take over," he said, setting the swing into motion. "We have boxes and crates of household goods she wants you to have."

"Thank you. I haven't had time to think of Stuart's house and the things I'll need."

"You would have been proud of your mother." He put his arm around Timothy and rested his hand on the boy's shoulder. "She pitched in and helped until she was exhausted. I had to order her home to rest." He smiled. "She was mighty fine."

Beth's heart filled with joy to realize her mother had changed, too, through the pain and upheaval their family had been through. "Oh, Papa, I love you both, and I'm so glad the secrets are all out."

"We love you too." He turned to Timothy. "What do you think about that?"

Timothy turned to her and grinned. Almost as if he were the one who had worked it all out.

Beth was soon back with Fanny. Martin left again, though Fanny protested. He wanted to work one more week for the railroad. The expenses of the new wing were piling up.

After a long week, Beth was ready for Martin to be home. The children asked, every hour, if he was on his way home yet. Beth took them to the pond to play.

Mandy dangled her feet while the boys stripped to their underthings and waded in. Beth joined them, holding onto

Mandy's hands as she kicked up water. They'd been playing for some time when the dog started barking by the house.

Beth had thought the dog was still with them, playing tag with the boys in the water. She peeked through the willows and noticed two men riding up the driveway.

She began pulling the children from the water. "Boys, get dressed right away. Tad, I want you to go out there and meet those men. Remember, don't tell them anything about the family. Don't forget."

He nodded, dried himself, and hurried to dress.

The men had reached the front porch by the time Tad ran up to them. Beth rubbed herself dry and pulled her dress over her damp chemise, straining to hear their words.

"Boy, where's your father?" one asked.

"What is it you want?" Tad said.

"Don't be insolent, now, boy," the man snapped. "I came to see your father."

"He's working, sir. Can I tell him what you're looking for?"

Beth peeked through the willows again. The men were looking around at the farm, especially where she hid by the creek. She rushed to button her bodice. She would have to go out there. Fanny would be lying down and something wasn't quite right with these men and their questions.

"Sam," she whispered, "take Mandy around to the back door. Don't let them see you and stay there. You hear?"

He nodded and left, holding Mandy by the hand. She wrapped a shawl to cover herself and took the path to the house. Despite her wet hair and rumpled, damp clothing, she stood up proudly. When she passed the man in back, she almost gasped aloud. John. She ignored him and forced herself to walk to the porch. There she turned and addressed the other man who seemed to be the one talking.

"What can I do for you, sir?" She stood next to Tad.

"You the woman of the house?" the man asked, a scar puckering across his face as he spoke.

"I work here." Her knees shook, but she willed it not to show in her words. "What is it you want?"

His raspy voice grated up her spine. "Looking for a bite to eat, miss."

"I'm sorry. Perhaps if you go on to town—it isn't far." She backed away, pushing Tad behind her.

The man studied the place—the horses in the pasture, the cows, and the fields. "Not very friendly, are you, miss," he said, walking his horse toward her.

The horse blew into her face, then tossed his head. She turned away and motioned Tad up onto the porch.

Beth's knees quivered, but when Tad was safely in the house, she faced the scarred man. "Sir," her voice cracked, and she stopped to clear it. "Sir, I believe it's time for you to leave."

"Come on, now, Suds," John said, "leave them alone."

Beth kept her eyes on the other man. The situation might go worse for all of them if the man with the scar found out she knew John. In the house, Tad called for his mother.

"Now, miss," the scarred man said, "you wouldn't want to turn away two hungry men with tuckered-out horses."

"I'm sorry." She glanced at the horse in front of her. He looked fresh and frisky. "Town isn't far."

"Hey, Suds, you know the boss wouldn't want us bringing attention to the spot where we've been camping," John said. "Let's get out of here."

The man with the scar looked her up and down, the gleam in his eye making her skin crawl. "I think she's alone, here, and I ain't afraid of that new boss man." He prodded his horse forward, backing her up against the porch.

"I told you, the boss won't like this," John snapped. "We're leaving town anyway. Let's get going."

Beth tried to step away, but the edge of the porch bit into the backs of her legs. In an instant, Suds glowered at her over the sights of a gun pointed right at her. She froze, not daring to breathe, staring into the black hole aimed at her face.

"Suds, let's go." John's voice dripped with exasperation.

Beth couldn't breathe as the black hole bore into her mind.

"We had this nice bit of skirt right under our noses." Suds sneered. "Too bad." Then he whipped around and turned the weapon on John.

Beth's ears roared. Gasping for breath, she grabbed the bridle of the horse in front of her and leaned on him to keep from falling.

What now? She peeked around the horse to see John glaring at Suds. His eyes held contempt and disgust but no fear.

From inside the house, the click of a cocking gun reached all who stood there.

Fanny shouted, "I have my sights trained on you, Suds, so put yours down and get out of here, or I'll use this."

"I won't be forgetting this." Suds' scar stood out as a vivid purple streak across his face. Wrenching the bridle from Beth's hands, he wheeled his horse around, holstered the gun, and rode away.

Beth's legs trembled so badly she could hardly stand as she met John's eyes. "Thank you," she whispered.

He raised his hand in a salute then turned his horse away.

"Be careful," she called.

He lifted an arm but kept his back to her, his animal moving into a canter and riding down the lane.

Beth swung around and found Fanny shaking behind her, shotgun in hand.

"Fanny, here, let me help you." She took the gun and helped the frightened woman to a chair. "Tad, get her a cool cloth."

"I thought surely we had enough to feed them." Fanny collapsed back in a chair. "To think, I almost let those men inside my house!" She gasped, clutching at the neck of her blouse. "How did you know?"

"One of them was John," Beth said as she lifted Fanny's feet onto a stool. "I didn't realize it until I got out here. The other man looked familiar although I don't remember the scar. I think they're the men who've been stealing livestock around here."

"Tad, go through the back way and get Mr. Morrison," Fanny commanded. "Ask him to come right away."

"Make sure those men don't see you," Beth added.

Tad jumped off the porch and disappeared around the corner of the house.

"Why do you think John helped us?" Fanny asked, her eyes hidden behind the cloth.

"I'm not sure," Beth said. "He told me not to believe all the things I would be hearing about him, but he has himself tied up with bad men."

Sam and Mandy emerged around the corner of the house.

"Sam, you and Mandy were good to stay out of the way. Go play on the swing now," Beth told them. "Let your mother rest."

She sat beside Fanny and waited for Mr. Morrison. When the sound of horses approached, she jumped to her feet, ready to use the shotgun if necessary.

Fanny snatched the cloth off her face then sagged back in her chair when she saw it was Mr. Morrison. "Oh good, Mr. Morrison's here, and his wife came too."

Beth tried to stop the shaking in her knees. Letting out a long breath, she bit her lip and returned the shotgun to its place inside the house.

"Tad said some man came and pulled a gun?" Mr. Morrison almost leaped from his horse. He helped his wife down, then turned to them. "Everyone all right?"

"Yes," Fanny said, "we're fine, but this has been a frightening experience." She went on with the story.

Beth listened to her tell what happened. When Fanny left out Suds pointing the gun at Beth first, she decided Fanny must not have seen that part. Well, Beth wouldn't tell her either. Fanny had been through enough for one day.

"Oh, dear me," Mrs. Morrison said. "Husband, you'd better send someone for the sheriff. There's something very wrong here, and we need to get to the bottom of it. A terrible disgrace—a woman threatened in her own home—and in her condition too." She made shooing motions at her husband until he left. "Now, Fanny," she said, "how about I help you lie down so you can rest. Beth and I will take care of everything."

Fanny let herself be shooed back into the house, and after a moment more to catch her breath, Beth began food for the men who would come to help.

Later, Mr. Morrison came back with more men and the sheriff, their expressions set with a resolve to keep their families safe.

Stuart arrived, too, rushed into the house, and pulled Beth into his arms. She allowed herself to lean on his chest and let his warm, strong arms bring her the comfort she needed. Stuart's beating heart was like a tattoo of constant devotion. Closing her eyes, she willed away the memory of Suds' lifeless stare over the sights of the gun barrel.

Neighbors milled about, and Stuart moved to hear how he could help. The men questioned her and made plans to begin searching the area. Tad kept to the porch and told his account too.

"I'm glad Martin comes back tonight," Mrs. Morrison said.

"Yes, me too," Beth said as she mixed up a batch of corn fritters. "It's frightening to be here without him now."

"I fear all this turmoil might have started Fanny's labor," Mrs. Morrison said.

"Really?" Beth stopped stirring. "Did she say something?"

"No. More like what I see on her face. I told her I would be here so that she could rest. I sent Stuart into town for the doctor."

"Oh, I didn't see that Stuart had gone," Beth said.

"I told Fanny we would have someone get Nora too."

Later, when the children had been fed and sent over to the neighbors for a few days, Beth cleaned up the kitchen again. Soon, Stuart arrived with Aunt Nora, and Beth hurried to the wagon to meet her.

"Mrs. Morrison thinks Fanny might be having the baby now."

"Not surprising, and it's time." Aunt Nora clutched Beth's arm as she stepped down. "How are you, dear?"

Beth compressed her lips tight to keep from bursting into tears. "Come on in and see Fanny."

Aunt Nora greeted Mrs. Morrison. "Ethel, how is she?"

"I sent her to rest. The children are over at Zick's. Her daughter is visiting, and the children are more than happy to have playmates for a few days."

"Good." Aunt Nora washed her hands in the dry sink. "Let's go see how our girl is doing."

CHAPTER THIRTY-NINE

Beth's eyes stung like she'd been in a sandstorm. She'd slept some but not enough. Fanny had gone into active labor in the early morning hours. Now, several women cared for her, while other neighbor women cooked or hemmed the diapers Beth hadn't had time to finish.

Martin had arrived home late the previous night, alarmed at what had gone on in his home. He'd rested with Fanny while he could but now paced—impatient and nervous for the birth.

Beth wiped a damp cloth over Fanny's forehead, then left the room to refill the bowl of water with a fresh, cool supply. She soothed her hair—she must look a fright.

The sheriff and his men returned from their investigation. Mrs. Sandsure and a woman Beth had never met brought coffee to the sheriff and the rest of the men as Beth listened to his report.

"We found a whole camp," the sheriff told Martin. "Surprised to find them right in this neighborhood ... that big slough west of here." He gestured to the marsh across the road. "A lot of cattle and horses have been held there by the looks of it."

Beth clutched her apron and bit into the cloth to stifle a scream. She'd come here to be safe, and all this time, they'd been only a stone's throw away.

"Mighty glad to know they moved out of our area." The sheriff raised a cup of hot coffee to his lips. "Someone is going to have to deal with them, but they've left here now."

Beth sighed. Was it finally over? The sheriff dipped his hand into a pan of hot corn fritters one of the women carried around. He downed it in two bites.

Stuart came to her, interrupting her thoughts. "Beth, the sheriff wants to speak to you."

Her shoulders tensed at the thought of facing the sheriff in front of all the men.

He took her hand, "It'll be fine. He just thought you deserved a report."

The sheriff stepped forward. "I was off the bat when I accused you of helping those yokels, miss. Turns out"—he consulted a notebook—"Leah, who works for the Ornsbys, was the one. She confessed she was jealous of you and thought this John fella was the man she wanted. I can't figure she knew enough to do any damage, though. She's right sorry for telling everyone you was involved."

Beth gaped at him, trying to comprehend what Leah had done. She'd attempted to ruin her reputation by telling people Beth was informing for a gang? No wonder Leah had kept her distance since they arrived.

"I'm right sorry you were bothered by those men, miss," the sheriff said, shifting his feet. "But you should rest easier now they're gone."

"Yes, sir. Thank you, sir."

"I'm wondering, though, is there more to the story than you're telling?" His eyes pierced her. "That Suds fellow was upset with you, and Tad says he pulled that gun on you first."

Tears welled up in Beth's eyes. Stuart came close and put an arm around her. She couldn't talk about that moment. If only everyone would let her forget. A loud agonizing wail from the house saved her from answering. The sheriff looked around, wide-eyed, and snapped his notebook closed.

"I guess it doesn't matter. Will keep you posted. Thanks for the victuals, ladies."

"You go be with Fanny," Stuart whispered in her ear. "I'll be here."

Ethel Morrison pushed the men out the door. "We women have work to do, so scoot."

Beth ran to Fanny's side, holding her friend's hand and mopping her damp brow while she labored to deliver the baby. She breathed when Fanny did. She panted when Fanny did. She held her breath when Fanny pushed. When the baby was born, he slipped into Nora's hands and began to cry.

"Oh my, you have a boy," Mrs. Morrison said.

"Lusty too." Nora turned him over and wiped him off with a cloth.

The blood finished pumping through the cord before she clamped it. She wrapped him in a clean towel and handed him to Beth. "Here, now, you hold him."

Beth gazed at the first newborn she'd ever held. His arms flailed, and he whimpered. She tucked the blanket tighter around him and cuddled him close against herself.

Suddenly, Fanny gripped Ethel Morrison's hands and groaned. "What's this?"

"I thought so." Aunt Nora pressed her hand around Fanny's abdomen. "You have more work to do."

Fanny groaned as she labored, and after more time, another baby appeared.

"Two, Fanny—both boys." Aunt Nora grinned. "My, my, what handsome lads."

"Two, Aunt Nora?" Beth said. "Did you know it was going to be twins?" She gazed from one to the other. They looked so much alike.

"I had my suspicions." Nora smiled as she attended Fanny. "Twins run in this family too."

Later, when they had the room straightened and Fanny dressed in a fresh nightgown, Beth placed the baby she held in his mother's arms. The women left the room so Martin and Fanny could admire their new sons and give the boys their first feeding. She joined Stuart on the porch where he waited for news.

"Twins?" Stuart surprised look was comical. "Are they big enough?"

Aunt Nora answered for all of them. "They're beautiful and healthy."

Lydia brought them coffee and the leftover corn fritters. "No wonder Fanny was so miserable."

"Yes, it explains a lot," Ethel said.

Stuart rubbed his hand over the back of his neck. "Now that I know everything is all right, I need to get home. Aunt Nora, Howard and I can check on your stock if you need us to?"

"No." Nora sat back and put up her feet. "Merin and Grant are still there, and they'll take care of everything."

"I thought they went home," Beth asked.

"Your dad is working on my house." Aunt Nora closed her eyes.

"Well good, but I still need to head home." Stuart took Beth's hand and walked with her to his horse. "Are you all right?" he asked as he put his arms around her.

"Happy, tired ... happy." Her voice muffled against his chest. "Will take a while for everything to get back to normal around here—if it ever does."

Stuart laughed and kissed the top of her head. "This will only get more interesting."

Beth would have been content to stay in Stuart's arms. His steady heartbeat felt more comfort than she thought possible. "Hope I get some sleep first."

He laughed again as he set her away from him and mounted his horse. "Go now while there are still plenty of women around to take care of everything. By the way, I did Martin's chores and put the milk in the cold house."

"Thank you." Beth watched him ride off and then wandered back to the house.

When Stuart visited later in the week, he admired the babies and even held them. Beth warmed to see him tuck one of the mites into the crook of his arm. He didn't seem at all frightened to hold the tiny infant but held him confidently. She wondered where he had gained such assurance, or if that was simply Stuart—solid, caring, reliable.

Later, they strolled to his horse in the darkening day, her hand snuggled in his. Beth looked around like she'd just woken up. "I don't know what day it is or even what time it is."

Stuart laughed. "This has been the strangest summer."

"I'll say."

"One thing after the other has happened. The first thing—I saw you."

Beth smiled at him as she studied the dark eyes and handsome face she had grown to love. More than anything, she wanted to marry this man and be with him always. At last, she knew what love was. Stuart taught her, Aunt Nora and her parents showed her, and even Fanny and Martin, with their steady relationship, had been an example of how to love.

"There was something about you from the very first," Stuart murmured.

"Oh?" She trembled. Stuart was a cautious man about sharing how he felt. He believed such things waited until marriage, but she wouldn't mind more words of love.

"Yes, and don't get shy with me."

"Why?" She smiled, hoping, probing for the words she longed to hear.

"You're too honest for that." He turned to untie his horse.

She toed the dirt. "A girl needs to hear things you know. Guessing isn't the way to know what someone is thinking."

"You're right, and I want to tell you what you mean to me." He leaned forward and kissed her on the cheek and squeezed her hand. "We'll have years and years together." He kissed her again and mounted his horse. "I almost forgot to tell you. Your dad is putting siding on the outside of the lean to." Stuart smiled. "I think they plan to stay with Nora over the winter. Guess who's helping him?"

Beth shook her head. "I have no idea."

"Timothy. The boy is glued to your father all the time—like his shadow."

"He spends time with Papa?"

Stuart nodded. "He's been around so much, his aunt, who he lives with, became worried he was being a pest. She came over to find out what was going on. When she saw your dad, she said he looks very much like her father."

"My goodness."

"Her father, Timothy's grandfather, died recently, but Timothy was with him until then. Your father is fond of the little guy and has taken the boy under his wing." He gathered the reins in his hand. "Works out well for everyone." He waved and turned his horse toward the road.

Beth waved to Stuart as he rode off. She turned back to the house. Timothy had been elusive. She shook her head. Maybe Timothy saw her dad as a substitute grandfather.

Beth hardly had time to miss Stuart as she washed diapers, gowns, and blankets—held, burped, and changed babies. When she tried to coax a smile out of each sober, little face, she knew she wanted children of her own.

Word spread, and Beth and Fanny had plenty of help. Neighbor women cooked, cleaned, held babies, changed diapers, and washed clothes. There was always food in the house and fresh diapers and gowns to use.

Beth received a letter from Aunt Nora that Lynn had delivered her baby too—a girl. Lynn and the baby were doing fine. The two would stay with Bernard's parents for an indefinite period.

Fanny rocked in a chair, feeding one of the babies. "I'm so glad. If she's with Bernard's parents, they'll make sure she's taken care of."

"I would think so. It's their grandchild." Beth's hand flew to her mouth. "My goodness, the little girl is my niece."

Fanny laughed as she lifted one baby to her shoulder and began to pat his back. "Exciting, isn't it?"

Beth stitched together the parts of a gown she was making. "Yes, it is. More relatives, like you and Martin. I want heaps of cousins." She grinned. "I wonder what I can make for her. I never thought I would have nieces and nephews as part of my life."

"You and Stuart will have children of your own before you know it."

Beth wanted children eventually, but first she and Stuart would have time to get to know each other better. Her parents didn't know him either.

"Speaking of that, when are you and Stuart planning on the wedding?"

"We thought Christmas would be nice," Beth said. "The babies will be older. My parents will have a place to live by then, or may be settled in with Aunt Nora."

"I'm sorry you have to make your plans around me." A loud burp erupted from the tyke at her shoulder. "My goodness, son." Fanny laughed. "I do appreciate it, Beth."

"Everyone has plenty to do. Stuart is having his housekeeper clean the whole house, and there are several major repairs he needs to do. He's planning to paint and rearrange rooms too. After the harvest is finished, he said he could get it done." Beth held up the gown. "How long will this fit?"

Fanny laughed. "A day or two, it seems. They are growing, aren't they?"

Beth nodded.

"No wonder. It seems all I do is feed babies."

"That is all you do." Beth laughed. She didn't mind the other work of cooking and caring for Tad, Sam, and Mandy. She could still get away for visits with Aunt Nora and her parents. She thought of her old home and all that had happened since she left. "I've been thinking about Alice."

"In what way?"

Beth laid the pieces she was sewing on the table and smoothed it. "These babies remind me of what she's going through. Having a baby should be a happy event."

"What about her parents?" Fanny asked. "Or will John's parents care for her?"

"Mother told me his parents went back east. I don't know about hers," Beth said. "She won't have the support you have. Even if John isn't caught, his involvement in these illegal activities will get around."

"I'm sorry for her," Fanny said.

"I wonder if there's something Stuart and I can do to help. If we could bring her here, maybe she could stay with Sophie? It would help them both if she needs someone, and Sophie shouldn't be alone."

"Oh, Beth," Fanny said, "that's a big step. Are you sure you won't resent her?"

"I don't see why. I don't love John and never did, but something about his last visit—protecting me—makes me want to care for Alice. Almost like keeping her safe until John can get his life together."

"Well, you surely saw more than I did. I saw a dangerous man, but at the same time I think it's a wonderful idea to make sure Alice has everything she needs. I'm sure to have baby clothes she can use." She smiled.

"Thank you, Fanny." Beth began to sew the hem of the baby gown. "I'll ask my parents if they know anything when I go visit them."

"God is good, isn't he?" Fanny wiped the mouth of the infant after another burp. "I'm so grateful I know God and his goodness."

"So am I." Beth filled her needle with a running stitch. "I learned so much from Aunt Nora when I got here. I was hurting from leaving home and had no idea what was going on. God showed me a little at a time. Now when I look back over the summer, I see God was preparing me for the news. Aunt Nora and her steady faith and love sustained me to handle the shock of it."

Fanny put the child in a nearby cradle and sat back down at the table with a bowl of potatoes. She picked one up and began to peel it. "God is like that, if we're willing to listen."

Beth laughed. "I can't say I listen as much as I should, and I struggle often with my emotions."

"Beth, none of us is perfect, but we continually strive to be more like Jesus. You've had much change in a few short months." She reached over and put her hand on Beth's shoulder. "I love you, cousin, and I'm not blind to how much this hurt you."

Beth swallowed down the tears that surged and bent her face to her sewing. After a moment, she said, "Fanny, you know I love you and your family. I'm not unhappy about anything I learned. Mother and Papa were good parents, they've always been good to me. Though I wish a few things could have been different, I'm lucky in so many ways."

"It's good to remember no one has a perfect life," Fanny said. "No matter how hard we try, we will have trouble, but God will give us the grace to handle whatever comes, if we keep our eyes fixed on him."

EPILOGUE

Beth's hands shook when she tried to do the buttons of her wedding dress.

"Never mind." Sally brushed away her help. "I'll do it." Her friend slipped the buttons through their loops and leaned back. "You look beautiful. Just wait until Stuart sees you."

"Thank you, Sally. You're a good friend." Beth smiled. "I'm so happy my mother and father are here. I have friends and even relatives to wish me well. I can hardly believe it."

The music began and Beth's hammering heart settled into peace. The time had come.

Sally left the room, and her father stepped in. He took her hand and tucked it over his arm. "You ready?"

"Oh, yes." She looked up into her dear father's face. "Thanks, Papa. Thank you for everything."

"You're welcome, honey." He smiled and leaned in to give her a kiss. "Let's not leave that groom waiting."

Beth walked with her father to the front of the church, her eyes on Stuart. When her father put her hands in Stuart's, Beth trembled. Her experiences thus far had prepared her for this day—the ups and downs, the joys and sadness. She silently gave thanks to God for all of it. This new life would have more challenges, but God and his faithfulness would be with them through it all.

ABOUT THE AUTHOR

Maggie R. McKenzie is a member of "Write Now" writers group and American Christian Fiction Writers, and treasurer of ACFW Minnesota N.I.C.E.

Born and raised on a farm in Minnesota, Maggie grew up hearing and researching the varied history of her family. This began a lifelong love of pioneer history. Maggie and her husband reside in Minnesota. She is a mother and grandmother. Her interests include genealogy, quilting, weaving, and gardening.